# AS THE CROWN FALLS

## KATIE BACHELDER

This one's for my little sister, Evie.
*Ír liora.*

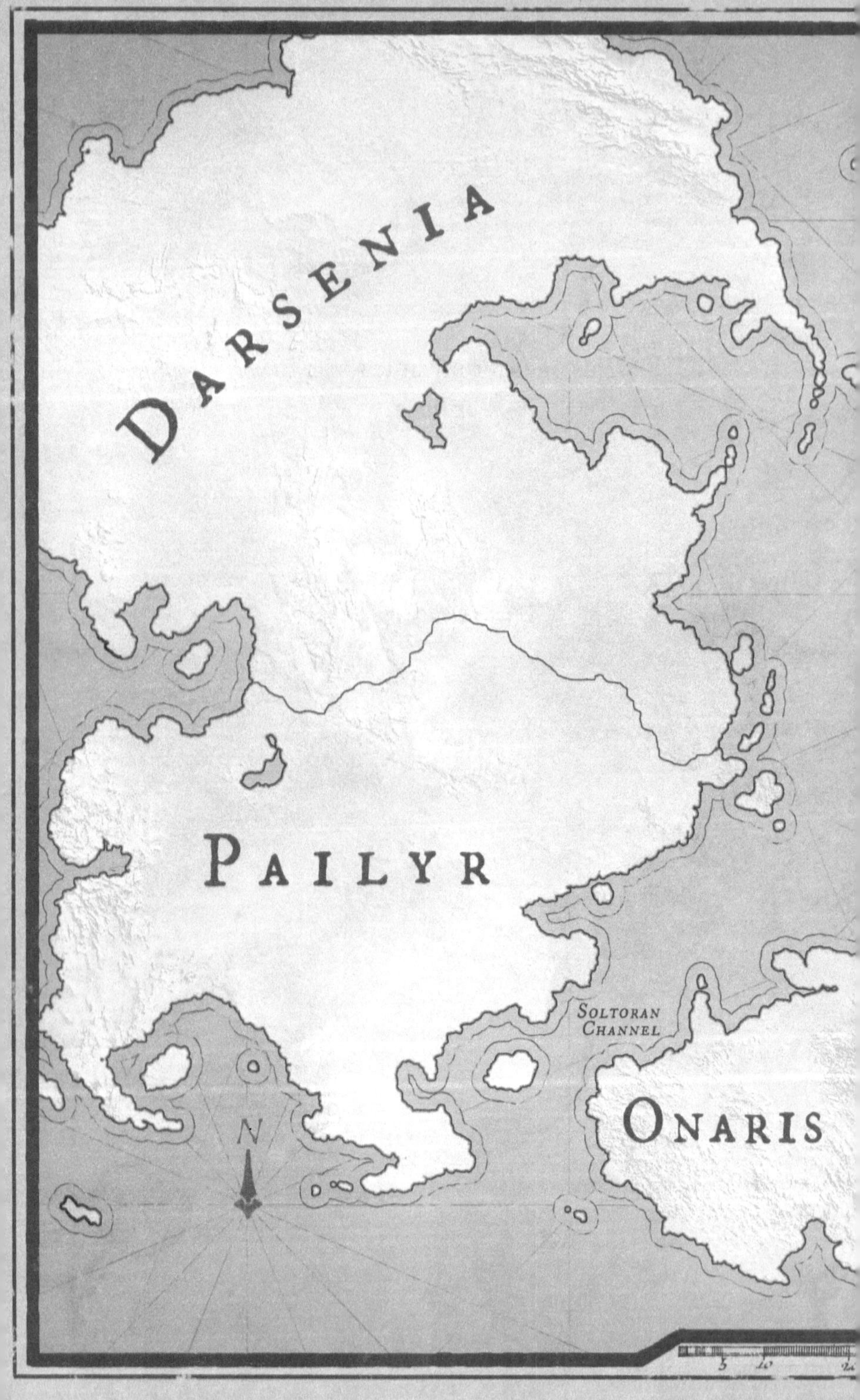

DARSENIA
PAILYR
SOLTORAN CHANNEL
ONARIS
N

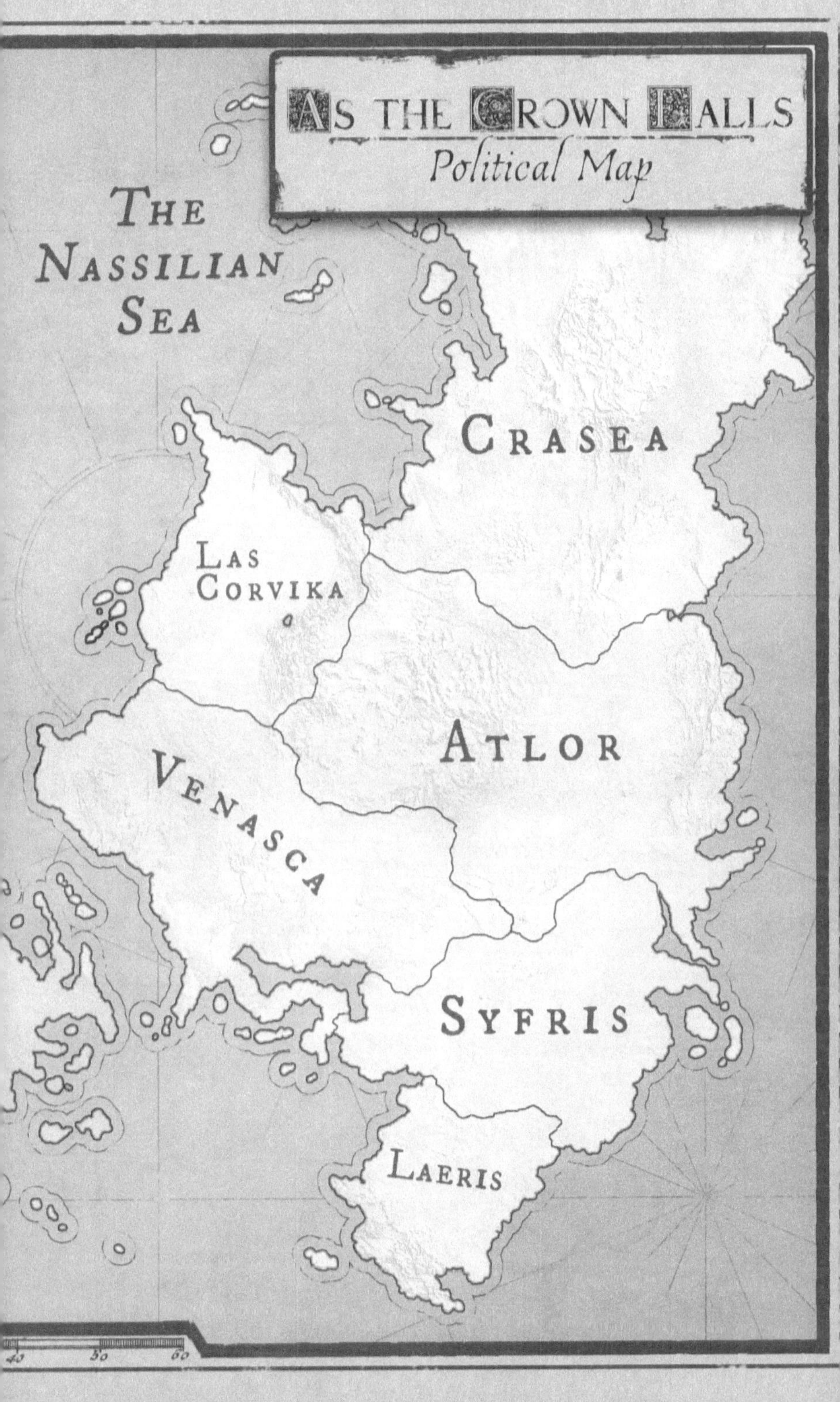
As the Crown Falls
Political Map
THE NASSILIAN SEA
CRASEA
LAS CORVIKA
ATLOR
VENASCA
SYFRIS
LAERIS
40
50
60

Las Corvika
Map Key
CAPITAL
City
Town
Fort
Rebel Camp
Les Dorent
Mod Adeirno
Obele
Mod Redel
Gonvelle River
Ait River
Mod Vjenaro
Bergev Mountains
Toritet
LES STELVO
Haveil
Medore
Kullen Hills
Bijal
VENASCA
ATLOR
N

# CHAPTER 1

Zyre loved reading dusty old tomes about battles as much as the next person—which was to say, not much at all. The sounds through the window of her office in the guard tower were not helping, either. Chirping birds kept swooping past, drawing her attention back to the two ships sitting in Nolasi's small harbor.

The first was a Corvikan merchant vessel named the *Embrunis*, dwarfing a port that rarely had to hold more than the locals' fishing boats. The deck bore massive crates, but Zyre would bet good coin that they were empty. Thanks to their spies, her family knew there were royal soldiers populating the ship, more than any merchant vessel had any right or reason to hold, unless it was a warship pretending to be something else.

Most of the soldiers were staying below deck, so it was hard to gauge the numbers. Zyre's family might not have known at all that something was amiss except one of their allies at court had sent them a warning. Now it was a waiting game. When those soldiers stopped hiding, that was when Zyre's family would truly be in trouble.

Zyre grabbed her spyglass and opened it with a *snick*. More soldiers were beginning to show their faces, meandering about the *Embrunis* in plain sight. Not enough to worry over, not just yet. But enough to stay alert.

Not for the first time, Zyre was reminded of an old adage from her mother's homeland: Be wary of secrets, for they multiply. It was one of the few Crasik sayings she knew.

She didn't know where it had all started. Where her father, the baron, had kept his first secret that had led to this, to his treason. It certainly hadn't been for her. But it didn't matter where it had started, because all it would take was for one secret to be let loose and it would all be over. Everything would unravel.

Zyre was not the biggest act of treason, but her identity would be the easiest to find out. Everyone knew her as Zyre Mescal, *sjarvisk* retainer to Baron Arnaud, and Kadj as her powerful soulbeast, but Kadj was a farce. Their bond was little more than superficial, a spell done up by some *kjarnik* to hide the fact that she was actually both an *aljarne* and an Arnaud, a deadly, dangerous combination.

Zyre had no idea what a proper *sjarvisk* was like or how the bond worked between one and their soulbeast. But those soldiers might. And if they started to think too hard about her magic, they might start to question everything else about her. That was not a risk her family could afford.

"We should sail away, eh, Kadj?" she crooned, looking down at her tiger as he lay supine on the wood floor. "Sneak onto that Venascan ship and go on adventures just like Coroneir and her owl?"

Kadj chuffed half-heartedly.

She laughed at him and looked again at the port, staring

longingly at the second ship that had claimed its own corner of the port in the early hours of the morning. The *Telaña dir Ansol.* It wasn't anything fancy, flat and slow and squarish. She was pretty sure the Venascan vessel had already dropped off its cargo; Remy had gone out to speak to the captain this morning and come back with a wagon full of crates.

Zyre drew the spyglass to her eye for a closer look, watching the Venascans strut around on their deck like the world was theirs for the taking. She smiled at them. Oh, to have that confidence.

As she swept the spyglass back toward the *Embrunis,* though, all of her lightheartedness died away.

Soldiers in dark Béranger green weighed down a rowboat as it was lowered into the water. Zyre's heart skipped a beat. They wouldn't be making landfall unless—

She scanned the deeper waters, hoping against hope that it wasn't true. But there, in the distance, just as she'd feared, was the black speck of another ship bearing down on the island. It took ages for it to cross the distance, but as it drew near, she took note of the masts plastered with sails, its form sleeker than the *Embrunis* and coming in fast. Eventually, she was able to make out the details of the sail, painted green with a gold shape in the center. She didn't need to wait for the gold to transition into the griffon's silhouette; it would be from the royal fleet, sure as water was wet.

"Kadj!" she barked as she collapsed the spyglass. The tiger rolled to his side, then scrambled to his feet as she dodged his massive paws. Their informant's reports had been true. The Béranger prince was coming.

She ran out of her office and thundered down the steps, taking them two at a time. At the base of the guard tower, Captain Merytz sat at a table with some men, cursing over a dice roll. The captain was young, perhaps only a few years older than Zyre herself, and good looking in the traditional sense. He had the telltale bronze skin of a Corvikan, though his pale hair was rather unconventional.

He was the first to see her. He scrambled to his feet, his cheeks burning as he fell into a succinct quarter bow. He even added the honorific, a fist placed over his heart. Merytz offered her a hopeful smile.

The poor fool. She'd blushed the day Remy had suggested the captain might be fawning over her. Neither her brother nor the captain knew Merytz had no chance of capturing her heart. This particular secret was not so big or catastrophic as her others, but that hardly made it easier. Part of Zyre wished he knew she was noble-born. It would have been far easier to explain.

The men with him followed his lead, falling into a half bow to make up for their lack of rank, and had the decency to look embarrassed. Dicing while on duty was bad form, after all.

Zyre returned the quarter bow to Merytz. Then, as she rose, she said, "The griffon has come to port."

He barely flinched. *Oh, but he is good*, she thought.

Then again, they'd been told this might happen.

Zyre left the guardhouse to warn her father. Merytz took command of his men, his sharp orders following her out.

With Kadj at her side, she ran up the stone road. It wound past the hilly terrain that covered most of the island, but even with the slow incline, Zyre felt the familiar burn in her legs as she came to the manor. There was no one guarding the stableyard, where the road ended, and though the halls were no less populated than usual, they felt hauntingly empty as she ran through, even as servants and guards hastened out of Kadj's path.

A few hallways later, Zyre found herself in front of a pair of doors inlaid with the family crest, two fish in midair, facing one another. Beneath it were the words *Eris bi Eljers*. By Skill and Valor. Zyre rapped her knuckles against the door.

"Enter," came the booming voice from within.

She swung the door open to find her father, his hair graying at the temples and his thick brows hiding eyes haggard from a long day of looking at papers. He sat at his desk with a pen in hand. Zyre knew better than to be fooled by his scholarly appearance, his skin light from time spent indoors and his frame undeniably wiry. Jervin Arnaud could still hold his own against the best of them.

There was no one else in the office, which came as a relief, because it meant there was no one Zyre had to pretend for.

"Zyre," said her father, frowning. "Aren't you on duty this morning?"

"The *Aretmor* is approaching, and the *Embrunis* is starting to land its troops."

Jervin Arnaud leaned back. "Fidou's information was good, then." He scrubbed at his face with a sigh. "All right. Find your brother, and meet me at the stables. And, Zyre? Be ready. If swords are drawn, we'll need you."

Zyre didn't have the courage to tell him that the idea of fighting turned her stomach. It would hurt her father to think Zyre wouldn't help, especially when she could do so little for her family as it was.

When Jervin twitched his fingers in a clear dismissal, Zyre found herself bowing, making it almost to the half before she stopped herself. With a wince, she turned around awkwardly and left her father. Kadj trailed behind her, looking up at her with confused yellow eyes. She scratched his head, right between the ears, and then hurried through the manor.

It did not take her long to find Remy. He was outside in the training yard, as he often was around this time of day. Sweat ran down his pale face and stuck his dark hair into clumps. He moved with a practiced grace against a bronze-skinned guard.

At the side of the match sat Remy's lovely, if quiet, wife, Damari, her skin a dark shade of brown and her thick black hair bound by braids behind her head. Young Bernard, Zyre's nephew, sat on Damari's lap, seemingly content with crumpling the maroon fabric of Damari's skirt while he chattered nonsensically.

It was the unfortunate nature of sword practice that it was not some lonely affair, which meant that, here, she was not Zyre Arnaud, youngest daughter of Jervin Arnaud. Here, she was the *sjarvisk* Zyre Mescal, serving her betters.

The recruit whom Remy was fighting noticed Zyre's arrival and barely deflected Remy's attack.

"*Vinje* Arnaud," she said sharply.

Remy's sword jolted mid-swing. "Zyre," he said, turning.

She fell into a quarter bow, as befitted a person of her rank given to the son of her supposed employer. "Baron Arnaud requests our immediate presence in the stableyard. We are being graced by the presence of the royal family."

Her brother's expression darkened. He accepted a towel from a servant and scrubbed his face clean of sweat. Damari set Bernard on his feet, reaching for the sword propped against her chair. Remy took it from her, ruffled his son's hair in a painfully heartwarming gesture, then motioned for Zyre to follow. As she did, Damari quickly began spouting orders at the guards and servants.

Remy led them through a shortcut around the house. She could hear men and women moving quickly, both inside and out. A group of guards ran past them, back up the path toward the house.

"This feels like a bad idea," Zyre said when they were out of earshot.

"What does? Playing like the loyal followers of a usurper?"

Zyre scowled at his tone. "Remy, the *Aretmor* is a proper Corvikan naval vessel. Why bring additional men on a *merchant* ship unless they plan on double-crossing us? They know more than Father thinks."

"Keep your voice down," Remy chided, although there was no one around them. "Zyre, you have to be careful right now. This goes beyond any person's pride. If they find out that you're an *aljarne*, if you give them even a hint that you are more than who you say you are, that's treason on its own merit."

"I'm well aware," Zyre answered coldly. She knew better than anyone the price of her magic, even bound as it was to Kadj.

Her brother's eyes frosted over. Perhaps he expected her to say "Yes, *Vinje*," or "No, sir," at his every whim. But they were alone, and she was granted precious few opportunities to be herself, even here. Everyone had spies on everyone, or so her father always said.

Remy's expression dulled. He grabbed her arm. "I just need you to promise me something. Mother and Father and I, we chose to go against the regis. You didn't. If you don't want to get involved, I wouldn't blame you. Whatever Father thinks, we can win this fight without you."

She yanked her arm free. Whatever her family chose, she would back them. It was the least she could do.

Captain Merytz was already waiting for them, joined by Guardsmaster Telsadt. Twenty unadorned guards stood under their command, all with horses at their side. The courtyard could barely contain them all.

Most of the mounts, of course, shied away from Kadj, but it was relegated to stomping hooves and nervous snorts. No horse in the Arnaud stable would toss their rider because of the presence of a soulbeast. To neglect that part of a nobleman's horse's training was like neglecting to train them against the scent of blood or the flash of steel or the sudden shift of their riders.

A stablehand held her horse, a stout black mare Zyre had named Telpari. Kadj sniffed Telpari's flank, and the mare snorted, stamping her hoof. Zyre patted the mare to calm her, then gestured to Kadj to leave the poor horse alone.

It did not take long for her father to arrive. Ivanya, her mother, was with him, wearing a resplendent dark blue dress with wide skirts and lithe shoulders that catered to the current fashion. As always, it fit well against her Crasik form, flattering against her light skin and her towering frame. She said something softly to Jervin, and Zyre found herself wishing her mother had come to the stables armed, if only for the impression that everything was well and truly under control.

As if she sensed her daughter's discomfort, Ivanya glanced at Zyre. She flashed three hand gestures at Zyre in quick succession. Nothing in Ivanya's posture or expression suggested the gestures were anything other than commands, but then, none of the guards knew how to read them. Secrets upon secrets.

Her words were none other than the family's crest. *By skill and valor.*

Zyre nodded, straightening. When Jervin swung into the saddle, Zyre leapt atop Telpari like she was about to take the horse into battle. Then prayed hastily against that possibility.

With everyone mounted, Jervin heeled his horse into motion, and the company fell in line behind them.

⁂

The path led them straight into Nolasi and toward nearly two dozen soldiers bearing the green uniform of the royal family. Four awaited them at the main entrance of the town. Their surprise and unease only added to Zyre's mounting concern.

They bowed to Jervin and Remy, a good sign if nothing else. She did not think they would show any such honorifics to traitors. Unless it was a farce.

"What is the meaning of this?" her father demanded coolly.

"We have been sent to secure the town, my lord," the guard with a round face said. "To ensure the safety of the prince and princess."

Remy stiffened.

Jervin seemed not to notice, his expression as unreadable as stone. "Lead me to the man in charge. I'd like to speak to whoever thinks I cannot control my own town."

Behind him, Zyre scowled at the reins in her palms. She didn't have much of a head for politics, but even she knew Rasin's presence would be nothing more than an underhanded trick.

The man with the round face bowed again, signaling to the rest of his unit to remain. Zyre held her breath, expecting her father to snap at the guard, but he didn't, and she couldn't see his face enough to know what he was thinking.

The streets were a tangled web full of ramshackle houses, many of which had small fishing boats tied down out front. The quiet thunder of marching Béranger troops ricocheted between the buildings. A small pack of dogs scampered down a nearby street, flashing just outside of Zyre's periphery. A few citizens were tailed by a dog or a cat or had a bird settled on their shoulder, but whether they were pets or familiars was unclear. Neither *kjarnik* nor their familiars were kept track of in Las Corvika.

*How nice it must be for them,* she thought, staring at the reins in her hand. *Had I been born a* kjarnik, *there would be no need to pretend. I could stare down the prince, perhaps curse him with some bad luck so he might fall off his horse right onto his pretentious face.*

They came upon the docks in a moment of relative stillness. Small fishing boats were scattered across the shore, of course, and men in billowy shirts and close-cut pants went about their business, minding the entourage only enough to give them a wide berth. The only thing that broke the stillness was the uniformed soldiers standing guard. One had his back turned, sweeping a spyglass back and forth across the sea. Inspecting the fishing boats, Zyre surmised.

With so many horses, Zyre's party attracted the attention of the soldiers quickly. The man with the spyglass didn't bring it away from his face until they were almost upon him, and then he turned. The man was surprisingly young, maybe Remy's age, late twenties. He had a knot on his shoulder that, at first glance, looked like Guardsmaster Telsadt's. But, no, it wasn't quite the same. Telsadt's knot was missing a few loops.

"When I heard a member of the royal family was visiting our shores, I had not expected it to be the Commander. To what do we owe the pleasure?" Jervin said to the man.

The man collapsed the spyglass with an expression so unwavering it could have matched a stone. "Baron. I did not expect you to arrive so quickly." His measuring gaze was an insult in and of itself. "You may dismount and wait for him here."

Well. That was a blatant slap in the face. But she knew who the man was now. The Commander? That would be Prince Nyli Béranger. And this man with extra knots was Nyli's Guardsmaster, the head of his honor guard. He would have no name, bound not to Las Corvika or even Regis Notoyem Béranger, but rather to Nyli, and Nyli alone. It was how this man could give commands to her father; honor guards held all of the authority of their charge, at least when it came to ensuring their safety.

In this one man alone sat some of the foundations for her father's own secrets, his treason. A position at court that should have been his, denied to him. An honor guard that should have been his, refused to him. It probably stung just as much as Zyre having to bow and scrape to her own father, cast out of the family in all but the loosest sense.

Merytz made a move to dismount first. She and Telsadt followed quickly after, as did the mounted soldiers behind them. Only then did her brother and father swing down from their horses and settle for the wait.

Royalty did not bother with hurrying. *Nobles*, Zyre thought, having experience with waiting on her own family, *admittedly have a habit of the same, but royals are definitely worse.*

They were left to twiddle their thumbs for at least half of an hour as the *Aretmor* dropped anchor and prepared a boat. Zyre was right. It had been a ship from the royal fleet after all. Zyre watched curiously through her own spyglass, ignoring the glares from Nyli's Guardsmaster, as the royal siblings managed to crawl into the rowboat with dignity intact. More troops filed into the boat after them until Zyre wondered if it would even stay afloat. How convenient it would be if the ropes snapped and the siblings drowned. It was unlikely, but Zyre could hope.

One last man stepped into the boat before it cast off, a stag climbing in after him.

Zyre paled.

A *sjarvisk*. They had expected the family to be accompanied by one, but Zyre had prayed their fears would prove wrong. No one would be better equipped than a *sjarvisk* to realize there was more to Zyre than anyone let on.

Zyre pocketed the spyglass and put a steadying hand between

Kadj's shoulders. The tiger's tail flicked, but she could tell he was agitated. Tholjun's blood, they all were.

Men continued to come and go, reporting to Nyli's Guardsmaster. Nolasi had been quieted, everyone sent home. It angered Zyre that her townspeople could be sent to their rooms like unruly children, but it was not her place to countermand an honor guard's orders.

When the royal boat hit the docks, Prince Nyli and Princess Rasin stepped out, somehow the very definition of composed. Prince Nyli's gaze swept across their group, his mouth turning downward into a shadowed grimace. Their party fell into the proper bows, the regular soldiers falling into the full bow, while she and Merytz bent to the half. Jervin and Remy went only into a quarter bow, pressing their hands against their hearts in the added honorific.

As she rose, she got a chance to look at the royal siblings. Prince Nyli was not a particularly handsome man. There was something about the sharpness of his jaw or the gleam in his dark eyes that made him look more like a hungry wolf than anything else. The princess, on the other hand, was not so much beautiful as she was pretty, though Zyre thought Princess Rasin's brown eyes were a flattering shade. She stood a good several inches above Zyre, slightly taller even than her brother, but beyond that, they looked quite the same, right down to the copper hue of their skin.

A strange expression, almost pitying, swept across Rasin's face as she looked at Zyre's brother. It was so fleeting that Zyre by rights shouldn't have seen it at all. Zyre toyed with the possible implications as her father welcomed the party to their island. If Aljeya were here, of course, she'd have understood it all. Her sister had been made for the court. But Aljeya, as the recognized daughter of House Arnaud, had been married politically to an Atloran nobleman several years ago. Zyre was on her own here.

"A pleasure to welcome you to Lasinia, my prince," Jervin said.

"The Crown considers it crucial to keep an eye on all edges of its borders," Nyli replied. He could have just as easily said "The farmers require rain for their crops" with that tone, as if his words hadn't been laced with a subtle threat.

"And we do our best to ensure its security," Jervin replied coolly. "As your Guardsmaster is seemingly unaware of, not trusting my own men to secure the town for your arrival. It would have been far easier, of course, had we known you were coming."

Rasin smiled. It bordered on vapid, but one stolen glance at Remy had that vapidness melt away. Her expression turned stony. "The *Embrunis* was supposed to herald our arrival. Alas, I hear they were held back several days by slow winds and bad weather."

"An honest mistake." Jervin's tone suggested he was not fooled. A merchant ship as their herald? Why not another ship from the royal navy? Anyway, if the ship was supposed to serve as herald, why wait several hours after docking to come ashore? Why not send a runner immediately to the Arnaud estate? But perhaps this was what it meant to play Court; everyone pretended to be stupider than they were, and barely veiled insults were the norm.

The last two on the boat, the *sjarvisk* and his stag, stepped onto the dock. As he followed the rest of the men ashore, Zyre watched. He held that selfsame arrogant demeanor that Zyre had expected from the royal family. He wore Béranger green, but his uniform was made out of silks rather than the good linen that the rest of the soldiers wore, and the griffon faced a cougar on its hind legs. So. This was Comte Pierre Duvachelle's *sjarvisk* nephew.

His cold eyes scanned the soldiers until they landed on her, almost as if he was looking for her specifically. It was an uncomfortable gaze, the kind that made Zyre want to squirm. She didn't give him the satisfaction.

Jervin's spare guardsmen passed their mounts over to the royal siblings and the ten honor guardsmen they had between them. The Arnaud men then fell in line with the rest of the Béranger troops. Zyre watched, curious to see if the *sjarvisk* also would demand a mount. But no one offered, and the noble-born *sjarvisk* surprisingly seemed unconcerned.

Frowning, Zyre swung back into Telpari's saddle as the rest of the Arnaud guards remounted, and the party began to wind its way back through the too-quiet streets of Nolasi. Hopefully, the guards left in the town would allow those poor fishermen to return to shore.

The royal *sjarvisk* rode behind her, and she dared not glance back at him for fear of rousing his suspicions, but it took quite a bit of willpower.

Then they came upon the manor, and everyone's attention fell to Baroness Ivanya and her daughter-in-law, Damari, with Bernard at her side and a whole gaggle of servants who hurried to help with the horses, bowing and curtsying to the full. Ivanya and Damari, of course, went only as low as a half curtsy, with the added honorific. Bernard almost managed to pull a proper half bow, and despite the circumstances, Zyre was more than capable of appreciating just how adorable her nephew was.

"A warm welcome to our island," Ivanya said as she straightened.

Zyre situated Telpari so that, as she dismounted, she could steal a glance at the royal *sjarvisk*. He looked as imperious as before, his nose in the air. He did not glance her way. She patted her mount and kept Telpari between the two of them.

A servant came up to take her horse's reins, and she passed them over reluctantly. As the stableyard cleared of horses, there was nothing to separate her from the rest of the party, or from the *sjarvisk*. Her mother shot Zyre a worried glance, but she had her duties to see to. The gestures she flashed at Zyre were so quick and subtle Zyre almost didn't catch it. *Be careful with him.* She didn't even stutter in her flippant conversation with the royal siblings.

As her family took Nyli and Rasin inside with their honor guard, Zyre realized she'd waited too long to follow after Merytz or Telsadt for an assignment. The *sjarvisk* crossed the distance, eyeing Kadj almost hungrily.

"A tiger soulbeast," he declared. "Those are quite the rare sight in Las Corvika."

"And a stag." Zyre crossed her arms, refusing to be intimidated by this man. "How original."

The man shrugged. "The soulbeast makes the choice, of course, not the *sjarvisk*, and my Modél is strong in his own right. My name is Ljerson."

"Zyre," she replied. "Zyre Mescal." As soon as she said it, Zyre cursed herself. He hadn't given his last name. He hadn't asked for hers. "Now, if you'll excuse me, I have duties to see to."

He followed her. "Allow me to join you."

"Isn't your job to stay close to the prince and princess?" It was an effort to keep her voice steady.

"Do I wear the uniform of an honor guard?" He sniffed. "I am to make sure the island is safe, and there is no better way to do that than to ensure the Arnaud guards are playing their part, same as the Bérangers."

Her panic grew. Dare she deny him? Dare she not? She spun on him, doing her best imitation of her mother in one of her fits of anger. "Are you implying we don't know how to do our jobs, Master Ljerson?"

"It's not that—"

She didn't give him a chance to finish. She didn't dare. "I don't know how you do things in the capital, but around here, we don't go looking over other people's shoulders and making them feel incompetent. You want to tell me that Nolasi isn't safe for the royal family, that our men are not equipped to handle a few peasants? What, do you think someone here wants to kill the prince? Well, do you?"

Ljerson blinked. He put a hand on Modél's flank. "One would hope not, Miss Zyre. Very well. Go about your business. But I will be checking up on you and your guards later. I wouldn't be doing my job if I didn't."

With that, he led his soulbeast toward the manor. Luckily, Zyre's legs managed to wait until he was out of sight before they decided to turn to jelly.

Taking a steadying breath, Zyre left the stableyard and walked briskly around the house, where she found Telsadt giving direction to their men.

Once the last man was addressed, Telsadt motioned for her to follow, and the two of them found a little privacy a short way away.

"The *sjarvisk* is going to be a problem, isn't he?" Telsadt said, eyes flickering toward a few soldiers chatting together a stone's throw down the hall.

"I fear he might be." Zyre crossed her arms, more than a little uncomfortable just thinking about the man. "He tried to stick his little talons in me, saying something about how it's his job to inspect our defenses and make sure his prince is safe."

Telsadt very nearly bared his teeth. "That task belongs to the honor guard, whom I will speak to shortly. I doubt he knows about you, my lady," he said, lowering his voice, "but he will be looking for any hints of disloyalty."

"Oh, I am well aware. I managed to keep him away from me for the time being, but he will be looking for me later, I think."

"That works in our favor." The grizzled old man scratched at his scruffy beard in thought. "I need to send someone back into Nolasi. Discreetly. There's a lot of movement happening down there, but we've been told to keep our troops on the estate to better protect the prince and princess. It's rotten is what it is."

Zyre forced herself to ask the question weighing heavily on her. "Are they going to attack?"

Telsadt shrugged. "If they do, they'll find us ready. But your father believes Prince Nyli got ahead of himself. The prince can't arrest anyone without proof, and he wouldn't go through the effort of being sly if he had it. He wouldn't have brought his sister if they weren't trying to unsettle us."

Zyre's indignation flared. Sometimes, she hated being right.

House Arnaud had swallowed their pride for twenty years in the name of survival, weathering insult after insult. But Remy and the princess had fallen in love shortly after his introduction at court, and their *regis*, Notoyem, was not known to be a forgiving man. The Arnauds were exiled from court with Remy under orders to marry a Venascan woman, one who wasn't even noble. And then, the final stinging insult: Notoyem had named his *son*, Nyli, the General of the Royal Forces, a title normally reserved for the barony.

"Well," Zyre said, trying to tamp down the bitterness, "it's troubling to me that they brought so many men. I think they fully expect to make us trip."

"It's our job to make sure they don't. Go down to Nolasi. Try not to be seen, but if you are, tell them the baron sent you to ensure the town was secured."

Zyre bowed to the quarter, out of respect rather than obligation. She clicked to Kadj and left Telsadt to his duties.

She wasn't a complete fool, though. She made sure Ljerson was nowhere in sight before she scampered down the winding road toward the small fishing town.

# CHAPTER 2

The streets of Nolasi were notably quiet. Zyre should have been able to hear the general hum of conversation, the occasional shout, something. But she found that prowling Nolasi in secret was easier than she'd expected, because it was also, weirdly, still empty. Zyre and Kadj padded under the small shadows of the buildings as she tried to get a feel for what the Béranger soldiers were doing here. She dodged around a corner as a guard turned onto her street, and, with a frown, she watched him pass. *Why are you patrolling Nolasi, soldier? What do you hope to find?*

As soon as he was out of sight, Zyre and Kadj pressed onward, though Zyre was more mindful of her step. The only sound that covered her own footfalls was the intermittent marching of passing troops, and that was not much consolation.

She needed to get higher up, though she hated to leave Kadj. Nearby was a low roof with a cart parked beside it. Darting a glance up and down the street, she bent down to Kadj's level. "Don't be seen." She mussed up his fur with a smile and then made for the cart. Barrels were tied down in its bed. Good for an extra boost, but not so good for the way down. She'd deal with that later.

Checking her footing, she slowly went on tiptoes, reaching for the ledge and grabbing it, barely. Propelling herself up, she managed to haul herself onto the thatch roof. Zyre kept low, testing her footing before she put her weight down anywhere. Something flashed in the corner of her eye. She had her hand on her sword hilt before she realized it was nothing more than a gull.

Then the main road came into view, and Zyre's heart nearly stopped. She had to count, then count again. Fifty men in green stood at the ready within a stone's throw from the docks. That alone would have matched the number of men her father had, but the Bérangers had brought so many more. The fishing boats had been cleared from the harbor, and the two rowboats still fighting the waves were filled with green. Zyre withdrew her spyglass from her pocket. Not just Béranger foot soldiers, then. One of the boats bore two more *sjarvisk,* one with a badger sitting on his lap and the other with a snake. Worse, the rowboat hadn't even come from the *Aretmor*. It had come from the *Embrunis*.

*How many men are stationed on that merchant vessel?* This didn't feel like men coming to shore to pass the time, not with the villagers sent home and the streets kept tightly patrolled. This felt like an invasion.

Telsadt had been right to send her.

Zyre crept backward and barely paused to grimace before swinging off the roof. Her foot hit the wagon bed hard. She stifled her groan, taking more care as she hopped off the back of the wagon and fell into a low crouch next to Kadj. As if sensing her mood, he lashed his tail sharply, his lips curling back into a snarl. He looked fierce like this. Wild. Hopefully she would not need his anger, or her own.

Zyre traveled with Kadj back the way she'd come, mindful of the handful of men patrolling the streets. Her skin itched at the idea of taking the road up to the house, but it was the only route from the town. The hills were just too steep in some places to leave it. The road would wind around them, and in those curves, she could find places to hide if she was careful enough, but she was beginning to realize just how reckless it had been to sprint down here in the first place.

Zyre crept around one house, and then another, getting closer to the main road. So far, there was no one in sight, and the men at the docks were lost to Nolasi's own curves. She crept closer still. It would have to be good enough. She checked one more time for soldiers and had to duck down when a pair crossed the main road. As soon as their backs were to her, though, Zyre breathed in deep and then sprinted toward the road.

No soldiers cried out. No one chased after her. The two of them could make it back to the house with no one ever the wiser.

Or they could've if two figures hadn't suddenly appeared around the next bend. *Thalja have mercy*, Zyre thought, her tongue heavy in her mouth. There, coming toward her, were Ljerson and his stag. That bastard was getting on her nerves. Did she have time to flee? No, they had definitely seen her. The *sjarvisk's* eyes were dark with suspicion.

Pulling her shoulders back, she reminded herself what Telsadt had said and took comfort in the fact that, worst-case-scenario, Kadj was a tiger and could rip Modél to shreds. She motioned Kadj to follow, and Zyre did her best to strut toward the *sjarvisk*. Ljerson, at least, had no problem thinking he owned the place, and he didn't even belong here.

Trying to calm her hammering heart, she waited until she was within reasonable distance before saying, "What brings you down this way, Master Ljerson?"

The *sjarvisk* and his soulbeast fell to a halt, and Ljerson leaned against Modél. Was she crazy, or did his gaze flicker toward the town? "I could ask the same of you, Miss Zyre. I'm beginning to get the impression that you're avoiding me."

If she hadn't been so afraid, she might've taken offense to that. As it was, it was a tremor she had to fight to keep out of her voice, not anger, when she spoke. "Last I checked, I didn't have to report my every coming and going to you. But if you must know, my tiger was getting restless and I was—"

"Do you take me for a fool?" Ljerson snapped. "A fellow *sjarvisk*?"

Zyre wasn't sure what he meant, so she tried to shrug nonchalantly and brush past him. Ljerson stepped in her way. He grew deathly calm, an unnatural, predatory stillness falling over him. "Here's how it goes. You've been inside that poor excuse of a village, and you know what's going to go down, I'm sure. You're smart enough to figure that out, at least. I can't let you go warn the Arnauds, which makes your choice very simple: Align your loyalties with your regis, with your *country*, or feed the crows. It makes no difference to me."

Zyre could see it in his eyes that the idea of killing her did not trouble him, and that made her more terrified than anything else. She forced her voice to remain even. She could still talk her way out of this. He was just trying to trip her. "The Bérangers have no grounds to arrest Baron Arnaud."

"I would not be so sure about that."

Ljerson stepped forward, a fist forming at his side. Zyre didn't give him a chance to call to magic. A chill went down her spine as she summoned her own. Her vision took on an orange tint as small spheres of sunlight leapt into view. The ones near Ljerson's hand began to tremble, and she yanked them back. The particles stampeded toward her, rolling and tumbling like the waves that crashed into Nolasi's port. Flame snapped into existence above her raised fist, and Zyre suddenly found she could not slow the deluge.

With a startled cry, Zyre very nearly threw it at Ljerson. But that terrifying look in his eyes, that willingness to kill—Zyre's stomach churned at the thought. She raised her fist toward the sky, and a great blast of fire rent upwards, exploding above their heads. Distantly, shouts sounded from Nolasi.

Ljerson cursed under Tholjun's name even as Modél charged toward them. Zyre threw herself backward, clawing at her magic, not knowing what to reach for. A streak of orange and black crashed into the stag before he could reach her. Kadj roared. Small bouts of flame sprouted between them as Modél dug his antlers into Kadj's side, and the ground trembled.

Water droplets appeared above Ljerson's hand and solidified. Zyre called to fire, clawing at it as she tried to gain her footing. Not a single sphere answered her summons. Ljerson began to bring his hand back, preparing for the throw.

Her sword. She still had her sword. Her fingers scrambled at the hilt, knowing she probably wouldn't be able to reach Ljerson in time.

The sharp ice projectiles darted forward.

Zyre screamed for Kadj.

Then something shot past her periphery. A great blast of fire cascaded past her, burning the ice shards to mist.

Both she and Ljerson looked up, following the direction of the fireball. Perched on the hill was a woman, tall, with dark hair in tight coils. Everything about her, from the darkness of her skin to the baggy sailor's clothes to the lithe sword glinting at her waist, screamed she was Venascan. But that was not what had distracted the *sjarvisk* or stayed his hand.

There was no animal at her side, no soulbeast like Kadj; Tholjun's blood, there wasn't even a cat or dog. But if they had any doubts the fireball had come from her, those were quickly dispelled when another bloomed above the stranger's palm.

"*Aljarne*," Ljerson hissed.

Zyre's heart skipped a beat. *Someone like me*, she thought. *What are the chances?*

The fire winked out, and the earth exploded between Zyre and Ljerson. Zyre stumbled backward. "Kadj!" she shouted. Modél's antlers dug into his stomach, but the tiger lashed out with his claws, managing to break free. Blood dripped down his fur. He ran to her, his ears swiveling. In the stillness, the sound of footsteps thundered down the path.

The woman slid down the hillside, landing with a jump right next to Zyre. She pulled her strange triangular hat a little farther down her face and sneered at Ljerson.

The *sjarvisk* scowled. A great fireball exploded above his hand, almost as large as his head. Sweat beaded down his face at the effort. Modél lunged toward them as Ljerson launched his fire. With sharp, deft movements, the Venascan directed her own magic. A large rock flew out of the earth, and right after, water appeared, elongated, and solidified. The rock exploded as the flame crashed into it, and the ice flew around the collision. Ljerson and Modél threw up a shield of air, but Ljerson's was too slow. The ice crashed into his chest, his throat. He fell backward, dead before his hands could even claw at the wounds.

For a moment, the stag froze, his eyes turning white as they rolled backward into his head. Then Modél bucked, kicking wildly, looking for a way out.

The Venascan waved her arms, and the unbound stag sprinted off. Zyre had to hold back Kadj to stop him from chasing the beast. She made the mistake of looking at the dead *sjarvisk*. She felt the sudden, inescapable desire to rid her stomach of its contents. There was just so much blood. And his eyes… Zyre had never seen a dead man's eyes before.

"Come with me."

A hand pulled her away, nearly yanking Zyre's arm out of its socket. The soldiers. They were getting closer by the second.

She whispered a quick prayer to Tholjun for Ljerson. It was one thing to hate a man and yet another to see him killed. Then she hurried after the other woman, crawling up the steep hillside to hide behind its crest before the soldiers stumbled upon the murder. The Venascan kept moving, sticking close to the road but hiding from sight, yet Zyre could still hear the men when they found Ljerson's corpse, knew it as soon as one shouted for the area to be searched.

Remy's warnings rang in Zyre's head. Her father's men were terribly outnumbered, and she might have just forced everyone's hand.

The Venascan kept them moving away from Ljerson and from Zyre's home, yet not quite toward Nolasi either. Zyre was just about to demand an explanation when the woman finally slowed, turning them toward the fishing town. This was not good. Whatever the woman had planned, Zyre had no intention of fighting in the streets. She should be with her parents, her brother.

"My ship is down there," the woman said, directing her attention to Nolasi. "I say we force our way through, get back to my ship, and hightail it out of here. I can do nothing more here."

Zyre frowned, but it didn't seem like the last part had been meant to be heard. "I have no intention of sailing away from my home with a total stranger, however indebted I am to them for saving my life. I need to return to the Arnaud estates to… to protect my employers." The lie stumbled off her lips, but the woman seemed not to notice.

Instead, strangely, she laughed. "The Arnauds? I would not

worry overmuch about them, *majican*. You, on the other hand, just killed a royal *sjarvisk*. At least, that's what they will think. If I were you, I'd be a little worried about my own hide."

Kadj flattened his ears, mirroring how Zyre felt. Her family was entrusting her to help them fight against the Bérangers, to make sure they were able to get away. Whatever misgivings she had about killing, she could get past them if it meant protecting her family, keeping them safe. "The soldiers…" she tried to say.

"Will be marching toward the manor," the woman finished for her. "Look."

She spun Zyre around, positioning her to better see Nolasi through the two hills they hid between. Zyre took out her spyglass and inspected the scene. Her view was blocked by the outer buildings, but there was a sliver of the main roads visible, and in those, she could see the troops moving.

"The fighting will have started now. I don't think they were going to wait much longer anyway. There'll be a skeleton force to protect the harbor, but once we fight our way past, they should be too preoccupied with their own quarry to worry about a single trade ship leaving."

The woman strode forward, but Zyre hesitated. Her orders were to protect her family, and who else, if not her, could even these odds?

Ahead, the woman noticed Zyre hadn't followed and stormed back toward her. "Listen, if you want to go back to your post, good for you. Honor and glory and all that. But if you go back, you die. That magic of yours will do you no favors, and those soldiers will go no easier on you than that *sjarvisk* did."

The image of Ljerson's corpse crumpled on the ground came back. Zyre would never forget that, would she? And she could have killed him if she'd wanted, if she'd just sent that fire at him rather than the sky. Gods, in all her years of training and in all of her father's careful planning, it had never crossed their minds that Zyre might be more liability than weapon, more coward than killer.

And she owed it to them, didn't she, to fight? She had more than just her faulty magic; she was a passable swordsman. She'd been waiting twenty years to be of some use to her family, and now they actually needed her, and here she was, wishing beyond reason to follow this stranger, to sail across the high seas like she'd dreamed? Had the gods sent this woman to test her?

Or to give her a way out?

The Venascan threw up her hands in defeat and stalked off.

*Thalja, I hope this is a sign from you*, Zyre thought desperately.

She hurried after the woman, crossing onto Nolasi's cobblestone streets, one hand on Kadj's shoulder as he limped along stoically. Her companion did not even try to be discreet. Yet it was as the Venascan had said; the town had been nearly emptied of soldiers already. Zyre tried not to think what that would mean for her family.

They almost made it to the docks before they stumbled across anyone. Two patrolling soldiers stepped onto the street they were on, nearly running headfirst into the strange *aljarne*. For a moment, the two just stared in surprise, mostly at Kadj. Then one reached for the horn hanging at his side.

The Venascan exploded into action.

The sun glinted off of her sword as she pounced. The soldier dropped the horn, his sword only halfway drawn when the Venascan's weapon drew a sharp red line across his chest. He let out a pained gasp as he fell. The Venascan turned her sights on the second soldier. As she slashed at him, he dove to the ground, colliding with his fallen partner. The soldier grappled for the horn, slicing the rope to free it from the dead soldier, not caring about the blood smeared on it as he brought it to his lips. The *aljarne* threw her hand out at him, and a gust came from nowhere, sending the man backward.

Zyre swallowed her surprise and grabbed the fallen horn before the man could regain his footing. The *aljarne* passed her periphery. Zyre watched in alarm as the other woman strode purposefully toward the soldier. The man skittered away, his eyes wide with terror.

"Wait!" Zyre exclaimed.

The woman didn't listen. She raised her sword.

With a squeak, Zyre flung her hand up in a desperate attempt to signal the woman to stop. Her arm pebbled from a chill, and a blast of air billowed from her palm. The woman didn't even see it coming. She crashed against the wall with a cry.

"Sweet Thalja!" Zyre cursed, rushing over to the other woman.

But she was succinctly shoved away as the woman scrambled to her feet. She advanced on Zyre, a fire in her eyes. The tip of her sword pointed at Zyre. "What in Dûl's name was that?"

"Are you mad?" she demanded, unfazed. "There's no need to kill a soldier on the ground!"

"Are *you*?" the other woman growled. She gestured wildly at the vacant place the man had just been. "I'm not trying to fight off the entire force your prince brought with him, and I certainly refuse to do it single-handedly. But I just might have to now, because you can bet your friend right there has just warned everyone in earshot."

Zyre spun. Surely the man had not fled so quickly. But the street was empty save the two of them and Kadj. "I didn't think…"

"No, you didn't. I'm risking a hell of a lot for you, *majican*," the *aljarne* snarled, her Venascan accent growing thicker. "You pull a stunt like that again and I will throw you into the sea or truss you up and hand you over to the soldiers myself. I will not have you put my operation at risk. Are we clear?"

Too ashamed to ask questions, Zyre could only nod.

"Good."

A horn blew only a few streets over, near the docks, and the *aljarne* cursed in Venascan. Whatever it was, it sounded colorful. "All right. Stealth be damned. It'll be a race now. I hope your magic isn't completely useless."

Well, Zyre hardly would have called them being stealthy before, but now they truly did run as if Tholjun himself were on their heels. A few soldiers caught glimpses of them in their mad flight, but Zyre understood the stakes. The horn would rally what soldiers could come to the docks. However many had been left behind to guard them, it would be difficult enough for the *aljarne* to get the three of them through *without* the added reinforcements.

Suddenly the houses ended, giving way to grass and sand. Ten men in leather armor barred their way. Their eyes fell on Kadj, and then on Zyre. For once, she wished she'd been able to have a smaller soulbeast, one that could fit in her sleeve. She had never expected to face a day where her *sjarvisk* identity would put her in danger.

One pushed his way to the forefront. "The docks are closed. No one in or out."

"I'm afraid that won't work for us," the *aljarne* replied coolly. Flames appeared above her palm, flickering until they rounded out into a fireball intense enough that Zyre could feel it where she stood.

The soldiers glanced uneasily at Kadj, but they held their ground. The one in front drew his sword first, but the others were not slow to follow. The *aljarne* sent the fireball flying, and it struck the man in front. The force of it sent him reeling backward, screaming. The scent of burning flesh was acrid. Another soldier very nearly lost his footing as the first man's flailing arm crashed into his side. Kadj leapt forward, his bared teeth still red from Modél. Zyre scrambled to call magic to her. The *aljarne* pitched another fireball at the group of soldiers and stomped against the ground immediately after, sending a ripple in the earth to slow the charging mass down.

Finally, Zyre's vision turned silver. The magic responded to her fear, rushing toward her like metal to a strong magnet. Air swept around her, the wind billowing against her clothes, her hair. It took everything she had to aim it at the soldier in front of her, and it crashed against him with enough force to send him skittering across the surface of the sea.

The *aljarne* stared at her, her gaze hard and suspicious, but only for a moment. Kadj leapt off of a bloodied soldier, and two other bodies had already been left behind, but the handful that remained regrouped, their sights set on Zyre.

The *aljarne* drew her sword, and Kadj spun around in an effort to reach Zyre.

Then two bodies spat out of an alley, both of them looking like Venascan sailors, taking the soldiers by surprise. Several of the men branched off to face the woman and the newcomers. One soldier kept his sights on Zyre, his griffon emblem seeming to run across his chest with the movement. Zyre's eyes widened. She abandoned her magic and reached for her sword as he closed the distance.

His sword glinted as it arced toward her. She knew her own would not make it up in time.

Then the man stumbled, his entire body falling toward her. Zyre twisted out of the way as he fell to the ground, his neck pooling with blood from Kadj's teeth. Her heart raced as she looked at her surroundings. The *aljarne* had killed the second, and the two strangers had taken out the third between them.

The aljarne's breath was as ragged as Zyre's, although perhaps for better reason. She turned on the two newcomers. "*Ír dezi ke oveleori ed baraschion sil iezt geor mod,*" she snapped.

"*Es mueven estad gerroten,*" the shorter of the two—though still a few inches taller than Zyre—replied.

Zyre listened blankly, her nerves still trembling. All she understood was *baraschion*, ship, and right now was probably the worst time to be having idle conversation.

The *aljarne* shook her head. Turning her dark eyes back on Zyre, she said, "Come on."

She seemed unconcerned about the blood that got on her boots as she stepped over the bodies, and her two companions cared just as little. Zyre very nearly threw up as the ground squelched beneath her boots. She used Kadj to steady herself, but they had to hurry to keep up with the other three.

It was a relief to step onto the docks, her feet thudding against the sturdy and bloodless wood below.

She was really doing this, then. She was really running from her family. Whether she was a liability or not, there was honor in facing impossible odds. There was no honor in retreat.

A handful of soldiers spilled onto the beach as the *aljarne* leapt into a rowboat, her companions already working on casting off. Zyre jumped into the boat with a yelp, but the *aljarne* caught her, her grip surprisingly strong.

Zyre turned, half-afraid that Kadj would refuse to make the jump, or that even if he tried, he would not fit. But she had barely had the thought before the tiger landed easily in its center, the boat sitting low in the water. The *aljarne*'s two companions found their seats and withdrew the oars as the soldiers made it onto the dock. The *aljarne*, at the head of the boat, put her hand in the water, and they began to move slowly toward the strange flat ship, the words *Telaña dir Ansol*—the *Water Spider*—written in silver on its side. The oars propelled it forward even faster, and they were out of reach before the soldiers even made it halfway.

She held her breath, fearing they would jump into one of other boats tied at the docks, but they stood at its edge for only a moment before one of the men barked an order and the soldiers retreated.

The *aljarne* spoke quietly to her companions in Venascan, glancing at the prince's ships that towered not far away. Zyre left them to it, scooting a little closer to Kadj. Blood dripped into a little puddle between his paws. She pressed her fingers carefully into his fur, feeling for the wounds. Kadj flinched and let out a low growl.

"You're my brave boy, *ehzi*," she crooned softly to him as she tore off a strip from the bottom of her dress. Laying even more compliments at his feet, she pressed a wad of cloth against the worst of his gashes, ragged from Modél's antlers. He chuffed uncomfortably, but she continued without breaking stride, tying a light blue strip around his middle, securing the bloodied wad in place.

"You need to clean his wounds," the *aljarne* said coolly.

Zyre raised her eyes to meet the other woman's, fire burning in her blood. "Do you have any cleaning supplies aboard this little rowboat of yours?" The woman didn't answer. "I thought not."

Kadj would need stitches, too, but that would have to wait at least until they got onto the woman's ship.

"Why did you come to Nolasi?" she found herself asking.

The soft conversation died away. The *aljarne* studied her, her deep brown eyes threatening to unseat Zyre. "Trade."

Zyre snorted. Now that she held anger in her fist, she found she couldn't let it go, or didn't want to. "If that's the case, you should not have intervened. What do you gain from this?"

The woman managed to look imperious, even sitting at an

awkward angle, her hand still in the water. "If you don't want my help, I can take you back to shore. Let the prince have you."

The very idea was enough to snuff out Zyre's burning. The woman had a point. She forced herself to untangle her fingers from Kadj's fur.

"That's what I thought," the woman said. Her dark eyes searched Zyre, cold and measuring. "How can you wield so much magic?"

"I don't know what you mean," Zyre replied evenly.

The woman remained unconvinced. "I have met a man with a lion soulbeast. It was a brief encounter, but I know for certain that his magic acted nothing like yours."

Zyre scowled into the water. All she had were secrets and flimsy lies. They were never meant to hold up to scrutiny. They weren't supposed to need to. "I was just born with a lot of magic, I guess. But I can never guess how it'll respond, so if that's what you're after, you're in for a mighty disappointment."

The boat fell under the shadow of the *Water Spider*, and conversation died away. She could hear footsteps thundering on the deck above. The *aljarne* withdrew her hand from the water, and her oarsmen helped slow the boat down so that when it hit the side of the ship, Zyre only swayed a little in her seat. Ropes shot down from over the railing, and the oarsmen quickly tied each one around either end of the boat. Kadj slid toward the lip of the vessel and rested his head on the side as he watched the water slowly, haltingly, be pulled away from them.

An older man, wiry like a cable despite his gray hair, with skin such a dark shade of brown that it looked almost blue, helped the *aljarne* onto deck. He said her name. Neelie. The two strode toward the helm, already deep in conversation, leaving Zyre to hold that name unspoken on her lips, like a secret.

The two oarsmen leapt out with ease, and for a moment, Zyre

feared they'd leave her and Kadj to find a way off the boat on their own, but they didn't. Their grip was steady as they each took a hand and helped pull her over. She didn't jump so much as float ungracefully. Kadj favored his side in his landing. She hurried over to him and whispered praise in his ear. Then she turned to the sailors and found their backs to her. "Wait. Now what?"

One, the shorter one, glanced at the woman. Now that the *aljarne* was on the ship, Zyre realized she emanated an air of authority. Her rescuer was not just an *aljarne*, she was also a captain of the ship. *Thalja have mercy*, Zyre thought. The short sailor said, "Go belowdecks. Wait with our cargo. I'm sure she'll be down to see you when she has time." His accent was so thick that it took her a moment to untangle what he'd said. By then, he'd hurried away.

The woman, Neelie, barked orders at the sailors, all of whom wore similar outfits to hers, save the hat.

Neelie glanced at Zyre.

Feeling her cheeks growing warm, Zyre decided to follow the sailor's advice. She fled below deck.

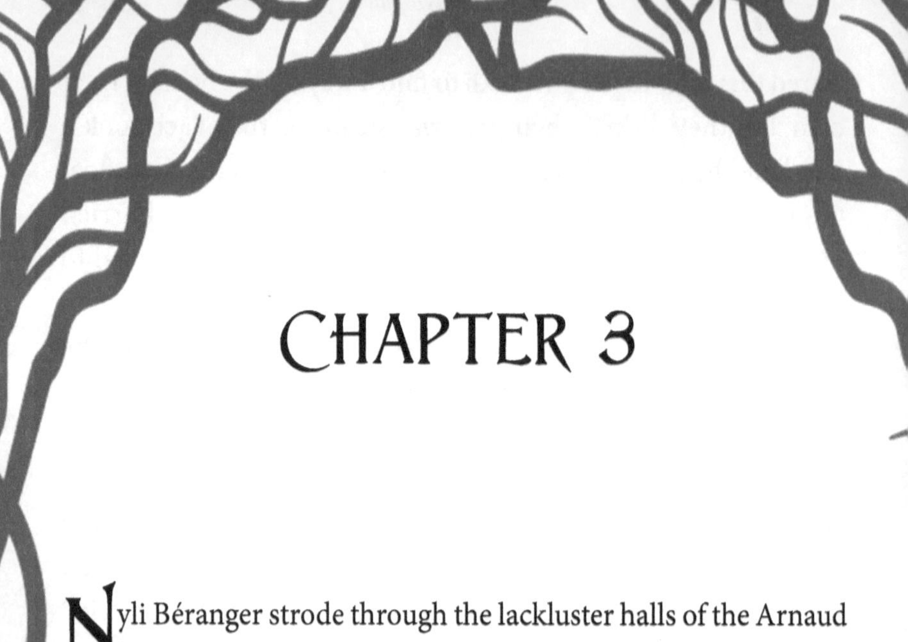

# CHAPTER 3

Nyli Béranger strode through the lackluster halls of the Arnaud house, trying to understand how a thing could fall apart so quickly. Two guards stood at the end of the hall, where a set of double doors would lead to the dining room. There, a messenger had told Nyli, his sister was waiting with a report for him.

Neither Nyli nor his honor guard had to break stride before the doors were open wide enough to admit them.

There were smears of blood on the floor but no bodies. No dead ones, at least, which was a relief from the horror of the corridors outside. Even with the Arnauds' servants, Nyli's men outnumbered Jervin's, but it had still been a bloodier battle than Nyli might've hoped.

Instead, the room was occupied by five living people. Nyli dutifully noticed Rasin, who lounged at the head of the table, inspecting her nails as if she owned the place. Baroness Ivanya Arnaud, *Vinje* Remy Arnaud, the Venascan wife, and Jervin's grandson had been collected. The baroness held a collected air as befitted her station, as if her entire world wasn't crumbling down around her. Remy appeared to have sustained some wounds in the fighting, but he'd taken after Ivanya in his stolidness. He kept flicking glances at Rasin, disappointed, of all things. The Venascan woman seemed to be the only one who wasn't holding up very well, looking ill, her gaze fixed on the table in front of her.

All of this was secondary to the one person he needed to be in this room who wasn't.

"Where's Jervin." It was a question, but at the same time, it wasn't.

Rasin glanced up from her nails. Her expression grew as hard as steel. "We're looking for him."

That was not the answer he wanted to hear. Nyli put his arms behind his back, forcing his expression to remain neutral as his brain ran ahead of him, already thinking of the excuses and half-truths he was going to have to tell his father to mitigate the damage. But every lie he came up with, he could hear his father's cutting reply. *Sloppy, unprepared, useless. Weak.*

More than a dozen Arnaud troops had been armed with various *kjarnik* weapons. At least three had used knives that had corrupted the bloodstream of several of his soldiers. A handful had wielded weapons with an almost eerie precision. Even in the chaos, Nyli's men had recognized them as enchanted. This, at least, was an excuse that would temper his father's anger.

"We found the comte's cousin," Rasin added. "Ljerson. It looks like the Arnauds' girl was better than we anticipated. Well, that or someone managed to get the jump on him *and* his soulbeast, enough to…" She trailed off and made a stabbing motion.

He'd been stabbed? Nyli hadn't thought the girl had it in her. "Where are the other two? Master Roch and Master Elowarin?"

Rasin sniffed. Nyli knew her enough to know it was a front. Whether it was out of spite for Remy or just to keep Ivanya from getting her hopes up, he didn't know. "They are searching the island for any stragglers," she said icily. "They'll find the baron and the girl and do what needs done. It isn't over yet."

It did the job. Baroness Ivanya stiffened. He only granted her a moment of attention, long enough to feel smug. Ivanya thought she was smart, didn't she? The Arnauds had hidden their treasonous activities behind a facade of complacency for years, letting others do their dirty work. Well, maybe Jervin and the *sjarvisk* girl had given them the slip thus far, but Nyli and his men had control of the harbor. Nyli's quarry could not remain hidden for long.

He would not suffer his father's rages for the likes of Jervin Arnaud.

The fast clatter of running feet echoed down through the doors, and Nyli turned only a moment before they burst open. The soldier who entered bowed, working around his heavy breathing. "Your Highness, pardon. A ship has been spotted leaving the harbor. The Venascan cargo ship, the one called *Telaña dir Ansol.*"

Nyli's stomach fell to his feet. "How?" he asked, but the word was hollow, offered out of instinct more than anything else. *Weak. Useless. Stupid.*

"I'm afraid I don't know, Your Highness. We saw from a distance, and I was told to warn you immediately."

He cursed, refusing to look at the baroness, knowing what smugness he'd find there. "Have the horses saddled," he barked to the messenger. The man made another hasty bow and took off running.

Nyli spun, knowing that his perfect courtly mask was slipping. He was losing control of everything.

"Guards," his sister said sharply. He barely hid his flinch. Rasin's honor guard stepped forward, just within his periphery. "Wait with the prisoners. Nyli, with me."

She glided over the floor, raising her skirts so they didn't get bloodied. Nyli glared at the baroness and her son before following after his sister into the hall. She shut the doors, but even then, she kept her voice low. "Keep your head, Nyli. We don't know if Jervin is on that boat."

"Best to assume he is." His palms were beginning to hurt, but he found it harder than it should have been to unfurl his fingers.

Rasin raised a hand in acquiescence. "I know, but don't bet all of your money on a single horse. And don't assume the worst. Our ships can easily overtake a merchant vessel, especially one weighed down by cargo. Go, find out what there is to learn at the docks, and if you need, call some men back to the *Aretmor* to send them in pursuit. We'll get him, Nyli, whether he's on the island or on that ship."

"We'd better," he grumbled, though he was careful not to direct his anger at his sister.

With Rasin to watch the prisoners and keep the men organized, Nyli went to the stables. He and his honor guard swung into their saddles, the horses dancing nervously beneath them. He quieted his mount with a firm hand, then kicked it into a canter. With the wind in his face and the horses' hooves crashing against the dirt, Nyli found his fears being carried away from him. Plans within plans. The Arnauds were not the only clever ones here.

⁂

Jervin Arnaud followed a deer path through the hills. He'd left the sound of shouts behind him, but the patches of blood on his clothes would not fade so easily. Zyre had done a good thing today, warning their family, though he'd have words with her about subtler signals. The ensuing fight that had broken out had split him from his family, and the only reason he'd gotten away at all was in thanks to Captain Merytz. Whether Ivanya or his son had also seen the signal in time remained to be seen.

Merytz raised a hand, suddenly, and Jervin obliged the

command. The young man had already proven himself, and if the gesture was better fit from an honor guard, well, Merytz was currently the closest thing he had to one right now. Jervin quieted his breathing and reached for his sword, straining his ears for whatever had caught Merytz's attention. And, yes, he heard the quickly approaching rhythmic footfalls of soldiers.

Merytz gestured for the hill, and they both scrambled out of sight, leaving the deer path to hide behind the hillside.

The soldiers drew near, and Jervin carefully looked above the grassy earth, marking the number of troops and what weapons they had. Five, two armed with bows, two with spears and one… Jervin smiled. One was a known ally from his years at court. Roch Allais, a *sjarvisk* with a badger soulbeast, and one of their most reliable messengers.

The creature turned its head and looked right at Jervin. His heartbeat grew as thunderous as Tholjun's laugh. A surge of doubt burst in his chest despite himself.

Roch Allais swept his gaze across the path, and, almost carelessly, his eyes latched onto Jervin's. The *sjarvisk* gave a subtle nod, little more than a random bob of the head. His companions did not look Jervin and Merytz's way. They continued on until they passed out of sight.

Jervin exhaled. Good old Roch.

Beside him, Merytz was tenser than a bowstring. They waited behind the hill until they could no longer hear the soldiers, and then waited a little longer still. Then Merytz signaled for them to keep going.

They followed the deer path closer to the cliffs on the west side of the island. The deer path had forked in several places, disappearing almost completely in others. He had to hope Roch had led the Béranger troops down the wrong paths. The *sjarvisk* would not know of Jervin's escape route, but, well, logic would have likely sent him elsewhere. Deeper into the hills, perhaps.

A steep path led them down the face of the cliff, Merytz trailing behind now, in case they found themselves being followed. The cavern at the base of the path remained hidden for the moment, as did the ship tucked inside it, but Jervin knew it was down there. He had been preparing for this possibility for quite some time now. He hadn't had walk down this path for a very long time, however, and he was beginning to feel a little compassion for all of the servants who had made this trip frequently in order to make sure an emergency flight would not find Jervin and his men without supplies.

"Are the men ready to sail?" he asked Merytz, then bit back a curse as he nearly lost his footing.

Merytz reached out to steady him, though by then Jervin had already managed well enough. "As long as they're able to follow orders, sir."

They walked a few more paces in silence.

"If I may, sir?" the captain hazarded.

Jervin did his best to wave on Merytz, though it was a little hard to focus on anything besides not slipping to his death. He half wished they'd been able to keep a ship somewhere a little more accessible, but then Nyli or his scouts probably would have found it, rendering the whole endeavor moot.

"Are you sure we can trust them? Mercenaries?"

"Their employers and I go way back," Jervin replied calmly, although slightly out of breath. "They have no personal stake in this and have no reason to betray us."

Merytz grunted noncommittally, clearly unsure if he believed Jervin but unwilling to argue further.

Down and down they went, sometimes Merytz keeping Jervin from pitching forward, sometimes Jervin offering the young captain a steadying hand of his own. The crashing of the waves grew louder as they drew near. Then it wasn't just the sound, as sea spray flew skyward and splattered across their clothes. It was a relief to step into the cavern, where the water was almost still. Light filtered into the cavern, though the sun stood at the opposite side of the island and it was more shadow in here than anything else.

A small vessel stood anchored near the cavern's shore. Men lounged on the deck, though as soon as they saw him, they scrambled to their feet. Jervin was surprised that the crew were not all dark-skinned Venascans. There was at least one towering pale-skinned man with features that reminded him of his wife and a handful of other sailors who could not be placed even by Jervin's well-traveled eye.

With one last glance over his shoulder to make sure they weren't being followed, Jervin waded into the water, grimacing at the cold that washed into his boots. The ship had a shallow enough belly that it was close to the shore, and Jervin only had to go up to his midriff in the water. Their escape vessel was called *Thalja's Breath.* He could only hope it had the speed implied from its name.

The sailors helped him and Merytz climb over the side of the ship, and then they bowed. A man stepped forward, his sun-dark skin mostly hidden beneath a billowing white shirt. "Greetings, Baron Arnaud. My name is Brandt, and I'll be captaining this vessel." His Venascan accent was surprisingly mellow.

"A pleasure to meet you, Captain," Jervin said politely. "Has anyone else come? My wife? My son? A *sjarvisk* with a tiger?"

The man shook his head. "None but you, I'm afraid."

Jervin sighed. It was as he'd feared. But perhaps they were just held back, not far behind. "How fast do you think she can run?"

At that, the captain grinned, and it looked almost feral. "Fast enough."

"Then unless fate forces our hands, we'll wait until nightfall." If Thalja shone down on him today, if even for a minute, an hour, then the rest of his family would come. "After that, we'll make for the mainland."

Captain Brandt nodded, bowing in a curt quarterly fashion.

It was time to stop hiding in the shadows.

The ship rocked underneath Zyre, and she put a light hand on Kadj's shoulder to steady herself. They went below, where a handful of men scuttled about doing what Thyljal-knew-what. She pressed herself against the walls as they ran past, but it was out of instinct more than anything else. The crew thundered above her head, making hasty preparations to cast off. It struck her that she had no idea where they were going.

Swallowing, Zyre found, was nearly impossible. Her throat burned. She made it to the other end of the hallway, somehow, and down a flight of stairs that ended at a door. Swinging it open, she found mountains of crates and boxes, stacked well above her head, with aisles just wide enough for her and Kadj to fit through if they went single file. A small lantern, carefully secured to the wall, was her only source of light.

Zyre shut the door as soon as Kadj was through. The latch clicked, a definitive sound that signaled just how alone she was. The reality of what she'd just done crashed into her. Suddenly, she found she did not know how to breathe. She fell against the door, no longer certain she could trust her own equilibrium. As her breathing came out in spurts and gasps, she slowly sank to the floor, reaching for Kadj. He pressed his head to her hands. She clung to him like a lifeline, fighting to remember how to breathe, how to think.

*What did I just run away from?*

Well. That was a devastatingly easy question to answer. She had just left her family to the prince. They needed her and her explosive magic. Surely, her father had not anticipated this. And she had left them to their fate. *Eris bi eljers* indeed. She had shown neither skill nor valor today.

Someone knocked on the door, and Zyre cursed as she sucked in an unsteady breath. "A moment!" she called to the newcomer, hoping they could not hear the quiver in her voice. She rose, scrubbing her face, then straightened her muddied and bloodied uniform. Then she opened the door.

It was the woman, Neelie. The captain. She held something up, and in the lantern light, Zyre saw a small metal pendant in the shape of a raindrop. Neelie hesitated, then said, "For your tiger."

Zyre stared at the pendant in confusion.

"It's *kjarnik* magic. Do you know how it works?"

Zyre shook her head, inspecting the engravings on the pendant with an avid curiosity that, somehow, managed to ground her. It was fine work. She didn't know anything about *kjarnik* magic besides the fact that used a *leiks*-like bond with domestic types of animals and it was woven into metal in some specific way that resulted in a spell of some kind. She didn't know if the skill of the metalwork made a difference, but everything from the fine chain this pendant hung on to the etchings on it that made it look like an *actual* drop of rain would have made the piece valuable even without the spellwork.

Neelie offered the pendant to Zyre, and Zyre let the cold metal fall into her waiting palm.

"Without *kjarnik* magic, you'll need a drop of blood to activate it. You'll press it to your tiger's wounds, and it should heal him."

Zyre almost reached for the knife hidden on her person, then she stopped herself. She was on a strange ship by the favor of a strange woman—an *aljarne*, it seemed, but that only made matters more complicated. It might be best if Zyre did not show all of her cards.

"May I borrow your sword?" she asked.

Neelie barked out a laugh. "To prick your finger? I think not." She whipped out a knife, though where she'd been hiding it, Zyre could not have guessed. So. Neelie had more than just her rapier. That was good to know. The woman was still laughing as she offered the knife, hilt-first, to Zyre.

The grip was smooth, clearly well-worn from use. Zyre tossed the blade in the air, testing its grip, and, if she was being honest with herself, showing off a little. So what if she didn't know what Neelie wanted or if she was trustworthy. In the cargo hold, with no one chasing after them or trying to kill them, Zyre realized the other woman was quite pretty, with dark brown eyes that could have swallowed her whole and beautiful high cheekbones.

The knife descended, and she caught the tip of the blade between her fingers, pleased when she did not feel the sharp sting of a cut. Merytz had taught her that one on one slow summer day. She risked a glance at Neelie through her eyelashes, but the woman still seemed caught up in her joke. Zyre blushed and carefully pressed the edge of the knife against her thumb.

Blood welled up in the small wound and then fell, cascading until it splashed against the metal raindrop. Zyre hastily checked her grip on the chain. The metal piece did nothing for a moment, and then it was as if Zyre had caught a small sun. She cursed, putting her free hand in front of her eyes as she hurried toward Kadj. The tiger growled in displeasure, turning his face away from the beacon. She pressed the metal between the fabric and his wounds, and the bandages muffled its light, barely.

After a few moments, the light grew dimmer, then flickered.

Kadj chuffed. The light faded completely, the metal raindrop regaining its silver sheen save only for a spot of rust-red blood.

Zyre carefully slipped a finger under the fabric, feeling for the gash. There was nothing to show for Modél's antlers beyond a line of skin that held no fur. She turned, a thank-you on her lips, but Neelie's gaze was sharp and suspicious, and suddenly Zyre felt like there was not enough space between the two of them.

"There's something you're not telling me about your magic, *Magi* Zyre," she said, her voice as sharp as the edge of her knife.

"We've only just met," Zyre replied, keeping her tone level. "You don't know anything about me. What is this? Are you part of the rebellion? Why are you *helping* me?"

Neelie snorted derisively "I've never seen a *kjarnik* charm glow like that for a *sjarvisk*," she said, pointedly changing the subject. "Not even for my mother. Why is your magic so explosive, *Magi*? Why can you not control it?"

The best answer seemed to be silence.

"Look," Neelie said, sounding vexed. "I know you have no reason to trust me, but I'm not your enemy. I can help you better if you're honest with me." Her eyes lit up, and Zyre knew she had figured it out. "You're an *aljarne,* aren't you?"

Zyre's fingers tightened around Kadj's fur. Angrily, she said, "*Aljarne* don't have soulbeasts. That's why they go mad."

The other woman flinched. "Of course *aljarne* don't have soulbeasts. My mistake." With one last grimace directed at Zyre, Neelie reached for the door.

Cursing because she still needed answers, Zyre swallowed her pride and said, "Wait. Where are we going?"

"Bijal. You will be safe from the prince's reach there."

With that, Neelie stormed out of the cargo hold and slammed the door between them.

Zyre found she could not breathe easy until the other woman's footsteps had faded.

***

The truth of it was, Neelie's suspicions only seemed far-fetched because, in all instances but Zyre's, what made an *aljarne* an *aljarne* was their lack of soulbeast. When they called, magic answered, no *leiks* to an animal required, and no sleight of hand with a knife, no fancy magic, no poison in an animal's food could sever an *aljarne* from their abilities. But it burned, that power. It rolled across them, like wind cutting away at a rock. The rock could withstand the wind, but not forever, and eventually it wore the *aljarne's* sanity away.

Zyre let herself fall to the floor—deck?—at Kadj's feet. He lay his head on his paws and closed his eyes. Within a matter of heartbeats, he was asleep. She put her head in her hands and forced out a long, unsteady sigh. No one was supposed to be able to find out the truth of him, yet in a matter of hours, she'd already drawn the suspicions of two people. Knowing that one of those people was dead made it worse, not better.

Part of the whole charade had been a matter of practicality. A noble-born *sjarvisk* raised brows, perhaps, but beyond the noble blood, they were no different than any other *sjarvisk*. But all *sjarvisk* were, according to Corvikan law, property of the regis, to be loaned out to noble families at his discretion. Noble-born *sjarvisk* always remained with the regis, and that was where the practicality came in. With nearly a hundred *sjarvisk* milling about the palace grounds and city proper, her secret would not have lasted long.

She simply had no frame of reference regarding the differences between her bond with Kadj and a normal *leiks*. She'd have said something or done something, and they'd have uncovered the truth, and she'd have been executed. *Aljarne* were just too powerful and, eventually, too unpredictable. When they snapped, it was said an entire city might fall.

Now, here she sat, terrified and ashamed, and angry at feeling terrified and ashamed. Zyre could see now that her father's plan had been a foolish one. Had she been in full control of her magic, she might've been a force to be reckoned with. Maybe she really could have taken Nyli's men all single-handedly. As it was, though? Well. She could have been run through with a sword while trying to call her magic, and she'd have been lucky enough to kill even one man with it.

The frustration built, pressing against her ribs, threatening to break them. Chills ran down her arms, and she wanted so terribly to just let her anger out in a single blast of… of something. Instead, she rolled to her feet, needing to move if only to prevent herself from breaking apart the ship that was supposed to be her salvation.

Fearing what would happen if she let herself dwell, Zyre forced herself to move, walking toward the towers of crates and boxes. There really was nowhere else for her to go down here. *Well*, she thought, *I may not be able to figure out how my family is doing right now, but perhaps I can at least learn a little something about my rescuer.*

The light from the fire cast shadows on the stack closest to her. The topmost one was an open crate.

Long bottles sat nestled against each other, the bases wrapped in thick cloth and the thin necks revealing a dark liquid inside. The cap was sealed in wax, pressed with a silhouette of a bee. She didn't know what exactly it meant, but the dark liquid was almost certainly wine, and the bee was likely meant to identify what vineyard it came from. Zyre was half tempted to unwrap one of the bottles to see if the label had any identifying marks—and truly, it might've come from anywhere; even Las Corvika had its own vineyards, though she knew from her mother that although there were some things Las Corvika did well, wine was not one of them—but if anything wound up out of place, Zyre was the only one Neelie could blame.

Zyre meandered to another crate farther from the door. The lamplight barely shone this far in, and she had to strain to see. The one she chose had a lid, but after feeling around the edges, she found a latch, and it was easy to open. She whistled appreciatively. The vases were wrapped carefully, but what she could see was enough to identify them as Pailyran. Pailyr was well known for its arts in general, but Zyre happened to know that the district of Vresaeli was widely regarded as the most adept at creating beautiful ceramics. She wanted nothing more than to unwrap them, to run her fingers over their smooth surfaces, along whatever patterns had been painted there. Had her mother been here, Zyre knew for a fact that Neelie would have risen in Ivanya's estimation.

The crate beneath was thin but long, and it looked promising.

Zyre would have put good money on it being paintings. Taking care with the pottery, she hefted it to the floor. She tried to pry off the lid and was surprised when it did not budge. But searching for a latch proved useless. Finally, she accepted defeat, squeezed around the crate of pottery, and unfastened the lantern from the wall. Kadj did not even stir.

Armed now with the light, she discovered that the reason she couldn't find a latch was because it had been wedged against the neighboring stack in the most inconvenient way possible. It took some straining and nearly getting her fingers stuck, but the latch clicked, and the top swung open without protest.

Zyre's jaw fell. Not paintings, then.

Instead, the silver glint of steel peeked out beneath a covering of straw. She reached out, then stopped herself, listening to what was happening above her. Feet no longer raced across the deck, from what she could hear, but that could have meant anything. Perhaps Neelie would storm back down here with the rest of her crew and demand the truth from her. Would Neelie be afraid of a fellow *aljarne*?

Before she could stop herself a second time, Zyre brushed the straw away. The metal was engraved. It was done in Venascan design, heavily reliant on linework. Vines crawled up the steel of all the blades she could see, although the exact nature of the patterns varied with each sword.

Enchanted swords. Only Regis Béranger could commission such weapons in Las Corvika, and something told her that Neelie did not have the proper paperwork for these.

Curious, Zyre shot a glance at the door, acknowledging even as she did so that the gesture was useless. Then she called to magic, felt her skin pebble as it answered her. The strangest wave of colors eddied and swirled across the entire length of the blade. Against her better nature, she picked one up. The colors didn't fade or flash, but the hilt grew warm and hummed beneath her fingers. Zyre quickly set the blade back down, not knowing how enchanted blades worked and not willing to test it.

What had Neelie said, right before they'd run? *I can do nothing more here.*

A hundred questions raced through her head. If these were weapons meant for Nyli, why send them to Lasinia? Which meant they were likely for Zyre's father instead. Indeed, Remy had gone to the *Spider* as soon as it had docked; surely it had not been to investigate the lovely Pailyran artwork. Did this mean her father had anticipated enchanted weapons and hadn't gotten a chance to fetch them? Or were these particular ones bound elsewhere?

At least one thing Zyre could be relatively sure of, though. The *Water Spider* was a pirate ship, and Neelie was its pirate captain.

# CHAPTER 4

There were no other crates of illegal weapons. At least, not ones that were easy to access. So, after a little more digging and finding more common goods like fabrics, fruits, and spices, Zyre fought back another yawn as she admitted defeat and returned to Kadj's side. She didn't know how much time had passed but doubted it was more than an hour. Things had certainly quieted on deck. Fastening the lantern back in its place, Zyre sat against Kadj and closed her eyes.

In the silence, there was no avoiding the subject anymore. The chaos of the fighting played on an endless loop. She saw the soldier in Nolasi fall, struck down by Neelie's sword. If it wasn't that, it was the soldier she'd blasted across the water—had he even survived? She'd been so focused on other things she could not remember if he'd resurfaced—or Kadj ravaging the other soldier on the beach.

*They were going to start a fight anyway,* she told herself harshly. *They probably would have died either way. Or, if they hadn't, they would have killed people* you *know.*

It wasn't enough. It still felt like her fault.

In the end, after an unknowable amount of time, her exhaustion pulled her under, and her mind fell quiet at last.

What woke her, some time later, was the thunder of footsteps on the second level of the ship and the strained voice of one of the sailors. Zyre, dragged from sleep, barely heard the Venascan words, muffled as they were by the wooden floor. But she did, after a moment, catch that word *barcaschion* again. *Ship.*

Zyre prodded Kadj until he opened his eyes and, with some reluctance, rolled to his feet, stretching. She didn't wait for him. She left the cargo hold and found Neelie stumbling shoeless and hatless out of the captain's quarters. Neelie spared Zyre a look, but she didn't say anything. Zyre followed her silently up the steps onto the deck, Kadj trailing silently behind them.

The ship was rife with activity. Some of the sailors were tending to ropes or climbing the masts, but most were manning the massive oars that sped the *Water Spider* along. They were well and truly at sea now. Zyre was farther from home than she'd ever been before. There was nothing, absolutely nothing, but water and sky.

Neelie had climbed up the steps, where the wiry old man from before waited for her. The man gestured behind the ship and passed her a beautiful spyglass made of gold.

Zyre hesitated at the base of the steps. "What is it?"

"A ship," Neelie replied, bringing the spyglass away from her eye. "A big one."

Throwing decorum and etiquette to the wind, Zyre jumped onto the raised section of the ship, strode past the great wheel that the old man tended to, and joined Neelie at the railing. The other woman offered her spyglass, but Zyre refused it in favor of her own. Even with it, the sea was endless, the skyline unbroken by land or vessel. Then the metal dug into her nose as Neelie pushed the focus of the spyglass a few inches to the left.

There. Yes, in the distance was the silhouette of a ship.

The harder Zyre squinted, the more certain she was that the ship looked familiar. "Is that…?"

"The *Aretmor*? Yes, I think so."

Zyre brought the spyglass down.

Neelie had crossed her arms in front of her chest, still frowning. "This doesn't bode well."

"How certain are we that they're pursuing us?" Zyre asked.

Neelie rolled her eyes. "Do you see any other ships they could be chasing, *Magi* Zyre? The sea is too big for this to be happenstance."

It was not the answer she was hoping for. "But why? Why go through such effort for a single *sjarvisk*?" Surely, the prince did not know who she was. But… What, did she think he would have just pointed at her, shouting *I know you're their daughter*? Nyli was cunning, clearly. He must've known more than he was letting on.

She feared, though, what their pursuit meant for her family. They wouldn't bother to chase after her, no matter what secrets they knew about her, if her father and the others had managed to get away. Without her father, Zyre could have the power of all three gods combined and it still wouldn't matter. It was Jervin alone who could upset Notoyem's claim to the throne.

Neelie said something. It took a moment to sink in.

"Outrun them? Are you mad? That's a proper warship!" Zyre regretted saying the word "mad" as soon as it was out of her mouth, but, really, it *was* a crazy plan. She didn't have to know much about ships to recognize that the *Telaña dir Ansol*, the *Water Spider*, had been built for efficiency, not speed. And the *Aretmor* had heavy artillery. If the *Spider* tried to flee, the warship would rain destruction upon them all.

"If I let them catch up, they will search the ship, *Magi*. I can't guarantee they won't find you." Neelie scowled as if she were being forced to eat rotten food.

"Why do you care so much?" Zyre demanded. "Why did you risk your life for me back in Nolasi?"

Neelie spared her a look of disdain. "Do you have a death wish?"

"No, but—"

"Look, I have my reasons. If that's not sufficient enough for you, then by all means, your ride out of here is on its way."

Zyre scowled at Neelie, then, after a moment, looked away.

"All right, then," the captain said.

Zyre thought about the contraband below. The captain surely had motivations beyond keeping her safe. "Then what do we do? If we can't outrun them, our best bet is that we give them what they want: the chance to find what they are looking for." Her stomach grew a little queasy. *I can't guarantee they won't find you.* If they did, it was either submit to her own execution or risk drowning them all in her efforts to fight back.

The captain shook her head. She muttered something in Venascan. Zyre waited as Neelie barked a few orders at the older man. Raylir, she thought Neelie called him. Then Neelie gestured for Zyre to follow, and the two of them ran below deck.

Once in the cargo hold, Neelie led the way through the stacks of crates, not bothering with the lantern. A small fire flickered above her palm. Zyre held her breath, hoping that nothing looked out of place to Neelie's discerning eye, but the other woman said nothing. Instead, they came upon a wall along the side of the ship. Neelie bent down and pressed the wood. A two-slat-wide section swung open on silent, invisible hinges, revealing a secret compartment. Her heart sank.

"Maybe we had better try to run," Zyre offered.

Neelie frowned as she glanced over her shoulder impatiently.

"You should turn me over," Zyre said softly. "I'd rather you didn't, of course, but you've already killed men for me and put yourself at risk when you barely even know me."

"Don't be stupid," Neelie snarled, spinning back around. Her intense gaze threatened to bury Zyre. Her tone remained as firm as steel even as she continued, "Some fools will never understand that a *majican* is more than their magic. A *najik*, an *aljarne*, is more than the madness that will corrupt their mind; they are everything that comes before, every good deed and brave action. I will not have my fellow magic-users chased down like rabid dogs."

An understanding passed between the two of them, and Zyre felt terrible for doubting Neelie. The least she could do was be brave enough for this.

*Eris bi eljers*, Zyre thought to herself, then ducked into the crawlspace, pinning her legs against her chest to make room for Kadj. Neelie nodded to herself, then closed off the crawlspace. Zyre's world went dark.

She wedged herself into a corner and hated how the wood dug into her back. It was impossible to get comfortable. Kadj's presence almost seemed to make things worse, making the space even smaller.

It had been years since she'd been confined to secret compartments and forgotten passageways, in the months after her magic had begun to manifest in noticeable forms but before a stranger had come to Lasinia with Kadj in tow. Her parents had let loose a rumor that Zyre Arnaud, the youngest daughter of the baron, had passed from a ruthless illness. They'd mourned in public while Zyre hid. For months. That alone nearly drove her to madness, with nothing but her worries and her loneliness.

Zyre shifted again, closing her eyes, though it made no difference.

*This is the last time*, she told herself. *I am done running away.*

⚜

In the dark of the crawlspace, time moved with unerring slowness. Zyre had no idea how long it might take for the *Aretmor* to catch up to the *Spider*. The minutes dragged on. Eventually, everything quieted.

And then she heard them. Boots too loud and self-assured and rhythmic to be the sailors'.

Zyre barely breathed.

The door crashed open. A man yelled to search *everything*. Kadj tensed under Zyre's grip, and she barely swallowed a whimper.

They came into the cargo hold, their voices growing louder, the storm of boots pressing through the aisles, boxes scraping against each other. Amidst it all, Zyre heard Neelie's voice, quivering with barely contained anger. "As I told you, Captain, there is no one aboard my ship save my crew."

"Then explain the men you killed back at port," another, deeper, voice demanded.

Zyre's arms felt as weak as half-dead weeds. She eased one hand from Kadj to the hidden knife, hardly daring to breathe.

"I will not have Corvikan half-wits trying to keep me from my ship," Neelie snapped. "I have deliveries to make, some of them perishable. Do you know how much money you can make on rotted fruits, Captain?"

"Watch your tone, Venascan."

"Hey, be careful with that! That one crate is probably worth more than what you dogs make in a year."

"Captain!" a man barked. "Look at this!"

Amidst the ruckus of the rest of the troops, Zyre had no idea what they had found. It was perilously close to her, but she did not think a soldier had found the hidden compartment. Neelie said, "I have papers for those."

Zyre strained her ears, wondering if the Corvikan men had found the enchanted swords Zyre had stumbled across earlier. She stayed frozen in place. The boots seemed to be everywhere, covering whatever it was the captain replied.

Then Kadj stiffened, half of a heartbeat before a latch sounded and a line of light burned against the wood panel on her right. The tiger bowled into the half-open door, and the soldier behind it barely had time to curse as he fell. Zyre let her instincts kick in, and she slipped the knife out, rolling into the open space. A good eight men crowded the cargo hold with her and Neelie, included the decorated Corvikan captain. All eight had their swords out even as Kadj lifted his reddened maw, tail flickering dangerously. Neelie exploded, drawing her fist sharply to her chest and then flinging it out. A dozen ice arrows flew, feathering three of the soldiers. They crumpled to the ground without a word.

Zyre jumped to the nearest one, dancing around his sword, her heart hammering. The steel sang. With a scream, Zyre let the knife fly as she dodged the sword once more, contorting herself. The knife missed his heart, but the sailor cried out, dropping his guard as he reached instinctively for the blade protruding from his shoulder. She turned her momentum back to him, lunging forward, fingers grappling for the knife. They both fell back, and only a stack of crates kept them upright. The sailor's warm blood smeared across her fist as she yanked out the knife. With a yell, he arced his sword for another blow. She buried her knife right between the ribs, just as Merytz had taught her.

Her stomach threatened to betray her, but she swallowed the bile and took his fallen sword. Neelie was hard-pressed fighting the captain of the *Aretmor* and another, her rapier a constant flash of silver even as bubbles of fire, air, and water flew wherever her sword was not. Kadj had his teeth sunk into the seventh sailor's leg, ignoring the punches the man landed on his side. The tiger shook his great head.

Whatever was left of her breakfast made it halfway up her throat. She found herself looking at the eighth sailor. The man raised his sword, then let it tumble to the ground as he darted toward the steps.

"Zyre!" Neelie shouted, barely deflecting a blow from her adversaries.

But Zyre was already dodging upended crates and askew boxes, chasing the man. If he got above deck, if he warned the *Aretmor*, the warship's ballistae would tear the *Spider* to pieces.

She scrambled after him, letting her magic crawl up her arms, down her spine. The sword was a weight in her hand, and she dropped it. As he scaled the steps to the main deck, Zyre drew close and leapt across the distance, crashing into him. Distantly, Zyre heard the man gasp for air as his chest collided with the steps, but that was secondary to the shouts that rose across the ship. She looked up. The Venascans drew weapons, colliding with the Corvikan sailors on board.

Zyre scrambled to her feet, barely evading a knife thrust from the downed sailor. Men in Béranger green began to thunder across the deck of the *Aretmor*. A single voice raised itself above the chaos. "Artillery! Move! Sink the Arnaud traitor and everyone with him."

*No*, Zyre thought, desperately looking for some way out of this. Men screamed and died around her. Blood crawled across the deck like small waves devouring a beach at high tide.

Feet pounded behind her, and a squeak escaped her throat as she bolted to the side. Her pounding heart felt a little relief as Neelie appeared, bloodied but alive. She took one glance at the

*Aretmor*'s deck, then turned to Zyre. Enemy sailors ran toward them, ready to engage. "If you have big magic hiding in there, *Magi*, now's the time to use it."

Swallowing her panic, Zyre darted around the incoming group of soldiers. She ran toward the *Aretmor*, not entirely sure what she was going to do once she was on its deck but knowing that if she didn't destroy those ballistae, Neelie and her crew would die, and it would be all her fault. She leapt onto the gangplank, letting her vision turn orange as fire offered itself to her. The *Aretmor* would not sink this ship.

A sailor yanked at the wooden plank beneath her. She stumbled, barely catching her footing. Another man ran over to help him. The ground buckled beneath her, and she fell.

Zyre crashed into the water, her magic escaping her grasp as the frigid sea swallowed her whole. It took everything in her not to scream. She pushed herself to the surface. Crossbow bolts dove into the water beside her, and by instinct, the magic crashed back into her, the air turning silver. Bolts raining down upon her head shattered on impact of the air shield. Zyre spat out the salt water as she struggled to stay afloat. And then an absolutely mad idea appeared in her mind's eye, a gift from Tholjun himself. Sucking in as much air as she could manage, she flung the air up. Then she dove, following the barnacles down toward the belly of the ship.

Her magic answered her summons so virulently that it staved off the chattering of her teeth. Her vision, already blue from the sea, turned a dark indigo, almost black, as she called to water. Zyre didn't try to bring the entire sea around her, uncertain she could even if she tried. Instead, she turned as much of it to ice as she could manage, praying to Tholjun that her magic would not explode. The ice coalesced into a sharp point, bigger even than Zyre herself.

Using a motion that jettisoned her backward toward the

*Spider*, she launched the great ice spear at the base of the *Aretmor* and watched as it tore into the belly of the ship. There was a loud, terrible groan. Then, as her vision went spotty, she made the ice melt. The sea rushed in, the force of it tearing at the edges of the massive hole so that it grew even larger.

The crossbow bolts continued to cut through the water. Her head pounded almost as harshly as her heart. She needed to breathe. She needed to get above water. Zyre kicked, scrambling for the surface, her magic ready to fling shards of ice toward the green-clad sailors as she burst above the water. The men cried out in pain and surprise as her weapons found their mark, but she could still hear the grinding of the ballistae as they were loaded and aimed. Zyre could not help but tread water, horrified at the destruction she had caused.

"Sir! We're taking on water!" someone screeched aboard the *Aretmor*. Already, the ship was visibly lower.

"Zyre!" a familiar voice called. Neelie leaned over the railing of the *Spider*, breathing heavily, a hand clutching her other arm. "Get out of the way."

Having some idea of what was about to happen, Zyre swam back toward the *Spider*. She didn't see the first blows land, but she could hear the screams of the Béranger men as magic ripped into the *Aretmor*. A Venascan sailor flung a line at Zyre, and she took it, letting the man haul her up, some sick part of her wanting to see the damage that Neelie was inflicting on the other ship. Zyre never would have thought one could hear a ship sink, but the wood groaned as the water clawed at it, and the men shouted, trying in vain to stave off their demise. By the time two sets of strong hands were hauling her back into the *Spider*, what remained of the *Aretmor* above water was inexplicably burning, the acrid scent bombarding Zyre's nose.

She barely managed to twist back over the railing before everything spilled out of her stomach and into the sea.

Neelie barked something at Raylir. The Venascan words rolled off her tongue too fast for Zyre to understand anything, but she knew what the woman was saying. *Get us out of here.* The first mate hurried to the helm, and both he and Neelie shouted at the sailors as they scrambled to get their oars back in place. Neelie took the steps two at a time and came beside Zyre as she turned away from the railing and braved the carnage on the deck.

Those of Neelie's crew not occupied in putting space between them and the floundering *Aretmor* were working together to haul the dead green-clad sailors over the side. It was a punch in Zyre's gut, a display of disrespect that she dared not voice and was afraid to dwell on.

Zyre started as a hand fell on her shoulder. Neelie stood at her side with a grimace. Dark red stains had smeared across most of her shirt and trousers, though Zyre was relieved to see few injuries. "That was impressive, *Magi* Zyre. I was afraid you didn't have it in you."

It seemed like an odd compliment, saying someone did a good job at killing, so she ignored the comment. Pulling her divided skirts above her ankles, Zyre stepped around the bodies and the blood. She dared not count the fallen or the wounded. Her head was still pounding, and she was not sure her heart could take that kind of knowledge.

The remnants of Neelie's crew were below deck, carrying out the dead from the cargo hold. Zyre found she could not stomach the thought of returning there. She darted into the first room she walked past. Kadj bounded in right behind her. Zyre almost turned and left when she realized she was in the captain's quarters, fitted with a small writing desk bolted to the ground and a bed shoved into the corner. She passed up both, opting instead to lean against the frame of the closed door, doing her best to breathe.

What a hollow, hollow victory. She had just sentenced a hundred men, maybe more, to a watery grave. There really was blood on her hands now. She feared she would not be sleeping anytime soon.

But the magic from the water had been the biggest she'd ever done before, and Zyre began to feel the effects all at once. Blessed blackness took over midway through a thought.

*Thalja's Breath* cut through the waves with all of the speed that Captain Brandt had promised. The dark night sky reflected Jervin's sour mood. No one had come to the ship's alcove before night fell, and there was no ignoring what that meant. The Béranger brats had gotten their hands on his family or had killed them.

The small ship crested the waves effortlessly, and in the familiar pitch and fall of the deck, he listed what he knew. Notoyem Béranger was known for his temper, but he was a man easily distracted by the delights his power had given him. It was a toss of a coin if he would execute Ivanya and Remy as traitors or try to use them against Jervin. There was a very real possibility Notoyem would kill them one at a time, pushing to see how far Jervin would go before he caved against the regis's wishes, but that was only if he could decide who to kill first, and on that front, Jervin hoped his wife and son could stall with their resourcefulness. Ivanya was as fierce and cunning as she was beautiful, and Jervin held on to the hope that Rasin held some loyalty to Remy.

And Zyre. He didn't know what had happened to her. She had tried to warn him; Jervin was sure of it. Perhaps she was the very reason he'd managed to give Nyli the slip. If she was alive, she must be in the prince's clutches as well. All those years hiding her identity, keeping her on Lasinia and away from the capital, could go down the drain in one fell swoop.

Captain Merytz approached with a bow.

"Any sign of pursuit?" Jervin asked distractedly.

"No, my lord," Merytz said. Even in the dark, he looked a little sickly. The man had not taken well to ships. "The captain says if they had caught sight of us, we would have seen them by now."

Jervin nodded thoughtfully. Sailing out of the alcove and onto the open sea had been harrowing to say the least. Even with night already upon them, there had been a good chance they'd be heard over the water and the prince's ships would pursue them. As *Thalja's Breath* had followed the coastline of Lasinia in order to set the right course, Jervin had seen Nolasi's docks well lit by torches, and one of the ships was barely visible by the pinpricks of light on its deck. The other, the *Aretmor*, Jervin was sure, was so dark and quiet that it could have just as easily not been there at all.

If it wasn't in the harbor, though, that did leave the question of where it had gone and if it would likely appear somewhere near them. That Corvikan merchant vessel, the *Embrunis*, the *Thalja's Breath* could outrun. The *Aretmor* was another matter entirely.

"Thank you, Captain. You may return below deck if you wish."

Merytz took his offer gratefully.

Jervin turned back to face the sea. It had been far too long since he'd sailed to the mainland. How many years had it been? Four? Five? Certainly, not since Notoyem had learned of his daughter's interest in Remy and the Arnauds' subsequent expulsion from court. Oh, how close they'd gotten to worming their way back into the regis's good graces and unifying the two factions dividing Las Corvika. Instead, their country regressed while the likes of Venasca and Pailyr pulled quickly ahead. Las Corvika was eating dust and growing weaker for it.

With a scowl, the baron looked skyward and muttered a prayer under his breath. Then he pivoted and made for the stern, dodging quick-paced sailors who would just as likely curse at Jervin as they would step out of his way. He was well familiar with these Venascan ships. Trotting up the four steps that allowed the captain to overlook the rest of the deck, Jervin strode up beside Brandt. "How long until we reach land, Captain?"

Brandt's focus settled on a young sailor fumbling with the wrong hitch knot. The captain shouted colorful instructions at the sailor, who corrected his mistake then quickly scurried off. "Five days if the wind holds true," he then said calmly.

Well, then. An additional two days to arrive in General Mahieu Tavere's encampment, and then they could begin planning. It would take the royal brats just as long to reach Les Stelvo; Tavere's encampment wasn't that far away from the capital. Still, it would be a long wait.

"And your so-called Viper? Will she meet us there?"

The Viper, who had captained the Venascan shipping vessel in his harbor, was originally supposed to have sent all of the weapons to Tavere, but that plan had been forced to change at the last minute when Jehan Fidou had warned them of Nyli's abrupt departure. Now that the entire plan had been torn to pieces, the fate of his already-paid-for merchandise remained unclear. And they *needed* them if they were to stand a chance against the defenses of Les Stelvo and the regis.

The captain only shrugged. "I cannot speak to her intentions, Baron Arnaud. All I know is what my eyes told me, which is to say she is no longer at Lasinia."

Jervin searched the man's voice for any trace of betrayal. Adreia herself, best known as the Pirate Queen, had sent Brandt to them. But it had been many years since he and Adreia had seen each other, and perhaps her alliances had shifted.

"No matter," Jervin said calmly. "We will make do whether we have her cargo or not."

If allegiances *had* shifted, that could easily mean he was walking into a trap. The *Aretmor* could be following behind, just out of sight, waiting for Jervin to lead them to his rebel army. Well, even if that was Notoyem's hope, he would not find them easy prey. Twenty years, they'd been fighting the Bérangers' claim to the throne. Sometimes covertly, sometimes less so, but Notoyem had broken tradition by seizing the throne, and Jervin had lost far too many friends and family as it was to sit idly by and let it happen again.

No, if Regis Notoyem Béranger was ready to get his hands dirty, Jervin was just as ready to oblige him. He would bring the usurper's little empire to its knees.

# CHAPTER 5

Neelie, daughter of Adreia, daughter of Caelan, trudged off the deck of the *Telaña dir Ansol*, making her way below to her quarters. She'd been fighting off yawns for the past hour, and her body felt so heavy it was as if her bones had been replaced with steel. She'd used big magic today, more than she'd normally risk, even at sea. She was exhausted enough to ignore the bloodstains decorating the floors. Someone would have to clean those soon, she thought tiredly. A project for another day. One of many.

Her hand was on the rough wood of her cabin door before she realized it was closed. She always left it ajar, trusting her crew completely. None of them would have shut it. So… A Corvikan sailor hiding from the carnage, perhaps? Shutting her eyes, Neelie gathered her strength for one last fight. Easing her sword out of its scabbard, she pushed the door open and jumped through.

She very nearly tripped over the tiger's great slumbering form, half propped as he was against the doorframe. *Magi* Zyre slept with her back pressed against the wall, a hand clutched against the scruff of the tiger's fur. Despite the noise, neither of them stirred. They'd both used pretty big magic today too.

Neelie stayed in the doorway for several seconds longer than she probably should have as she debated whether or not she was angry at the breach in privacy. With a quiet sigh, she made up her mind, returning her rapier to its scabbard. She was too tired to care after all. Leaving the other woman where she slept, Neelie stumbled into bed and was asleep in seconds.

When she woke several hours later, she didn't know if it was to the cold, wet nose that pressed against her hand or if it was the soft curses that streamed out of Zyre's mouth. She yanked her hand back, surprised at how disconcerting it was, even now, to wake up with some sharp-toothed animal staring at her. Zyre's tiger—if it *was* actually Zyre's in the way a soulbeast *was* to a *majican*—flicked his tail curiously. Neelie sat up, groaning. She would not have minded another few hours.

"I'm sorry for intruding on your room," the *majican* said, making curt gestures at her tiger. "I didn't even hear you come in."

"No, you would not have."

Zyre made for the door, but her hand hovered above the knob as she hesitated. Slowly, she turned back toward Neelie. "Captain, I can't thank you enough for everything you've done for me in the past day. I doubt anyone else would have done the same. But I can't go to Bijal. I need to stay in Las Corvika, to free my… my employers from wherever they were taken."

Neelie sighed. "I can't land *es Telaña* on the Corvikan coast, not after our involvement with the *Aretmor*. She needs to get out of their waters as quickly as possible. But don't worry; Jervin Arnaud made it free."

"What?" Zyre breathed, stepping forward.

Neelie scooped up her boots and began the process of yanking them on. "The *Aretmor*'s captain wasn't looking for you. He was convinced the baron was hiding on my ship." She stood upright, her other boot in one hand. "Why do you care so much, *Magi?*

You're free. You can stay in Bijal and make a living for yourself, unbound to any king or pompous nobleman."

Zyre scowled. "What about everyone else? Ivanya, or Remy? What about Damari and her son?"

"How would I know? Does it look like I have magic eyes to see more than I should not?" she snapped, then realized how that sounded and quickly pummeled her temper into submission. "Bijal's as good a place as any to learn where your baron landed, and it'll be a short sail home from there. I think he can handle himself until then."

"We'll see," she said icily as Neelie yanked on her other boot. Then Zyre reached for the door and walked out.

Neelie wanted to let her just walk off. It wasn't like she didn't have a million things to do already. But Zyre was hiding something, something big. And Neelie thought she was past caring—she'd accepted long ago the dangers that came with her *najik* magic and the battle-hunger that would inevitably take her mind—but Zyre was proving her wrong. No *majican* could sink a battleship single-handedly.

But no *najik* could have done it and stayed sane.

With a curse, Neelie scrambled out of her room and chased the other woman down.

Zyre was halfway to the cargo hold already.

"*Magi* Zyre," Neelie called, letting it boom in the confines of the hall. The other woman jumped halfway to the ceiling. Neelie closed the distance between them, passing a few crewmates on their way to eat or sleep or take a shift at the oars. She followed Zyre below, keeping her anger from boiling at the chaos of broken crates and products that she found there. They were going to lose a lot of money on this venture. But it would be worth the cost if she learned of some way to protect herself from the madness of their shared magic.

Shutting the door behind them, she turned to the other woman. "I know you aren't who you say you are." The other woman opened her mouth, but Neelie cut her off with a gesture. "Don't lie to me. Please. I have spent my whole life thinking there is only one place my magic can take me. *Aljarne* are killed for it where you're from. Where I'm from? As good as. And most places are the same. You owe it to not just me, but to all your fellow *aljarne*, to share that information if it's true."

Zyre stared at her, and Neelie knew she was weighing her, deciding whether or not to trust Neelie. She cast a silent prayer to Skï, begging the goddess that all of these risks she'd taken on Zyre's behalf would pay off now. She would write off all of her losses, every single piece, if Zyre would just say the words.

"He is my soulbeast," she said finally. "It's true; I was born an *aljarne*. I think I still am one now, except I've been bound to Kadj. But it does me no good, Captain. I've never heard of a *sjarvisk* or *aljarne* having trouble with controlling their magic like I do, and some days, I wonder if it's because I'm not supposed to have a soulbeast, and the gods are angry for it."

A stubborn rock wedged itself in Neelie's throat. She had never imagined there might be a way to cheat her fate. It was the price they paid for their power. "How is it possible?"

The other woman shrugged. "A *kjarnik* came to the island many years ago, when I was five or six, and bound me to Kadj. The *kjarnik* was from far away. Onaris, I think."

"Onaris?" Bonding a *najik* to a soulbeast would require no small amount of magic, and there were only two people in the world who might have been capable of it. "Did he have a dog with him, by any chance?"

"It was a long time ago," Zyre replied. "I'm afraid I don't remember."

Neelie's breath caught in her throat. Maybe it didn't matter.

"Come with me to Bijal," she found herself saying. "It won't be as safe or isolated as your little island, but my people will protect you. I know someone who can help you with your magic."

Zyre blinked, eyes shining in the lantern light with newfound hope. "Really?"

Neelie nodded. "Then you can go rejoin your employer and help him free the rest of his family if you truly desire."

Zyre smiled. It was quite a beautiful smile, too, if Neelie was being honest with herself. Then, too quickly, it faded. "Is it actually dangerous, Bijal?"

Neelie grimaced. "For an *aljarne*, it is. For *sjarvisk*, not so much, but there are a lot of *sjarvisk* and *kjarnik* in the city, and even an *aljarne* with a soulbeast will find the city is willing to swallow them whole."

"You're an *aljarne* though, aren't you?"

Well, that was no lie. Neelie laughed darkly. "Bijal is mine. People have tried to take it from my family and me, and those people are dead or wishing that they were. Never you fear, *Magi*. The streets of Bijal are not dangerous to me or to my allies." With a shake of her head, Neelie made for the door. "Just think about it."

Neelie left, not sure how Zyre or her tiger could stand the gloom, and wound her way back up to relieve Raylir. There were rites to see to in regard to their fallen, the cargo hold to clean up and determine the damage, and a whole fistful of other things that now needed tending to, but even with all of them weighing on her mind, Neelie found herself smiling.

⁂

Zyre spent a considerable amount of time below deck, trying to stay out of the way, fearing perhaps that the crew blamed and hated her for the deaths of their crewmates. But she did sneak up onto the stairs when they sent the dead into the sea. They'd been wrapped in green cloth and hoisted reverently over the side of the ship while the crew sang. It was haunting and eerie, and although she could not understand the words, it pulled at her heart.

Once the death rites were over, Zyre returned below deck, facing the disaster of the cargo hold. The blood and bodies had been cleared away in the morning following the sinking of the *Aretmor*, but the mess of broken boxes and crates had been wholly abandoned. Feeling like she owed Neelie, she started righting the boxes, checking what was inside for damages.

This eye for art was one small thing Ivanya had been able to pass down to her. Zyre had always shared her mother's passion, and one summer in particular, when Jervin and Remy had been visiting court with most of the Arnauds' servants attending them, Ivanya had taught Zyre everything she could.

Zyre was glad to use that knowledge now. It kept her busy. Some of the crates had not been touched at all, but the contents of others were beyond repair.

At one point, Neelie sent down some men to assess the damage. At first, the two men tried to force her out of the hold. Realizing that they probably just didn't trust her with the contraband, Zyre clawed at her memories for a scrap of Venascan. "*Ethere. Velguir. Cor su perima.*" *Wait. Follow. Please.*

The men warily eyed Kadj, who was getting antsy, and finally they caved.

Zyre led them through the pathways she'd begun to form until she got to one of the crates from earlier, the lid askew, revealing the enchanted swords. The taller one stared at her as if he didn't know what to make of her. He muttered something to his companion in Venascan. They exchanged some sharp words, and then the taller one nodded to Zyre.

After working with them for a few hours, when they realized

Zyre knew what she was doing, they even started to let her direct most of their work. The men still kept to themselves, joking with each other as they did, but if Zyre needed their help lifting some of the boxes or keeping the items organized, they would help her, she in broken Venascan and they in halting Corvikan.

She couldn't hide in the hold forever, though. Drawn out by her own hunger, Zyre followed her nose until she found the kitchen. Like the two sailors, the cook didn't speak much Corvikan at all, but he was surprisingly friendly, even awed. Zyre got the queasy sense it was because of what she'd done to the *Aretmor*, but he let her taste the food he was cooking, and since neither spoke each other's language, at least they didn't talk about it.

Other sailors came and went in between their shifts. Curiosity got the better of her. Shyly, she began interacting with some of them. One in particular, Neelie's second-mate, a younger man named Bo who shared Neelie's oval-shaped face and tall frame, happened to know almost as much Corvikan as Neelie. When he sat down next to her with a plate of seasoned salmon, he asked her questions about her life back home and how she'd gotten so good with art in between her guard duties. The questions stung, but only a little, and she only had to skirt the truth a little.

Eventually, feeling restless, she braved the decks with Kadj, finding clear skies and calm waters. It wasn't as difficult as she'd feared, staying out of everyone's way, and she found that she loved the way the ship rose and fell with the waves.

⁘

The ninth day after leaving Lasinia found Zyre sitting by the helm, wearing a spare outfit lent to her by Neelie—her own was bloody and sweaty and utterly disgusting—and not minding it was too big for her. Leaning against the railing, she watched with some amusement as Captain Neelie hovered over Bo, teaching him how to be a captain. There was a lot of playful shouting involved, and even with the crew trying to teach Zyre some words in Venascan, she was pretty sure she was mishearing the two of them. She certainly didn't understand the joke in being called the equivalent of a rat-faced gizzard.

In the mast, one of the men shouted, pointing ahead of them.

With a shake of her head, Zyre withdrew her spyglass and scanned the horizon, not really expecting to see anything in particular except perhaps the distant silhouettes of merchant vessels. It had become something of an enjoyable pastime.

But Zyre did not see any vessels. Instead, she saw a break in the skyline. She got to her feet for a better look, ignoring Kadj's annoyed snort. Neelie saw where her attention had fallen and, with a silent gesture, asked for the spyglass. The captain looked ahead of them, and her mouth quirked into a miniature smile as if of its own accord. She snapped the piece shut and handed it back to Zyre.

With a few nasty words thrown at Bo, she chased him off the wheel and shouted, "*Vierno adelne!*"

For a fraction of a second, everyone paused, looking past the bow. Several of the sailors let out an excited whoop. Neelie barked off instructions too fast for Zyre to interpret, preparing the ship for port.

"I'll get out of the way," Zyre said to no one in particular between Neelie's shouts. She only got two steps before the other woman grabbed her arm.

"You won't be in the way," she said idly, though her focus remained glued to the deck. "Raylir!" The wizened first-mate looked over his shoulder from his position at the base of the helm. "*Uda moteya, cor su perima.*"

Raylir scaled the steps with practiced ease and took over at the wheel while Neelie dragged a now-anxious Zyre to the corner. He didn't seem concerned, only curious—a good sign regarding the direction of this conversation.

"The Corvikan government has no jurisdiction here," Neelie began carefully. "That doesn't mean Bijal's *Freyr*, the man in charge of our city, won't pass you over the border if it gains him favor or saves him trouble. What's your full name, *Magi*?"

Her secret formed upon her lips. *I'm an Arnaud*, she wanted to say. Not because Neelie needed to know, but because Zyre wanted her to know. Neelie already held her most dangerous secret; what was one more? But after over ten years of swallowing this truth, keeping it from nearly everyone she knew, she found it was not so easy to speak it now. "Zyre Mescal," she said instead, using the false surname her father had given her as soon as she and Kadj had been bonded.

"Not anymore. From now on, or at least while you're in Venasca, your name is Ange Duval. Have a care. Don't call any unnecessary attention to yourself. Your tiger will do enough of that for you."

"I thought you said Bijal was safe?"

Neelie shrugged. "As safe as any city can be for a *majican* seeking political asylum. Just… Be careful. A cover story will help with that. Tormod went on at length about the help you offered with the cargo."

"Tormod?"

The captain pointed below, where Zyre found both of the men who had helped her in the cargo hold this past week. "You know about art. Let's say one of your country's lords sent you scouting for some pretty thing to decorate their fancy, expansive halls."

The derogatory tone was unnecessary, Zyre thought. There was nothing wrong with appreciating art, and if Neelie disagreed with that, then perhaps she ought to find different cargo.

Neelie must've noticed, because she added, "Look, *majican* and *wyrdi* are free to do as they like, but *najik* are a separate entity altogether. *Ed Vodaría dir en Loræden* keeps tabs on *majican* and *wyrdi* dealings, and if they start looking too closely at you, Zyre... Things would grow messy very quickly."

Neelie paused, eyeing Zyre to ensure they understood one another, and then she returned to the helm and let Raylir help below.

Slowly, the horizon grew quickly before them. Ships speckled the harbor, some farther out than others. Zyre saw sleek, almost sharp-looking vessels with sails the same shape as the *Spider's* and, closer inland, ones that resembled the *Embrunis*. A handful of ships looked similar to the *Aretmor*, barely, but Neelie confirmed absently that they belonged to the Venascan armada and that their presence was not unusual. Beyond that, though far fewer in number, were ships of various designs. Zyre didn't know from where they hailed, but she thought she recognized a few designs from contemporary paintings that suggested they were Darsenian or Pailyran.

As soon as the *Spider* had dropped anchor and assignments had been given, those not part of the skeleton crew all crammed onto either of the ship's two rowboats. It took some jostling for Zyre and Kadj to get onto Neelie's boat, but there was only so much a person could do against a tiger, and even though Zyre had gotten used to the crew, she had no intention of letting Neelie out of her sight.

The rowboats wove through the smaller ships and into the latticework of docks that reached out far into the harbor. There was some order to it, there had to be, but whatever it was, Zyre could not have guessed. But it didn't matter, because then they were on land, and it was too still for Zyre's liking, but somewhere

here they would get news of her family. It had been nine days. There had to be something.

The pier was understandably busy. They had to push through the comings and goings of everyone else on the docks, although once they were on solid ground, the path led directly to a squat pavilion where a man sat at a desk, writing furiously. People streamed past only at his behest. It was to this man whom Neelie led them, dodging what crowds did not get out of her way fast enough.

Despite the bustle of people, however, there was not currently much in the way of the line. Neelie's crew gathered off to the side, leaning against a building—the back of a warehouse, Zyre thought—and produced a cup and some dice from somewhere. They played while they waited, tossing small silver coins in the middle for stakes.

The game reminded her, suddenly, of Merytz. No amount of gossip would be able to tell her if he'd survived the fighting.

She wanted to dwell—it seemed cruel not to devote some thought to her friend—but it took all of her focus not to get lost in the sea of people. And before long, all thought of Merytz had neatly slipped to the back of her mind as she tried not to gawk. She'd been taught that the people in each country had characteristics that would identify a person's heritage: Crasik people tended to be massive and pale-skinned, and Pailyrans and Darsenians might have sharp eyes, and Onariseans had skin so dark that it could blend into the night. That was what she'd been told, anyway. But Bijal was a mystery. There were short people with dark skin and short people with light skin, and tall people of every hue, and so many of them wore clothes similar to Neelie's, a sailor's outfit, but whether that was an international thing or whether that made most of the sailors Venascan, Zyre had no idea. It made her head spin.

Even so, she loved it. She loved it all. Had the world always been so big? She'd been a fool to stay on Lasinia all these years. She should have left ages ago to see the world before her father's war yanked her back. Now she didn't think she'd have the chance.

If the appearances of her fellow travelers were a confusing mash-up, the sounds and smells were even more so. Heavy spices and what she was pretty certain was an aggressive amount of alcohol blended onto the thick ocean air. Music clanged, emanating from street corners and wafting out of inns. There were those on the street being trailed by dogs or cats or who had birds perched on their shoulders. There were two men with foxes trotting by their side, and another with a creature that looked like some strange kind of badger. She put a hand on Kadj and was surprised, too, to find that her own magic felt dull, and had been that way as soon as they'd left sight of the water.

The rest of the crew split off shortly after they left the pavilion, searching for a cheap tavern close to the docks, but Neelie and two crewmates—Sten and Tormod, the same two men who had helped Zyre with the cargo for the past week—led Zyre and Kadj deeper into the city. After passing several streets, they crossed an invisible line where it suddenly wasn't so difficult to push through the crowd. The streets were still heavily populated, mostly by tall darker-skinned Venascans in threadbare vests and dresses.

Zyre wondered if perhaps Neelie had brought her two crewmates to make sure no one robbed them until she realized several of the passing crowd nodded respectfully in their direction. Zyre and Neelie weren't just lucky in finding pockets of space to walk; people were intentionally moving out of their way.

The only ones who didn't seem friendly were the few white-clad guards who eyed the crowds suspiciously.

Neelie didn't seem bothered. She eventually turned toward a tall building that smelled of decent food rather than cheap ale, with the soft hum of music tumbling out of the open doors. And the *doors*. Zyre had always wanted to see a *ðedael*—the intricate designs carved into the door of a building detailing the history of those who owned it. At the center of this carving was a woman with hair curled above her head and a long tail where legs should have been. The inn's name was carved in succinct lettering below the finned figure. *Huerdi dir ed Níete.* The Siren's Haunt.

Ivanya Arnaud's subtle prison rattled down the crowded streets of Les Stelvo. The carriage was marked with the insignia of the royal family, and the horses that had taken her family, the royal brats, and the ridiculous number of soldiers on the two-day journey from the harbor to the capital were fine beasts. Sturdy. But, with the curtains of the carriage drawn shut and the pace slowed to allow the royal soldiers to return to Les Stelvo with them, it was obvious what Nyli was trying to do. He was hiding her family's arrest behind some kind of parade of soldiers, a show of force to the people while hiding his own failure.

It was one small consolation. Several of her preparations and plans had unraveled the moment the fighting had begun, but at least her husband had slipped away. If news reached their allies that the Arnauds were about to make their move, noble Houses might start to flock openly to his cause.

Ivanya eyed her guards, the two men and a *sjarvisk* woman with a woodpecker sleeping on her lap. She did not look at Princess Rasin, who peered out of her window in boredom, but she was still acutely aware of the younger woman's presence. It was not ideal; Rasin's alliances were foggy at best, and she was too intelligent to make an easy quarry for Ivanya's political schemes. If Rasin had been in the other carriage with Remy, things might've been different, but then, the princess had been avoiding Ivanya's son.

Was it because Rasin still loved Remy, or was it because she had grown to hate him?

The driver called out to the horses, and the carriage lurched to a stop. Rasin threw Ivanya a wary glance and then hopped out. Her honor guard surrounded her in seconds.

"Baroness," came a man's voice. Ivanya turned her head and found one of the two soldiers offering his hand to her. She did not sigh or glower or curse. She took his hand as if it was her due and let him help her out of the carriage. Remy stood beside his wife and son, his arm protectively around Damari's shoulders as he eyed their guards. The three of them stood in a small sea of green-clad troops, men who had been crammed into the *Embrunis* those seven days at sea and who had marched with them from there to Les Stelvo. Now they were waiting for Nyli to dismiss them, the little prince thinking he knew how to play at war. The royal palace had already swallowed Rasin and her retinue.

"Lieutenant-General," Nyli barked as he swung down from his horse. "Escort Baroness Arnaud and the rest of her family to the dungeons. Find a sequestered cell, and make sure they are carefully guarded." The wolf pup eyed Ivanya with his dull fangs bared. She kept her expression neutral. Nyli shook his head in disgust and strode off.

The men fell into a tight formation around them. There were not enough troops to fully hide the Arnaud family at the center, but there were enough that passing glances wouldn't find anything amiss. This was unfortunate. She needed them to be sloppy and arrogant. She needed witnesses.

Ivanya hated dungeons. Even excepting the personal distaste for the dank, putrid darkness, being in a cell would cut her off from any political maneuverings she'd need to do to get herself and her son free. If no one saw them walking through the commons of the palace, no one would think to look for Ivanya or her family below.

*I have something to work with; I just don't know what,* Ivanya mused. She was afraid, but she was from an ancient Crasik House, *Rosema* Zandua, and she had been raised to be above her fears.

Moving toward the east side of the palace, Ivanya's mind spun as quickly as her hurried steps. The Bérangers could use what members they'd snatched from House Arnaud to make a political statement. To crush Ivanya and Remy, especially, would jeopardize Jervin's claim on the throne. It wasn't that Jervin couldn't sire another son, but even the most unhappy of Corvikan Houses would weather a tyrant regis with two sons who ensured the continuation of his line. No one liked the idea of an uncertain succession.

They stepped into a beautiful garden with a great silvery tree at the center, its silhouette a strange mix of a willow and a redwood. A velídas tree, though much, much larger than the one the Arnauds had on their own grounds. It was old, too; four men could have stood inside the trunk had it been hollow.

They left the garden behind and found two large buildings taking shape. The buildings were connected by a short covered pathway. The one on the left was the *sjarvisk* barracks; the one on the right belonged to the foot.

*Of course,* Ivanya thought, somewhat desperately now, *House Arnaud has allies here in Les Stelvo.* They, at least, would know what rumors to listen for. It was only the question of how long it would take for their allies to realize Ivanya and her family were hidden right beneath their feet that worried her. And, of course, if this careful guard continued, it would not provide her allies much leeway to help them escape.

Most of the soldiers broke away, but the Lieutenant-General

and ten men followed the periphery of the barracks until they reached a smallish shed-like building. A man lounged by the door, opening it for them. The building was only the entrance, Ivanya knew. A staircase led down, down, down. Already, she could whiff the foul odor of the dungeons. Here, where no one but soldiers could see, she wanted to balk. It would be so easy for Notoyem to snuff their family line out, just as he'd extinguished the ancient House Ermengarde. That it was not politically in his best interest made no difference.

*Soldiers are the worst gossips, Ivanya*, she told herself fiercely. *If you're not going to perform for them, you may as well not perform for the nobility.* So she straightened her back, gave her son and daughter-in-law encouraging glances, and followed the Lieutenant-General down the steps before anyone could think to start shoving.

The staircase led them to a large, cavernous underbelly that was cordoned off with wooden walls and iron gates. Near the base of the stairs was a large office where half a dozen guards were on duty. Their party halted while the Lieutenant-General spoke quietly to the officer in charge, a severe-looking man who went by Captain Liem. Liem studied the four of them with a predatory gaze. Ivanya matched it, noting his sword, his baton, the heavy chairs he and his men sat in.

The Lieutenant-General took his men and withdrew, stomping up the stairs. Liem shoved Ivanya forward the moment he was gone, and she seized the moment. With a scowl, Ivanya spun around. Her fingers wrapped around his sword hilt before another blow landed, this time in her stomach. The sword clattered to the ground as she fell.

"Mother!" Remy shouted, pushing toward her.

Liem's men stepped between the two of them while the captain glared down at Ivanya. "I suggest you not try that again. As far as I'm concerned, you're no longer high and mighty nobility, and while I cannot kill you without my regis's say-so, I can still make your life—and your *family*'s life, I might add—*very* miserable."

He snatched his sword off the ground while one of his men hauled Ivanya to her feet, pinning her arms behind her back. It was undignified, but worse, left her little room to maneuver. She couldn't even sign to Remy to tell him to remain calm. *Tholjun burn him*, she cursed. It had been a foolish plan; they'd never have made it out of the palace, let alone the city, but she would not walk to her death with her tail tucked between her legs.

They were taken to the last cell, the one farthest from the stairs and the one that overlooked a terrible room—its door left wide open—with a table and some vicious-looking tools. Ivanya and her family were not the only ones in the prison; three had rough livery, servants who had probably upset the regis over something or another, and one held a miserable-looking minor lord she didn't recognize. All were in cells nearer the staircase. If the torture chamber was meant to be a threat, Ivanya heard it clearly.

# CHAPTER 6

For Neelie, the inn *Huerdi dir ed Niete* was full of familiar faces: people who owed her family a favor or who had sailed under her mother's fleet or helped her father on one occasion or another. She stepped inside, and the silence fell like dominoes. Men who had taken up Onarisean ink hid the telltale flashes of the raven tattoos that marked them as her father's men, *Hædros dir en Schadra*, Men of Shadow. Those who recognized her raised their mugs and called out a greeting.

Hæfnir, the inn's owner, a tall if heavy-set man with a proper Venascan braid in his beard, strode toward Neelie and her three companions and bowed. "Captain Neelie! I did not expect you back to Bijal nearly so soon!"

"Yes, well, unfortunately, business proved less fruitful than we'd hoped. The Coral Room, if you please."

Hæfnir bobbed his head in commiseration and gestured for them to follow. "Certainly, certainly."

*Magi* Zyre did not follow right away. Her attention had gotten snarled on their surroundings. *Foreigners*, Neelie thought, but the comment had little bite. With a sigh, she tugged Zyre along, gesturing for her crewmen to get settled.

It was an overall aesthetically pleasing room, with beautiful Bijali wood-stained furniture, but its beauty wasn't why Neelie had brought them to *ed Huerdi*. Hæfnir had long proven loyal to her family and discreet in Shadowmen dealings. The Coral Room belonged to her family and them alone. They paid good money to keep it empty for occasions such as this.

"I'll bring you two ladies wine," Hæfnir said with another small bow.

"And water, for the tiger, if you please," Neelie said as she slid into her seat.

He bowed again and took his leave.

Zyre gave Neelie a strange look before she settled into a chair opposite her. The tiger disappeared under the table, though Neelie heard him flop onto the ground. "So, what happens now?"

Neelie held up a finger. Just because she trusted Hæfnir and most of the people in the common room did not mean she wanted to risk letting Zyre's secrets fly out to the first curious ear. Hæfnir did not take long to procure the drinks, and as soon as they were served, he shut the door behind him and left them to their private conversations.

"It's no small thing, what you can do," Neelie said finally, slipping easily back into Corvikan. "As I said, I know people who might be able to help, but I don't know how long it might take for them to unravel the mystery. In the meantime, you'll stay here, in *Huerdi dir ed Níete*. An old friend of mine will be stopping by. His name is Modorin Kal, and he will make sure you don't do anything stupid that will get yourself caught."

Zyre's expression flattened. She took her wine and downed half of it in one go. It took most of Neelie's self-control not to grin. At least *Magi* Zyre had no compunctions about alcohol. Neelie didn't trust anyone stringent with their drink.

"I get it," she said gently, because she did. If it were her family in trouble, she'd be eager to get back to them. "But we came straight from Lasinia. Anyone who knows anything about it will probably be a few days behind. Regretfully, I can't stay with you the whole time until then."

"What am I supposed to do until then?" Zyre demanded, keeping an admirably tight lid on her panic.

"I wouldn't leave you stranded in a new city; don't you worry. Modorin knows the city almost as well as I do. He can act as a guide, if you'd like, and can make sure no one bothers you while he's at it."

A familiar hunger lit up Zyre's expression. She hastily took another swig of her drink. "I would love to have a guide," she admitted.

With a laugh, Neelie sent her wine down her throat. It was not the swill they served at the docks. It was good: sweet, with an earthy base. "You should take the opportunity to see the sights. Bijal has a lot more to offer than that small island of yours." She placed her emptied cup on the table, then rose. "I'll be in touch."

Neelie patted Kadj on her way out, winding back down the hall and into the common room, where she found her two men. "Stay until Modorin Kal arrives. Then enjoy your leave." After the unexpected skirmish with that warship, her crew certainly had earned it.

"Thank you, Captain," the men said eagerly.

Neelie found Hæfnir in the middle of refilling cups. He gave her another bow. A good man. He'd find a room for Zyre and Modorin, even if he had to house them in his cellar. That again nearly sent another grin worming its way onto Neelie's face. Modorin would hate that.

The streets of Bijal were busy as usual for this time of year. Even in the Deckhand's Quarter, where money had little to do with trade, there were so many people on the road that few recognized her or were able to step out of her way even if they did. It was all very familiar, and, better yet, the only language she heard on the street was the sweet curl of the Venascan tongue. This was an old part of town, and many of the people here could trace their families back multiple generations.

As Neelie reached Vantero Street, crossing into the Shadow Quarter, her father's territory, she saw a cluster of men in clean uniforms with a sea serpent embroidered on the collars. They strolled down the street, arms resting on their sword hilts, their expressions guarded. She slipped down a side street without a second thought and paused at a cart of linens. The man at the stall said something to her, but she ignored him, and he caught the hint.

Troops wearing the crossed swords of *Freyr* Honir had been speckled throughout the city; she'd counted more than eight just by passing through the Sector of the Gulls, and in the Deckhand's Quarter, three. The presence of High King Inoger's sigil was another matter entirely. Soldiers did not belong in the Shadow Quarter. Her family had paid good coin to keep it that way. Unfortunately, Inoger's men were far harder to bribe than the locals.

She had missed quite a lot in her few weeks at sea. And now the *Spider* was sitting hot in the bay.

Mercy to Skï, this was not good. She'd have to send word to Raylir, get a skeleton crew together to sail the *Spider* away from Bijal for the time being.

Neelie pushed the tip of her hat down and fell into a dismissive slouch before returning to Vantero Street.

The soldiers didn't see her, or if they did, they did not think her worth their attention. But she kept her hand on her sword and her magic close until she reached her destination.

The Shadowmen's headquarters resided in an unadorned building that doubled both as her father's main office as well as the family's home. Most called it the Raven's Head. The *ðedael* bore dozens of designs inlaid within more designs: the crescent moon nestled against the sun—Skï's mark—hanging from the lowest branch of a tree that grew on the back of a whale. Woven into the design too was a bloodied knife, a ship. And, at the heart of it all, the raven, her father's mark. Not all who saw it would recognize the bird, but those who did would know what it meant.

Neelie opened the door to the office, the sounds of the street replaced by the shouts and footsteps and general clamor that came with the family business. The gambling and betting that bred from here was considered the more *lawful* half of their business and paid for the bulk of Shadowmen wages, building boats, and bribing city guards, among other things.

The snobbish city guards did not take kindly to that part of the business, though, and if they found the *Spider*'s cargo, Neelie would have a hard time talking herself out of it. Even more so if Inoger was poking his nose where it didn't belong.

The men and women populating the Raven's Head stopped whatever it was they were doing as she walked past them, waving hello and calling her out by name. She ignored most of them, offering a brisk smile to only a few.

Her father, Hosvar, was in his office, as she expected him to be. His raven, Berhôt, sat on her perch above Hosvar's head, her black feathers almost blue in the light. Neelie sauntered through his half-open door and cleared her throat.

Her father looked up from his desk, his spectacles sliding down his nose. His long coiled hair was pulled back into a bun. Thick white strands streaked past his temple, but that was nothing new. He had not aged too much in her short trip away.

It wouldn't have killed him to look a little more surprised at her premature return, though.

"Neelie. I wondered if you'd be hitting our docks today. A

little earlier than planned though." His unspoken question was obvious.

"I ran into some unforeseen complications, and the *Telaña* is still hot. So imagine my concern when I found city guards, men with *sea serpents* on their collars no less, patrolling our streets." She crossed her arms. "What's happened?"

Hosvar sighed and gestured at the door. Neelie shut it, then fell into the seat opposite him, propping one leg over the arm of the chair. "*Freyr* Honir is to blame, I'm afraid," he said at long last.

Neelie barked out a laugh. Her father was joking with her. Honir had never been more than a gnat buzzing around the room. He liked to play at being king, but his control over his own men was flimsy at best, and until recently, the only city guard that had stepped foot in the Shadow Quarter were loyal to Hosvar's coin and were only playing at anything else.

"Your brother and I are handling it. What happened on Lasinia?"

"The Bérangers got there quicker than anticipated. We were pursued by a Corvikan naval vessel, though, so I have to assume Brandt's mission went well. They thought we had Jervin Arnaud on our ship." She paused. This was the part where she should tell Hosvar about Zyre and her magic, but the question was, would he believe her?

"What happened to the Corvikan ship?" Hosvar prompted, misunderstanding her hesitation.

"It met an untimely end."

His eyes narrowed. Two words hung between them. *Big magic.* Or, more aptly, *dangerous* magic.

"I had help," she said finally. "A woman by the name of Zyre Mescal, one of Jervin Arnaud's employees. She has a tiger soulbeast."

"I've heard of her." Hosvar scratched his chin. "Rumor says

she has no control over her magic. I hope you didn't take any undue risk for her, Neelie. I know you like to play the part of the hero, but your magic is not free to use."

"I'm well aware," Neelie replied, resisting the urge to roll her eyes. She did not help her fellow magic-users just to be a *hero*. That was vain and arrogant and unseemly. "Father, she's not a *majican*."

He blinked. If she'd had any doubts as to which *wyrdi* had done those impossible enchantments, Neelie was certain now that it hadn't been her father. "But you just said—"

"I know. I need to speak to Kaspar Gehrig. I think he's the one who did it."

"Neelie, Gehrig would have told me if he had managed to do something like that."

"Would he have?" she shot back. "You have a *najik* daughter. You both were friends. And it has never been done before. Zyre doesn't even know if it worked. Maybe he didn't want to get your hopes up or replicate it if he wasn't sure what the effects would be."

Hosvar ran a frustrated hand through his hair. Berhôt squawked from her perch and flew down to sit on his shoulder. "What, exactly, do you hope to gain? He cannot replicate the feat, not without Mauel."

"I know, but that's not why I need to speak to him. Or, at least, not the only reason. Zyre wants to fix the false *leiks*; I think it's affecting her magic. He might know why."

"Fine," Hosvar said with a sigh. "Gehrig is helping me with a project by the warehouses. I'll talk to him when he gets back. Leave your friend here, if you must, but you? I need you to take your ship back out to sea and put its cargo in a safe place until things calm down here."

Neelie crossed her arms. "Are things really that bad with Honir?"

His expression was answer enough.

"Then I am duty-bound to stay."

His shoulders fell. He opened his mouth, and Neelie knew that if he spoke, he would find some way to see her off. She stopped him before he had the chance. "Look, we've been dealing with this goon for as long as I can remember, and he hasn't gotten the upper hand yet. I don't care what his motives are, and I don't care why High King Inoger has reinforced Honir's men. The Shadowmen are stronger than they've ever been. We'll beat him again, and this time, we'll crush him so thoroughly he won't be able to find his way back out of the mud."

Hosvar laughed, and Neelie suppressed a smile at the sound. "You sounded just like your mother right then, do you know that?" The laughter lines faded. "*Freyr* Honir knows the Shadow King has a *najik* daughter. He knows roughly what she looks like. He'll be searching for you."

"Let him find me," Neelie replied, surprised at her own vehemence. She had her sword, her magic, her intellect. That was all she'd ever need.

Hosvar, who knew she was Adreia's daughter to the core, understood.

Master Hæfnir did not know any Corvikan, Zyre surmised as he gestured for her to follow him out of *En Kurat Thola*—she didn't know what color *kurat* was, but the room's walls were painted a reddish color—several minutes after Neelie had left her. She trailed after him, listening to the rowdy Venascans in the next room over, their voices growing fainter but the smell of food growing stronger. From the kitchen came the scent of fish and sharp spices that Zyre couldn't put a name to by scent alone.

The kitchen was populated by two girls and an older woman. The girls darted around the kitchen under the watchful eye of the gray-haired, well-padded elderly woman with olive skin more akin to the eastern Corvikan border than any place in Venasca.

Hæfnir spoke to the gray-haired woman, gesturing at Zyre before slipping back to the common room. The woman, Kaari, took one look at Zyre, barked a few commands at the two girls, then smiled. She bobbed a perfect quarter curtsy, just as any Corvikan innkeeper would offer newly arrived guests. "A warm welcome, *Magi*. Allow me the honor of your name."

Zyre found herself swallowing down a lump in her throat. She hadn't realized how much she'd missed hearing her native tongue without a Venascan accent, but now, even Kaari's rough eastern Corvikan lilt sounded like honey. It threw her so off guard that she very nearly gave the woman her "real" name, but she caught herself just in time. "Ange Duval, madame. And this is my tiger, Kadj."

"Ange. Lovely name, that." She smiled warily at Kadj but did not draw close. "Come. We have a few rooms available. Not very big, mind, but…" Kaari trailed off.

"I'm sure I'll find them more comfortable than the confines of a ship," Zyre assured her.

Kaari smiled. She took both of them down the service halls, up several flights of stairs, then turned down a hallway filled with numbered doors. The room labeled thirty-one swung open beneath Kaari's fingertips, and as they stepped within it, Zyre realized that the woman hadn't been lying about the size. A small bed was wedged in one corner, and a simply wrought wardrobe had been placed beside a small window that let in the dusty summer breeze. There was nothing else.

Still. It was better than the incessant gloom of the cargo hold, and no one had died in these rooms. At least, not that she knew of, and she certainly had no intention of asking.

"Is there any luggage I can have brought up for you?" Kaari asked politely. Surely, though, she knew the answer.

"No. I didn't… I didn't have time to pack anything, unfortunately."

Indeed, Kaari seemed unfazed. "Yes, that is often the case with the *sjarvisk* whom *Nagi* Neelie brings through here. You look about the same size my daughter used to be. I may have a few of her old dresses lying about that you can borrow for the time being, if only to get your own clothes washed. They'll be a little out of fashion, I'm afraid. I'll have a tub brought up so you can wash the sea air off you."

At this point, Zyre didn't care if Kaari put her in a two-hundred-year-old dress. Even with Neelie's clothes, she felt like a dozen baths would not be enough to make her feel truly clean, not of the salt water, the blood, the heavy ocean air. "Thank you, madame. You're too kind." Zyre cocked her head to the side. "What did you mean? That many of the *sjarvisk* whom *Nagi* Neelie brings are like me?"

Kaari chortled. "She likes to pretend she has no heart, but it would require more than my fingers and toes to count how many poor souls Neelie has given safe harbor to here in Bijal. My husband Hæfnir and I have promised a place here in our inn for whatever poor souls she brings. They've come from all over, as north as Crasea and as south as Laeris. She's even helped a few from Pailyr and Darsenia, though most times, you magic folk are going the opposite way."

All over? Yes, Crasea was fickle with their magic-users. It was said they nearly worshipped their *kjarnik*, but *sjarvisk* and *aljarne* were another matter entirely. Laeris was a surprise, though. She'd have thought them too wrapped up in their endless civil war to care that much about magic.

"If you'll excuse me," Kaari said politely. "I must return to my duties. But it was a pleasure to hear my native Corvikan tongue. I hope we'll get to speak further. In the meantime, I'll send for that tub."

The woman strode out of the room, her heavy footsteps fading away down the stairs. Not long after, Hæfnir and another man who smelled strongly of horses brought in a copper tub and hefted it into the middle of the room. One of the girls from the kitchen helped carry water buckets up the stairs to fill it, but Zyre's heart sank at the lack of steam rising from the tub.

"Excuse me," she said before the girl could dart off. "The water is still cold."

The girl stared at her blankly.

"Um. Hot. *Oriete?*"

The girl replied in Venascan, too quickly for Zyre's unpracticed ear, but she caught the word "*loræden*"—*magic*—and a few choice insults muttered under the girl's breath. Well, her meaning was clear enough. Now the girl probably thought she was lazy and entitled for asking. Zyre sighed and waved the girl away. Suddenly, a bath did not sound like such a pleasant idea.

She looked through the window and found it showed nothing more than an empty alley and the next building over and decided that, since the hot air was likely the only source of heat she was going to get for the moment, it would be best to just leave the window open. Still, she took care not to get undressed right in front of it. High up or no, there was no reason to risk a passing stranger seeing her while she was indecent.

She put a hand in the water to brace herself for the chill, and was pleasantly surprised to find it tepid. *Bless these Venascans and their summer heat*, Zyre thought with a smile. She still had to get in slowly to adjust to the temperature, but once she was in, it was as refreshing as a pond on the hottest day of the year. Zyre reached for the soap that the kitchen girl had left behind and began to scrub away the dirt and grime and salt she had gotten far too used to. Kadj padded across the room in a few short strides and put his head on the rim of the tub, looking quite envious.

Once Zyre felt clean, she let herself relax. She sat with her head against the back of the tub until a knock on the door interrupted her quiet. She quickly scrambled to her feet, the water threatening to slosh over the side. "Just a minute," she called out, reaching for her towel.

"I brought you a dress," said the voice on the other side of the door.

Zyre breathed in a sigh of relief, and once she was suitably dry, wrapped the towel around her chest and opened the door a crack to let Kaari into the room.

The woman slipped in with the fabric draped over her arm. "I hope you found the bath pleasant enough," she said amicably. Then her eyes narrowed after a glance at the tub. "Oh. Did it take me that long?"

Zyre swallowed and cast about for something that would explain the lack of heat above the water. "I like cooler baths in the summer," she lied.

Kaari nodded as if she should have expected as much. "Yes, well, then I'm glad Hæfnir talked me out of heating it for you. 'She can probably do it much faster,' he said to me, 'and that way she can get the temperature just right.' I should listen to him more, I suppose." She laughed boisterously.

Kaari thrust the dress toward Zyre. "Here, try this on. Oh, and there's a man waiting for you in the common room. His name is *Magi* Modorin Kal. He's a friend of *Nagi* Neclic's."

Zyre accepted Kaari's offering with profuse thanks. The inn-keeper's wife turned her back but remained in the room.

Zyre inspected the dress in her hands and grimaced. It was not one single piece, but three. Four, if she counted the shift that Kaari had been kind enough to provide. She took it to the bed, mindful of the window, and laid out the pieces. The skirt and blouse were cut from the same fabric, a soft purple color, the dye spread unevenly across it. The fabric was very light, as was the floor-length overcoat that went atop the outfit. It was unlike anything she was used to wearing at home.

She let the towel fall to the ground and started with the shift. The outfit was not particularly difficult to untangle. It fit well enough, although even with the waist tightened with the draw-string, the skirt was a little loose. The overcoat, a pretty gray, had a belt that went around the waist, fastening it over the blouse while the skirt beneath it was left on display. Fortunately, each of the layers was made of a light fabric, and it wasn't nearly as hot as she'd feared.

"It's beautiful, madame," she said, trying to visualize how it looked on her.

Kaari was kind enough to look over her shoulder before turning around completely. "It's a little loose," the woman clucked. "But serviceable all the same."

She gestured for Zyre to follow, and with Kadj at their heels, they took the main stairs that led directly to the common room. The boisterous conversation hadn't gotten any tamer in her time upstairs, and in the sea of faces, she had trouble finding Sten and Tormod. Kaari disappeared before she could ask, so Zyre waded into the fray. She searched until she recognized one of the crew, a man with a sharp jaw and thick black hair tied back in a bun. Tormod. Sitting with him was the other sailor, Sten, his head completely free of hair despite the fact that he couldn't have been older than his mid-twenties. They had spoken very little Corvikan on the *Spider*, but they had been kind.

Zyre did not recognize the third man at the table, which meant he must have been Modorin Kal. Even sitting, he appeared to be rather short, and his tan skin and short-cut sandy-colored hair stood out in this room of dark-skinned, black-haired Venascans. It seemed safe to bet that he was Fresian.

As she drew near their table, the three men rose from their chairs. A small ball of orange and black fur tumbled off Modorin's lap, taking the shape of a fox.

"You must be Ange Duval," Modorin said in near-perfect Corvikan, with only the slightest dip of his u's. He bowed his head, sweeping fist from brow to heart. "It's a pleasure to make your acquaintance."

"And you must be Modorin Kal." She returned his strange honorific with a quarter curtsy and hoped the two gestures were comparable.

Tormod spoke to the Fresian, gesturing in Zyre's direction. Modorin waved his hand, replying yes—ïz—in Venascan. Tormod and Sten both offered clumsy bows before taking their leave.

That just left the four of them—Modorin, Zyre, and their two soulbeasts. She took a moment to study her new companion. He was handsome, she supposed, in the traditional sense. He certainly wasn't much older than her. Mostly, she just found his fashion interesting. He wore a wine-dark tunic that went down to his knees and baggy breeches similar to what the *Spider*'s crew had worn, paired with a Venascan-made rapier belted at his waist. Around his neck was a leaf-green scarf with impressive stitching.

Modorin gestured abruptly for her to sit. She got the impression that he had been sizing her up too.

Kadj positioned himself regally next to her chair. Modorin took the place opposite her, and his fox disappeared under the table somewhere. Zyre kept her legs still, fearing she might kick him on accident.

"So," she began, steepling her fingers in front of her. "What is it, exactly, that you do, Master Modorin?"

The man only shrugged with a knowing grin. "Whatever it is Neelie asks of me."

*Interesting*, Zyre thought with a sinking feeling. *He gave her no title.*

Modorin leaned back in his chair. His smile had vanished. "I heard you got caught in the middle of a war between two noble families and that you're lying low for a bit because your magic doesn't act the way a *sjarvisk's* magic should."

There was nothing in his tone that suggested he knew more, which was fortunate. It meant she was right, that Neelie was good at keeping secrets. "I suppose I should take advantage of the situation," she said, choosing not to correct him. "I've been in their employ since I was young, and it's left little opportunity for exploration." Neelie had been right about that, at least. Zyre wasn't sure that sitting in her room, worrying over her family, was going to do anyone any good.

"Bijal's as good a place as any for that," Modorin said.

"I need to send some messages and find a seamstress," she continued, nodding. "Perhaps we can do some sightseeing in the interim."

"Your wish is my command, Miss Duval."

Zyre wanted to wipe that stupid grin off his face, unsure if he was making fun of her. But her heart, the traitor, thought that perhaps this strange, extroverted character might make for a re-freshing change to her quieter, professional friendship to Merytz. *I think we might get along just fine, Thyljal willing*, she thought, suppressing a smile.

# CHAPTER 7

Nyli stood in an empty hallway, staring at the inscribed door before him. The family's sigil stood proud, and beneath its clawed feet, their motto: *Oderta neg rasin det pieterad.* Beware the fury on the winds. Judging by the number of honor guards occupying the hallway with him, Nyli knew that a whole family's worth of fury was waiting inside for him.

He hated the room. It was where Notoyem's first wife, Elodja, had spent all her time deftly politicking with or against the fellow ladies of the court before she fell to poison. If there was one person in this world whom Nyli's father truly loved, it was his first wife, and he was far less predictable in this room steeped with memories.

Nyli could hear Luc, his half-brother, even in the hallway, and it didn't bode well. He sounded like he was trying to live up to that infamous Béranger fury. Were they fighting over Nyli, perhaps? *I told you we couldn't trust him with this, Father,* he imagined Luc was saying. *He can't even do the easy jobs without bungling something.*

Oddly, Nyli couldn't hear his father's voice.

One of the guards shifted uneasily behind him. Steeling his

resolve as best as he could, Nyli pushed the door open and strode into the room.

"What possible benefit could be had from keeping them alive?" Luc was saying with disgust. He leaned beside a shuttered window, but even still, his presence was like a spiked wall, immovable yet deadly. He had, after all, learned to loom menacingly from the best of them.

Notoyem lounged on a couch opposite Rasin. Unlike Luc, his presence was… small. Unassuming, for now. "We're not killing them. Not yet, at least. Have you no care for your sister's feelings?" he admonished as the door swung shut behind Nyli. His father craned his neck over his shoulder. "Nyli. Took you long enough."

There were no barbs in his father's voice. And yet, under his father's scrutiny, Nyli still couldn't help but shrink away.

Luc sneered across the room at him before flicking his gaze to their sister. "Rasin, if you're still clinging on to some romantic feelings for Remy Arnaud, then there is no help for you."

Their father sat upright on the couch and gestured for Nyli to take the spot next to him. Warily, Nyli did. Explanations and excuses formed on Nyli's tongue as he waited for his father's temper to show.

"You left Les Stelvo with over a hundred men, a warship, and three *sjarvisk*. And yet apparently you were still not able to outsmart a powerless man past his relevancy."

Nyli tensed for his father's anger. The quiet tone was always temporary. Notoyem would want him to admit his mistakes outright. It would be better in the long run if he did. But the Béranger wrath always bubbled underneath the surface, waiting for one accidental jab to let it out.

"I brought his wife and son. He can do nothing against us for fear of our retaliation."

Notoyem stiffened. "His wife and son?" he repeated dangerously.

Even Luc flinched. Nyli hated him for it, just as he hated how quickly his brother could shrug it off. "Ivanya and Remy Arnaud are only useful to us, *Butcher*, if Jervin Arnaud knows we will kill them if he doesn't comply."

The nickname was a slap in his face.

Notoyem glared at his eldest son. When he turned his attention back to Nyli, it was clear he was making an effort to contain his anger. "What can I do with a baroness or their *vinje*, pray tell?" The tension in the room spiked as his control began to fray. He'd never been good at holding it for long. The whole room, even Luc, fell still. "Do their allies and their rebels require permission from Ivanya or Remy Arnaud before they breathe?"

*One of these days*, Nyli thought, furious at his own timidity, *you will insult the wrong people and find that fear is not enough to keep the knife from your back.*

"Father," Rasin said softly. Notoyem turned his trembling wrath on her, but she met his fiery eyes and hardly blanched. "It is not a matter of the power they hold over their countrymen. You're right; it's Jervin Arnaud we need for this to end. It's Jervin Arnaud who would lead the rebel army against us, if he dares. But if he loses his family, he loses support. No one will want to back a nobleman who doesn't have an heir."

"See?" Luc butted in. "Even Rasin wants to see Remy dead."

Rasin looked at their brother through heavy eyes, though Nyli doubted Luc noticed. "No, I don't." She turned back to Notoyem. "Think about it. We can lure Jervin here with a promise of safe passage and the guarantee of his family's release if he just swears more stringent oaths."

"I've already been merciful with that backstabbing traitor

once," Notoyem snapped. "That man will die. And soon, Tholjun willing."

*Be careful, be careful,* Nyli thought to his sister, wishing she could hear him. She knew as well as anyone just how far Notoyem could go when he was angry. He would much rather weather their father's fury than see Rasin's safety compromised.

She carried on, though, confident in her ability to spin their father's mood. "I know. But it will tempt him. He will think himself clever. He will think that if he swears the oaths, he will get out of the capital alive so he can reunite with his troops, and with his wife and son riding behind him, his claim could not be stronger. He'll be so proud of this sneaky plan that he won't see the headsman until the axe begins to fall."

Notoyem blinked. He looked at Nyli as if to say, *See, that is what a proper Béranger acts like. Smart, decisive, bloody. Unlike you.*

*It was the girl,* Nyli wanted to say. *It was the girl, and Ljerson's pride. Had they just stuck to the plan...* He bit the words off before he could actually say them. Ljerson was under his command; his failure belonged to Nyli.

"In the meantime," Nyli began, building off of Rasin's plan, "we know he has an army. We need to set our forces to finding them and destroying them. That will make the other Houses think twice about rising against us. I can lead the forces dedicated to the search."

"You?" Luc drawled. "You're the one who screwed up the first time. No. I'll deal with Arnaud's men."

"I already have a plan," Nyli said, pointedly not looking at his brother. He didn't actually have one, but he could be a quick thinker when he needed to be.

Luc barked out a laugh, but Notoyem's glare silenced him. To Nyli, he asked, "And what, pray tell, would that be?"

In his periphery, Nyli saw Rasin's eyes flashed worriedly, and he wanted to tell her it was all right; he had no intention of killing anyone he didn't have to.

"How much information do you think Ivanya Arnaud would pay for comfort?" he asked pointedly. "And how much do you think she would pay for Remy's life?"

Notoyem's eyes glinted, and Nyli knew he had him. He laid out the rest of it, what little he was able to come up with on the spot: drafting a small army to deal with Jervin's hidden troops, pulling as much information from Ivanya and Remy as they could by tricking them, crushing Jervin Arnaud's soldiers—and truly, there couldn't be that many—and leaving Ivanya indebted to the crown for letting her son live. Remy would swear stricter fealties to the crown to appease the Arnaud supporters, but with his power mitigated.

"It'll never work," Luc sneered. "We'll send a firmer message if we have them executed. They are rebels and traitors. If we let them live, we are telling other families they can get away with the same."

"Be quiet," Notoyem snapped in a tone that brooked no argument, even from Luc. He looked to Nyli. "Very well. But every day we give Jervin is a day he can gather more troops and support against us. I will give you ten days to get him here and to find out where the rest of his men are located. Ten only. If you cannot prove your competence by then, I must assume you are intentionally sabotaging the family and you will no longer be welcome in Les Stelvo. Both of you are dismissed. Rasin, stay. We need to discuss the matter of your marriage."

Nyli darted a glance at his sister, but he could not disobey a direct order from their father. Rasin straightened her shoulders, not a crack in her composure. He prayed to Thalja that Notoyem would go easy on her.

Luc had no such compunctions about leaving her to her fate,

storming off with a deathly glare sent to Nyli on his way out. But as Nyli followed him out into the corridor, Luc didn't look back, didn't exchange any harsh words or threats. He just walked off, his men in tow.

Nyli's honor guard peeled themselves from the wall and fell in line behind him. He barely noticed. The assignment was a gift, an offering, but it also felt like a test. Ten days to search the entirety of Las Corvika? One might think his father was setting him up to fail.

Except Nyli had been set up to fail the moment that, three years prior, the title of General of the Royal Forces had been thrown upon him. Whatever Luc said about Nyli's capabilities, he had yet to lead the country to ruin. Far from it. He might have even delayed a war long enough to gather men for the crown.

Nyli wound his way through the palace, ignoring the servants, clerks, and nobility roaming the halls. He pushed open the doors to his own chambers and stopped short. His grievances and fears melted away, for there, reading by the light of the window, was Kuval Duvachelle. He was the comte's youngest son, a man who had no right to be as handsome as he was. Tall, with olive skin and sweeping brown hair, and deep, deep eyes that cut past every single mask Nyli had ever worn.

Nyli hastily shut the door behind him before his honor guard could see and then strode across the room so fast that Kuval barely had time to mark his place. He helped pull the other man out of the chair, the book thudding against the floor as Nyli let Kuval drown him in a sea of hungry kisses. "You shouldn't be in here," Nyli said, or tried to.

Kuval broke away. Nyli's traitorous body thrummed, desiring more. Somehow, he managed to restrain himself from closing the distance Kuval had put between them. "Why didn't you tell me you were going to arrest the baron?"

"I'm sorry," Nyli said, and meant it. Jervin had spies in the court; it would be stupid for him not to. It had taken quick thinking to get the ships supplied and manned without anyone getting hold of that information. "Had I been less quick, Jervin and his family might have been dust in the wind by the time I got there. Besides, Father's eyes are on me, Kuval. I can't risk losing you to him."

Kuval did not seem mollified.

With a sigh, Nyli led him back to his seat and gently pushed him down into it. Then he hooked the leg of a nearby chair with his foot and dragged it close. The rest of his kisses were going to have to wait. If anyone could help him figure out how to find the baron in ten days, Kuval could, and being included in this now was the only gift he could think of. Remy Arnaud could probably have helped him too, he was willing to concede, but Nyli did not think the man would be affected by his charms. Besides, Kuval was far more pleasing to look at anyway.

The dovecote was the first place Zyre asked Modorin Kal to take her.

Zyre hadn't seen her sister Aljeya in five years, not since Aljeya had come home to celebrate the birth of her first child, a daughter. Traveling from Atlor to Lasinia Island was no quick or easy journey, even with a small retinue. But they'd always been close, as close as Zyre's secrets would allow, and she was the only family member Zyre knew the location of. Thalja willing, Aljeya would even have an army to march across the border. After all, what was the point of marrying into powerful families if not to have their support in a time of crisis?

It meant heading back to the Sector of the Gulls, and without

Neelie to push them quickly by all the sights, Zyre could actually stroll through Bijal's exciting streets. They didn't even get out of the Deckhand's Quarter before something had caught Zyre's ear.

Musicians played at the next corner, and it was nothing like she had ever heard before. Eyes widening in excitement, Zyre snatched Modorin's arm and hauled him closer. A few others had stopped on the street to listen, slapping their hands against their leg in time with the two drummers. A low, ethereal hum hung in the air like a fog, though whether it was from the drummers or the listeners or both, Zyre didn't know. But one of the musicians held a metal piece against his mouth, flicking a smaller metal tab that twanged.

It was nothing like Zyre had ever heard before. It did not ebb and flow like a courtier's song. The song called to something in her soul, something brutal and deadly. She had half a mind to dance, she a puppet and the music the hand that controlled the strings.

She watched in an awed silence as the drummers continued to strike their great drums. All too soon, though, the song faded away. The watchers' arms fell still, except for the coins that a few threw at the musicians.

At that, Modorin pulled her away. Kadj, the traitor, seemed just as eager to be going. Zyre could hear the musicians start up another song as the two of them walked away with their soulbeasts, and she longed to stay and listen.

"Why aren't they playing in taverns and inns?" Zyre asked, throwing one last glance over her shoulder. "Wouldn't they make more money there?"

"Agnir is a month of musical celebration in Venasca," Modorin replied conversationally as they continued their way down the street. "*Preze od Kerig.* Right now, there are more musicians than taverns and inns. They'll prove their worth, and the best from each neighborhood will play for *Freyr* Honir at the end of the month for a prize. It's all fun and games; a lot of amateurs will play on the street for the hell of it, drinking and partying. It's a riotous good time."

Curiosity getting the better of her, Zyre asked with feigned indifference, "Are you well acquainted with this holiday?"

Modorin looked at her drolly. "Is that your way of asking if I was born in Venasca?"

Zyre shrugged.

"The answer is no. I wasn't born in Venasca, I mean. As for how well *acquainted* I am with the holiday," he said with a pointed look, "well, however much acquaintanceship one can get out of three years."

"Does that mean you're a traveler? Captain Neelie made it sound as if the two of you are good friends."

Modorin barked out a bitter laugh. "Neelie and I are good friends, yes, but it's not because we went gallivanting across the world. She loves the sea, and I have found it a bitter enemy."

"How long have you known Neelie, then?"

"Three years ago, give or take a few months." He chuckled at the memory. "It was down at Yeog-ka. I think it was actually one of her first commands."

Yeog-ka was a large trading post much like Bijal, located off the coast of Syfris, near the southern border.

A pair of guards appeared up the street, and suddenly Modorin was leading her down an alley. He said nothing about the abrupt change of direction. "I don't know how familiar you are with the laws and history of Syfris, but *bolfendari*, what you call *sjarvisk*, are required to put in at least eight years of military service. I found it didn't suit me, and found in Neelie a way out. The short trip to Bijal made me second-guess myself, I'll tell you that much," he said with a laugh. "I was puking out every bit of food I put in my stomach. But when we made it, she set me up with someone who could teach me Venascan, asked if I would work for her family if she was willing to send some of the money home to my family. I've been here ever since."

Modorin gestured suddenly to a towering building down the street. "Do you have any money? For the messages?"

Any questions Zyre might've asked died on her lips.

Oh. Of course they would charge for the service. Crestfallen, she said, "I suppose we should have gone to the bank first."

The other *sjarvisk* shrugged, shoving a hand deep into one of his pockets. "My mother always said being lazy only creates more work, but I disagree in this case. Here." He withdrew a small flat silver *silse* with a flying horse impressed on the surface. "You can pay me back when we reach the Archway. How many messages do you need to send? They'll usually charge a *volir* for any day-bound notes."

"Just the one," Zyre replied, gratefully taking the coin from his palm. The *silse*, a moderately cheap metal, would have given her enough money to send out two notes with a half-*volir* left over, but she was ashamed to admit she didn't know where she would even send another dove. She would not have minded sending a message to her father to let him know where she was, but she did not know where he might be heading. Remy would have, but Remy was not here.

That easily, her good mood slid off her. Was Remy with their father, on the run? She dreaded to think of any one of her family in the royal family's clutches, but even that was better than the other alternative.

*I should have stayed on Lasinia*, Zyre thought, toying with the metal coin in her hand. *If Remy is dead, it'll be my fault for not sticking to the plan. I ran away.*

"*Magi* Zyre?"

She didn't have the heart to look at Modorin, so she simply closed her fist around the coin and said, "Right, then." She left him waiting for her outside the dovecote. She didn't expect it to take long.

The building wasn't particularly tall, but a great wooden dome poked against the sky. The entrance had a pair of doors designed with dozens of birds connected by whirling winds. Kadj leapt inside after her. There, she found a hallway with another set of doors at the opposite end. Zyre could hear the cacophonous cooing as soon as she set foot in the hall.

A man waited there and opened the second set of doors for her, allowing her into the main dovecote. She nearly lost her breath at the sight of it. A great open room presented itself to her, a handful of desks placed at intervals around the circumference, shuttered windows behind each of them. Men in cream-colored uniforms helped transcribe messages from their various patrons as birds soared around the dome, dove toward the desks, or settled into their roosts. And in the middle of the chaos, populating the space between the desks, were dozens of men and women from all over the world depositing messages.

It was clearly a hub of activity, and Zyre could not reconcile the practiced movements of the scribes with the chaos of the birds. Kadj flicked his tail, more excited than agitated, though a passing scribe looked nervously at him. She put a hand on his shoulder, willing him to behave.

Shaking her head to steady herself, Zyre found a man who appeared unoccupied. Better yet, he looked a lot like her: olive-colored skin, dark brown hair, bright round eyes. If the gods were good, he'd speak Corvikan. Otherwise, she might have to fetch Modorin after all.

"*Púo irudavit?*" the man said, not looking away from his desk right away. Then he saw her soulbeast and gave a start.

"Corvikan?" he hazarded. He sounded like he might've been from the south, but Corvikan was Corvikan. Zyre nodded in relief. "My sincerest apologies, *Magi*. Greetings! What can I do for you? A letter?"

"Yes, actually. I would like to write a letter to Aljeya Nyelin of Atlor."

"Certainly, certainly. Shall I write it for you?"

Zyre shook her head, wondering idly about the customers that frequented this business, how often Corvikans came this way. "If I could just borrow a piece of paper and something to write with, I would like to write it myself."

With a careless shrug, he set the supplies on her side of his desk and returned to his work.

It was not a large piece of paper that he gave her. She supposed it was unfair to expect the dove to carry anything larger. Still, it was no easy thing, deciding what to say. Worse, Aljeya would expect it to be ciphered. After a moment, the key came back to her mind: "Kiss the Willows," the title of an old Corvikan lullaby.

"May I have a piece of scrap paper?" she asked the scribe.

He looked up from his work, mildly irritated at the interruption. But the expression disappeared in an instant, and he provided it for her.

Zyre did not have a head for ciphers and had to use her quickly drawn reference sheet for most of the message.

"Hope you are well," she began. "Arnauds charged as traitors. Jervin free? Rest of family's fates unknown. We could really use you. I wait in Bijal for further word. —Z"

Well, it certainly wasn't poetry, but she hated ciphers, and anyway, it would be enough, surely, for Aljeya to understand.

Zyre cleared her throat, and the scribe looked up. Seeing she was done, he wordlessly sprinkled sand across the page to dry the ink, then sealed it with a small blob of wax.

The man made his demand for the price. It was a single *volir*, just as Modorin had said it would be, and once the man had given her the change, he sought out a roosting dove and fastened the note to the bird. He carried the dove to the window and gently tossed it into the air. Zyre watched as the creature flapped its wings and turned eastward. Then the man quickly shut the window before any other birds could get any ideas.

Before she left, she had the man burn her cipher reference sheet for her. She thanked him profusely, but despite his initial fervor, he seemed eager to see her on her way.

With a roll of her eyes that she took pains to make sure he didn't see, Zyre returned to the bright, hot Venascan streets. Poor Modorin waited across the way in a meager shadow, looking as if he might melt despite the shade.

Before they went to the Archway, Modorin led their small party to a cluster of stalls that carried a surprising selection of cuisine. Zyre could hardly tell which scents were coming from where. One stall had dried fish hanging from the side, and another had braided Corvikan bread. She found herself drawn toward her native food, but she hesitated when she saw Modorin head straight for another stall, one with food she didn't recognize. He called out over his shoulder, "Do you want anything?"

"What do they have?" she asked, curiosity getting the better of her.

"They have a killer *mendui* here," he said, leaning on the counter in a way that made the vendor look a little annoyed. The man wore a similar type of scarf as Modorin, and they exchanged a few words in a language she didn't understand. Fresian? The vendor's expression warmed.

Zyre hated to interrupt, but her stomach insisted. "I've never had *mendui* before."

Modorin grinned. "No time like the present. They're really good."

"I'll pay you back for it," she promised. He just waved her concern away.

A few minutes later, Kadj and Sarol had already scarfed down some extra meat from the vendor, and Modorin and Zyre wove through a ravenous crowd until they spilled back onto the main road. They picked at the food—which was a Fresian form of dumpling with a thin shell, stuffed with a mixture of different meats—while they made their way through the district.

The Archway was apparently close to the docks, and the farther away they got from the Deckhand's Quarter, the more mixed in everything became, as if there hadn't been enough chaos at the dovecote or the food stalls. Once again, Zyre was astounded by how different everyone looked. There'd been nothing like this on Lasinia; the whole district was a microcosm of the world.

It wasn't all beautiful, of course. They saw no fewer than three fistfights break out, though they never seemed to last long. And, for the first time in her life, Zyre witnessed someone stealing someone's purse, the silver gleam of a knife cutting the strings. She even saw one dark-skinned Onarisean chasing a cluster of Crasiks out of his shop. But there was something grounding in these conflicts. None of these people knew or cared about the war that was about to break out in her home country. For them, it was life as usual. It shouldn't have been a comfort, but in a way, it was, because it meant there was more to her world than just the constant struggle for power.

*I want it to see it all.* The thought tumbled into her heart with greater force than she would have expected. But it was true. It was overwhelming, and she loved it. Her old Corvikan dresses paled beside the cut and colors she found here. The voices cascaded against each other, a dozen languages with a hundred dialects, and musicians fought to be heard over them, over each other. It was chaotic. It was beautiful. *What other secrets is the world hiding from me?*

Zyre should have left home sooner. She could have sailed the seas like Neelie. Las Corvika couldn't kill an *aljarne* they couldn't catch, and she could have outsailed them all.

They turned down another street, one crowded with animals joined by their *sjarvisk* and *kjarnik*. There were others populating the street with them, trying to shuffle past the madness to get to wherever it was they were going, but the *sjarvisk* and *kjarnik*'s destination had been cordoned off, and the street was growing so clogged that it was impossible to move.

Ahead, a dozen soldiers in white-clad uniforms stood before a massive building that put the dovecote to shame. Two stories tall and in traditional Venascan build, the center of the *ðedael* was the crossed swords that Modorin had said belonged to *Freyr* Honir. The soldiers waiting outside, however, bore a different sigil. The sea serpent. High King Inoger's crest.

"That's *Ed Vodaría dir en Loræden*," Modorin said quietly. "The Guild of Magic." Zyre almost didn't hear him. His expression grew dark.

She followed his gaze to the doors, where *sjarvisk* and *kjarnik* waited to be allowed in or out. A man with a leather cuff around each of his wrists spoke to a woman with a bird fluttering around her head. Zyre could barely make out a sleek black dog at the man's feet. She strained her eyes, but it wasn't until they moved a little farther up the street that she made out the designs on the cuffs. More sea serpents.

"Does he work for the king?" Zyre asked, following Modorin's lead to keep her voice low. "He's wearing Inoger's crest."

"*High King* Inoger," Modorin corrected, casting a nervous glance around them. "And yes, he does. Dûl! This doesn't bode well. I'm going to ask you to return to the Siren's Haunt as soon as your business at the Archway is finished. The dresses will have to wait, I'm afraid; our friend needs to know Inoger has sent *ed gortien* to the city."

The woman with the bird gestured for the man to follow. They walked inside, and the soldiers blocking the way went with him.

"*Gortien?*" Zyre asked, glad to finally be moving again.

Modorin glanced at her, his dark eyes burning. "Many countries kill *aljarne* the moment they find them, afraid of the destruction they will cause when they go feral. High King Inoger and his predecessors decided that was wasteful. Instead, whenever they find an *aljarne*, they pair them with a specially equipped *kjarnik*, called their *gortien*, who watches them, helps them with whatever task they are assigned, and the moment they start to slip…" He mimed a knife across his neck.

A chill ran down Zyre's spine. "How do they know someone is an *aljarne?*"

"Normally, someone reports a person using magic without a soulbeast, and *Ed Vodaría dir en Loræden* investigates. If they find the claim is true, they'll request *ed gortien* from the capital. But *someone* thinks she is safe on her streets. She truly believes Bijal to be her own personal kingdom—flashing her magic around carelessly." He looked over his shoulder, though the Guild was already blocked from view. "I fear he is here because he already knows about her."

Zyre put a hand on his arm, asking him to stop. A few threw dirty looks their way, but she ignored them. "I have never met someone as fierce or deadly or commanding. You know her better, I won't deny it. But she saved my life on multiple occasions. I have seen what she can do."

"She's got a big head is what she has," Modorin mumbled, but there was the smallest glint in his eye.

She grinned. Sometimes, Thalja graced her tongue with the right words.

They kept moving. The Archway wasn't much farther. It was no grand thing, though: The doors themselves had a curved edge, almost circular, with intricate designs that held none of Venasca's noble sigils. Instead, it was just the moon nestled against the side of the sun, sharing the sky with clouds that poured out coins instead of rain. There were more images, but she couldn't quite decipher them. Venascan art was a language in and of itself.

Modorin agreed to stay outside, and so Zyre trotted up to the door of the Archway, Kadj on her heels, and hefted open its doors. She nearly ran into someone on their way out. She apologized and darted out of their way. The Crasik woman—at least, Zyre assumed she was Crasik; she was certainly tall and pale like Ivanya—just shot her a look before continuing on her way.

Grumbling under her breath, Zyre stepped inside and immediately felt underdressed for the occasion. Bless Kaari for the clean outfit, but the men and women in this place were clearly of a higher status than those who lived in the Deckhand's Quarter. Most of the people she'd seen at the Siren's Haunt probably couldn't afford even half of the fabric it took to make one dress she saw in here.

Eventually someone hurried over to her, a squirrelly woman wearing the brown and silver livery of the guild. She inspected every inch of Zyre's front, crinkling her nose at whatever it was she found. "Welcome, miss, to the Archway. Under whose account are you here for?" Her Corvikan was thick and unflattering, as if she did not even care to make an effort.

"Jervin Arnaud," Zyre replied flatly. "Guardian of Lasinia Island, Defender of the Odyri, and the Steward of Ermengarde. I am his *sjarvisk*."

The attendant frowned. She muttered something under her

breath, then, with as false a smile as Zyre had ever seen, gave a halfway decent quarter curtsy and said, "Right this way."

The woman brought them to a lightly furnished room with a chair on either side of dark-wooded desk. A man sat at the head of the desk, peering over stacks of papers set before him. Zyre decided not to even bother guessing where he was from. The floor was almost completely covered by rugs, and the walls by paintings that looked to be a speckling of prominent Pailyran artists, though she was pretty sure the one of the burning boat had been painted by Corsovo, a Laerian. All of them were current, which made them worth less, but a few of them, she knew, would likely gain quite a lot in value in the next hundred years.

The woman spoke quietly in Venascan to the man, and he, studying Zyre and not seeming to like what he found, waved her in. The door shut behind the attendant before Zyre had fallen all the way into her seat. "This is not the normal way for Baron Arnaud to address matters of his accounts," he began without preamble. "I'm afraid I must ask for the passkey before we can begin discussing financial matters."

"Valor?" she hazarded. That had been their cipher key for some time, when the need warranted one, and even after they had changed to a new one, it had been used to some purpose or another.

But the man only bent his head to the side. He rose, not even fazed by Kadj as the tiger watched his every move. He returned to the desk with an unfurled parchment. "What's your name?"

"Zyre… Mescal."

The man searched the document, nodding slowly. "Yes. Your name is on here. It's the stipend you're looking for, I presume?"

"Please," Zyre said through her teeth.

He passed one of the pages to her. "As you can see, your allotment is seven *barset* per week, which amounts to one hundred and forty *silse*. It will cover room and board for a respectable inn, though nothing fancy, and there should be enough left over for any business you may need to see to. Is this satisfactory?"

*Hopefully*, Zyre thought, but that wasn't the right answer. "Certainly," she said.

Once everything was sorted, Zyre left the Archway with her purse full. Modorin, of course, was waiting not far off. She flipped him a *silse*, which she hoped would cover both the note and lunch. "Do you think we'll have time later today to go wandering again?" she asked as they began walking.

Modorin grimaced. "Don't worry, there'll be plenty of time for sightseeing later."

Sighing quietly, Zyre bit her tongue and contented herself to take in the sights as they walked back to the inn.

# CHAPTER 8

Jervin Arnaud heard the trill of a tufted boor-hawk as he and
Merytz rode under the crisp canopy of the summer forest. The
call was repeated again, farther away, and again farther still. Jervin
let out a sigh of relief and ran his thumbs along the heavy straps
of his pack. Merytz walked beside him with an equally heavy bag,
doing an impressive job of hiding his fatigue.

It had been a tense journey, but the birdcall signaled that they
were near the end of it.

"I owe you my life tenfold," Jervin said, breaking their silence.
And it was true. Merytz had been instrumental not just in getting
Jervin off Lasinia but also in the arduous journey between here
and the coast. Jervin had been toying with an idea for some time
now. "You should know that before the Massacre of Kullen Valley,
Regis-Uncrowned Louis Ermengarde bestowed upon the Arnaud
family the Right of Precedence. And although I'd set that knowledge aside in the name of peace, it appears that the gods are now
in favor of allowing me to set things right."

Merytz walked on, frowning

Well, the laws of governance and the passing of titles was not
a topic most soldiers, even skilled captains such as Merytz, were

well educated on. When a regis died, the crown passed down to his eldest living son. Well, it needn't go to the eldest—there were instances where it had skipped the firstborn or even the second—but that was a complexity a guard like Merytz certainly would not understand. On occasion, though, the gods decided that the ruling family no longer deserved the title of regis. The regis would bear no sons, or if he did, they met untimely ends. A relative of the regis attempting to take the throne was considered going against the gods' wishes; catastrophe had followed more than one greedy relative who had tried.

To appease the three-faced god, Las Corvika's nobility had put forth the idea of the Right of Precedence. The ruling family would name which House could assume the throne should their own line fail, thus appeasing the gods while keeping some control over the future of their country.

Fjeron Tavere had been regis. A halfway decent king, by Jervin's estimation, but when his sons started dying, people grew worried. Fjeron had already given House Ermengarde the Right of Precedence, had even confirmed it, with witnesses. Then he had fallen ill.

Some stories said Notoyem was in the capital at the time. Some said he'd merely been on a nearby estate belonging to a minor House loyal to his own. Either way, he had not been far from Les Stelvo at Fjeron's untimely passing and had seized the throne as if the Right of Precrence were his.

Louis Ermengarde had raised banners to claim the title that should have been his. House Arnaud had sworn themselves to him. He'd been a good man. He would have made a great regis, had Notoyem not played his foul trick. An uncrowned regis's Right of Precedence might not have the law behind it, but it held the same weight of expectation.

Notoyem wasted money on parties and on drinking and insulted and exiled those who tried to keep the country together.

Louis's Right of Precedence meant it fell to Jervin to right Notoyem's wrongs.

"Do you plan on taking the throne?" Merytz asked finally.

Jervin shook himself, clearing his thoughts. "Yes, I do. And I'll need an honor guard if I'm to claim the title of Regis-Uncrowned. I would have you at its head, Captain."

A man suddenly appeared, almost out of thin air. He wore green and brown to match the forest around them. The small silver rose identified him as a soldier of General Tavere's, a distant cousin of the old regis and current leader of Jervin's army. The scout before them was old, his hair almost completely white, but he had the hard features of a seasoned soldier. The man inspected Jervin and Merytz. It struck Jervin that news must not have reached Tavere yet.

Merytz stepped in front of Jervin, all traces of exhaustion hidden away. "You have the honor to be in the presence of Baron Jervin Arnaud, guardian of Lasinia Island, Defender of the Odyri, and the Steward of Ermengarde."

The grizzled soldier gave a full bow at that. "My name is Noam Rodier. I will take you to General Tavere, if it pleases you."

"It does," Jervin replied, his tone even.

Noam bowed again before gesturing for them to follow.

Merytz leaned close to Jervin, his voice kept low as he said, "Pardon, sir, but it would be the greatest honor to lead your guard."

It did not take them too long to stumble upon the outskirts of camp. It was sizable, all considering, and as Noam led them through the warren of paths, Jervin was proud to see how tidy everything was. Tavere had helped Jervin undermine Notoyem's rule these past twenty years with fast strikes in pivotal locations. Their rebel army posed as bandits, the troops spread out across

Las Corvika, camps fading out of sight before any of Notoyem's men could track them down and find the truth of it. Any resources they captured from Notoyem, they certainly put to use boosting Jervin's own claim.

Jervin could only hope that his patience and beaten pride had earned them enough to give them a chance.

Tents began to appear as they drew nearer to the central part of camp. They would belong to the men of rank. One bore the flags of House Arnaud, Tavere, and Ermengarde stacked atop each other, though there was no wind to give them life. It was to this tent that Noam led their party of three. Dismissing the old scout, Jervin strode into the tent.

A handful of men were already inside, but if any of them had served during the Succession, Jervin only recognized one of them. Tall, with his short dark hair tied back at the top of his head, a dark blue uniform sporting a dozen honors, Mahieu Tavere looked every inch a general. He and the rest of the men studied a map with small markers spread across it, yet they noticed Jervin quickly.

Tavere's eyes narrowed, and then, in a flash, it was replaced with a broad grin. The general gave him a half bow with the honorific hand over heart. Distantly, Jervin was aware of the others giving him the three-quarter bow, and he studied them as they did. They'd be captains or lieutenants. Of the five, three were old enough to have served in the Succession. The other two had to be Remy's age, or perhaps even younger, although as they rose from the bow, Jervin noted a hardness in their eyes that told him they were boys no longer.

"Dismissed," the general barked to the others. The men filed out quickly. An otter trailed after one of them, sniffing at Jervin's dirt-fringed pants.

"Wait outside the tent," Jervin muttered to Merytz. The captain bowed and slipped away.

"How bad is it, then?" Mahieu asked once they were alone.

Jervin drew closer to the map. In addition to the camp they were in now, there were four different encampments, one of which was stationed on the opposite side of Les Stelvo. Another was in prime position to harry trade routes between Obele and the capital. A third was positioned near the Bergev Mountains, close enough to the Duvachelle stronghold to cause them grief, and the last was in the north, near the sea, ready to do the same for the Villeneuves.

The number of pieces representing Béranger men were scattered across the board, their presence in all of the major cities and old outposts. They even had the audacity to occupy the ruins of Mod Adeirno, abandoned after House Ermengarde fell.

Jervin scowled. The regis's occupation of Louis's old home was salt on a much bigger wound. Jervin's forces were, all told, slightly larger than what Notoyem held the capital with, but even that was not a particularly soothing balm. One needed far fewer men to defend a city than one did to attack it. It would take effort and a substantial amount of funds to besiege Las Corvika.

He looked up from the map at Mahieu. The old general stared back at him, waiting. "I'm a wanted man," Jervin said finally. "The rest of the Arnaud family has been taken prisoner. We need to act, and swiftly. How much of a financial reservoir does the army have?"

"At its current size? Three, maybe four, months. I can have my attendant get you a copy of the numbers."

"Please. And how close are we to toppling Houses Villeneuve and Duvachelle?"

The general grimaced. "We'd expected to have at least another year or two to chip away at them. They're hurting, but they still have enough resources to back their regis."

The young Béranger brat had upset their carefully laid-out plans, of that there was no mistake. But a commander must be fluid, ready to change strategy at the first glint of steel. "We'll make do. The Bérangers only pushed themselves closer to their own demise."

No more compromise with Notoyem, he swore to himself. No more backing down. He had promises to keep. He would sit on the throne if he could, but even if they failed at that, he would not rest until Notoyem and his sons were dead. Jervin would meet his gods content that House Béranger, at least, was stripped of what they had not earned.

***

Zyre paced back and forth in her room. Her shadow was almost as tall as she was, though at this point, it was barely discernible from the darkness cast upon the room. The sun had only just begun to set. For the last half hour, she'd had nothing else to do but watch the shadows lengthen. If Modorin took much longer to return, she might lose her mind.

"That's it," she said aloud. She had to get out of this room. "Come on, Kadj, let's go."

Kadj chuffed in annoyance, but he rolled lazily to his feet and padded behind her as she thundered into the common room. Despite the late hour, or perhaps because of it, the room was full of people. They sat around tables with tall cups in their hands and large stacks of thin, round bread. A musician played, though the song was softer, tamer than what the street performer had played earlier that day. Some of the men conversed, but most were tossing about dice. Kadj drew eyes, but then, he always did, and at least no one glared at her in here.

One of Kaari's kitchen girls brought her a drink. "*Medias,*" Zyre said, thanking her in Venascan. The girl just dipped into a polite curtsy and hurried off. With the cup in hand, Zyre found an empty chair at a gambling table, taking it as a good sign when the present occupants did not curse her off.

Whatever game they were playing looked nothing like the dice games that her father's men had played in their downtime. They would rattle the dice in an empty cup, lift up the cup just enough for them to glance at the dice, and then call off a number. Then the cup and its hidden contents would be passed off to the next player, who would roll the dice and call out another number. Except, sometimes, the next player didn't make the roll. They'd look at the hidden dice and would usually pass coins to another player. Once, though, the player looked at the dice and rose out of his chair so fast it nearly toppled backward as he yelled in victory.

It was some sort of game of bluff, though it took Zyre ages to figure it out. She was just getting to the point of wondering if she knew enough Venascan to play when Modorin returned.

He wasn't alone.

Zyre tried not to stare at Neelie, who'd changed into a more fitted shirt, a beautiful blue that reminded Zyre of home, and a flattering black overcoat with Venascan vines embroidered on the hem.

The pair wound through the common room. Neelie greeted a few men at the table before turning her attention onto Zyre. "Come on. We're going to look into this magic of yours."

Zyre blinked. "Didn't Modorin tell you about… the *kjarnik*?"

"He is not here for me," Neelie replied with utter conviction. "As I told this idiot, *Freyr* Honir knows it would mean an all-out war if he tried to touch anyone in my family. We'll be fine. Now, do you want your magic fixed or not?"

The answer was a resounding yes, so Zyre downed the rest of her drink and motioned for Neelie to lead the way. She groaned as the room spun a little, relying on Kadj to steady her.

They headed northeast, traveling under lamplight. Worst of all, they traveled in silence. It seemed too good to be true, that her magic might be fixed tonight, and a little surreal that it should be happening now, after Modorin had left to deliver a warning.

Her nerves settled a little as she realized they were moving through the outskirts of the city. Wherever they were going, it would be far enough away that her magic wouldn't hurt anyone if it got out of control. Even when the buildings began to dwindle, giving way to a long beach sparsely populated by spindly pines, they pressed onward. It was well and truly dark by now, and only a small flame floating above Modorin's palm gave them any light to see by.

Zyre called to her magic, letting it thrum in her blood, waiting. Outside of Bijal-proper, her magic felt more like she was used to. It answered her the way it might've on her family's estate or even in the fishing town of Nolasi. Less present than out at sea, though.

Eventually, a dark silhouette in front of them took the shape of a cluster of trees. They pushed through it, and a cove opened up before them. Two men waited. One, a tall man, bespectacled and with a braid in his beard, had a large black bird perched on his shoulder. The other held a torch that illuminated his dark features, and Zyre sucked in a breath. It'd been years since she'd seen him, but she remembered his face, his dark skin and shaved head and his deep brown eyes.

To her horror, Kaspar Gehrig offered the perfect Corvikan half bow.

"You honor me too greatly," she said quickly.

"I wasn't expecting to find you in Bijal, *Vinjess* Arnaud," Gehrig replied with a voice as deep as thunder.

"You mistake me," she said quickly, unwilling to risk a glance at Neelie. "My name is Zyre Mescal. The only *vinjess* was Aljeya Arnaud, but she has since been wed."

Gehrig looked at the man with the bird on his shoulder. The light of their torch cast a forlorn pallor across Gehrig's features. He snapped something in Venascan, but there was no mistaking the anger lacing his tone.

The other man, the one with spectacles perched on his nose, only frowned darkly.

Gehrig started walking toward her, and then, to Zyre's horror, continued *past*, toward the city.

If he walked away, she might lose her only chance to fix what was wrong with her.

Praying to Thalja that she wasn't making a huge mistake, she said, "Wait!"

Gehrig looked over his shoulder at her expectantly.

"I'm *not* a *vinjess*. But…" Zyre breathed in deeply, ready for the plunge. "I am an Arnaud. And I do need help."

She glanced shyly at Modorin and Neelie and quickly looked away. Neelie, especially, looked wounded, as if Zyre should have told her from the start that she was an Arnaud. What did she expect? For Zyre to lay every single secret down at her feet? For eleven years, she'd kept her head down, acted like it hadn't bothered her when her own parents' eyes passed over her like they didn't see or when she'd been left behind time and time again. She hadn't been able to join her family at court seven summers ago or be there at her sister's wedding.

There had to be a reason for it all. There had to be a reason for all of the secrets and lies and tears at her heart.

Her knees threatened to buckle. *Thalja's mercy*, she thought, reaching out for Kadj. *I did not think I had it in me to be bothered by this anymore.*

Kaspar Gehrig glanced at the bearded *kjarnik*. With a sigh, he returned to their small group. "Show us," he said.

*You knew the biggest secret first, Neelie,* Zyre thought quietly, stepping toward the water's edge. *I hope that's enough to placate your wounded heart.*

Her magic rippled down her arms as Zyre let the night take on a blue tint. The water in the dense coastal air asked for direction, but that was small, effortless. She reached for the water pooled in the cove, and with one firm gesture, her magic exploded out of her. Like a wave crashing in reverse, the sea rolled backward in an arc. It retreated farther and farther.

For one blindingly exhilarating moment, Zyre wondered if she might manage to hold it after all.

But as the sea wall grew, it bucked under her control. She could either let it come crashing down or try to control the fall. But before she could decide, something snapped, and the great wave broke free of its own accord, roaring toward her. With a yelp, Zyre turned and brought her hands to protect her head, but the water never came.

She looked back.

The water was held back, a great wall with small rivulets rolling down its face. Modorin and Neelie controlled the sea as it slowly crept back to the way it had been. Sarol and Kadj stood at attention near the water's edge, playing their part.

She turned to Gehrig and curtseyed bitterly to the half, returning that honor back to him. "It was not a lie, what I said. I haven't been Jervin Arnaud's daughter since the day we learned I was an *aljarne*." Zyre glanced at Neelie, hoping she took the words to heart. "I have not been much use to my family for most of my life, but a war is about to start, and I want nothing more than to be able to help them."

*I won't run away again,* she swore. *If I have control of my magic, I won't need to.*

The *kjarnik* said something to Gehrig in Venascan. Neelie made a reply, and the *kjarnik* shrugged. Throughout the whole conversation, Zyre stood awkwardly. Modorin wasn't far off, playing with Sarol. They caught each other's gaze, and Zyre looked away.

Gehrig and the other man—Hosvar?—let their conversation die away. Hosvar, the man with the bird, brandished a piece of metal in the shape of an uprooted flower. Holding the piece toward Zyre, he closed his eyes and muttered a few words under his breath. Zyre stared at the charm, her hand frozen halfway to it as she debated whether he wanted her to take it from him.

Then the air suddenly felt cold, though no wind messed with her hair or caressed her skin. Zyre wrapped her arms around her chest. Her borrowed overcoat did nothing for her as the temperature continued to drop. Kadj pressed against her side, his head burrowing against the curve of her ribs. His fur didn't offer her desperate fingers any warmth.

Hand shaking, she searched her companions for any explanation and found them staring at her curiously. The cold did not touch any of them. Even Sarol slouched at Modorin's feet, unconcerned. Hosvar's eyes darted around Zyre and her tiger, frowning. Then the cold faded as quickly as it had come.

"*Id ed pejo ledri es wydonis dir ed furto,*" he said to Gehrig.

Zyre looked to Modorin. He wouldn't return it, choosing instead to study Sarol. "He says your magic is getting stuck to Kadj," he whispered.

She was pretty sure *furto* meant "octopus," but figured it was maybe better not to ask.

"*Probua ed lesyra dir zkife,*" Gehrig proffered. Disk of reading?

Hosvar waved him off impatiently, reaching into his jacket with his other hand. He withdrew another charm, indeed in the shape of a disk, and held it near her.

She waited, bracing herself for another onslaught of magic, at least until Hosvar gestured sharply in front of her and she realized she was actually supposed to take this one. Her cheeks burning, and fully grateful for the scarce light, Zyre snatched at the disk.

She couldn't help but gasp.

Her magic swelled of its own volition, and colors swirled in front of her eyes from silver to blue to yellow and back again. Yet it did not lunge at her, the magic. Instead, almost sleepily, the little particles rolled toward the disk, spun around its circumference, and then lazily went on their way, dissipating.

Zyre was so distracted that she didn't notice Hosvar brandishing the uprooted flower until the temperature dipped a second time. It felt like an eternity, those few minutes while Hosvar studied her magic. Even so, when he put the flower charm away and her fingers began to thaw, she was loathe to give the disk back. She'd never done anything like that before. Her magic had never been so calm. When Hosvar gently pulled the charm from her fingers, it felt like he was ripping away something vital.

Hosvar returned to Kaspar Gehrig, and they began to speak to each other in Venascan. Modorin wouldn't interpret, and since it seemed like the two of them would be preoccupied with their own conversations for some time, Zyre plopped onto the sand next to Kadj.

Then, thank Thalja, Neelie fell gracefully into the sand beside her. Modorin took Neelie's other side, lounging on his back so he could stare up at the sky. Sarol settled in by his feet.

"Suddenly a lot of things make sense."

Zyre glanced at Neelie, and the other woman shrugged. "Remy

Arnaud is your brother, I suppose." Neelie scrunched her nose in distaste. "I had thought you might be his mistress."

Zyre didn't know whether to be disgusted or enraged on her brother's behalf, so settled for both. "Why?"

"He asked me to look out for you, to get you off Lasinia if everything went wrong. Anyway, it also explains your determination to find the baron."

Zyre grimaced.

"You're going to find him, aren't you? You want to have full use of your powers so you can use them on the battlefield," Neelie hazarded. Her eyes had gone hard, bitter. "Do you think yourself capable of that?"

"I don't have a choice," Zyre told her softly.

It was the harsh truth. She did not think she could live with herself if something happened to her family because she refused to lend them aid. However much it hurt, their actions had saved her life, and quite possibly her mind. Besides, they were her family, whether she could announce it to the world or not.

"It's not a good idea to be a *najik* in the middle of a battleground," the other woman warned.

"You're one to talk," Modorin muttered.

"Oh, shut it," Neelie snapped, spraying sand at him. But after a moment, she cracked a smile, and so did he.

"*Magi* Zyre," Hosvar called.

Neelie rolled to her feet and, to Zyre's surprise, offered her a hand up. She took it, and before Zyre could let go of Neelie's hand, the other woman tightened her grip and said, "Just remember that royalty comes and goes. A throne never belongs to someone forever, and this thing your father is chasing is a temporary thing that will cost a lot of blood. Help your family, but remember when you do that there is a whole world out there and enough causes to fight for to last more than three lifetimes, many of which are far more noble than mercurial shifts in power."

Only then did Neelie's fingers unfurl themselves from around Zyre's wrist. Baffled, she turned toward the *kjarnik*, trying to put Neelie's words away for later.

Hosvar began without preamble. "Your magic is unreliable because your connection to your soulbeast is rudimentary and unnatural." Hosvar flicked an apologetic look to his friend, but Gehrig only shrugged, and Hosvar pressed on. "It's quite possible that the only solution to the explosive nature of your magic now is to break your connection to your soulbeast and allow your *najik* magic free as it was meant to be."

"Lose Kadj?" Zyre blinked. "Isn't he supposed to serve as a buffer?"

The expression he wore looked a lot like pity. "That's the choice you're going to have to make."

Well, that was an easy answer. No, absolutely not.

*Your magic is useless otherwise*, part of her thought savagely. *Or did you forget all those times you tried to help only for your magic to blow up in your face? What good are you with unbridled yet unreliable power?*

"My daughter knows where to find me once you've made your decision," Hosvar said gently.

"Thank you." Turning hesitantly to Neelie, she said, "It's really late. I'd like to return back to the Siren's Haunt, if that's all right."

Neelie looked to her father—her *father*; that was an unexpected turn of events, and one that brought with it a bucketload of questions, such as what her relationship with him was if she was so quick to suggest that Zyre abandon her own father—and, at his gesture, nodded. "I have some things to get done, but Modorin will take you. I'll check back in sometime tomorrow, if I can."

"Be careful, Nee," Modorin warned. "I'm serious. Even if that *gortien* isn't here for you, it doesn't mean the city is safe."

Neelie rolled her eyes. "I appreciate the concern, but I'll be fine. We haven't lost the city to him yet."

Modorin scowled, but he didn't argue. He led Zyre back toward the great black silhouette of Bijal, leaving Neelie behind.

# CHAPTER 9

Every bone in Zyre's body ached as the early morning rays pulled her away from sleep. Whether it was from all the walking or from the magic of last night, she didn't know, but she'd have given a pretty penny to fall back asleep. Kadj appeared completely unfazed, however, peering happily out of the window. The edge of his tail flicked back and forth as he caught whatever scents were to be had in the Deckhand's Quarter. She smiled, but the memory of the meeting on the beach turned her joy hollow. Thoughts from last night came rushing back to her.

She should have known the only solution would be to break her bond with Kadj. But what would happen when she did? How long would she have before the madness claimed her?

Zyre pushed herself off the bed, perhaps more forcefully than she needed to, but she couldn't stand the idea of just sitting there fretting. She threw on her outfit from yesterday, then clicked her tongue for Kadj to follow her.

The two of them trotted down the steps. Zyre scanned the common room for a place to sit and found Modorin tipping his chair back to talk to a man at the table behind him. She walked over and sat down next to Modorin, surprised at the number of empty plates and bowls already stacked in front of him.

"Did you feel the need to feed an army?" she asked dryly once Modorin turned his attention away from his fellow conversationalist.

"What?" Modorin replied haughtily. "I got hungry waiting for you to wake up."

One of Kaari's girls arrived at the table with a cup of hot tea for Zyre and bobbed a curtsy when Zyre asked for some breakfast. Once the girl was gone, she turned her attention back to Modorin.

"I feel I owe you an explanation."

Modorin cocked his head. "For?"

Drumming her fingers against the side of the table, Zyre cast about for the right words. "I don't want you to think I was lying to you specifically. This is no small deception my family has pulled off, and I've spent most of my life knowing what might happen if I told my secrets to the wrong person. It's just…habit, at this point."

"We only met yesterday, *Magi*," he said with an uncomfortable shrug. "Tell you what. To make us even, I'll give you one of my own secrets."

"Technically, I shared two," she blurted, trying for that easy wit Neelie and Modorin shared.

Modorin laughed. "You know what? I think I have an even better idea. Have you heard of *Holte Barol*?" He explained the rules to her, and she realized that it was the game she'd watched yesterday afternoon. He lit up like a sunrise when he realized she had a basic understanding of the rules. "Obviously, people will normally bid money, but I think it'll be more fun if we trade secrets. What do you say?"

"I say that it's a terrible idea and I'm all in," she found herself saying with a laugh. After all, Modorin already knew she was an *aljarne*. He already knew she was a nobleman's daughter. What major secrets were left to share?

Within moments, Modorin had procured a cup, a set of five dice, and, somehow, even more food, though that last, at least, he deigned to share. "Winner gets to ask a question, and the loser has to answer," he said as he scooped up the dice and started rattling. "Sound fair?"

"Will you take it easy on me since this is my first game?"

"Not a chance," Modorin said with a laugh as he slammed the cup upside down. He glanced at it. "Eighteen."

Zyre took the cup off of him, trying to discreetly count the dice before she rolled her own. She thought he was right, which didn't tell her much about his style of bluffing. "You just told me you owe me a secret of your own." She counted the pips. *Twelve. Off to a great start.* "Twenty-one."

He looked at her suspiciously. She returned it with a challenging glare of her own, more for the secret he'd promised than for the lie she'd just told. He swiped the cup from her and didn't even bother to glance at its contents before shaking. He set the cup down. "Twenty-two." Modorin announced, then pushed it over before she could call his bluff. "I'm no liar. Whoever loses, I'll still give you a secret. This one round, anyway."

"Then tell me now." She considered calling his bluff anyway, then shook her head and rolled. It would be just her luck that the one time she called his bluff would be the one time he wasn't actually lying. *Eighteen. Tholjun's blood. Does anyone actually ever not lie with this game?* "Twenty-five."

"Bluff," Modorin said instantly.

Grumbling, Zyre withdrew the cup and revealed her lie.

Modorin smirked. "All right, here's my question: How the hell did you live under your family's own roof, with all those servants and guards and stuff that all nobles are supposed to have, and keep your magic a secret?"

"Zyre Arnaud is said to have died at a young age from a terrible fever." She spoke with a false, haughty air. Smiling bitterly, Zyre scratched Kadj's ears and said, "I had to stay out of sight for almost a year. A few adjustments to my hairstyle and the cut of clothes I wore, and a tiger cub to boot, was all it really took. There were a few entrusted with the secret, but the Arnauds haven't been able to keep a large staff in such a long time, anyway, which I suppose made it all a little easier for the rest."

"I have trouble believing you looked *that* different that no one could tell."

Zyre shrugged. "I've learned that people often see what they want to see."

Modorin let the topic go with a grunt.

"My turn. Why do you know Corvikan? Is it common for people in Syfris to learn it?"

"Ah! And that is easily answered." He scooped up the dice with ease, rattling them idly. "I happen to have a very good head for languages. It didn't take me long to learn Venascan, and once that was down, I figured Corvikan would be an easy next step. I'm actually learning Atloric now." He presented her the cup. "Here, you go first this time."

They played several more rounds, and Zyre was so engrossed that she was able to forget everything else. Her next loss, Zyre told Modorin all about her sister, Aljeya—how she would stick up for Zyre and bring her books to read in that year of isolation. The loss after that, she was asked about her brother Remy, and she spoke of how he would tease her endlessly, but kindly, and how she had always believed him when he'd told her as a kid that he wouldn't let anyone take her away. In exchange, Modorin divulged information about his home, located in the small town of

Gorad-Eum along the Xertse River. He had three brothers—two of them older—and two younger sisters, all of whom he missed terribly.

By a stroke of misfortune on her end, Modorin glanced at his roll once and crowed, "Ski's pips! Ha! I won!"

She'd just rolled what she claimed was a twenty. "What? What does that mean? A thirty or something? I call bluff."

"Not a thirty. A fifteen, but most importantly, the roll is consecutively one through five. You owe me a secret," he said, revealing his dice.

"But fifteen is less than twenty!" Zyre protested.

"It's a winning throw, no matter what. That's why they call it Ski's pips."

Considering how often he'd seemed to be winning, this seemed an unfair addendum. With a sigh, she asked him to give her his question.

"If your family wasn't stuck in this civil war of theirs and you could be doing anything in the world, what would it be?'

"I'd like to visit Pailyr, I suppose," she said honestly. "One of the few things my mother was able to pass on to me was a love and respect for all forms of art, and Pailyr is supposedly second to none. I'd love to see the whole world, but if I could only choose one place, it would certainly be there."

Zyre rattled her dice and began the game anew.

Their very next game was interrupted, however. A boy, no older than fifteen, hurried into the common room and asked for Ange Duval. Zyre waved the boy over and accepted a piece of paper off of him. He stood there for several moments expectantly. Realizing what he was after, Zyre fished through her pocket until she had her fingers on one of the smaller Venascan coins.

Once he was gone, Zyre inspected what he'd offered her. It was a note, sealed with the linework that stood for sigils in Atlor. This particular design belonged to the Nyelin family, to Aljeya. She broke it hastily and winced at the stream of unintelligible letters she found there.

"Any chance I can get some scrap paper and something to write with?" she asked.

Modorin flagged down one of the serving girls, and in a few minutes, Zyre had the key written out and was scribbling Aljeya's message.

"I don't know what you're doing in Bijal," it read, "but if you're safe from the Béranger family, all the better. I have received word from the baron that he escaped unscathed but that the baroness, *vinje*, his wife, and their son were all taken to the capital. Their lives are at the mercy of the regis, whom we all know to be mercurial. You may be better off staying where you are. I will see what we can do from here. Stay safe. —A"

"What does it say?" Modorin prompted softly.

It took some effort to look up from the note. "I really thought that maybe my whole family got away." She handed him the note. It took all of her self-control not to rush out of the inn then and there. Zyre could not run all the way back home, and even if she did, she had no idea where to go. "I've been so selfish, acting like I have time to consider Hosvar's offer when my mother and brother could be executed any day now."

Modorin set the paper down. "Have you made up your mind? About Kadj?"

"How can I?" Zyre wanted to scream. "How can I possibly? If I accept Hosvar's offer, I actually stand a chance of helping my family survive this, but— Gods, how *selfish* I am." Her internal war from the night before reared its ugly head. A good daughter would do anything to protect the family, sacrifice anything. So why, *why*, did she hesitate?

She never should have run from Lasinia. She should have

stayed and fought. And if it had led to her death, well. At least she could face her gods with pride.

Needing to do *something*, Zyre let Modorin take her through the city again. They visited a seamstress, both because Zyre was in need of clean clothes that would actually fit her and also for the gossip Modorin promised they'd find there. The word there was that civil war was looming in Las Corvika, but High King Inoger was more preoccupied with issues of his own to offer any aid to either party. That information was a relief, Zyre decided afterward, though she'd been foolishly hoping for something a little more substantial.

Afterward, they went to the docks to see if any of the sailors had heard anything. The Sector of the Gulls was as untamed as it had been in her previous pass-throughs, but even sailors' knowledge was limited. There were little signs of rebellion every-where—old Corvikan flags were being flown... towns troubled by massive groups of bandits were suddenly unable to find any proof the bandits had been there in the first place, as if the earth had swallowed them whole. But no one knew where her father might be, and no one could think of any reason that Notoyem had kept his prisoners alive.

Some hours later, Modorin dragged Zyre back to the Siren's Haunt in defeat.

If the common room had been nearly empty when they'd left, it was practically dead now. The breakfast and lunch crowds had long since left to tend to their duties, and it was too early for the dinner folk to be in. It was even slow enough that one of Kaari's girls had propped herself on a chair, feet on the table, fanning herself with a simple ridged fan. The people she was with seemed not to care, though no doubt Kaari or Hæfnir would, were they here to see it.

Of course, her eyes snapped open with their arrival, and, blushing, she scrambled to her feet, bobbing a polite curtsy. She spoke to Modorin in Venascan, but all Zyre needed to hear was *Nagi Neelie* and *en kurat thola* before she was striding off to the Coral Room where Neelie had deposited her less than twenty-four hours prior.

Modorin's footsteps were slow and far behind, the way a person might walk when they knew a friend would wait for them regardless. Perhaps someday, Zyre would have a friend like that, but friendships were the furthest thing from her mind.

The truth was, once she stood in front of Neelie, she knew the words she needed to say would stick to her mouth like bitter honey. It wasn't just about losing Kadj—and she would, sure as day, because once the *leiks* was broken, there'd be nothing to keep him tamed and at her side. It was also the madness, that ever-looming threat. Remove the *leiks*, and she'd lose herself eventually someday. Dying seemed a better option.

But if she died, her family would lose one of the greatest weapons they had in their arsenal. She didn't mind the idea of dying in order to stay true to herself, but she refused to risk *their* lives for her own pride. After a lifetime of keeping her distance from her family, taking this risk was one thing Zyre could do.

Building armor around herself, she shoved the door open with the intent to say as much.

She did not get past the first syllable. Neelie stole it from her.

"I was quite certain I'd have to wait here all day for you to return, *Magi* Zyre."

"I had some errands to run."

Modorin finally caught up to them, shutting the door without pausing to ask. He glanced curiously at Zyre, which she promptly ignored, even as he stepped around her to take a seat. "Been here long, Neelie?" he inquired.

"Long is a relative term. For a lazy rapscallion like yourself, no, not overly. For a busy woman with half a dozen things I must get done by day's end?" She smirked as if to say *one point to me, none to you.* It was all a game, one that Zyre wasn't in the mood for. But then Neelie turned her dark eyes onto Zyre, and whatever bitter words might've formed on her tongue died away. "Aren't you going to sit?"

With some reluctance, she did.

"Have you thought about your answer?"

Zyre bit back a laugh. It was *all* she could think about. "It's an impossible question," she said. Zyre flicked a gaze at Modorin, pouring himself a cup of wine from the pitcher someone had left for them. Then she studied her fingernails, jagged and torn. She thought of Aljeya's note, of her family's safety, and of her heart. "Neither answer is a good one, is it?"

"Perhaps," Modorin said, pitching headlong into the conversation, "Some spare opinions are in order. As the most famous *najik* at present, we mere mortals beseech you to share yours."

Neelie cursed him out so thoroughly in Venascan that Zyre nearly blushed. She had half a mind to join in, though. Maybe he was trying to help, but this wasn't the type of situation made better by jests.

When she fell silent, Modorin grimaced, looking properly chastised. There must've been a question at the end of her tirade, however, because he said, "I'm a *majican*. What do I know of great magic and madness?"

"A coward's answer, and you know it," Neelie snapped.

Zyre pulled the pitcher toward her and poured wine into a sizable cup.

Scowling softly, he said, "Finc. Would I keep Sarol, if I were in Zyre's position? Honestly, it does not seem like a hard choice to me. Sarol's magic has saved my life on many occasions, and I like being able to rely on my mind."

"But you wouldn't be able to rely on your magic," Zyre noted. "As *Wyrdi* Hosvar said, the nature of the made-up *leiks* is what makes my magic unpredictable. And I can't afford it to be. My family's lives are on the line."

Modorin raised his cup. "Good point, to which I say, magic is not the only weapon a person can learn."

Well, that was unhelpful. Passable as she was with a sword, most of the men in her father's camp would be far better, making her presence redundant. It was her magic that made her the most dangerous. "And you, Neelie? Do you agree?"

"I'm too sober for this," Neelie grumbled. She gestured to the pitcher. Zyre let it slide down to her. Neelie filled her cup, drained it, then filled it again, nursing her drink close to her chest. "I've never had a soulbeast, never felt like I was missing out for the lack. I can walk into cities that a *sjarvisk* couldn't because even if people are afraid of magic, they will never know I have it so long as I'm careful. It's a well-kept secret, an explosion tucked away for emergencies. But," she said, drawing out the word.

Neelie grimaced at her cup, then let its contents pour into her mouth. "But I will pay for it someday, and the cost is no small thing. You are lucky in that, *Nagi* Zyre. You have a buffer. That stunt you pulled on the *Aretmor* alone probably would have cost me my sanity, but it didn't even touch you."

Zyre's eyes fell to the table, tracing its lines and whorls with her gaze so Neelie did not know how sharp her bitterness cut.

Silence reigned for several minutes, each an eternity unto itself. Apparently, not even Modorin felt comfortable enough to break it.

In the end, it was Neelie. "I have grown too reliant on my

own magic, maybe, but if it were me, I'd much rather have full use of it. If my family were in danger, and I did not do absolutely everything in my power to make sure they were safe, I would regret it for the rest of my life."

The words dug in deep. Neelie had hit the one thing Zyre could not shake. Had her entire family escaped Nyli that day, she'd have left them to their own devices. But she at least had to see them freed. To do otherwise was unconscionable.

*I love you, Kadj,* she thought at him, though of course he couldn't hear. *I have to do this.*

"I need the *leiks* broken."

Neelie's lips became a thick straight line. "Then I'd best go tell my father." She emptied the remaining contents of her cup into her mouth. "Modorin, I'll see you later."

And just like that, Neelie was gone.

Ivanya would never admit it, but she was terrified. Béranger troops marched her, Damari, and her grandson out of the dungeons, through the dim grounds of the palace, and into the palace proper. No one would answer her questions about Remy—why he was being left behind—or where they were being taken now. In the silent, barren, eerie hallway, she could only imagine they were being marched to their deaths.

Their guards did not take them to the throne room, or even to the courtroom. Instead, they wound through the section of the palace reserved for major Houses.

She knew the direction they were being taken, but her mind could not make sense of it. Were they being lulled into a false sense of security? Surely, they were not being taken to their old apartments.

*I have to be wrong,* Ivanya thought. *If I'm right, that only means there will be a heavy price to pay.*

Four men with the knotwork of honor guards stood at attention in front of the Arnaud apartments' main entry. She didn't need to see the two fish or the House words carved into the wood to know it was theirs. The honor guard, though, belonged to the regis. Ivanya was going to have to act for all she was worth.

The honor guard opened the doors and ushered the lot of them inside. The regis's back was to them as he inspected, somewhat unsteadily, artwork that Ivanya had picked out long ago.

As soon as they were shut within, the regis turned. His bloodshot eyes swept over them all. To Damari, he said, "Your son should be in bed. Take him to the sleeping quarters so I might have a few words with the baroness."

Damari's eyes widened, and she glanced at Ivanya questioningly. The guards gave neither of them much choice, though. One of them pushed her. She let them lead her to the spare bedroom, looking over her shoulder apologetically as Ivanya was left alone with the drunken regis.

"Ivanya Arnaud," he said, his tongue slow from the drink. His hungry gaze, however, was not. She took heart in the guards who remained with them. "It is true what they say. The years have only enhanced your beauty."

"And it appears," Ivanya replied, "that the years have not touched your wit."

Notoyem did not notice the insult. "I suppose you're wondering when your husband will come to the capital to rescue you."

"It has only been a day since our arrival, Regis. Give him time."

Yes, there was that infamous anger. He crossed the distance between them in three long strides. The guards instinctively stepped aside, doing nothing as his bony palm struck her face. His voice trembled in his anger as he said, "I do not need any further proof of your family's misdeeds, Baroness. Your son lives by my mercy. Your grandson. You. Do not test my patience."

"Of course not, Your Highness," she said. It took most of her willpower not to bring a hand to her cheek. She would not give him that satisfaction.

Content, Notoyem retreated. "You have been brought here on my good graces. Truly, I want nothing more than for peace to befall our country. So I have come to a decision. I'm willing to forget it all—the treason, the army your husband has set against us, even the grab for power when he tried to shove his son at my daughter—as long as he is willing to get on his knees and ask for my forgiveness."

"Forgiveness," Ivanya echoed.

"Yes," Notoyem said slowly as if she were the dull-witted one. "I can't let this go unpunished, after all, can I? No. I am willing to let him, and the rest of your family, live, so long as he asks. You will have less power, of course, because I can't trust you anymore, and he'll have to swear more oaths, but you all will live."

No, that was far too easy. He wanted something from her.

Ivanya smiled vapidly. "Why, Regis, your mercy is truly unrivaled."

The regis looked at her skeptically, but he'd never been smart enough to see through her. "I took the liberty of having some paper and ink left in your desk, Baroness. Should you wish to tell your husband the good news and end this war faster, you need only to write the letter out and instruct one of our men where to send it."

*There it is*, Ivanya thought. They didn't know where Jervin was. But if they thought she would reveal his location, accidentally or otherwise, they were stupider than they looked. "I'm afraid I don't know where he is right now, Your Highness, but surely if you spread the word across the country, it will bring him in. Better yet, it will prove to all Corvikans just how merciful and kind you are."

His mask slipped, revealing burning embers in his eyes. Of course he didn't want everyone to know if he could help it; if he went back on his word, his rival was still dead, but it wouldn't look good even to the commoners. "Well. Be that as it may, it'll be quicker if we can send a letter directly to him. If you remember where he is, you'd best be quick to pass it along. And Ivanya? My mercy, like my patience, grows thin. I know your son has participated in the same acts of treason as your husband, and if Jervin is slow to pay his dues, young Remy will be asked to pay the bill. And it will not come half as cheap."

Notoyem made sure she understood his threat—and she did, loud and clear—before he stormed out. She bobbed a small curtsy, if only because the guards were watching. The soldiers eyed her suspiciously but followed the regis out, stationing themselves just outside their doors.

Ivanya stood rooted to the spot for several minutes, fearing the guards would storm back in with a sneer and return her, Damari, and her grandson to the dungeons. But they never did.

Once she was sure, she pressed farther into the apartments, noting dully that what few windows they'd had were now boarded over. Deeper in, through the sitting room, she finally caught the sound of quiet humming. She followed it into the small bedroom, where Damari rocked a restless Bernard. Damari caught her eye, and Ivanya nodded in answer to her unasked question. *He's gone.*

Then Ivanya retired to the master bedroom and lit a candle, searching for some tools she could use to help their escape.

The room was not quite how they'd left it. Everything that had made it cozy had been stripped bare, from the floor rugs to the ornate wardrobes to the beautiful wall hangings. It was just the bed now, with the blankets and pillows all in order, thank Thalja, the night stand, and a chest with only two changes of clothes tucked inside. Of that last, she recognized neither and didn't hold her breath for the fit. The fireplace was empty—not that it mattered in the summer heat—and there was nothing in here that could have been used as a weapon. The only thing that seemed remotely out of place was the silver wash pitcher that sat oddly on its tray.

Well, it wasn't ideal, but Notoyem had unwittingly given her more power by bringing her here. She'd make full use of it. Starting with what little bath she could make with the water pitcher. When she went to pour the water into the bowl, however, she saw something.

It was a white square, folded up to fit under the belly of the pitcher. She swiped it and set the jug back down. Unfolding the paper square revealed a rough sketch of a tree and, below it, a shadow that looked suspiciously like a crown. It was a note, a promise: She still had allies at court. Moreso, her allies knew she was there.

Ivanya put the corner of the note into the little candle's flame and set it to burn in the cold fireplace. Then she strode into the sitting room, happy to find that it was at least a little better furnished than the bedroom. There, she found a writing desk filled with the promised pen, paper, and ink. She appreciated the irony as she used Notoyem's "gift" against him. She was not much of an artist, either, but she made do.

Once it was finished, Ivanya sat back and inspected her handiwork while the ink dried. It was a small school of fish caught in a fraying net. Through the smallest slit in the bottom, the fish were making their escape.

Ivanya folded the paper into a small square and, once she was done with the pitcher and bowl, carefully wedged her reply beneath the pitcher. Feeling a little less hopeless, she got into bed and let sleep take her.

# CHAPTER 10

A figure fell into step beside her as Neelie wound her way through the tangled warren south of Cade Street. Neelie very nearly slipped a knife between the hooded figure's ribs until she saw the familiar sword strapped to his back. Dropping her hand away from her sword hilt, she seethed. "Ren, I swear to Skï, one of these days I'm going to stab you and I'm not even going to be sorry."

Her brother just hooked his hood with a finger and pulled it down, revealing an uncharacteristically stern expression on his dark features. His short hair was in need of a trim. "Father told me of *Magi* Modorin's warning. Honestly, Neelie, if anyone should be trying to disguise themselves right now, it's you. There's a *gortien* in town, and Dûl take my soul if he is not here for you."

"Don't lecture me."

"Lecturing would imply I thought I had any chance of changing your mind," Ren said, rolling his eyes. "Where are you off to?"

Neelie considered not telling him, as a repayment for him being an insufferable brat, but sometimes it paid to take the moral high ground. "I'm off to meet Vidar to assemble a crew."

"For something of Mother's, or is it one of yours?"

"Mine. One of my informants crossed paths with a Crasik *majican* in need of safe haven. My informant is going to help them reach the coast; I just need to tell them where to meet the ship."

"I thought Raylir usually put your crews together?"

Ahead, a group of Venascans stood rigidly as they talked together. Their eyes darted watchfully over those who passed by them. They bore no uniforms, but Neelie could smell the soldier on them. She gestured to Ren. They both ducked their heads and turned surreptitiously down the next side street. No one gave them any odd looks, and, thank Skï, they weren't followed.

"He's off finishing the last assignment for me, with the enchanted weapons owed to the Corvikan rebels," Neelie said finally. "But trust me, Vidar knows his way around a ship and crew almost as well as Raylir."

Ren just shrugged. Her elder brother knew something of ships and the fortunes that their mother chased on the open seas, but Ren had taken after their father in this regard. Just because he knew something of that part of the business didn't mean he forced himself to get invested in the particulars. "Are you sure now is the time to be sending any of our men out of Bijal? Or our ships?"

"No, but I'm going to do it anyway. Don't worry; I already informed Father."

"Well, speaking of your little enterprise, I hear your latest damsel knows something of artwork."

Neelie shoved her older brother, not that it did any good. He was as solid as stone, but it was the principle of the thing. A few people passing by them shot the two of them a glare, but Neelie paid them no mind. "Don't call her a damsel, Ren. She took down a Corvikan naval vessel almost single-handedly."

"The Las Corvikan navy is a joke," he said, though he couldn't hide his surprise. "Either way, it's not her magic I need her for; it's her expertise."

Hardly mollified, she motioned for them to turn down another street. They were getting near Vidar's home. "I thought you had someone for that."

"Soderi?"

It was Neelie's turn to shrug. She was as well versed in Ren's side of the business as he was in hers.

"Out of town on some business of mine. I've been expecting this drop, but Soderi left before Inoger's men came swarming. Now I'm sitting on hot goods with no way to know their worth."

Vidar's squat little house appeared. The man himself was outside, tending to his vegetable patch. He saw her and waved, a gesture she returned before focusing back on Ren. "Last I checked, Father had a whole slew of men who could do your appraisals for you. This can't be the first time you've needed to get rid of something while Soleri was out of town."

"Soderi," Ren corrected, and got another shove for his efforts. It was a small one, though. "And we think Honir's men got to one of them. We just don't know which."

"Dûl's bones," Neelie cursed. "I say we storm his fancy little mansion and pull him down from his brittle throne. I'm getting tired of dancing to his music."

"You and me both. Regardless, if your Corvikan's numbers match up with our fencers, we know they're loyal. If not..." He drew a neat line across his throat.

With a sigh, Neelie said, "I'll speak to Zyre."

Before she could get more than two steps away from him, Ren had closed a hand around her arm. Her brother's expression was curious, and she wasn't ready for the question she knew was about to spill out of him. But in the end, it wasn't a question, just more lecturing. "You're awfully protective of a girl you barely know. I doubt I need to tell you, sister, that now is not a good time to be getting distracted by matters of the heart."

"You have a funny way of asking for help," she said, glaring at him. Ren dropped her arm. He meant well, but good intentions did not take the sting out of an insult. "Don't belittle me, Ren. I am not the type to waste my time on lost causes. My head is clear."

Neelie left him behind, but not quickly enough that she didn't hear what he said to her back. "You wasted your time on Modorin Kal, didn't you?"

She threw an obscene gesture over her shoulder to let him know she'd heard, then put the whole thing out of her mind. Ren did not catch up to her. She stepped up to Vidar's fence, casting a last look behind her, but Ren had already disappeared.

With a sigh, she stepped through the open gate.

⁂

Wasting her time with Modorin Kal was a far different variety than with Zyre Arnaud. Modorin was neither a seafarer nor adventurer. Neelie, on the other hand, was not the type to sit still. And it pained her to admit, but Neelie did not like to love from afar. Her parents had a peculiar kind of romance, somehow more passionate for all of her mother's comings and goings. But the mechanics of it made little sense to Ren and none at all to Neelie. She had tried for nearly a year to love Modorin. He was handsome and fiercely protective in ways that only sometimes bordered on offensive. Not to mention, his wit was of the same language as her own.

Modorin was the first person she'd ever smuggled out of a country. It had been one of her first commands of a vessel, and she'd had something of little consequence to get into Syfris, to test her abilities. Modorin had been a wrench in her plans, of course, but she'd been in this underground world all her life. She'd completed her mission, snuck Modorin aboard her ship, and set sail without any officials thinking they ought to pry into her business.

He hadn't known where he wanted to go, just that he didn't want to stay in his country. There were jobs to be had in Venasca, and she didn't have supplies or a proper ship suited for longer voyages anyway, so he consented to go to Bijal. It didn't take long, though, to learn that Modorin was not the type of person well suited to the rolling decks of a ship at sea.

At least he was pleasant company when he wasn't puking his guts out. Once they arrived home, Neelie even went out of her way to spend as much time as possible helping Modorin get acclimated to the city. One thing led to another, then next thing she knew, it had been over a year since she'd been at sea.

Love, however, was a strange beast. Ballads like "The Tragedy of Signele and Borhad" or "Egyll's Rescue" made love seem easy to identify, but they never actually defined the term for laymen like Neelie. She did love Modorin. She didn't love him like she loved Raylir, her parents, or her crew, and that made her think perhaps the love she felt for him was romantic. Then business took her from Bijal, and they both chafed under the pressure of romantic expectations.

When she suggested they give up, Modorin was heartbroken, but he saw the sense of it, and eventually both of their hearts—raw from giving up on something that, while it made little sense, did give them some semblance of happiness and normalcy—mended. Friendship chafed less.

Zyre was just another question. Neelie couldn't stop thinking about how willing the woman had been to give up her very life rather than put Neelie in unnecessary danger.

Neelie's family did good things with the money they accumulated. Yes, they did bad things to get it, sometimes to good people, but always to take care of their own. Many families in both the

Deckhand and Shadow Quarter had skirted utter ruin thanks to the goodwill of her mother and father. But the pressure to do good, to help her family and the downtrodden of Bijal, weighed down on her. It wasn't that she didn't want the best for her *Hædros dir en Schadra*, her Shadowmen. It was just that there was a whole damn world out there that needed saving, and she wanted to be the one to help save it.

It was why she couldn't get Zyre's offer out of her head. *You should turn me over. You've already put yourself at risk.* She couldn't remember the last time a stranger had prioritized Neelie's safety over their own; always, it seemed, it was the other way around.

If Corvikans weren't so prudish about "unnatural" romances, she might've kissed Zyre for those two sentences alone.

⁂

Although Neelie sent a message to Modorin at the Siren's Haunt as soon as her business with Vidar was dealt with, it took a few days to get everything in order.

*Freyr* Honir's men were proving to be more troublesome than expected. Two days after Ren asked for her help, she waited in the Sector of the Gulls for Modorin to arrive with Zyre, keeping a low profile so the white-clad guards didn't look too closely at her. Neelie hated hiding, but for all her bravado, she had no intention of picking fights. Especially in the Gulls, where there were too few Shadowmen to back her.

Modorin was punctual as usual, with the Corvikan *najik* along with him. Zyre's quizzical expression was strangely endearing. Their two soulbeasts trailed behind them.

Zyre was still wearing Mistress Kaari's dress, and it sat on her as well as Neelie's outfit had. *Well, maybe not quite so well,* she thought, then immediately stopped herself.

"Are we here for me?" Zyre asked carefully.

They stood in the Shadow Quarter, near where it bumped against the Sector of the Gulls. All of her family's warehouses were scattered along these few streets, close enough to the bay that on especially quiet nights, the crash of the waves could sometimes be heard. The warehouses didn't have *ðedael*, of course, as they were not places of residence, but her father's buildings had the raven's mark etched in the doorknob.

"It's no small thing you've asked my father to do," Neelie replied. "Even with Kaspar Gehrig, it could be several more days at least before he has anything to show for it. No, this is something else entirely."

She gestured for them to follow her and strode down a nearby street that was more alley than anything else. The other two hurried on her heels, and she explained as they went.

"My family has a habit of finding odds and ends in places they really have no right to be, and my brother found some interesting pieces of treasure that he cannot determine the value of. I figured a lady's daughter would know, and that a lady's daughter might likewise be bored of sitting in her room with little to do."

"I'm not a lady's daughter," Zyre said. "Only a baron's."

Modorin peered curiously down a hallway as they passed. "The outing is definitely a change of pace, at least. Zyre had me accompany her to the dovecote two days past, and we haven't really had cause to go anywhere since. It's all been lessons in the Venascan tongue for her, and she's even more brutish about snack breaks than you."

"Oh, please. I swear, if it were up to you, we'd never get anything done," Zyre retorted. "Besides, I never said you had to stay with me. Just because I was not in the mood to go anywhere doesn't mean you were stuck with me. I could have found other ways to occupy my time."

"And miss the opportunity to steal all your little secrets? How else would I have learned Kadj once chewed off a chunk of your hair and you had to get it cut boyishly short?"

Zyre colored visibly in Neelie's periphery. It was endearing. "Yes, well, I should thank you. How else would I know you ate so much *mendui* on your eighth birthday that you threw up all over that childhood crush of yours?"

"That was private!" he said in mock indignation.

"Luckily for both of you," Neelie interjected with a laugh, "I happened to know that one."

Modorin turned red. "How?"

She grinned wickedly. "You're incredibly chatty when you're drunk."

Modorin spluttered indignantly, but they had drawn up in front of Ren's warehouse. Neelie ignored her friend as she unlocked the door and swung it open.

The warehouse was not lit, but Modorin lent them his fire, and they traveled down a short hallway. The back of the warehouse butted up against an inlet, but most of what could be found in that half of the building was legal, things like food and fresh water stores, although some of it was fabrics, timber, and various feeds for soulbeasts and familiars.

They went past all that and filed into an office space, winding around its furniture and its stacks of unprocessed crates, stopping at a stone wall with cracks and fissures that, if one followed the right parts of the web, might have looked like a door. Neelie withdrew a small, thin metal cutout of a bird in flight and fitted it into a part of the fissure that was about shoulder-height. There was the familiar pop, and Neelie pushed the door in.

Behind her, Zyre laughed in delight.

A smile wormed unbidden onto Neelie's face, and she was grateful her back was still turned so Zyre couldn't see.

If the main warehouse was dark, the hidden room was positively gloomy. Near the front sat some boxes with a red strip of cloth lying across the top, as Ren promised it would be. Neelie removed the cloth with a flourish, allowing Zyre to peer inside even as Modorin brought a now-lit torch from its stand by the door. Neelie studied Zyre, watching as the other woman blinked and reached her hand into the box, pulling out a small sphere with intricate metal inlay. She held it tenderly. With her other hand, she twisted the small knob on the top of the sphere, and the ball unfolded into four pieces.

"Where did you find this?" Her tone was half awed, half accusatory.

"Do you know what it is?"

Zyre carefully clicked each of the four pieces back into place and set the sphere, whole once more, back in the box. "They were the height of fashion in Las Corvika two centuries ago. It was called a *mutalguen*, a perfume ball. They were outlawed in 1237 after Ordyl the Red enchanted three of them to kill his political opponents and nearly became the first *kjarnik* to sit on the Corvikan throne."

"Does *that* have any enchantments?" Modorin asked. Neelie rolled her eyes as he retreated a few steps.

"Bring that light back; I need it," Zyre said testily. "And no. I don't think it does. If it was enchanted, it would hum. Wouldn't it, *Nagi* Neelie?"

"It's true," Neelie confirmed, though she was half lost in thought. Ren hadn't told her where he'd gotten the cargo, but if it was as hot as he claimed, it was probably from a Venascan ship. So. Did its previous owner know it could be turned into a weapon? Had it been bound for Venasca, or had it been on its way to another shore? If they could find who had wanted it, they would probably find the person willing to spend the most to get it back. "What is it worth, then, *Magi* Zyre?"

Zyre gestured at the torch. Modorin passed it over without a word, letting Zyre inspect the *mutalguen* in its bed of straw. "It looks like it's in good condition. I didn't see any rust or any signs of the mechanisms breaking down. Someone who knew its history would probably be willing to pay five gold *delars* for it."

Neelie whistled appreciatively. For such a strange small thing, that was worth quite a lot. She did some quick math in her head, converting the Corvikan currency into Venascan. Twenty-five *barset*, when the metal, melted down, would likely be worth little more than a tenth of that, and only if it was made out of silver like it appeared to be.

It was made out of metal, though. Perhaps this Ordyl the Red could serve as inspiration. Weapons were always worth more than mere artifacts, even old ones.

The three of them unburied other artifacts in that crate and in the ones stacked beneath it. Almost everything within them were Corvikan, with the exception of two ceramic pieces that Zyre guessed were Pailyran. The *mutalguen* had been a lucky find. Everything else in the boxes was of a more mundane nature. Jewelry, a few gilded weapons, even a metal bracelet that *did* hum in Zyre's hand when she inspected it. All of it, Neelie wrote down to be given to Ren. She was in the process of scribbling down notes of Zyre's last find when Zyre, rummaging through the final crate, gasped.

Neelie tensed, reaching for her magic. Maybe someone had known Ren would make the grab. Maybe they'd planted an enchanted explosive.

But when she looked at Zyre, all the woman held was a sheathed sword.

Zyre didn't say anything, not at first. Her attention was set wholly on the scabbard, inlaid with dark blue gemstones, on the hilt, half a fish visible to Neelie. The metal rasped as she pulled it free. Even Neelie knew what the words etched on the side meant. They were House Arnaud's, written in old Dosperic. *Eris bi eljers.* By skill and valor. Not particularly inspired House words, but old, older even than the *mutalguen.*

Modorin, sitting on the floor nearby so he could pet Sarol, pushed himself closer to the two of them.

"Neelie, where did your family find these?" Zyre breathed, eyes glued to the sword.

A chill ran down Neelie's spine at the informality. "My brother could answer that question better than I, I'm afraid."

"This is an old family sword. My family lost it during the Succession. It belonged to my uncle until he fell in battle. We thought Regis Béranger had it melted down to make a new sword, truth be told," Zyre said, staring at the weapon's fine edges, the words written upon the metal. She barely spoke above a whisper. "Whatever you're planning on doing with this, *Nagi*, I beg you not to sell it. My family would pay to have it back in their hands. I would. That I found it here and now is a sign from the gods, from Tholjun himself. My father is waging war, and he will need this."

Modorin threw a look at Neelie as if to say *I can guess how you got it. You'd better give it back.*

Neelie let her lip curl back in a mock snarl. *You put too little faith in me.*

Zyre hadn't seen Modorin's expression, but she raised an eyebrow at Neelie, then darted a glance at the *majican.* With a sigh, Neelie raised her hands in surrender. Ren was going to kill her. "Then I suppose we'd best ensure it is returned to its proper owner," she said.

Zyre sheathed the sword and hugged it against her chest. She wasn't going to like what Neelie said next, but someone had to be the voice of reason here.

"*Magi* Zyre, I can't let you go walking around with that sword in your hand. It would put my family in a lot of danger, and more than that, it would put you in danger too. Or do you want the wrong person looking into why a Corvikan *sjarvisk*, one with a tiger soulbeast no less, is carrying around a lord's family heirloom?"

Zyre's free hand darted to her tiger's side. "You stole it, didn't you? Or had someone else steal it for you? All these Corvikan treasures, and you're going to sell them. Did you know this sword was in here, *Nagi*? If I hadn't been brought along, what would you have done with it?"

They both knew the answer to that question, so Neelie played it safe and didn't answer. "I can get it to your father." She did not reach for the blade, but she wanted to. Zyre's accusatory tone stung far more than it should have. "It'll be safest for everyone that way, and that's what you want anyway, isn't it? To get it back to him?"

Zyre's grip tightened around the sword. Her mouth opened, fire in her eyes, and Neelie tensed for a fight. But then, grace to Skï, Zyre closed her mouth, frowning. The fire dimmed. "I don't plan on being in Bijal long, *Nagi* Neelie. Can I ask you to keep it until I leave so I might bring it with me?"

"It'll take you at least a week just to get to the border if you were to leave right now. Wouldn't you rather send it to him tonight?"

Zyre blinked. "Tonight?"

"Yes." Neelie straightened her papers and placed them in the crate with the *mutalguen*, returning the red strip of cloth over the box. Modorin, reading her mind, hefted one of the boxes and began to restack them as Neelie said, "I'll come fetch you tonight, and you can see it off."

"Is this some kind of *kjarnik* magic?" Zyre asked, her brows furrowed.

That made Neelie laugh. "No. It's just *magic*. Have you never heard of Velídas?"

Zyre sneered. "Of course I have. It was an ancient tree that Teirolac ventured through to save the world. But it made him go mad."

Neelie had no idea what in Dûl's name she was talking about. Modorin didn't either, though he looked on the verge of asking. She quickly silenced him with a gesture before he could derail the whole conversation.

"It's not *an* ancient tree. It's a network of them. Somehow they're connected to each other, spanning across the entire world. Soulbeasts and familiars can travel across the world in less than an hour. They've been used to send messages. I happen to know for a fact that your father's men use them to communicate with other branches of their rebellion. My father has access to a tree of his own."

"I don't believe you." Zyre crossed her arms in front of her chest. "Maybe you just want to keep it so you can sell it to someone at an exorbitant price."

Neelie wanted to shove her. She might've, had they been even a little better acquainted. "Oh, yes, that's just part of my elaborate scheme. By offering to give it to your father, I'm guaranteed to earn a hefty bit of gold for a sword only Jervin Arnaud could possibly want."

Zyre deflated. "I'm sorry," she said quietly.

*Rats*, Neelie cursed, now angry at herself for losing her temper. "Come on," she said, hauling the last crate back up since it was apparent Modorin had given up on helping. Zyre leapt forward to help, and once the crate was in place, Neelie motioned toward the door. "It's a nice day out, and I hear you like to explore. How would you like to be shown the best parts of the Shadow Quarter?"

"Nice day out to boil a person alive," she heard Modorin say to Zyre behind her. The other woman laughed. A flash of something that was *not* jealousy stirred quietly in Neelie's chest. She put on her captain's stony exterior, and once the room was put to right, she led them out of the warehouse into the warm Venascan sun.

The Shadow Quarter was full of men and women loyal to Hosvar and their family. The stark difference between the orderly streets of the Serpent's Quarter and the sprawling neighborhoods of the Shadow Quarter or even the Whale's Belly in the southern part of town showed just how much *Freyr* Honir cared for the lower classes. A lot of people in the Shadow Quarter owed their lives, their homes, their well-being to the success of Neelie's mother and father. They didn't care where the money came from or how much of it had questionable origins.

As a result, Neelie barely got a stone's throw from the warehouses before she recognized a youngish boy hurrying past her. She caught his arm, pressed five little *silse* coins into his palm, and asked him to deliver a brief message to Ren. The boy was more than happy to oblige.

⁂

The Shadow Quarter was one of the louder districts of the city. There was music playing, street vendors selling food, kids squealing as they chased each other, mothers screaming after them. Zyre's mouth seemed stuck in a perpetual small *o*.

Neelie smiled as Zyre watched a group of street musicians play "Sigaard and the Snakes." The vocalist clearly knew Neelie, but though her eyes flashed in surprise, her voice did not waver.

*In the depths of that shifting pit,*
*The cold scales of Dûl's veins*
*Writhed against the fated hero,*
*Their white fangs promised pain.*

The jaw harp fascinated Zyre. Neelie wasn't sure Zyre even knew what the song was about or if she just liked the primal drumming, the rhythmic twang of the metal harp. The vocalist sang of Sigaard as he felt the venomous bite of one of the snakes in the pit and turned to his music as a last resort. The snakes fell asleep, and a great eagle heard Sigaard's music, rescuing the hero from the pit only for him to die of the poison.

As the song faded to silence, Zyre clapped excitedly. But the musicians hadn't been blind during their performance. The harpist held out his hand, the metal harp in his palm. "Do you want to try?" he asked in Venascan.

Zyre looked back at both of them, uncertain, first at Modorin, then at Neelie. But who was Neelie to rob Zyre of this?  With a sigh, she nodded. Zyre's eyes lit up, and she said, "Ïz." It was kind of cute, her tongue slipping over the accent, but there was no mistaking what she meant. It was even cuter when she added, "*Medias.*"

The musicians pressed in around Zyre, teaching her how to put the harp against her teeth so she didn't chip any, laughing good-naturedly as her first attempts produced some rather abysmal sounds.

"Neelie." Modorin's tone was sharp, pulling her away from Zyre. She carefully followed his gaze and found white-clad men farther down the street.

That quickly, her joy turned to icy hatred. More of Inoger's men had flooded into Bijal in these past few days. Where once no soldier would have dared show their face in the Shadow Quarter, it seemed she could not go a day without seeing several.

So far, none of them had tried anything. They were smart enough not to. Right here, armed with her sword and her magic, surrounded by people who would have leapt between her and any trouble Honir threw her way, she was untouchable. The soldiers passed them on the street, her hatred mirrored in their eyes, but they did not say a word as they walked out of her view.

Neelie hated to think about it, but she really was afraid that one of these days her *Hædros dir en Schadra* would not be enough to protect her.

"Put your hood up, for Skï's sake," Modorin hissed at her. "One of these days, they're not going to just walk by."

"They'll see what happens when they do," she hissed back.

Modorin shook his head. He held his fists at his sides like he always did when he had to stop himself from saying something sharp. With one last glare at her, he threw a pained smile at Zyre and said with a levity that sounded impossibly fake, "Come on, Zyre! You haven't even seen the smallest portion of the Shadow Quarter. I told you, Neelie, it's impossible to go anywhere when she's tagging along."

His tone suggested she was supposed to laugh, but she could only bring herself to roll her eyes. "I'm hungry. Let's find something to eat."

Zyre's face fell, but she returned the jaw harp to its proper owner, saying *medias* again. Neelie threw her arm around Modorin's shoulder, ignoring how he stiffened beneath her, and then threw her other around Zyre's. They turned down the next street.

Something made her look back, though, right before the buildings obstructed her view. A man had appeared not far behind them, a fine pendant hanging around his neck and a black dog trotting at his heels. His gaze swept the street, latching eyes onto hers. Neelie's heart skipped in her chest. *Ed gortien.* A man of the king's. His lips turned downward into the slightest frown, and she knew that he was waiting for her to misstep.

"Are we going to find another food stall? I'm feeling adventurous," Zyre said excitedly as Neelie ushered them down a side street, fearing *ed gortien* would follow.

Neelie only paid half a mind to what Modorin replied. She had to hope *ed gortien* would stay within the law, that he would not arrest her unless he had seen her do magic and was certain she had no soulbeast linked to her. Still, it shook her more than she cared to admit. Neelie made sure to take extra turns to shake off any tails and found herself trekking halfway across the district before she felt safe enough to sit down for a meal with her friends.

If Modorin thought she was being paranoid, he was wise enough to keep his mouth shut.

# CHAPTER 11

The seventh rising of the sun since returning to Les Stelvo lit up Nyli's room, pulling him from sleep. He seemed to be getting precious little of it recently. Ivanya was proving far harder to crack than Nyli had hoped. The closest they'd gotten to an answer had been three days ago, thanks to Captain Liem's hard work on Remy. Even then, it had been vague. Liem said Remy swore to Tholjun that he'd only ever seen the maps in passing and held only a vague idea of the inner workings of the bandit army. "South" was all they'd gotten. So south was where they'd been looking.

Now, Kuval lay sprawled out beside him, taking up far more than half of the bed. An arm was flung over Nyli, and his mouth was half open, a small droplet of drool collecting at the corner. On any other person, he probably would have been disgusted, but this was Kuval, and if anything, it struck Nyli as funny that a man so cautious and reserved and knowledgeable awake could look so disheveled and untidy while asleep. It was endearing.

The door slammed open, and the spell was broken. Instinct and fear had him reaching for Kuval, ready to push him onto the floor. He could almost feel his heart with his tongue, it was pounding so hard. But then his brain caught up to his fear, identifying the intruder as his sister.

Kuval was not so quick on the uptake, diving to the floor of his own accord. His messy hair stuck above the top of the bed.

"Did you never learn to knock?" Nyli snarled at his sister. He rolled out of bed to help Kuval find his clothes.

His vitriol bounced off of Rasin without leaving a mark. "Father wouldn't knock."

Beside him, halfway to putting on his pants, Kuval stiffened.

It was partially true. Father wouldn't knock, although his honor guard would. Enough time for Kuval to dive under the bed unseen, maybe, if he was quick. The regis's honor guard would enter with or without Nyli's permission, and if any of them saw, Father as good as knew.

Nyli pulled his shirt over his head and tried not to think about what would happen then. He still had nightmares sometimes about the last time the regis had gotten it into his head that someone was ruining his son.

He knew he should care. He had no grand delusions about his ability to protect Kuval—fifteen years later, and he would still be as helpless against it as he'd been the last time—and he *did* care. He *did* worry about it. But while Notoyem Béranger could make his son live in fear, the gods themselves couldn't stop Nyli from loving Kuval anyway.

His pants fully on—unfortunately—Kuval sat on the edge of the bed and tended to one of his shoes.

"Both of you are far too careless, you know," Rasin said quietly. "It's not just Father you have to worry about."

"Why are you here, Rasin?" Nyli demanded.

"Ah, yes," she said, brightening. "One of my informants found something."

"Jervin?" Kuval asked before Nyli could, jamming his other shoe on.

Rasin shook her head before Nyli had a chance to actually get his hopes up. "No. Well, maybe. We found the girl. Well, we found the tiger, and where there's the tiger, there's the girl, and, with luck, Jervin."

Now his heart was well and truly thrumming. They had three days to find the baron. Time was running out. Maybe Thalja did favor him with her mercy on occasion. "Where?"

"A day's ride south, in Medore."

Medore? He frowned. That was a nothing town. It made some excellent linen for the rest of the country, but beyond that, it could have burned to the ground and no one would notice. "Does Father know?" he asked.

Rasin again shook her head. "Best to make the grab and surprise him, don't you think? Then, if it turns out to be wrong, he never has to know."

"Your foresight is as admirable as always," Kuval said, sounding like he actually meant it. Or maybe he was just trying to win Rasin over.

Rasin just rolled her eyes like she could see right through him. "We should take a few *sjarvisk* with us and no others. It'll be faster that way, and we'll need as much magical power as we can muster so the girl doesn't take us by surprise again."

"All right. I'll meet you down at the stables in ten. Have the stablehands saddle up twenty horses."

Rasin blinked. "It's just one girl."

"I'm not taking any chances, not like last time. And it might not be *just* the girl," he replied, ushering her out of his room while being careful not to let either of their honor guard see past the door. "I'll bring the *sjarvisk*. Just have the horses saddled."

"Fine," Rasin harrumphed. "But if you're not there in ten minutes, I'm leaving without you."

Nyli shook his head, calling the bluff, and shut the door in her face. Then he steeled himself and turned apologetically to Kuval. "Maybe we could pose it as a hunting trip," he offered.

"If only it was known around the court that I love a good hunt," Kuval replied sardonically. He crossed the distance between them, planting a soft kiss on Nyli's mouth. "It's okay. We both have our duties to see to. I knew what I was walking into with you."

Nyli opened his mouth, on the verge of saying something he probably shouldn't. Instead, he resigned himself to saying, "If all goes well, I'll be back by tomorrow night. That's all. Medore isn't far."

"It's not the distance that worries me," he retorted, although Nyli knew that was half a lie. It was also sweet, even after all this time, that Kuval still worried over him.

Nyli extricated himself from his love. "When I get back, the last dregs of a dying rebellion will be in hand. Las Corvika can finally settle into some peace. And you and I? We'll have a lot more time to ourselves afterward, I think."

"That'll never be true, and you know it," Kuval said, but he didn't sound bitter. In fact, he laughed, pushing Nyli toward the door. "Now you'd best hurry before your sister grows impatient."

Nyli let the smile stay in place until his fingers were on the doorknob. With his back turned to Kuval—he hated whenever he had to play the part of prince in front of the other man, feigning indifference—-he wiped all emotion from his face and did his best to put it in a box in the recesses of his mind. It would not do to give anyone reason to ask why Nyli Béranger was smiling, not until Jervin Arnaud was in his hands, anyway.

He left Kuval, trusting the man to find some way to slip away unnoticed.

Despite the early hour, the castle was busy. Servants, most of whom were in livery matching Béranger colors, scampered up and down the halls. Clerks and attendants moved through, too, doing whatever it was they did in the castle. They bowed and curtseyed to Nyli in passing, dipping to the full to show their respect.

The Royal Palace itself housed a grand total of seventy-three *sjarvisk*. Considering whom Nyli was going up against, he half wished to bring the lot of them, and a branch of soldiers to boot, but that would only slow them down, and he could not risk tipping Jervin off. So they would bring Nyli's and Rasin's core honor guard—five men each—and eight *sjarvisk*. Twenty people making a trip to Medore could cover such distance with enough speed to catch the rebels by surprise, if Tholjun favored them.

Nyli went to the barracks and found the man in charge of the *sjarvisk* troops, a lieutenant by the name of Segal. "I need your eight strongest *sjarvisk* in the stable in five minutes, Lieutenant," he said once they'd seen to the formalities.

"They'll be down in three, Your Highness," Segal replied. He went to fetch a runner, and Nyli took his leave. He wouldn't put it past Rasin to leave early, just out of spite.

***

Nyli sat on a powerful roan stallion just outside of Medore as the sun dropped perilously close to the horizon. Two of their *sjarvisk* were in town, searching for information while their wolverine and hawk soulbeasts waited impatiently with the rest of their group.

Nearby, Rasin stared off into the distance, lost in thought.

It struck him that he hadn't been a very good brother these past few days. What with Notoyem's sudden desire to find a husband for his daughter and Remy's "return" to court, Rasin had very good reason to be distracted.

Nyli kneed his stallion a few steps closer to his sister, giving them at least a modicum of privacy. "How bad was the marriage talk?" he asked.

Rasin started. "What? Oh." She wrinkled her nose. "He said he'd been humoring my reservations for a long time now but implied the longer I wait, the less desirable I am and the harder it will be to find a decent husband. I was half- tempted to say, 'That's fine by me. I don't want a husband at all.'"

"Even Remy Arnaud?" he offered.

She just glared at him. "That ship has long since sailed, Nyli."

Nyli let it go. There were days they could tease each other about their relationships, but with Remy's life held by the whims of their father, now did not seem the time. Instead, he just stared at the leather reins in his hands. "Do you think that all love that is true and wholesome must wither away, that marriage is nothing more than bitterness and betrayal?"

"I have to hope not." Rasin straightened her bodice with a frown. "There's a danger in drawing any conclusions about life just based on the experiences that Father has had."

"He loved Elodja well enough."

"Yes, well, according to all the rumors, Elodja matched his temper perfectly." Rasin sniffed. "May we all find our Elodjas and save all the Maryns of the world from utter destruction."

Nyli scowled at her flippancy. Maryn, their mother, hadn't been *destroyed*. That implied some sort of careless mistake, some tragedy. It had been quite the opposite. It had been intentional, and it was unforgivable.

But in Notoyem's court, there was nothing to be gained from confrontation, and so his anger and guilt festered, and fifteen years later, Nyli still grieved.

A stir some distance away drew both of their attention for a moment. Slowly, he was able to make out two people as they made their way back to the group.

"They will want me to sire heirs, whoever it is," Rasin said quietly. "And I'm not sure I am willing to do that for anyone. I'm not even sure I'd have done it for Remy, even knowing the political ramifications."

"Father will not make you marry a terrible man," Nyli replied before the scouts drew too close. "And if he does, I swear to you, it will not be a long marriage by far."

"He would not know a terrible man if he looked in a mirror."

To that, he had no answer.

By then, the scouts had drawn close, and the rest of their party was pressing in to hear the news. There was nothing for it but to drop the topic all together, which was fine by Nyli. However much he loved his sister, he didn't quite get her hesitations, and talking about it was usually just as awkward as it was now.

The scouts both bowed to Nyli and Rasin once they had closed the distance, and then the man made his report. The woman gave a ghost of a smile as her wolverine waddled over to her, but she kept at attention like a proper soldier should.

"The girl with the tiger soulbeast has taken up residence at an inn called the Dancing Feather. They say she's been here for two days. Unfortunately, there's no man matching Jervin Arnaud's description, but it is said that there is a man being given sanctuary in the town's chapel. No one would describe him."

Nyli frowned. If the traitor had managed to find sanctuary, why hadn't the *sjarvisk*? Medore was too close to Les Stelvo for its citizens to be superstitious about magic or soulbeasts. "Does the girl have any men with her?"

The scouts shook their heads, but again it was the man with the hawk who answered. "The town says there are a lot of newcomers right now, all at the Dancing Feather, but Medore only has the one inn, and they have not all come on the same day as the girl."

That meant little for someone as clever as Jervin Arnaud. "Rasin, take your guard and a *sjarvisk* to the chapel. Promise them a sizeable donation should they let you search their grounds. I'll take the other seven to the inn."

His sister just grimaced. Distasteful, yes, bribing the mouthpieces of the gods, but he was certain that Thyljal, goddess of creation, and Thalja, goddess of mercy, would appreciate the end of war and bloodshed and forgive them of whatever means it took to accomplish peace. And Tholjun? Well, Nyli was likely about to appease his bloodthirstiness.

Their group split up. The man with the hawk had been assigned to Rasin, so it was the woman with the wolverine soulbeast who led Nyli's group down the main road. The citizens took one look at them, at the handful of soulbeasts that accompanied the group, and wisely hurried out of the way.

The Dancing Feather was not far, unsurprisingly. It was small, not even two stories high, though sprawling, with no evidence of a stable out back. Its front door was cracked open, letting out the scent of cheap smoke and weak ale. Nyli dismounted and tied his roan stallion to a wood post. The others followed his lead. Two of his honor guard peeled off to guard any other possible exits. The other three fell in tight around him, followed by his seven *sjarvisk*.

Conversation died immediately as they filed into the common room. His scouts had spoken true; the Dancing Feather was packed full.

Still, a tiger was hard to hide despite the throng, and Nyli quickly found the girl in the back, sitting alone save for the soulbeast beside her. Her eyes fell on his, and he knew immediately that it wasn't Zyre. Her hair was too light, her face too round, and her thin form nothing but muscle.

The girl rose with the speed of a viper, a bright orange flame streaking toward Nyli. Whatever happened to the flame, Nyli couldn't figure out beyond the fact that it never landed, because the next thing he knew, the common room fell to pandemonium. The entire population began streaking toward them, rushing for the door. Their screams bounced against the walls, clashing with the shouts of his men.

One of the *sjarvisk* to his right fell, red blossoming against his side. Nyli stared in surprise at the vacancy in the man's eyes, but his attention was swiftly pulled away as the man's soulbeast, a great black bear, roared wildly, lunging at the nearest Medoran. An owl shrieked above their heads with the reckless abandon of another soulbeast unbound.

He did not remember drawing his sword, but it was in his hands. His *sjarvisk* were preoccupied, trying to subdue the bear and to combat the sudden flashes of knives from the fleeing patrons. The girl with the tiger jerked her hand once more toward them, and Nyli knew there would be no one to block the magic for him. He braced himself as a gust of wind raced toward him, knocking him off his feet.

A guard crashed against his side, very nearly getting skewered by Nyli's sword in the process. Then a rumbling flew past one ear, and a roar past the other. Broken bits of furniture buried into the girl and her tiger before the flames even had a chance to crash against them.

By then, Nyli realized, the rest of the people were either gone or dead.

Nyli returned his sword to its scabbard, his heart fluttering wildly. He helped one of his guards back onto his feet. Then, scowling, he knelt down next to the nearest enemy corpse and lifted the man's coat. Beneath it, stitched over his heart, was a silver rose. He checked a few others, just to be sure. They all bore the rose, the insignia of House Ermengarde.

Stepping over the other bodies and around the tables and chairs separating them, Nyli searched the dead *sjarvisk*. The girl was not so careful with her allegiance. A band around her arm held the same stitching as the rebels. He turned to face the others. "Some of the traitors will have gotten away in the chaos. Take your soulbeasts and find them."

The *sjarvisk* leapt to obey.

The innkeeper peered sheepishly from the backroom. Nyli's guards hauled the man over and shoved him into a chair. Nyli strode coldly toward him. There was no way this man had been ignorant of the plot. "What do you know of this attack? Who were all those men? Who was the girl? Tell me!" Nyli snarled.

"I don't know, m'lord. Your Highness," the innkeeper spluttered. He was middle-aged, not old enough for Nyli to know one way or the other if he might've fought in the Succession. He was skittish, darting glances at the door. "The *sjarvisk* arrived the day before last, asking for a room for herself. The others… They were strangers, Your Highness, but I thought they were just Corvikans returning from Venasca or something. I swear, Your Highness, on my life! I did not know they would do this thing! You must believe me. We don't accept the violent type here!"

Nyli looked at the man in disgust. He gestured to his honor guard and turned away. The man continued to squeal his promises as he tried to delay the inevitable.

He took the chance to study their losses. The unbound owl was nowhere to be found. It had probably flown out over the heads of the stampeding crowd. The black bear was a still form not far from the *sjarvisk* it had been bound to. Whether it was a sword that had killed it or a well-placed magical blow, Nyli didn't know. And, he surmised, it probably didn't matter. An unbound soulbeast was as useless as a dead one.

The bear wasn't the only animal casualty; the wolverine was dead, too. Its *sjarvisk*, the female scout, cried, hugging its body against her chest.

So. He'd lost three *sjarvisk* today. Without her soulbeast, she would not be able to wield magic any longer. The woman would be given a severance pay and would be allowed to return home to grieve over her lost animal.

Several minutes later, Rasin strode into the inn, looking surprised to see the carnage.

"Please tell me Jervin Arnaud was in that chapel," Nyli said, his voice as hard as steel even to his own ears.

His sister shook her head. "A man on the run from a murder charge. I have the *sjarvisk* guarding him." She gestured to the dead. "Rebels?"

"I think it was supposed to be a trap. More than a few got away in the confusion. I'll have to stay in Medore for another day or two to chase them down. Tomorrow morning, though, you should head back to Les Stelvo…" He trailed off. It would be easy for the rebels to hide in the dark. But he was so close to finding Jervin. This trap had to have breadcrumbs for him to follow. "I'm not sure how many *sjarvisk* I can spare you."

Rasin nodded thoughtfully. "I should be fine with my honor guard and the *sjarvisk* you just lent me. We'll be safe. I'll tell Father you're chasing down a lead here. Just… Make sure you find one, Nyli. Time is running out."

Nyli bit off a sharp retort. He had no desire to return to the capital empty-handed. It was not something his father would forgive.

This was shaping up to be one of the best days ever for Zyre, though she would never in a hundred *million* years admit to it. Finding *Eris* was the first really useful thing she'd managed to do in Bijal. Maybe finding it was even enough to balance out her cowardly flight. And, since today marked the second full week since Prince Nyli's attack on her family's estate, Zyre had a good feeling. It was a sign from the gods.

The second reason for Zyre's good mood came in the form of the tall Venascan and short Syfresian who led her around what they'd called the Shadow Quarter. Well, Neelie said *burriot dir schadra*, but Zyre knew what it meant. There was something almost intimate about getting to see the place where Neelie had grown up, where she was most herself. The people of this district showed Neelie more respect than the entire town of Nolasi ever gave the baron. Here, Neelie wasn't just a *najik* or a captain or the daughter of one of the most powerful men in the world. She waved at people. She pressed coins into beggars' hands. At lunch, she asked after the innkeeper and his family.

It was so surreal, so unexpected. Zyre had never really had the chance to learn what it meant to fit in somewhere, but Neelie seemed just as home here as she did on the deck of a ship, and because Zyre was with her, it felt like Zyre belonged by extension.

The sun was beginning to fall as Zyre and her friends started heading back home, a place Neelie called The Raven's Head.

When they came upon the building, Zyre wondered if she'd been mistaken at calling it Neelie's *home*. It had a busy feel to it. A half-dozen people—four men, two women—leaned against the exterior of the building, chatting. One was a *kjarnik*, if the black cat was anything to go by. The small congregation nodded at Neelie as Zyre followed the other woman into the house.

They stepped right into an open room full of desks, many of which were occupied with folk playing at dice. The air was laden with smoke and cheap ale and the dull buzz of a room full of boisterous, half-drunk men. There were more than a few animals, too, birds settled in the rafters and a few cats and dogs, even a rabbit. There were soulbeasts, too, a badger, a boar, and even a strange goat-like creature with a narrower face and slightly longer horns. Most people bore the characteristics of Venascans. Regardless, all of them had at least a handful of tattoos. *Wyrdi* Hosvar's raven was visible on more than a few.

The farther Zyre and her friends pressed into the building, the more it took on the shape of a homey place, one used to housing more than a small family. The dining table was longer than the one Zyre had seen her family sit at, and her father had a large table for possible state visits. They passed a pantry and two bedrooms—the doors were only partially opened, but they did not look used—before finding themselves back out in the warm night air. Unlike the rest of the house, the yard was quiet and empty. A fence ran around its perimeter, but what grabbed Zyre's attention first was the tree at its center. It was not a particularly old tree; its tallest branches did not go far above the fence. But it was the strangest thing Zyre had ever seen. It was silver, and its branches were heavy with whitish leaves.

"Sit tight," Neelie said. "I'll be right back."

Zyre barely noticed her leave. A chill ran across her arms, past her neck, though no wind touched her. It was the tree. Magic incarnate. "The epic of Teirolac described Velídas as a place where magic was tangible, like diving into the sea," she said. There was no purpose to the words; she was more speaking *at* Modorin than *to* him. "'A beautiful sea in which to drown,' or so the story says."

She tore her eyes away from the tree, gauging Modorin's reaction, wondering if he knew how much of the story was true or false.

He came to her side, thoughtful. "Beauty is not something to chase. It is temporary. It is not worth dying for."

Zyre shrugged. "It wasn't the beauty Teirolac was chasing. The world was ending, and his lover, the renowned traveler Coreneir, didn't have the magic to stop it. It was irony, you see? Velídas showed him the innate beauty of the world, and it drove him mad. He could not save the world because he loved it too much."

"That makes no sense," Modorin said.

Her feet hurting from all the walking, Zyre plopped into the grass next to Kadj. Modorin gave her a funny look but joined her anyway.

"It's possible to love a thing too much. Sometimes it hurts more than anything else. Or do you disagree?"

Modorin's eyes went distant. "That's a special kind of hurting," he agreed.

Suddenly Zyre felt like they weren't talking about magic or strange trees. He was thinking of home, and then she was thinking of it too, of listening to the ocean far below from the cliffs by her house, of watching Merytz and the other guards play at dice at dinner, of riding Telpari down to Nolasi to keep the peace. Lasinia was beautiful in the fall. The leaves would be changing colors soon, and she would not get to see it.

The sound of footsteps tugged Zyre impatiently out of her melancholy. Neelie held the sheathed sword in her hands, and several coils of rope hung off one shoulder. "Well, you two look like someone stepped on your soulbeasts' tails."

"Your compliments are like rain on parched soil, as always," Modorin deadpanned, rolling easily to his feet. He offered a hand to Zyre, and despite having a few inches on him, she found herself flying upright.

"So how does this work?" Zyre asked, directing her question at Neelie.

In response, the other woman transferred the entire weight of the sword onto one hand and let the rope slip down her other arm, falling into her waiting palm. "Well, assuming your bond to Kadj gives him access to Velídas, we'll tie it to your soulbeast's back and have him travel through. He'll find someone to take the sword, and then he'll come back the same way he came."

"I thought you said it was a network of trees. How will he know how to reach my father's camp?"

"I don't know! Soulbeasts just *do.*"

*He's not a regular soulbeast,* Zyre wanted to point out. Neelie knew more about it all than she did, of course, but it seemed risky to assume the journey would be the same for Kadj as it would be for Sarol or other soulbeasts. Who was she to argue, though? "Very well. If you're sure."

"Don't take this the wrong way, *Magi* Zyre, but I'm not entirely sure of anything when it comes to you. Come on. We need to fashion a harness for Kadj, and he'll probably take it better if you're helping me."

Neelie was right about that, because even with Zyre helping secure the sword to Kadj's body, the tiger flicked his tail angrily, sniffing the ropes the way he'd sniffed her hair right before he'd chewed through half of it. After several minutes with all three of them messing with the knots, the sword was secure, and there was nothing else keeping Kadj from walking through the tree. Zyre stepped away from him. The tiger just stood in place, tense, only his tail flicking.

*Great, another thing messed up by a fake* leiks, Zyre thought to herself, hating how her face grew warm. "Kadj, find my father. Find Jervin Arnaud." She pointed to the tree and willed him to understand, as if the bond were nothing more than a mental connection between them. Kadj didn't move. She tried something else. She gestured for him to follow and came beside the tree. If Kadj knew he could step through it, he clearly didn't want to.

"Let me send Sarol with him," Modorin offered.

Neelie just shrugged.

Zyre watched with some fascination as Sarol bounded to Kadj's side. She would never admit it, but she was jealous of Modorin's control over his soulbeast. Or perhaps *control* wasn't the right word. Communicate, maybe. Sarol sniffed the tiger's ropes, but his teeth didn't worry over the rope. Instead, he trotted toward the tree. He didn't even slow as his head neared the trunk. Then the tree itself seemed to swallow him whole. Kadj made a noise, raising his paw against the silvery bark.

When Kadj had both front legs propped against the trunk, everyone finally comprehended his hesitation. Velídas was closed off to him.

"Dûl's bones," Neelie muttered. "Modorin, you may as well recall Sarol. And please, go grab Oharyn."

"Why me?" Even as he said it, Zyre watched the somewhat disorienting motion of Sarol stepping through the tree as if it didn't even exist.

"Because I had to go inside last time," she retorted. "And Zyre doesn't know who Oharyn is."

With an exaggerated eye roll that one only found with close friends, Modorin strode into the house, Sarol at his heels. Neelie and Zyre got to work untying the knots they had just done.

Oharyn, it turned out, was the woman with the strange goat-like soulbeast. Zyre liked the woman's braids, though she kept the thought to herself. Oharyn didn't ask questions or anything of the sort, just helped Neelie fasten the sword to her goat-creature. They tucked a piece of paper against the rope, too, since no one would know where the sword was coming from. Neelie spoke to her in their native tongue, saying her father's name, saying Las Corvika. Somehow, it must've been enough, because the creature trundled off, and the tree swallowed it and the sword whole.

Zyre hoped Neelie was right about how quick the whole

exchange would be. Oharyn's soulbeast was not nearly as big as Kadj, and the sword was clearly heavier than it was used to carrying.

She also feared, for reasons even she knew were illogical, how her father would react when he received the family heirloom. She imagined him saying, *I need you for this war. Why are you putzing around in Bijal, wasting time, when the regis continues to destroy our country and hurt our family? Are you truly so eager to turn strangers into friends that you would forget your family?* Well, perhaps he wouldn't say that last part, but it didn't stop her thinking it.

Enough time went by that Neelie got up and lit the torches—with flint, not with her magic, which Zyre found odd—and the shadows grew ever longer. But less than an hour later, the soulbeast emerged, the ropes hanging loose on its frame and only a small piece of paper—a different shape than the first one, though—tucked in the space between where the rope pressed against the goat-creature's shoulder blade. Oharyn passed the paper to Neelie, who in turn passed the paper to Zyre.

"I'm glad to hear you escaped Nyli's raid," it said. "I doubt I have to tell you we need you. Please return to Las Corvika forthwith. We sit in the shadow of the Bérangers. —Jervin"

Zyre went to the nearest torch and burned the letter. *I'm working on it,* she wanted to say.

"What did it say?" Neelie asked.

"He was just telling me where I could find him," Zyre said, which was a partial truth, and it was all the easier to sound convincing after her practice at *holte barol.* She wanted to send another letter through, demanding he tell her how he was, if he was well, if he'd managed to get away from the raid uninjured. But at least he was alive.

"Hmm," Neelie said, but didn't press. "Modorin, do you feel comfortable taking Zyre back to the Siren's Haunt?"

"It's not so late as all that," Modorin replied, which Zyre took to mean, *too much later, and the streets won't be safe, even for a friend of Neelie's.* Or maybe it had to do with their arguments with the city guard.

"Then you two probably should head back." She smiled, but it didn't reach her eyes. "Zyre, I know you want to return to your family as quickly as possible. I'll get an update from my father and send word tomorrow."

"Thank you," Zyre said, and meant it. She'd made her choice, and now she wanted to see it over and done with.

# CHAPTER 12

The Áit cut across the lower half of Las Corvika with such force and determination it was as if Thyljal herself powered the river. Jervin's army was positioned near one of its few forks, the Gouvelle, though the smaller river wasn't visible from where they stood. A patch of forest and the fringes of their newest camp blocked the Gouvelle from view.

Today marked the seventeenth day since his departure from Lasinia, which meant that it was also the seventeenth day his wife and son had been the captives of the regis and his shifting whims. He hadn't been able to get news on them these past few days, and it was a relief to know the communication could be re-established now that they had a stable camp again. Jervin could give them hope. *Eris*, in his hands where it belonged. Enchanted blades, delivered as promised. And if the location of his daughter wasn't ideal, well, at least he knew she was alive. If nothing else, Ivanya would take heart in that.

At the head of their forces, ten thousand strong, Jervin watched as a *sjarvisk*, a man with a black sable, stepped up to the banks of the river. The ground rumbled in protest. Suddenly, a thick, solid beam of packed earth rose above the water. The river crashed against the barrier, protesting futilely.

Jervin heeled his mount forward. General Tavere and Captain Merytz flanked him, and behind them, four other men hand-picked to serve as his momentary honor guard.

There was something satisfying about hearing the men move out behind him, following him across the bridge with the synchrony of a well-trained army.

On the other side of the river, a man ranked as lieutenant waited for them with a *sjarvisk* of his own. The lieutenant's name was Oretnir Valade, and he was responsible for the branch that had been stationed near Obele. He bowed. "Welcome back, sir."

Jervin studied Valade thoughtfully. He was a middle-aged man, perhaps old enough to have fought in the Succession, his black hair cropped short. His lieutenant knotwork was pinned above his heart where it should be, now that their days of banditry pretense were behind them. It filled him with pride. Maybe they'd had to rush their plans, but these men had been fighting for the cause for years. It was about time they were allowed to show their honors.

Jervin turned to Merytz. "Have someone fetch Lieutenant Vaudian." The settling of the troops could be overseen by someone else, and Jervin wanted to discuss plans of action with his highest-ranking officers. To Valade, he asked, "Is the war tent already set up?"

The lieutenant nodded. "It is, sir. It was set up last night."

"I'd like to be taken there."

Valade bowed. He waited silently as Jervin dismounted, glad to finally be on his own two feet again. He still wasn't used to spending all day in the saddle, and it had been a hard few days of travel. Merytz and Tavere followed suit, as did Jervin's new honor guard. All of them, of course, except for the one who had just left in search of Vaudian.

Jervin led his own horse until they reached the outskirts of the camp, where Valade grabbed the nearest soldier and had him lead their mounts to the closest horse lines. Everything had been set up with the five branches of their army in mind. It would lead to less chaos in the coming days, but right now, the half-formed pathways, the spread-out cooking fires, and the scattering of tents just made the whole place eerie.

The unpleasant blend of sweat and refuse was already present, unfortunately.

Tavere had had the foresight to send instructions regarding the setup of their new base through the velídas tree prior to their departure. Valade had followed them to the minute detail, setting up the important tents all at the center of the camp. The main infirmary, the war council, both Jervin's and Tavere's sleeping quarters, and the dovecote were already waiting there, forming a loose ring around the new site's silver tree.

Their small party entered the war council's tent and began unearthing maps and records while they waited for Vaudian. Luckily, it didn't take long for the lieutenant to arrive. Jervin spent a few minutes with each of them, overseeing the plans for settling down the troops. With *Eris* back in his possession and a dozen enchanted swords to enhance his best soldiers? It was as if Tholjun himself was looking down on them and smiling, saying, *Finally. It is time.*

When their business was complete, Jervin dismissed everyone except Tavere. The tent was spacious enough to fit all of the ranking officers of the army, which meant they had plenty of privacy once the others had left.

Jervin fell into an empty chair and readied himself for a possible fight. "I heard about Medore."

Tavere grimaced. "I shouldn't be surprised."

"That was a stupid waste of a good *sjarvisk*."

The general shrugged. "I know how Notoyem thinks. I couldn't waste the opportunity to take out one of the royals before we moved, especially since we won't get many other opportunities from here on out."

"But a tiger *sjarvisk*? How did you even know Notoyem would fall for that? That he would send *any* of the Bérangers?"

"I'd do it again," Tavere replied, indignation coloring his tone. "This is what you hired me for, Jervin. I've had to use every dirty, underhanded trick I could think of to level the playing field. Sometimes it's messy, and it doesn't always work, but it has to be done anyway. With luck, once the army marches together, we can leave all of that behind, but I won't apologize for working with what tools I had."

Jervin appraised the general severely. Their *sjarvisk* weren't so numerous that they could just throw them away. Especially not one as powerful as a tiger's *sjarvisk*. Finding their footing in their eventual battle against the capital would be difficult enough. "Is it true that Les Stelvo's defenses have been under repair?"

The general relaxed slightly. "Unfortunately. Our *sjarvisk* won't be able to pull the walls down with the new *kjarnik* enchantments, and even with the advantage of numbers on our side, I believe Notoyem has enough troops to hold the wall. If we're going to besiege the city, we need to make sure the rest of your family is out of the regis's reach beforehand."

"Jehan Fidou is working with a handful of our most trusted assets in Les Stelvo to see it done."

Tavere nodded appreciatively. In their circle, Fidou was considered one of their best allies at court, one whose loyalty they never had to doubt. Fidou had had to watch his sister become the second wife of Notoyem Béranger, mothering his two youngest children before being executed during one of Notoyem's more volatile moments. If anyone would see to the Arnauds' rescue, Fidou would ensure it got done.

Until then, besieging the castle was out of the question. Tavere and Jervin spent several hours considering their troops, their supplies, and their assets. Drawing Notoyem's forces out of Les Stelvo would have been the smart thing to do, but for the moment, both Jervin and Tavere agreed it was a bad idea. That very tactic had been what had ended the Succession two decades prior, when Notoyem had sent his troops to engage Louis Ermengarde's approaching army at Kullen Valley.

Even now, Jervin hated to think of it. Kullen Valley was a legendary battle, one that did not give Notoyem a good name. Tholjun himself was said to have cursed the regis's reign because of it.

Jervin had been held up for a few days trying to squash a small contingent of Villeneuve soldiers attempting to reinforce the capital, and he and his men had nearly ridden their horses to death trying to catch up to Ermengarde's troops. It was supposed to be the last battle, the one where Louis brought Les Stelvo to its knees and threw Notoyem off the throne that didn't belong to him.

Rumor couldn't quite seem to capture what had happened that day in the valley. Some said Notoyem hit the Ermengarde forces with a hundred *sjarvisk*. Some said it had only taken a few, strategically placed, to set off the trap Notoyem had cleverly set up for his foes. Of the few who speculated *aljarne* had been at play, most thought it was a handful of them, secretly gathered from around the country, maybe even borrowed from Notoyem's ally, High King Inoger.

Jervin, who had heard the sounds of battle and had drawn rein to inspect the field, knew for a fact it had only been one *aljarne*.

A single man, accompanied by several *kjarnik* and *sjarvisk*, had stood on an opposite hill. There was nothing that could have prepared Jervin for the absolute carnage one man could bestow; the *aljarne*'s companions certainly hadn't been there to help with the damage. The hills had collapsed under his earthquakes. Fire had rained down on the fighting soldiers, sweeping up Notoyem's own men without a care. Most of the troops in the valley had died that day, regardless of allegiance, including Louis Ermengarde.

Once the fire had gotten a life of its own, the *aljarne*'s companions had turned on him.

The amount of magic at that man's disposal was terrifying. Jervin still didn't know what the gods were trying to tell him by giving him an *aljarne* for a daughter.

When a contingent of reserve troops had stumbled across Jervin's forces, undoubtedly desiring to check the results of the battle, Jervin didn't even try to fight them off. There had been no point. Too few men and no banner to rally behind save the one burning in the valley below.

It had taken these past five years, exiled and away from the scrutiny of court, slowly collecting and training men so Notoyem didn't sense a thing. And for what? Fifteen thousand men couldn't take the whole country. It wasn't even enough to steal the capital from Béranger troops. And even forgetting all of that, it all still might fall apart if he couldn't get his family out of the capital alive.

The memory soured his already abysmal mood. Jervin was not pleased when a young man asked for permission to enter, bearing messages. "Lieutenant Valade asked me to apologize," the messenger said quickly. "These arrived over the past two days, and in all the preparation, he forgot about them until just now."

There were two notes, one bearing the Nyelin family's sigil, the other, *Rosema* Zandua's. The first, at least, was from his daughter.

*"I'm sorry to hear about the family,"* she wrote. *"If I could bring*

*the entire country to march against Notoyem Béranger, I would. My husband will speak to the city representatives, but he says he does not expect a favorable outcome. There are no rules to prevent me from coming, however, and I'll bring with me what personal soldiers I can. Expect me soon. —Aljeya"*

Jervin set the letter aside with a grimace and grabbed the second. The Crasik seal was a comfortingly familiar one that had come and gone with every letter Ivanya had sent to and received from home.

*"Jervin: It pains me to hear my daughter has been caught in Notoyem's trap,"* Doran Zandua wrote. *"However, Crasea has favorable agreements with your present regis and will not break them to offer their support to you. I will write to Notoyem and remind him of those agreements in the hopes he will be merciful, but there is little else I can do. I suppose there is little use in asking you to end this pursuit, so, barring that, I can only wish you well."*

With a growl, Jervin balled up that particular note and used a candle to burn it. "Even if Les Stelvo falls, we won't have enough troops to hold it against Duvachelle and Villeneuve should they decide to try taking it for themselves," he said angrily. "Not without reinforcements."

Tavere looked up from his reports. "Crasea and Atlor?" Jervin nodded. "I wouldn't put so little faith in our men. They're all seasoned warriors. We can make do without foreign help, and we'll look all the better for it."

"I hope so," Jervin muttered. The alternative was the ruination of his House. Maybe even his entire country.

⁂

The next few days did not hold the same allure for Zyre. Nothing could compare to that beautiful day she had shared with Neelie and Modorin. She felt miserable most of the time, impatient to be gone from Bijal, and afraid of the loss that had to come with it. The increasing presence of guards in the Deckhand's Quarter put Modorin on edge, and eventually, even Zyre began to understand his concern.

They couldn't explore Bijal with the guards breathing down their necks. A pity, because even her and Modorin's game of secrets could only hold her attention for so long. The more time she wasted at the Siren's Haunt, the more she found herself worrying about the war effort, and the more useless she felt.

A highlight of those days was the arrival of the outfits she had ordered. She wasn't allowed to go out and pick them up, of course; Modorin did all that for her. But there was something to be said about putting on clothes made specifically to one's measurements. Zyre put on one of the dresses cut in Venascan fashion and felt, for a moment, at least, like her entire world was no longer slipping out from under her control.

Neelie made time to stop by on occasion, keeping a hood up until they were safe in the Coral Room. She didn't visit often enough for either Zyre's or Modorin's liking, but both were more than willing to take a break from the monotony of each other's company. There was only so much time one could spend with someone else before getting tired of the company. Kadj and Sarol were not helping, either. Even soulbeasts did not do too well cooped up all day.

"When do you think your father will be able to help Kadj and me?" Zyre asked one day, not out of any particular impatience or malice.

"Are you so eager to be out of our company?" Modorin teased dryly.

Neelie just rolled her eyes at both of them, then said, "I don't know. It's no small magic. I've known my father to require days to create some charm or another. The one that took the longest was a defensive spell, and that took him nearly a week. But yours is something different entirely, and Kaspar can only do so much without his magic. And, I'm sorry, but it's not a huge priority right now with Honir pacing at the gates."

It seemed unfair to point out that Zyre herself was on something of a clock. *A week*, she told herself. *Or until things start to feel too dangerous here. I can't afford to get caught up in someone else's fight, not when my father is about to rebel against the whole kingdom.*

Not for the first time, Zyre wished she'd been born a normal *sjarvisk*. Who needed all this power anyway? What did it do a person beyond paint a target on their back?

⁂

Neelie strode through the winding streets of the Shadow Quarter, half lost in thought. The presence of white-clad soldiers in the Sector of the Gulls had really expanded in these last few days. It was beginning to feel more and more like a fight was going to break out. Neelie pulled her hood further down her face.

It was demeaning, scuttling about her own neighborhood like a mouse, but Adreia's ship was due to arrive any day now, and the whole family had decided it best not to start anything until she got there. This was a whole-family type of affair.

As Neelie turned down an alley, she heard another set of footsteps echo her own.

Her hair rose on the back of her neck. Neelie stepped a little faster, turning onto a main street. She very nearly bumped into a white-clad guard, wearing, to her disgust, Inoger's sea serpent crest. He wasn't even the only one on the street. She muttered an apology and continued on her way, checking that her hood had not fallen back too far in the near-collision. The streets were too quiet for her liking. Everyone in the Shadow Quarter was stepping a little lighter with so many guards now populating the city.

The footsteps were definitely still following her.

She grimaced, her anger getting the better of her. Neelie was not one to play cat and mouse, and if she were, she would *not* be the mouse.

Only a few hundred feet up the street was another alley, one that curved out of the view of prying eyes. Neelie made for it, not too quickly, not too slowly, reaching out for her magic. It was harder to grasp in the city and harder to hold on to, but at least it had never refused the call. What Neelie did not do was reach for her sword. Not yet, at least. She wanted to turn the corner and run her sword through him, but that would only work if he was unprepared.

She made the turn, and her pursuer followed. As Neelie took the curve, her hand slowly reached for the sword. Then she saw what was waiting in the alley and stopped dead.

In front of her stood a dozen men, all armed. Their uniforms held a mix of Freyr Honir's crossed swords and the High King's serpent.

She'd let herself walk right into an ambush.

Neelie pivoted, confronting the person following her. But it wasn't just some fool man, and her heart fell to her stomach. The man bore a neck-chain with the enameled sea serpent. A black dog panted at his side. The dog. How had she not heard the dog? This man wasn't just some city *wyrdis*. He belonged to the High King. *Ed gortien*, come to take her.

"Surrender, girl," the *wyrdis* said, though he was not much older than she. "You can't fight your way through."

Neelie barked out a laugh. "Watch me," she snarled.

Several things happened at once. The men drew their swords

and began the charge even as the *wyrdis*'s dog lunged at her. Neelie threw a hand toward the pair, air whipping past her fingers and sending both dog and human rolling backward. Then she pivoted again, ripping into the earth. She charged at the soldiers, transitioning between elements faster than she'd ever had to do before, drawing her sword.

Neelie needed to kill the *wyrdis*, or at least his dog. Letting her vision swing brown, she clawed at the earth with her magic. The stone pavement cracked, and the dirt began to roll upwards. The dog bounded another step forward, his *wyrdis* a few steps away, scowling. Trying to buy herself some time with the soldiers, she yanked harder on the earth, pulling it as high as she could before the dog could to crash into her. She pivoted blindly back toward the *wyrdis* as her vision swam. She swung her sword and felt the hilt smash into the dog's head, sending it sprawling. The beast lay dazed on the ground, unfortunately not dead.

The wall was not nearly tall enough, and the city guards were already struggling to climb it. It struck Neelie that now would be a good time to be afraid.

Hefting her rapier, Neelie lunged toward the *wyrdis*. He dodged her with an unnatural speed, throwing something between them that blasted air outwards and sent her flying. She crashed into the wall of a nearby building. *Get up*, she told herself fiercely. She tried. Her head pounded, her body refusing to obey.

The black dog stepped into her view, alert but not aggressive. It wasn't trying to kill her, after all, though she would have preferred that end to what his *gortien* had in mind.

Then the dog's *wyrdis* appeared before her. It struck her how dull his expression was, as if he had not once thought to be afraid of her. Silver flashed in front of her eyes, and a slurry of words slipped from the man's lips. The pendant in his hand shone, burning her eyes, and then it touched her skin and her vision went black.

⁂

On the thirteenth day since they'd landed in Bijal—the twenty-second since she had fled her home—Zyre sat underneath the windowsill of her bedroom, letting the mid-afternoon wind swirl around her. Modorin was lying on the floor, tossing an acorn he'd found. (The word for acorn in Venascan was *beikotel*.) She was secretly hoping he'd miss the catch and have the spiky bottom poke him in the eye or something. So far, no luck. Sarol sat on the windowsill above her head, looking more cat than fox, and Kadj was sprawled on the floor several feet away from Modorin.

Zyre didn't think anything of the hurried footsteps, expecting them to come and go like the rest of the traffic. Then Kadj's head bounced up a fraction of a second before a harried knock cracked against the door. He scrambled out of the way as it began to swing open, revealing Kaari's head. "Miss Zyre, *Magi* Modorin, sorry to bother you. Ren is in the Coral Room. He said it's urgent. He looked rather murderous."

"Who's Ren?" she asked Modorin.

The *sjarvisk* frowned at Kaari. "Neelie's brother," he said absently. "Come on. I have a bad feeling about this."

Sarol hopped off the windowsill, and Kadj came to stand beside Zyre. They left Kaari behind, thundering down the steps and past the common room. Ren had not shut the door to the Coral Room, and so Zyre saw the man pacing. He looked to be a few years older than Neelie, with his hair cut short. A sword was strapped to his back, a wicked-looking thing that was far larger than Neelie's rapier.

Ren stopped pacing. He glanced at Zyre, and for a second,

she feared he was going to throw her out. He certainly seemed on the verge of saying something. But then he saw Modorin. Neelie's brother spoke too quickly for Zyre to interpret much of anything, but she heard Neelie's name.

She also heard the word *gortien*, and a shiver traveled down her spine.

Zyre glanced at her friend, hoping for an interpretation, but all he gave her was his reaction. He grew still, tense, as if waiting for a blow to land.

"*Anodev*?" he demanded. *When?*

Ren snapped something else in response and motioned for them to follow. They took to the streets. The two men walked side by side, leaving Zyre to trail behind, searching for any signs of soldiers while she tried to pick apart that first thing Neelie's brother had said. But there were no soldiers. There was little in the way of music or people on the streets.

*I can't afford to get involved in this, can I?* She thought, her panic rising. She hadn't used her magic since that night on the beach, and until Hosvar's charm was ready for her, her greatest asset was unpredictable. She had little stomach for violence, and it already turned her gut to think about what she was going to have to do for her father. Besides, it wasn't her fight.

She couldn't. She wasn't brave like Neelie. She wasn't a fighter.

But Zyre had already run when her family had needed her most. Was she really going to leave Neelie to her fate without at least trying to see if there was something she could do to help?

The answer was no. *Had* to be. Not just because Zyre felt lighter when Neelie was around, and not just because Neelie had helped her when she shouldn't have. If for no other reason, Zyre followed Modorin because she could not leave another *aljarne* to some terrible fate.

They crossed the invisible line between the Deckhand's

Quarter and the Shadow Quarter, and as the streets began to grow more populated, Zyre caught sight of more than a few raven tattoos. The absence of Honir's soldiers was just as telling: he had taken Neelie in an attempt to goad the Shadowmen off of their home turf.

Something told Zyre, though, that the Shadowmen were more comfortable out of the Shadow Quarter than Honir believed. Looking around at the men and women armed to the teeth, just sitting and *waiting,* Zyre thought they looked more like predators than the prey Honir must've wanted them to be.

"Modorin," she called, trotting forward.

He looked over his shoulder, barely even paying attention.

Zyre took care not to step on Sarol as she came right up behind the two men. "Please, tell me what's happened."

Modorin seemed loath to leave his present conversation. "Neelie's gone missing. Apparently there was a skirmish a few streets over involving a *wyrdis* and some city guards. We think Inoger's *gortien* got to her."

It was as she'd feared. No, worse. They'd ambushed Neelie where she thought she was safest. *She should have been more careful,* she wanted to shout, but to whom? "What are we going to do? Tell me the Shadowmen are not going to just sit by and let them take her?"

Ren threw a glare over his shoulder. Zyre met it.

"*Wyrdi* Hosvar is calling all of his Shadowmen from across the city," Modorin said, glancing between the two of them. Well, mostly at her, warning her not to cause trouble. "We're going to find out where she's being kept, and we're going to break her free before Honir can send her off to the capital."

"Honir has decided to wage war," Ren added in Corvikan, his voice dripping with contempt. "We will answer it."

His response offered only a little relief, for now she had to answer a difficult question of her own: Would she join them?

She began to recognize their surroundings. The closer they got to the Raven's Head, the more congested the street became. *"Etherodden en ssamena"* was a chant that followed in their wake. *We await the call.* The Shadowmen were ready to pick up arms and fight. All they needed was direction.

It took Zyre's breath away. She knew Neelie was a captain at heart and could command people with ease, but to see that level of loyalty was astonishing. They were planning on fighting the city's *freyr* himself.

The Raven's Head appeared before them, guarded by armed *sjarvisk* and their soulbeasts. They saluted to Ren as the three of them strode past into the house proper. Angry voices greeted them. That first room was as full of people as it had been a few days past, when Zyre had seen her father's sword off, but where that had held an easy air, the people waiting now were silent, tense.

Hosvar was their center of attention, his raven perched on his shoulder. He wore no weapons, but it didn't matter. His stormy expression was enough for Zyre to realize why so many people feared to cross him.

At their arrival, he barked a few last curt orders and then gestured for the three of them to follow. They headed directly for the office. Hosvar shut the door behind them. He eyed Zyre, frowned, then strode to his desk. "I'm going to assume you're here for Neelie, *Magi* Zyre," he began sternly. "And not for your magic."

"My—" Zyre blinked. "Sir, Neelie put her life at risk to save me three weeks ago. Of course I'm here to help."

He nodded. Then he inhaled shakily. "I don't know where she is. We can't make any concrete plans until we know what we're getting into."

"Tradition dictates *najik* be held at *Ed Vodaria*," Modorin offered.

Ren shook his head. "For a normal *najik*, maybe, but for all of Honir's stupidity, he knows she would be easy pickings there. He wouldn't risk it. The dungeons, perhaps, or at one of the city barracks." He looked thoughtfully at Zyre, then spoke to his father in Venascan.

"Absolutely not!" Modorin snarled.

"What?"

Rather than answer, Modorin switched to Venascan and continued to yell. Zyre reached for Kadj. They were arguing about her. She knew they were. Part of her was afraid to press for information. If they were taking such pains to keep Ren's idea a secret from her, it couldn't be good.

Ren snapped something back, but before the argument could go any further, Hosvar raised his hand, and both fell silent. "Until we know where Neelie's being kept, this is a waste of time," he said, switching back to Corvikan. "Only the main barracks has a velídas tree."

Oh. "Kadj couldn't go through the velídas tree. We already tried."

Hosvar threw her a look. "Your tiger is not a proper soulbeast, *Magi* Zyre. Only one with magic in their veins can enter Velídas. A soulbeast or a familiar… or a *najik*."

Oh. *Oh.* They meant her. "No, I can't. I'm sorry, *Wyrdi* Hosvar. I want to help, I really do, but Velídas is a risk I cannot take." She could not afford to skirt madness like Teirolac.

"Exactly!" Modorin snapped. "Besides, while she's connected to Kadj, her magic remains explosive and unpredictable. She'd be walking into a well-defended building with no weapons to speak of and no backup. Neelie would not want Zyre to be thrown needlessly in harm's way."

Hosvar's dark eyes grew sharp. "Neelie's not here." His gaze fell past Zyre, to the door. Or, no, not the door, but rather to a pedestal with a bowl sitting atop it with little metal ships bobbing on the surface. "I don't think Velídas would hold much risk for you, *Magi* Zyre. No more so than it would be dangerous for a normal soulbeast. We will lose far fewer lives with your help."

"Wouldn't it be easier to ambush them on the road?" Zyre asked, her panic rising. "You won't have any defenses to break past."

"We'll have magic to face," said Ren, drumming his fingers against the back of the chair. "They don't like to keep magic-users in the barracks with the regular soldiers. There probably won't be more than five helping guard her no matter where they're keeping her. But on the road, she'll be surrounded by some of Inoger's best troops, and those men won't have any qualms about working beside a *majican*."

A knock sounded at the door. "Enter," Hosvar boomed.

A woman stepped inside, a hawk on an outstretched arm. She bowed briskly as she spoke. The *sjarvisk* was a few inches shorter than Zyre, very short by Venascan standards, and she wore a belt over an outfit that looked similar to the dress Zyre had borrowed from Kaari. A long, curved knife hung from her waist.

"*Medias*," said Hosvar. The woman took her leave. Hosvar ran a hand over his face and sat heavily at his chair.

"Honir can't help exposing himself to a defensive weakness," Ren said with bitter smugness.

Zyre looked to Modorin, frustration rising. She hated relying on the trickle of information they deigned to relay to her in Corvikan.

Her friend's shoulders fell. "The main barracks," he supplied. "Crawling with soldiers. The dungeons would have been easier to clear out."

Hosvar and Ren shifted back into Venascan, arguing heatedly. Modorin listened and made comments of his own.

Zyre lost track of the conversation quickly, and her mind began to wander. Her heart was telling her she needed to do something her brain did not wish to contemplate. It would be a huge risk to participate in this fight. A *huge* risk. People died in fights all the time, and if she was one of the casualties, her family's war would become that much harder to win.

It wasn't logical to want to help these people she had known for less than a month, but she did. Zyre knew for a fact that, after everything Neelie had risked to help her, she had to return the favor. If Zyre wasn't willing to get her hands bloody, then she was subjecting Neelie to a fate even worse, one where Neelie would be forced to kill, and it wouldn't even be on her own terms.

"Where is the velídas tree on the barracks grounds?"

The others were too preoccupied with their discussion to hear her the first time, so she repeated herself and ignored Modorin's disappointment.

Ren drew a map—Zyre didn't ask how he knew the layout so well—and she was relieved to see the tree was relatively close to one of the outer walls.

She was no tactician, but she'd learned a thing or two from all those dusty tomes she'd read in her guard tower. It was time to put her knowledge to use.

# CHAPTER 13

After two long hours cramped in that office, the four split to see to their duties. Hosvar and Ren had to see to their men, and Zyre and Modorin were in dire need of a food break. Luckily, Modorin was no stranger to the Raven's Head and knew right where to go. He hadn't spoken much during the meeting. That he was angry with her was obvious. He wanted her to sit back and do nothing. Maybe he thought she didn't have a right to care. And maybe she didn't. It wasn't like she'd known Neelie for very long. But Zyre *did* care.

Their noses led them near the kitchen, and the kitchen brought them to a pantry. Modorin fished out some fruits and a loaf of bread wrapped in cloth.

"Here, let me." Zyre held out her arms, an offer to help carry.

He seemed on the verge of refusing, but finally, with a shake of his head, he passed over the bread. Without a word, he turned back the way they'd come, leading her through the warren of hallways until they came to a room with its doors only half-closed, revealing a sitting room with plenty of chairs. Modorin pressed his back against the door but didn't push it open, not right away.

"Zyre," he began. She prepared herself for the argument. But he didn't say anything. He just shook his head, gave the door the shove it needed, then turned his back to her. The sitting room was decorated with a handful of paintings, the colors balancing each other out well, especially in the dim light. Surprisingly, a small clock that must've cost a small fortune sat in one corner. A circular rug lay at the center of the floor, and both Sarol and Kadj made a beeline for it.

Modorin dumped his fruits onto a small table and hooked his foot around the leg of a chair, pulling it out. He stared down at it, unmoving.

Zyre walked warily toward the table.

"It's just that you barely know her, Zyre," he said finally, so softly that she almost did not hear.

There it was, then.

Modorin grabbed a yellow pear from the pile and stepped away from the table, the fruit flying from one palm to another.

"That's a bit harsh," she replied sharply. "And anyway, she saved my life before she even knew me, so what's your point?"

The pear fell still with a resounding *smack* against his palm. "It's not about that. It just seems unfair that you would have to be the one to weather most of the risk. It should be me. I mean, what about your family? These kinds of things are bloody, and people are going to die. What if that person is you? What then?"

"I should be asking you the same question. You hate fighting as much as I do, don't you? Isn't that why you ran away from Syfris?"

His expression darkened, and she wished she could take it back. "I ran because I didn't like the cause I was fighting for. This is different. This is *Neelie*."

"Modorin." Her vision blurred. She wiped at her eyes angrily, determined that this would not make her cry. "I don't even know if I can call them my family. They never let me be part of it, not really, not when the wrong people could see and begin to wonder at all the things that didn't make sense. I know it was for my own safety, but it was a knife constantly digging into my skin to see them, to interact with them, to bow and say '*Yes, Baron,*' or '*No, Baron,*' to look into their eyes and see that they did not care about me. I think somewhere along the way, they forgot how to."

Zyre tried to keep talking, but her throat felt raw. She was afraid she truly might break if she said another word, might reveal too much if she admitted the way she felt around Neelie. Confident, steadfast, strong. She ran her hand across Kadj's head and tried to pull herself together.

With a shaky breath, she continued, before Modorin could say something sympathetic and destroy any chance she had at composure. "Here in Bijal, with you and Neelie, I am not the forgotten daughter of the baron. I can be just me. It's not that I won't go back to my family when this is all said and done. I have to, because for better or for worse, we share the same blood, and that has to mean something. But I owe Neelie, and it's for more than just saving my life. For her, for you, I'd put my life, my heart, my very sanity on the line."

She glanced at him through her lashes, carefully, so he wouldn't see. Modorin stared, taken aback. Perhaps she had gone too far, expressed too much. The whole concept of friends was still new to her. She certainly never would have said even half as much to Merytz.

Avoiding his eyes, Zyre instead set her focus on the bread she had brought. She unwrapped the cloth and pulled a piece off. Modorin absently reached again for the pear, biting into its soft skin.

For a long time, silence hung over them like a dark cloud. Zyre cast about for other topics, anything to break the silence and turn them away from her confession, but came up empty.

In the end, it was her friend who found the bridge across the chasm. Modorin exhaled, grimacing at the juice collecting on his fingertips. "Your loyalty is commendable, Zyre, and touching. Someday, I hope you'll find it in yourself to consider your own desires, to let people fight their own battles so you might find some measure of peace. I'm just worried you don't know what you've signed up for."

Zyre thought back to the day she'd fled Lasinia. She thought about the *Aretmor* and wondered if Modorin could ever believe she knew exactly what she'd signed up for.

She was grateful, though, that he didn't say anything about the reliability of her magic, or her lack thereof, because that was one thing she had no argument for.

"Do you think you can get through tonight without killing anyone?" Modorin asked before the silence could grow awkward again.

She grimaced. "I don't have much of a choice, do I?"

"I suppose not. Come on, let's go over the plan again."

It provided a much-needed distraction for both of them. They dove into the rest of their food as they broke down the plan. They went over it several more times, and when there was no question they had it down, they checked to make sure Hosvar needed nothing from them. But the *wyrdis* was preoccupied with the preparations, and Ren was nowhere to be seen. They retreated back to the sitting room, talking quietly. The sky grew dark. They lit a candle and waited as the hours crawled toward midnight.

⁂

When the clock chimed half-past eleven, Zyre found herself being shaken awake by Modorin. She hadn't meant to fall asleep, but by the ragged look on her friend, she hadn't been the only one.

The house was no longer silent. Voices and footsteps bounced off the walls from half a dozen different directions. She and Modorin prodded their soulbeasts awake, though the animals were looking infinitely more rested than the two of them. They left the sitting room, heading for the backyard.

The silver velídas tree rustled quietly under the soft wind. Torchlight cast short shadows around its base, as well as the sole occupant waiting for them there. Hosvar leaned against the tree, his raven perched on his shoulder.

The *kjarnik* held a short sword. "Ren will be waiting for you," Hosvar told Modorin. "You're going to have to hurry."

"Of course, sir," he replied. He faced Zyre. "Good luck," he said to her, wrapping her in a hug. She tensed, surprised. Then, with a smile she was glad he couldn't see, she returned the gesture.

When they broke apart, she urged Kadj to follow Modorin. The great cat blinked at her in confusion; she couldn't remember the last time they'd spent any amount of time separated. But Sarol chattered at him, and, with some hesitation, he fell in step behind Modorin. Her friend and her soulbeast both disappeared into the house.

For all her bold words, she couldn't believe she was really doing this. Part of her hoped the tree would not respond to her touch so she could run after Modorin and fight in a way that was not so likely to crush her sanity.

She set her shoulders and willed herself to be courageous. *Eris bi eljers.* Her family's words. *Her* words. She would live by them now, for her friends.

Hosvar stepped aside as she drew near. This close to the tree, she realized that the silvery bark was uneven, crackled. Its branches reached out more than up, the leaves smooth-edged and closely bundled. If that was all, she might have told Hosvar there and then that Velídas would not respond to her. But something stirred in her chest, like a root delving for water. She could feel it. The magic of Velídas was calling out to her.

"It's going to work," she said with utter certainty, drawing back.

If Neelie was to be believed, Velídas was not supposed to take long to walk through. The Shadowmen were all getting into position with Ren at their helm, and Modorin needed to move quickly if he was going to reach his own group of Shadowmen.

She waited, knowing they were all dancing with time. One misstep would jeopardize the whole thing.

Hosvar offered her the sword. "You should know that the city will not be safe when this is all said and done. I've prepared a ship with a good, respectable crew to take you back to Las Corvika."

Zyre blinked at the suddenness of the announcement as she belted the weapon around her waist. "I really… I had hoped to have the full force of my magic before I went back to my father, sir."

"And I hope to send you off with it yet, but do not hold me to it. It will depend the swiftness of *Freyr* Honir's reaction."

Her hand reached out for Kadj before remembering he was not there, and she laughed quietly at herself. If she got her wish, she would have to get used to the lack of his presence.

"It's time," Hosvar said.

Just like that, her good humor crumbled. *By skill and valor, Zyre,* she told herself fiercely.

She called to her magic, not to summon, just to hold. The velídas tree immediately lit up in her eyes, radiating color, burning like a beacon. It seemed wrong that it should be visible only to her, but Hosvar remained unfazed. The edges went fuzzy. She took in a deep breath, and then made the crossing.

It was like walking into a wall or falling into icy water.

The hair on the back of her neck, on her arms, on her legs, all rose with such a fervor that she feared they would yank themselves out. A roar thudded against her ears, her blood churned, and she found for one terrifying second that she could not even see. Magic crashed into her from all sides, pushing against her, pulling from inside her, and Zyre found she'd forgotten how to breathe. In its pulsing, Zyre did not know where she ended and the magic began, only that it felt like she was a vase full of cracks, its water quickly seeping out.

Out of instinct, she threw it all toward Kadj, letting it pass through her.

The waters quieted. She could still feel it, that inescapable mass of magic, hungering for her, but it was more akin to a wolf scratching at the door than it was to the wolf inside, teeth bared and already tinged with red.

The scuffle with magic had taken less than a few seconds, and now that it was settled, she studied her surroundings. It took her breath away. All around her, colors swirled, eddying into pools before being swept off by some unseen force. She looked down beneath her feet and found that it was not a road beneath her, but rather, the silvery crackled wood that made up the velídas tree. All around her, the paths branched, leading this way and that. Looking at each path, she heard a different song coming into focus above all the background noise.

As Zyre searched, trying to figure out which path to follow, her ears caught a familiar song, a lullaby.

> *The sun begins to set*
> *Though the owls are not woken yet.*
> *Inside it's nice and warm I bet*
> *Let's join together now*
> *Hush and kiss the willow*

She found herself stepping toward it. Something told her that the song would lead her to her father, and even after everything she'd said to Modorin, Zyre missed her family terribly. She missed her mother and the subtle hand signals they shared to lessen the sting of her isolation. She missed the sharp jokes her brother made, how he'd sometimes request the protection of the family *sjarvisk*, and her alone, so they might be able to have some time together, however strained it might've been. She missed her father's certainty.

It would be so easy to follow it to them, to her father, and leave everything in Bijal behind... to leave Kadj and her hopes of better magic.

But it was not her family she was seeking tonight.

Eyes burning, she turned away from the song, let it fade to a soft hum behind her. She needed to find Neelie. Song after song came into focus, many in languages she didn't even understand. Then, like a miracle, she caught a piece of a familiar, thudding song. A Venascan tune with the brilliant twang of the jaw harp: the one she had heard only a week ago on that beautiful sunny day with Modorin and Neelie.

Zyre's magic throbbed at the song, pulsing like an arrow, a tether. She followed it over other pathways, across the hollow, half-faded branches that Zyre somehow knew had been the gateways to Velídas trees cut down long ago. It did not take her far. The music grew louder, and suddenly, a silhouette of a tree appeared before her. The drums thundered in her ears. She inhaled, then exhaled, the sound drowned out by the noise. Then she stepped through.

Surrounded suddenly by a poorly lit courtyard, Zyre pitched forward. There was no constant tug and push of the swirling magic. The ground felt too still and the wind too calm.

A gray shape moved nearby. She strained her eyes, groping for her sword. A few paces away, a soldier in clothes white enough to form a beacon stood guard. He turned at the scrape of her blade.

She leapt, bashing the soldier's head with the hilt of her sword. The man crumpled to the ground without so much as a whimper.

Her heart pounding almost as loud as the music of Velídas, she knelt beside the man and pressed her fingers against his neck. The soft *thud, thud, thud* of his heartbeat pulsed against her fingertips. She breathed in a sigh of relief.

Tearing at the fringes of the man's clothes, she pulled free enough to bind him. Moving him was a lot harder. He certainly weighed more than she did, and time was not on her side.

Neelie's words echoed in her mind, those harsh words from their first encounter. *I'm not trying to fight off the entire force your prince brought with him, and I certainly refuse to do it single-handedly. But I just might have to now, because you can bet your little friend is about to warn everyone he can find.*

She couldn't afford for this man to wake up and warn his fellow guards, but she would not kill him.

With a last, desperate heave, she got him propped against the velídas tree.

Zyre called to her magic, wincing as the tree burned her vision. But when she called to earth, it answered, splattering across the guard's white uniform without burying him completely. Content, she turned her gaze across the courtyard. There was no one. For now, at least. She hefted her sword and moved on.

She kept the rising moon to her left, slinking through the courtyard. An empty training yard was just past it. It offered no cover, and beyond the field was the dim silhouette of a squat building nestled against the towering gate that separated the barracks from the rest of the city. The guardhouse was well lit from the entrance, and she could count four guards on duty, but that said nothing for who was inside the building.

Zyre knelt beside the small weapons hut. The door was locked, or else she might have considered investigating for spare weapons, but she couldn't risk the noise. Her own would have to do.

Then a great bell began to clang from far away, one for each hour. On the third chime, the ground began to shake. Zyre heard a soft *crack*, and then a horn, urgent, distinctive in its relative proximity. Ren and his Shadowmen were beginning the attack. She was right on time.

Three more men spilled out of the guardhouse. One barked a few curt orders in Venascan. Two men stayed behind. The rest ran toward the source of the noise, sprinting on the opposite side of the weapons hut. Zyre did not breathe easier until they were well out of sight. Then she gulped in air, readied herself, and launched from her hiding place.

The guards saw her right away, of course, and their weapons were out well before she'd crossed half the distance.

*Tholjun bless my hand. Give me precision and power to defeat my enemies.*

She summoned earth. The flare of browns seemed muted after Velídas. For a moment, the soil refused to budge. Then it snapped. The ground rumbled and cracked, exploding under the guards' feet. One flew. He crashed into the guardhouse with a sickening thud.

The second was on his hands and knees, his sword several feet away. He crawled toward it, his body swaying.

Zyre's vision turned blue, then silver. She crafted a pebble-sized bit of ice and sent it flying between the second soldier's eyes. His head whipped back as the ice made contact, and he crumpled to the ground.

She sprinted toward them, skidding across the last few feet. The second soldier's pulse flared beneath her fingers, and she made quick work of tying him up. The first guard was only a short distance away.

When she checked his pulse, a small part of her shattered. Dead men didn't need to be bound.

*Tholjun, forgive me*, she prayed.

Then came the worst part, for she needed the keys and didn't know which of them had it, if either of them did. She rifled through the dead man's pockets, ignoring the sense of wrongness that came off of a body.

Coming up empty, she returned to the bound soldier. He groaned as she searched him. Again, nothing. When one eye groggily opened, she quickly tore off an extra bit of fabric and shoved it in his mouth.

Zyre gave him one last pitiful glance and jogged into the small office. The gods favored her and let her find them quickly. There, hanging on a wall by the door, were the very keys she needed.

She returned outside, trying not to look at the dead man, and found the lock by the light of the flickering torch. The lock clicked and swung open with ease.

A great orange blur streaked toward her. Kadj nearly knocked her over in his relief. Modorin ran in after him with Sarol and five other soldiers. There were two men and three women. One, Zyre was surprised to realize, she recognized. Oharyn, with the goat-like soulbeast she now knew was called a chamois. Two others had soulbeasts. They would hold the gate if need be.

Modorin tripped over Kadj as he crashed into her, wrapping his arms around her. "You made it through."

"Yes," Zyre said, gently pushing him off of her. "We have to go."

Modorin spoke quickly to the Shadowmen, and they nodded. With a curt gesture, Modorin set off toward the main building, and Zyre followed after him.

*We're coming, Neelie.* With luck, though, she already knew.

Neelie sat in an office crowded with soldiers—one of whom bore the silver knots of lieutenant, which meant the office was probably his—two *majican* with their soulbeasts, and the *wyrdis* with his sleek black dog. The *wyrdis's* name was Bard, a fact which she neither asked for nor wanted, and he wouldn't shut his damn mouth. Had that damned *wyrdis* not done something to her magic, blocking it off from her somehow, she would have already shut his fool mouth for him.

"Truly, *Nagi* Neelie, I understand this seems like an insult to your person and your magic, but the High King puts these laws in place to protect *you* and the citizens of Venasca." Either he was dumb enough to believe the words he was spewing, or his time at court had already made him excellent at lying. Considering his youth, Neelie was willing to bet it was the former.

She gave him her fiercest glare. "Are you trying to talk me to sleep, *Wyrdi*? Because if we are truly setting sail first thing in the morning, you're robbing yourself and these fine soldiers of their rest."

"We're going to be partners, *Nagi*," Bard said, sighing in disappointment. He bent down just enough to pat his dog on its side. "Best get used to our company."

The great bell began to chime the hour. It rang once, twice, three times. Then the office walls shook suddenly, plaster flaking off and dust shaking loose. Before the bells had fallen silent, a frantic, clanging warning bell sounded. Neelie tensed, fighting off a victorious grin.

The lieutenant snapped his attention in the direction that the explosion had come from. "The Shadow King is here for her after all. Captain Ortigan, *Magi* Vigdis, remain with *Wyrdi* Bard. The rest of you, with me."

The room emptied, and Neelie smiled wickedly. She hoped her father did not expect her to sit around and wait to be rescued.

She gave *Magi* Vigdis and her badger soulbeast to the count of sixty. Lost in the chaos of the thundering footsteps outside, even Bard seemed to forget her for the moment.

The second *Magi* Vigdis and *Wyrdi* Bard made the mistake of taking their eyes off of her, Neelie launched out of her chair, shoving it toward the *majican* with every fiber of her being. She lunged at the captain, slammed a fist into his gut, and took his half-drawn sword out of his hands while he gasped for breath like a landed fish.

The sword slipped between the captain's ribs with ease and came back just as easily. Pivoting, she swept the sword in a downward arc, catching the badger in the neck before the soulbeast had a chance to dig its fierce teeth into her. The *majican* let out a sharp scream, lunging awkwardly for the creature.

Neelie sidestepped the woman, spinning the sword in her hand, testing its weight. Bard paled, his dog staying at his side, hackles raised and growling.

"I'm afraid we're not going to be companions after all, *Wyrdi* Bard." The man opened his mouth to say something, but she forestalled him. "Ah, ah, ah. I don't like killing *wyrdi,* on account it not being a fair fight, but you say one more word and I swear by Dûl I will run you through."

Bard swallowed visibly. She found some satisfaction in that.

The ground rumbled under her feet as she left the room. She slammed the door behind her and searched the hallway quickly. The door swung out, not in. There was a chair nearby. She rammed it underneath the doorknob.

Neelie left them, getting as far as the next hallway before a group of soldiers caught sight of her and stopped dead. She reached for her magic and hissed vexedly when it refused to answer her call. She spun on her heels and ran the other way. They chased after her, their dozen feet echoing her own. She cursed and bolted into a dark room.

The soldiers slowed, but by the time they'd caught up, she was ready for them. She cut down the first soldier with Ortigan's sword. He was dead before he even knew what hit him. The second managed to exchange blows with her, but he didn't guard his left and died for his mistake.

The third leapt through the doorway, over the fallen soldiers, swatting away Neelie's thrust with ease. He had a silver knot on his left soldier, marking him as a man of rank, a captain. He fought like one, too. Neelie was hard-pressed to keep him close enough to the door to discourage his fellow soldiers from following him in and surrounding her. Her sword met his, and he pushed off of her, sending her stumbling back. She barely managed to dodge his next blow.

Then she heard a familiar deep growl, and the man's eyes went wide as he was thrown onto the floor. Neelie sidestepped the tumbling man with a yelp.

Kadj, of all creatures, stood over him, his teeth dripping with blood. The soldier twitched and then grew still. Behind him, *Magi* Modorin finished the last two soldiers with a quick but efficient blast of fire. Zyre was not far behind him, her sword out but shining silver.

"I had it well in hand," Neelie said between breaths. But she smiled in relief. She was glad to see their familiar faces, more than she cared to admit.

Modorin flashed her a grin, then gestured for her to follow. She and Kadj leapt over the bodies, and Modorin and Zyre led her down the halls, storming down staircases, dodging a few fallen soldiers marked either by sword thrust or scorch marks.

They left the main building through a small entrance off to the side, where they slowed their pace, wary of the rushing tide of soldiers. The men ran past, oblivious of Neelie and her little group. Eventually, they came to a small training yard. A handful of familiar faces waited for them there, guarding their way out.

"Where is all that noise coming from? Is it my father?"

"Your brother," Modorin answered.

Neelie laughed. She saw the look Zyre flashed her, but she paid the other woman no mind. It was an inside joke, one that Modorin didn't even really understand.

They stepped over several dead bodies, and the Shadowmen gave way, allowing the three of them to pass through. Once outside, Modorin and Oharyn sent fire catapulting into the sky. Then, at Modorin's signal, everyone began to disperse. He threw her one last, touching look before the darkness swallowed him. Zyre stepped toward Neelie as if to follow her, but Neelie signaled for her to follow Modorin. The way Neelie was going, she doubted Zyre could keep up.

She knew the entire city like she knew her *Ansol*, her *Spider*, which was to say, very well. The streets were lit with dim lamps, but the alleys were not, and she dodged between both until she found easy access onto some poor soul's roof. Neelie leapt and jumped from roof to roof, keeping low. She heard the shouts of soldiers follow her below.

She kept forward, and before long, the sounds of pursuit faded away. Neelie paused for a breath, searching below. Either Honir's men had given up the chase, or they'd just fallen far behind. She reached for her magic again, just to see, and scowled. However long it took for *Wyrdi* Bard's magic to wear off was too long by half.

She hoped her brother had managed to disengage from the barracks, that he and his men had been able to get away. She hoped Zyre had not gotten lost in the warren of streets and that Modorin was taking care of her.

With a final deep exhale, Neelie checked again for movement below and, finding it empty, leapt back onto the street. In this respectable neighborhood, no one else was awake, or if they were, they wisely stayed clear. The Shadow Quarter was some distance away. Neelie kept running.

# CHAPTER 14

Zyre followed close behind Modorin in their mad dash from the barracks. She'd known it was a far run, but she hadn't anticipated her hungry, burning lungs. Birds flew overhead, first an owl and then a hawk, as they ran through the Serpent's Quarter, but there was no way of knowing if they belonged to Honir's men or Ren's. They ran only into one group of soldiers, numbering five.

Against two *sjarvisk*, the men must've known they had little chance of success. They did not fight with much conviction. Zyre was relieved. Her sword was clean, but if it remained so because Modorin did the killing, did it make her any less complicit? What did it mean for her conscience that she stood her ground while her friend and her tiger advanced on the enemy without hesitation, killing them with an ease that made her gut roil?

Modorin grabbed her arm and dragged her down a shortcut through the fringes of the Deckhand's Quarter. Slowly, things grew familiar, though the dark streets distorted shops she might've otherwise recognized with ease during the day. They drew nearer to the Shadow Quarter.

Suddenly, a chill settled over her. It was as if the air had been sucked out of the space, and in her sudden inability to breathe, she did not realize she was falling until she was already on the ground. She was only dimly aware of Kadj's paws thrashing beside her. They were close, too close, those claws.

It felt like it would never end, like it had been going on for an eternity and would carry over into the next, but in a few moments, Modorin was by her side, his hand around her arm. "*En ssorvælo enya es borde dir ed theurvo.*"

As soon as the last word passed his lips, the weight slid off of her. She let Modorin help her back to her feet. She gulped in air, hungrily, caring little for the fact that it was warm and heavy with the sea. When her breathing slowed back to normal, she glared at Modorin. "What in Tholjun's name was that?"

"A deterrent against *Freyr* Honir's men. You don't have the raven tattoo. That's the key in."

"You do?" She was a bit surprised. She had not thought he was actually a Shadowman, just a friend to one.

He nodded. "Come on. Just because Honir's men can't get through doesn't mean we should sit around. Besides, there'll be news at the Raven's Head."

"All right," Zyre said. Maybe it was the effects of air deprivation. Maybe it was shock. But when she glanced over her shoulder and found only an empty street, she couldn't suppress a grin. "I can't believe we did that. We actually got her out."

He smiled at that, even went so far as to throw an arm around her shoulder. "Yeah. You did good, Zyre."

It was such a… *brotherly* gesture that she was taken aback at first. It almost made her sad. But tonight, she didn't want to dwell on the past.

Modorin let his arm fall, and they jogged to the Raven's Head with their soulbeasts trailing behind them.

The closer they got, the more people populated the streets. They were all heading in the same direction; Zyre and Modorin were not the first to return. In fact, they found an impressive conglomeration of Shadowmen occupying the stretch of road just in front of the Raven's Head. The street lamps cast a light on the men and women, and Zyre's elation stumbled. Modorin's little party had managed to slip free mostly unscathed, but it was Ren's Shadowmen who had held the brunt of the attack, and it showed. Some were worse off than others.

*Kjarnik* pressed through the crowd with enchantments in their hands and their familiars on their heels, tending to Shadowmen or, on a rare occasion, to one of their soulbeasts.

"Come on. They'll be in the office," Modorin said, his steely voice suggesting he felt the same as Zyre. They'd sprung Neelie out, but it had been a costly night. Tholjun had gotten his dues for the victory.

The door of the Raven's Head was left propped open, and men's cries could be heard within. Healers stood over tables. Not all of them were *kjarnik*. Even with healing spells, there were limits both in supply and what it could do for patients who had lost too much blood or had wounds that cut too deep.

Not for the first time, Zyre thought about how much she wished battle magic did not exist, that there were only *kjarnik* with their quiet magic. It was all artwork, deftness, and skill for them. There was no finesse in blasting someone with fire.

She and Modorin filed into Hosvar's office and shut the door behind them. Neelie and Ren were already inside. The *najik* looked unharmed, though angrier than a hornet, and Ren, oddly enough, seemed the opposite—subdued, exhausted—though none of his injuries looked life threatening.

Modorin took the last empty chair and fell into it with a sigh. "Do we have a count yet?"

Kadj had already lain down near the door, his tail curling around the leg of the pedestal with the bowl of ships. She nestled against his side and found she felt utterly exhausted, though she had barely used any magic today.

"We won't know the full of it until morning, I expect," Hosvar replied. "At least three killed, one *majican* lost her soulbeast, and there are a few more who remain to be seen. As for the injured, well. You saw them on your way in."

A stray thought ambled into her head. "Your city's *freyr* has purposefully put himself in the corner." All eyes swiveled to Zyre. She hadn't meant to say it out loud. "I mean… while there is no denying the insanity of Venasca's *najik* laws, *Freyr* Honir acted within his legal right and duty, and our counter-attack, however justified, goes against the law. If he hates your family as much as you say, this will be what he uses as an underhanded declaration of war."

Neelie sniffed, begrudgingly impressed. "Well, I could see someone like High King Inoger being that clever, but *Freyr* Honir is not half as smart."

"He underestimates the people of Bijal," Hosvar added. "He supports the quality of life for the merchants and the aristocratic families of the city while people on our side of town struggle to make enough wages to pay for their homes, their food, their clothes. If he's angry that I am taking away his power by earning the loyalty of the people, well, he did that to himself."

Ren grunted agreeably.

"But it doesn't matter what Honir's reasonings are now. What matters is how he reacts. Neelie, too many people know you're *najik*. It's too big a risk; you cannot be in the city right now. You are to take Zyre back to Las Corvika, to her father."

Neelie tensed. "I will not." The rest of her argument, however, was lost to Zyre as Neelie switched out of Corvikan. Whatever she said, she was vehement. Hosvar answered swiftly, his voice growing thunderous, but neither Ren nor Neelie blanched.

Zyre glanced at Modorin, hoping for some hint, some window into the conversation, but he just looked studiously at Sarol, his fox sleeping on his lap.

A knock at the door quieted their argument. At Hosvar's gesture, Zyre rolled to her feet and opened the door a crack, careful not to disturb Kadj. Though, if the shouting had not woken him, she supposed little would right about then.

Zyre expected not to recognize the person waiting on the other side, but it was Mistress Kaari, of all people, backed by two men, one of whom was carrying a familiar trunk, the one from her room. Zyre blinked. She had not realized Kaari was a Shadowmen, but she must've been, to be able to cross into the Shadow Quarter. And desperate too, if the hour and the state of her hair and dress were anything to go by.

"Pardon, *Wyrdi* Hosvar, *Nagi* Neelie, Master Ren." She bobbed a respectful curtsy. "I brought *Magi* Zyre's things, like you asked, *Wyrdi* Hosvar. And it's a good thing you did, because I have news. My husband and I spotted *Freyr* Honir himself riding through the streets of the Deckhand's Quarter with a contingent of men."

"Riding this way?" Hosvar asked as Kaari's strongman set the box down beside Zyre.

Kaari shook her head. "It did not appear so, *Wyrdi* Hosvar. He seemed content to cause trouble in the Deckhand's Quarter, with your… known associates. Including us at the Siren's Haunt."

"Was anyone hurt?" Hosvar asked, seeming genuinely concerned.

But, again, the answer was no. "We got away with some broken tables and chairs, some of our food and drink 'seized' in the name of Honir, but little else. Hæfnir stayed behind to calm our guests, but he thought I should warn you."

"Thank you, Madame Kaari," Hosvar replied. "We'll pay for

the damages, of course, and you're welcome to stay here in the Raven's Head for the night."

"It's a kind offer, *Wyrdi* Hosvar," Kaari said with another curtsy, "but I should be getting back to my husband. I will send one of the girls over to help your healers, though."

Hosvar, Ren, and Neelie all muttered their thanks to Kaari, and then the woman took her leave.

As soon as she was gone, Neelie turned to her father. Zyre tensed for the argument to continue.

"I expected he would, Neelie," Hosvar said tiredly, cutting her off before she could even start up again. "Denied access as he is. It's nothing we can't handle. Now, *Nagi* Zyre, regretfully, there's too much I must attend to tonight, but tomorrow morning, I will sever your ties with Kadj, if you still wish to do so. Then you really must be on your way. Neelie, Vidar has assembled a crew for the *Lemanthus*. They'll be waiting for you."

"So I can't even gather my own crew now," Neelie growled.

"Can you even use your magic yet?" Hosvar snapped. Impossibly, Neelie's face flushed. "I thought not. Stop being so childish." He said something else in Venascan, something that made Neelie's shoulders fall. The room stumbled into silence for a moment. Neelie looked at her brother. Then, with a grimace, she nodded.

Hosvar mirrored the gesture. "Good. Now, Ren, I have need of you tonight, if you're up for it."

"I can be." Ren pushed himself out of the chair with a sigh. He grabbed his sword and slipped the strap across his back with a practiced ease. Saying something glib to Neelie in Venascan and getting a hand gesture that Zyre was pretty sure was considered impolite here, Ren laughed a hollow and exhausted laugh and then left the room.

As the door swung open to reveal the healers and the dying men, Neelie's brother didn't even pause.

Neelie rubbed at her eyes. "I'll talk to you tomorrow morning, then. Modorin, Zyre, come on."

Suppressing a yawn, Zyre shook Kadj gently. Modorin and a tired Sarol followed suit, falling in line behind Neelie.

"*Ír liora*," Hosvar said as they filed out.

Zyre looked back and caught Neelie's anger melting away. "*Ír liora téano*," she said softly. *I love you too*. Then she shut the door behind her, looking the very image of unhappiness.

⚬

The Raven's Head had a handful of guest bedrooms, but most were already spoken for by Shadowmen who resided in the next neighborhood over or Ren's *majican* sleeping off their big magic with their soulbeasts. Even then, three or four were going to be sharing a bed, according to Neelie.

"Luckily," Neelie added as they traipsed through the house, "there's more than enough space for you in my room. You too, I suppose, Modorin, but you're going to have to sleep on the floor."

"Yes, I'm an insufferable rogue who can't be trusted," Modorin replied flatly, a small flame resting above his palm, casting the hall in a dim light.

Neelie laughed, and it sounded genuine. "In that case, you'd better sleep in the hallway." Zyre couldn't tell if she was joking or not, but Modorin, at least, took it as one.

It struck her, then, what Neelie meant. Zyre, share *her* bed. She blushed at the idea and berated herself for it, hoping Modorin's flame was not bright enough for the others to see. *It'll be just like sharing a bed with Aljeya*, she told herself fiercely, *those times when the thunderstorms drove you from your own bed when you were five.*

Look at her. If this was how she was going to be thinking, she deserved to sleep on the floor more than Modorin did. And if they were departing in the morning, if Modorin was staying behind, perhaps it would be better off to let them share the bed. But Neelie had said Modorin would sleep on the floor, so Zyre could not protest.

Neelie's bedroom door was designed after the same fashion as Venascan exterior doors, which came as a surprise, because Zyre knew that designing the *ðedael* was costly. Neelie's was in the shape of a tree. A spider hung from the lowest branch, mirroring the tattoo on Neelie's forearm. At the carving's center, right in the heart of the tree trunk, the Venascan homage to Ski'tha had been etched in the shape of a crescent moon sitting snugly against the sun.

Neelie entered first, but Modorin, as the designated holder of their only light source, went in quickly on her heels and did the honors of sparking the candles within the room. There were no windows to open, no breeze to let in, but the night's relative cool pervaded the space anyway.

With the candles lit, Zyre was able to see the detailing in the room, and it spoke of a certain amount of wealth. A soft Atloran rug woven into Venascan designs rested by the end of the bed. There was a chair and a writing desk shoved against one wall, Venascan-made, of course, as no other country could do it better. Things were surprisingly tidy, too. No clothes scattered about, no mud on the floor.

And there were books, too! A whole shelf full of them! She was sorely tempted to go through them—what did Captain *Nagi* Neelie read when she wasn't pirating or killing men in alleyways?—but Zyre knew if it was a competition between nosing through a bookshelf and falling asleep, the latter would most certainly win.

She wondered, belatedly, if perhaps any of this had been stolen.

Zyre hung back toward the door, thinking, foolishly, that this was a hundred times more terrifying than stepping into Velídas or fighting Ljerson. Worse, Kadj wouldn't fit on the bed with them, and she hated sleeping without him at her side. She sat next to her tiger on the fine Atloran rug, fighting off her exhaustion.

Neelie unlaced her boots and set them next to her bed before falling gracelessly into it.

Modorin swung the chair out and did the same there. "Is it true, what *Wyrdi* Hosvar said about your magic?"

A rush of alertness snapped Zyre's eyes open.

Neelie didn't even bother to sit upright. "It's just a spell. It'll wear off."

"Has this happened to you before?" Zyre asked.

The other woman laughed bitterly. "Call it an educated guess. *Najik,* when found, get sent to the High King to serve their country until death or madness takes them. I'm hardly any use to His Highness if I can't use magic." Neelie propped herself up. "Are you going to sleep on the floor, *Nagi* Zyre?"

The formality of the question stiffened Zyre's resolve. She pulled her own shoes off, putting them on the opposite side of the bed as Neelie's. Then, taking care to stay as close to the edge as possible, Zyre awkwardly sat down. She gripped the side of the bed. "I'm sorry we weren't there to help you. It didn't seem like much of a fair fight."

Neelie sat up abruptly, throwing one long leg over the side of the bed. "I'm not some helpless damsel, *Nagi* Zyre," she said in biting tones. "You don't get to be where I'm at if you need some honor guard every waking minute of your life."

It was a slap in the face. "That's not what I meant," Zyre protested. "I know you're incredibly powerful, *Nagi* Neelie, both with your magic and with a sword. My brother is good with a sword, too, as is my father, and my friends in the guard. That didn't stop Prince Nyli. It's not a slight against your skill, *Nagi*; you're worlds better than me. Sometimes the odds are just too great to face alone."

Neelie, strangely, seemed a little flustered. "Well," she said, her tone level enough that Zyre wondered if perhaps she was just imagining things. "You had no reason to be there. Besides, you both stormed the bloody barracks on my account. If there was any debt between us, Zyre, it's even."

There, she'd dropped the formality. That was something.

"Modorin, it's late. Care to snuff the candles for me?"

The flames didn't so much as flicker.

"Modorin."

His slumped figure didn't stir.

"I think he fell asleep," Zyre said softly with a snicker. Neelie sighed and got up with a shake of her head. For herself, Zyre tried to get comfortable, hugging the side of the bed, wishing Kadj's slumbering form were within reach. Her thoughts raced, and not just from the bed rocking slightly as Neelie slipped back onto it.

Tomorrow. Tomorrow, she would say goodbye to Bijal, to the wonderfully loud streets with the musicians who played for festivities. She wondered if they would have their chance to play, still, with this thing with Honir going on. And tomorrow, she'd say goodbye to Modorin, because it seemed her newfound friend would not be accompanying them. What did one do with a friend when a whole country sat between them? She wasn't quite ready to find out.

And, tomorrow. Tomorrow would be the day she would finally see what it meant to be an *aljarne*. Tomorrow, Kadj might turn into a beast she no longer recognized. She regretted that thought. Life would be far duller without her constant companion, and the sting would no doubt grow when Neelie took her leave as well. Zyre's only real consolation was that she would be with her father before too long, and, with any luck, her old friend, Merytz.

Fortunately, she did not have a chance to dwell. Tonight had been a night of magic, and her trip through Velídas had been more draining than even her stunt with the *Aretmor*. For a few blissful hours, she slept hard and barely even dreamed.

⁓

When Zyre found herself conscious again, it was still dark. She closed her eyes fiercely. It was *way* too early to be awake. Worse, a song kept playing in her head.

> *A whisper in the evening air*
> *The wind rustles through your hair*
> *From here and there*
> *Don't be afraid; it's lovely*
> *Hush and kiss the willow.*

When she was little, she had insisted the song made little sense. It must've been in the weeks or months just before her magic had first presented itself, because she distinctly remembered her mother presiding over her bed, singing the soft lullaby. But, unlike now, the song had had no effect.

"No one would hug a *tree*, Mother. That's just crazy."

Ivanya had let her lyrical voice fade away, giving in to Zyre's protests. It was almost prophetic, the choice in song, because Zyre had learned the *willow* was actually a magical tree and that the song had supposedly been written in the days after Teirolac's tragic journey through Velídas. The song was a contradiction, both a warning against things that falsely promised safety but also a lament for losing the one place one belonged.

Now, as Zyre resisted the urge to toss and turn, all she could think about was home. It would have been so easy to follow the music. She hadn't realized her family estate *had* a velídas tree, but instinct told her that was where the song had been trying to take her. And now, on the eve of her departure from Bijal, there was an itch between her shoulders that demanded she see just what she'd left behind.

The bed creaked slightly as Neelie shifted, groaning softly.

Zyre wasn't the only one having trouble sleeping. "Are you awake?" she asked quietly, just in case she was wrong.

"Yes, unfortunately," Neelie groused. "Why aren't you asleep?"

"I think I need to do something."

⁂

"This is a really bad idea," Neelie reiterated for the fifth time as they stood in the dark, cool air underneath the velídas tree. "There will probably be soldiers prowling the estate, ones who aren't loyal to your father. Even if you're right, and you didn't just get lucky the first time through Velídas, there's no way to know you won't be *unlucky* once you get out."

Zyre wasn't stupid. She knew all this already. But she felt she'd left her courage behind, on Lasinia. She needed to take it back. So she just said, "Wish me luck." The tree flashed into a burning beacon as magic answered her summons, and before Neelie could answer, Zyre stepped through.

She was ready for it this time, the assault of shifting colors and thudding sounds. When the discordant threads slowly settled into discernable music, Zyre took a moment to steady herself and to listen for the one she wanted.

There. The words.

It was no easier to push through than the first time. At some point, she realized she was crawling on her hands and knees, though she didn't remember falling. The journey felt like the second eternity of the night, although the song never actually had time to repeat. The silhouette of a tree formed in front of her, a shadow of substance that was a welcome relief from the shifting lights.

With as much caution as she dared, Zyre left Velídas.

Immediately, the scent of wet ash clogged her nostrils. She didn't know where it was coming from or if anyone was nearby. In the dark, all she had to go off of were the sounds, and everything was eerily quiet. Even the soft tumbles of the wind sounded all wrong, and as she waited for her eyes to adjust, she began to wonder if she didn't understand Velídas at all.

Then, ever so slowly, the shadows took shape. Underneath the smell of ash was the soft scent of hay. The dark shape fifty feet to her left had to be the stables. But her mind refused to contemplate the bumpy, rough field in front of her. It wasn't until she walked closer—slowly, carefully, even though she heard no signs of patrolling soldiers—and put her hand on the closest pile that she realized why it was so quiet. Why Nyli hadn't left any men here to ensure Jervin didn't come back.

There was no reason to guard a ruin.

Throwing caution to the wind, Zyre summoned her magic. So close to the tree, her magic was more willing to respond, and once the flame was called, it was easy to keep it stable.

The fire cast a dreary glow on the ruins of her home. The secret passages she'd hidden in, the room she'd shared with Aljeya as kids, the very *art* that Ivanya had hand-selected… all of it, gone.

Zyre clambered over the remnants of the wall and went farther in. The destruction was evident everywhere. A horrible, cloying scent rose rise and fell as she searched the ruins, but it wasn't until she found a terribly misshapen hand poking out from some of the rubble that she really understood the extent of Nyli's cruelty. He hadn't even buried their dead.

*Tholjun smite the Bérangers*, she thought as she fiercely wiped off some burning tears. *Them and their damned wrath.*

Zyre let her flame flicker out, reaching for earth. She clawed desperately at it for several moments before it finally took, but when she tried to move one of the rocks, the earth rumbled so loudly that she fell and nearly hit her head. The pile of rubble tumbled into a landslide, burying the hand she'd been trying to unveil.

*They definitely heard that in Nolasi*, Zyre cursed. And if there weren't soldiers patrolling here, well, that meant nothing about the fishing town.

She had to scramble back to the tree in the dark, not trusting her magic to behave, and earned several nasty scratches for her efforts. She only looked back once, the sob she'd been holding back threatening to come unleashed. Then she forced herself through Velídas yet again.

Neelie waited for her on the other side. In the moments of pure darkness after leaving Velídas behind, Zyre only heard her scramble to her feet. "Are you okay? What happened? What did you find?"

Zyre didn't trust her voice. She just barged past, relying on her memory and vague outlines to keep her steady.

"Zyre, talk to me," Neelie insisted, her voice much quieter once they were back in the slumbering house.

She shouldn't have cared. Lasinia was her past, her lies, her secrets. She had a chance to create a future where she didn't have to hide. So what if Nyli had burnt it to the ground?

But Zyre had been right about one thing. She'd found her courage again. Seeing the rubble of *her* home set a seed of anger right in her chest. Nyli would pay. The Bérangers all would, for their crimes against her father, her brother, her home. The next time Zyre saw the prince, she would kill him.

She woke several hours later, just before the sun rose. The thoroughfare of the house had picked up enough that even Zyre was dragged back to consciousness. She rubbed her eyes, then became aware of a quiet popping sound.

Opening her bleary eyes with a groan, she found herself a little closer to the middle of the bed than she'd wished and scrambled backward, feeling very much, very suddenly, awake. But the bed was empty. Neelie sat in the middle of the room, half turned away from Zyre. With a soft *pop*, a fire appeared above Neelie's hand and then disappeared just as quickly.

"It's back," Zyre whispered. There was so much wrong in the world right then, but Neelie, returned to her home with her magic back under her command—that, at least, was *right*.

Neelie's latest flame disappeared with another soft, startling *pop*, and she dropped her arms into her lap, looking haughty. "Yes, well, took it long enough. Come on, do you want some breakfast?"

"What about Modorin?"

"Hmm." She grinned evilly. Striding up to Modorin on silent feet, she bent close to his ear and then shouted, "Get up, you lazy scoundrel!"

Modorin was up and flailing at the second word. Neelie laughed, and Zyre couldn't help it; she giggled too. The *sjarvisk* glared at both of them. "That's just not right, waking up a man like that," he said, yawning.

"I thought you might want breakfast," Zyre said, feigning innocence. Neelie just laughed harder.

"Come on, Modorin," Neelie said as she wiped away a tear. "I'm sure the cook will have some food to make you feel better."

Muttering to himself in Fresian, Modorin fell in line next to Zyre and they, with their soulbeasts, made their way to a large room furnished with a long table and enough chairs to fill it. Despite the early hour, many of the chairs were full, and not all of them by Venascans. Most of the room's occupants had visible tattoos, though, even the ones who weren't obviously a native to this country. Zyre recognized a few of them from last night, the Shadowmen or their healers.

The floor was speckled with soulbeasts and familiars, too. Ones that were stuck on the ground, anyway. A handful of perches had been installed to the ceiling, and Hosvar's raven, Berhôt, shared one such perch with a beautiful eagle owl.

Hosvar himself sat at the head of the table, deep in conversation with Kaspar Gehrig. Both glanced briefly as Neelie took her place at Hosvar's right but continued their discussion. Two women were already occupying the chairs next to Neelie, but they got up to make room for Modorin and Zyre. Zyre offered a clumsy "*Medias*," to which they smiled and bobbed their heads.

As she and Modorin sat, Zyre's hopes fell. There was no food on the table besides what was already on people's plates. It was quite the irony that even with the early hour, they'd somehow missed breakfast.

Before she could ask about it, though, two serving girls in unadorned linens appeared, balancing trays of food and drink for the three of them. Breakfast, it seemed, included several slices of buttered bread, a small bowl of porridge with strawberries—a small treat for her since they were incredibly hard to grow in Las

Corvika—a few strips of well-cooked bacon, and a cup of hot, bitter tea.

Eventually, Kaspar rose and left the room.

Neelie waited all of two seconds before grabbing her father's attention. They spoke quietly in Venascan.

Zyre turned to Modorin, determined to settle her question, to know just how broken-hearted she was going to be by the end of the day. "Will you stay in Bijal, then?"

He tore his attention away from Neelie's conversation. "Say again? Oh." He frowned, glancing at Neelie. Then he lowered his voice. "I don't know. It'd be nice, admittedly, to get out of the city and away from the fighting that's about to hit the streets."

"But?"

"But you're returning to your father, who is currently at the head of a rebellion. And if you come swooping in, you a fully re-alized *aljarne*, and bringing with you another *aljarne* and a rather powerful *sjarvisk*, well. He's going to be sorely disappointed, Zyre. I won't stay. I won't fight."

"I wouldn't ask you to, and my father wouldn't force you to stay for a cause you don't believe in."

He shrugged. "Hosvar won't want me to go anyway. It's no small thing, you know, fighting soldiers in the streets. They're going to need what help they can get."

"Would you want to fight for this cause?" Zyre asked, confused. He had, after all, deserted Syfris's army.

"For someone known as the Shadow King, Hosvar actually cares about the people in his district. Neelie got me out of Syfris, but Hosvar helped ensure I had everything I need. I suppose I owe him."

Out of the corner of her eye, she saw Hosvar rise. Berhôt flew to his outstretched hand. Chatter across the table stumbled as more than a few looked his way. He ignored them. Zyre, very much interested in whatever the two of them had been talking about, let the conversation between her and Modorin go. The *sjarvisk* seemed more than happy to do the same.

With the bird on his arm, he directed his attention to Zyre. "Finish your breakfast, *Magi* Zyre. I have a few things I need to tend to. But when you're done, meet me out back."

She nodded. Then the Shadow King strode out of the dining hall.

Unprompted, Neelie said, "Well, they put out an arrest warrant for me, and for Ren, and there's a bounty for information on anyone else involved. We have until midday to bring the wards down, or else *Freyr* Honir will bring his own *wyrdi* to unravel them. Either way, we need to be out of the city by then."

"What about your brother and the rest of the people involved?"

Neelie picked up her spoon and toyed with her porridge, the oats disgustingly congealed. With a grimace, she ate it anyway. "Ren will keep a low profile elsewhere for the next couple of days, just until things cool down. The *majican,* too, at least until we can say for certain if any of them could be recognized from the fight. The others should be safe so long as they're careful; Honir doesn't want the little men."

*Little men?* Zyre wondered. There was not a single 'small' man at this table, except perhaps Modorin. A Venascan turn of phrase, then.

But she knew one thing. If Modorin didn't want to get caught up in a fight, it was to her father's camp he must go, though it seemed that should not be the case. "If the *majican*"—she stumbled on the word but pressed on—"are at risk, Modorin is even more so. The both of us were seen running through well-lit hallways and stairwells. He may be in just as much danger as you."

Neelie set her spoon down and studied Modorin. Zyre held her breath. Finally, the other woman said, "Perhaps we can arrange for you to join us in our little escapade." She snorted. "If I'm going to be stuck in Las Corvika while all of the excitement is here, then I'm going to drag you with me."

"Do I get a say in this?" Modorin drawled. He did a good job at keeping his excitement—relief? Fear?—hidden.

"What part of 'drag you' do you not understand?" Neelie shoveled another spoonful of her porridge into her mouth before pushing the bowl away in disgust. "I hope you remember your way around an army camp, Modorin Kal, because that's exactly where the three of us are going."

Zyre beamed at Modorin, and her friend let slip a smile right back at her.

# CHAPTER 15

The thirteenth day in the capital dawned with hope for Ivanya. Pieces were falling into place, and if everything went according to plan, in four days' time, the family would be on their way to the safe confines of Jervin's camp. She looked up from her book. Damari sat on the floor with her son, both of them playing quietly with small twigs from the basket of kindling.

Ivanya had been unfair to Remy's wife. Damari had been the very last insult Notoyem had thrown at the Arnauds before Jervin had snapped completely, their regis not only refusing marriage between Remy and the princess, but also insisting that Remy marry some Venascan girl, and not even a noble one at that.

How disappointing it must have been for her. How excited she would have been to marry into Corvikan nobility, only to be shunned by them all.

When they got out of here, Ivanya planned on setting that to right.

"Damari," she began, but she was cut short when the doors flew open. Damari skittered back, her arms protectively around Bernard as two honor guards stormed into the room, followed closely by the regis himself.

Notoyem was not taller than Ivanya, thanks to her Crasik blood, but today his very presence was like smoke, rolling into the room, filling every nook and fissure with its suffocating substance. He wore a full suit of polished armor, its breastplate painted with the griffon, and a sheer cloak the color of burnt orange, an homage to Tholjun. His helmet was tucked in the crook of his arm, and his sword hung from his waist. Worst of all, though, was his terrible smugness.

Ivanya rose from her seat, doing her best curtsy with the book occupying one hand.

The regis sneered. "My son found your husband's rebels just as I said he would. You had your chance to save him. Now he's as good as dead. I hope you are prepared for widowhood, Baroness."

Her pride rebelled on instinct. The greatest prizes required the greatest risks, and widowhood was certainly a worthwhile price to pay for the chance at becoming queen, a *dirige* in the Corvikan vernacular.

"Your life, and the lives of the rest of your miserable family, will rely on my good graces," Notoyem continued. The sneer had fallen away, replaced by pity she did not want. "I shall give you one chance, and one alone, to prove your loyalty to my reign and your interest in keeping your family alive. How much do you know about the inner workings of your husband's army?"

"Very little, Your Highness. He never saw fit to share—" Her words were cut off as Notoyem was suddenly right in front of her, his fingers like a vice around her throat. Whatever kindness had been there before was yanked away, only to reveal that eternal burning anger.

"Don't play with me," he said.

Damari tried to intervene. A guard hauled her back as she screamed, "Your Highness, please! She cannot tell you if she cannot speak!"

Notoyem's attention flicked to the other woman, and then he snorted derisively. His hand fell away, and Ivanya sucked in a relieved breath, her throat burning as black spots skittered across her vision.

*Play with you?* Ivanya, still gasping, wanted to laugh. *You flatter yourself.*

Instead, she simpered, pretending that the regis had more of an effect on her. "But my husband…"

"Will be dead in a fortnight. Would you like your son to follow in his footsteps?"

Ivanya collapsed back into her chair, letting her book fall to the floor. "They have thirty powerful *sjarvisk* at their disposal, dispersed between the five branches of their army."

"Thirty!" Notoyem exclaimed. "You lie." His hands stayed at his side, though, and he did not advance.

"Yes, scattered amongst the five branches to do the most damage across the country. But we've had to operate in the shadows. We couldn't afford to make our army too big. All told, it is perhaps eight thousand men strong." Ivanya choked out a sob, her eyes watering through some effort. "I beg of you, Your Highness. Have mercy on my family. I only went along with this terrible plan because he is my husband and it is my place to support him."

"If I find out you're lying, I will make sure you watch the rest of your family die before you." Notoyem swept out. As he left the room, Ivanya heard him say, "Someone fetch me General Héroux."

The door slammed shut behind them, and a weight lifted from Ivanya's chest.

"Are you absolutely mad?" Damari hissed. She held Bernard protectively in her arms, and the poor boy trembled. "That was a terrible risk! What if he knew the truth? You would have shown your hand, and we would be dead! We certainly will be when he finds out your husband's real numbers!"

"By the time he learns the truth," Ivanya replied calmly, "we will be well out of Les Stelvo, and I may have just improved Jervin's chances considerably. Unless you think I should have encouraged Notoyem to call the many Houses' personal armies so that Jervin's own could be crushed? I doubt you would find it a pleasant future, answering to the whims of the tyrant once my husband fell."

Damari frowned. "I fear for my husband's life," she said, looking at her son.

"I'm glad. It means I'm not the only one worrying about him. But we do what we must." Ivanya brightened. "Besides, with Notoyem out of the castle and with most of his troops gone with him, our escape might've gotten that much easier. Have heart, Damari. We may get out of this yet."

⁂

Zyre's stomach roiled with a sudden, persistent fear as her companions finished their meals, and she found herself wishing, fervently, that she hadn't eaten anything. Almost two weeks, she'd waited for this, and now that the day had finally arrived… It wasn't that she didn't want it anymore. After what she'd seen last night, that couldn't be further from the truth.

It was just that her entire world was about to change. She was committing herself to Tholjun. To war. To death.

She kept a protective hand on Kadj's shoulder as she followed Neelie and Modorin through the house. Modorin flashed looks of concern her way, but if either he or Neelie sensed her hesitation, she was grateful that they kept their silence. Despite her fear, this *felt* right. She was tired of secrets and of explosive magic. She was ready to be *Vinjess* Zyre Arnaud, *aljarne* daughter of Baron Jervin Arnaud.

Especially after her late-night travels, Zyre was growing familiar enough with the layout of the house to recognize the path that would lead them to the backyard, to the *velídas* tree. Hosvar waited for them there, standing behind a makeshift table, but he was not alone. Old Kaspar Gehrig stood beside the *wyrdis*, their heads bent together in quiet discussion, and even Neelie's brother had come, though she did not appreciate the implications behind the presence of his swords.

There was an odd smell to the air, like rain, though there were no clouds to be seen and the grass held not a single drop of dew.

Hosvar took note of them, but his conversation with Gehrig did not falter. He picked up a piece of metal. There were a few last-minute things to prepare, and as soon as it became obvious that there would be a small wait, Neelie strode across the yard, joining her brother along the fence. Modorin hesitated only a few moments, beckoning Zyre to follow, but she held back. Right now, she could not have made small talk to save her life.

She gestured for Modorin to go ahead, and he did.

Instead, she walked toward the table, watching Hosvar work.

"I hope you are not angry that I'm about to undo your work," she told Gehrig.

"You'll forgive me if I am, a little," the man replied. Hosvar darted a glance at both of them but said nothing. "Your spell was my last great achievement as a *kjarnik*."

A thought struck her. "I will not lose my magic by breaking with Kadj, will I?"

Hosvar shook his head. "From what I saw on the beach, I don't think so. A soulbeast does not lose their magic when their human dies; it is only true when the opposite occurs, and you function as the soulbeast in this bonding. But, of course, there's no way to know. Anything could happen. If you are not prepared for the possibility that you might lose your magic, then you should reconsider this plan."

Hope, foolish, inexplicable hope, surged in her chest. She almost found herself asking, *could I really? Could I be normal?* But even considering the present company, it seemed unfathomable that she might ever consider such an outcome as good. Her magic was a part of her. She was not *Zyre* without it.

Instead, she said, "When a soulbeast loses their human, they go feral. What are the chances that either he or I go mad? Or both?"

"Animals don't *go feral*; they just return to their normal state. They have no magic, their aging returns to normal, and they're no more or less friendly to humans than their non-magic counterparts. But there is no precedent for you, *Magi* Zyre. No way to know what's coming," Hosvar replied.

"He came from an animal show," Kaspar said quietly. "Well-trained to do tricks, friendly with humans. None of that had to do with a *leiks*. With luck, he may simply lose some of his polish."

Zyre glanced at Hosvar, hoping for some confirmation. The *wyrdis* only grimaced and said, "I'm ready if you are."

Zyre looked toward her friends and found their conversation silenced. They knew. It was time.

"I'm ready."

"Then step back, please," Hosvar said.

Zyre and Kadj put several feet between them and the *wyrdis*. She put a steadying hand on Kadj's shoulder blades.

*Tholjun, give me fortitude. Let me be brave.*

Hosvar grabbed a metal disk from his table. He closed his eyes, muttered a few words. Berhôt cawed suddenly from high up on the velídas tree's silver branches.

*Thyljal, protect Kadj and help him remember who and what he is.*

The *wyrdis* drew his arm back, readying for the throw. As it left his fingertips, Zyre cast out one last, frightened prayer.

*Thalja, guard my future.*
*The disk hurtled through the air.*
*Tell me I'm doing the right thing.*

Then it stopped abruptly in the space between her and Kadj, still spinning, suspended several feet above the ground. Hosvar began to hum, the sound blooming from deep within his chest. It sounded familiar, like a song she'd heard one of the street performers play, but she did not know the tune.

Zyre continued to watch the disk spin, even as it felt like something was winding itself around her middle at the same speed that it spun. The *thing*, the strand of magic, began to tighten. For the second time, Zyre felt Hosvar's peculiar magic squeeze her breath right out of her. Her heart pounded so roughly in her chest that it almost threw off her balance.

She tore her eyes away from the disk, looking frantically for Neelie. A muted version of her own fear was mirrored on the other woman's face.

At her side, Kadj whimpered. It was a gruff, short growl. Ren reached quietly for his swords, drew them but did not advance. *Keep your mind, Kadj. If one of us is going to lose our sanity, it's supposed to be me.*

The tightness in her chest grew. She clutched at her shirt, wanting to be free to breathe the way she needed. Finally, she fell to her knees, crashing hard into the ground. She could feel the surge of magic, the wildness akin to Velídas, but this time, she could not find out how to ride the waves.

Black spots speckled her vision. Any second now, she was going to pass out.

Then, suddenly, something seemed to break. The invisible ropes of magic snapped, and Zyre inhaled hungrily, wheezing.

Slowly, her breathing fell back to normal, and something else grabbed her attention. It was as if something had awoken in her blood. Her veins thundered with it. Magic, raw magic, ready to be accessed, begging to be called.

So she did, and it answered her summons as naturally as a bud bloomed in spring. The elements appeared in front of her, casting her vision in shades of orange, then blue, then silver, then brown. Brown! Even the earth was more willing to listen.

The rasp of steel brought her back. Zyre found herself automatically stepping between Kadj and Ren. She would protect her tiger even if he had gone feral.

Then her mind caught up, realizing that the rasp was only Ren sheathing his weapons. Zyre spun, fearing to hope.

Kadj was silent. He lay on the ground, head on his paws, breathing too fast. She scrambled down to her hands and knees, perching beside him, hand outstretched, hesitating.

"Kadj? Are you okay?"

Zyre searched for Hosvar, her throat burning. The *wyrdis* leaned heavily on his table, his spectacles riding too far down his nose.

"What's wrong with him? Is he dying? *Wyrdi* Hosvar, please."

Neelie's father looked up, the exhaustion deadening his eyes. But it was Ren who answered. "It doesn't matter, does it, Father? Neelie, you need to go, and you need to bring your *najik* with you."

"Right now? But Kadj—"

"I'll take care of him," Gehrig said, tearing his attention away from Hosvar. "As I did all those years ago on our way to your island."

Leave? Kadj? She'd been afraid he'd be lost to her, and now that it was a possibility she could keep him, that he'd remain tame enough to stay, it was unfathomable. "I can't!"

Hosvar straightened. He pushed his spectacles farther up his nose. "Ren, go fetch Edny. She should be sleeping in one of the guest quarters."

Neelie's brother rolled his shoulders and stalked off.

Zyre didn't know who this Edny figure was. She waited protectively beside Kadj. If Edny was the one who would tear her away from Kadj, she'd be in for a surprise.

Sarol poked his nose against the tiger's face gently until Modorin stooped down and brought his fox into his arms. Modorin stayed near. Zyre was grateful for it. She ran a worried hand over the length of Kadj's side, felt as his breathing slowed, but only just.

A pair of footsteps drew near. Neelie put a hand on Zyre's shoulder. The gesture was awkward, lacking comprehension, but at that moment, Zyre was just glad the other *aljarne* was not trying to draw her away. Kadj was still *hers*. Maybe not her soulbeast, not anymore, but he was still her tiger, her one constant companion growing up. He had protected her from her own magic, both from the madness and from the explosive power of it. He had never looked through her as if she were nothing.

When Edny came, she brought with her a tall black and brown dog. She nodded to Zyre as she knelt next to Kadj. The woman's dark eyes were rimmed with exhaustion, her hair a wild black expanse atop her head. Yet she moved with a determined fluidness as she drew out a pendant and pressed it against Kadj's side. She asked a series of questions, directed both at Neelie and

Hosvar. Zyre searched for Modorin, begging for an interpretation, for news, but his attention was locked on Edny.

Wishing her Venascan were better, that they didn't talk so fast, she bounced on her heels, searching their tone and their expressions for bad news.

After a few minutes, the *kjarnik* left.

"Well?" Zyre demanded.

Modorin threw Neelie a weighted glance, then answered, "Zyre, we're going to have to leave without him."

She sat down heavily on the ground.

"He's going to be okay," he added quickly. "But that was no small spell, and he's just had magic stripped out of him. He needs to be able to sleep, and Edny thinks he may need time to adjust to the fact that he has no magic."

"He should be with me," Zyre insisted. "He'll take it better if I'm by his side. And I can't leave him in Bijal! Who knows when I'll be able to come back? And with everything happening here, it's not safe."

"It's far safer here than it'll be in a war camp."

His words cut deep. He would know. Of course he would know. But it was *Kadj*. He'd been by her side for eleven years. How could she leave him now?

"Zyre," Neelie said softly. "No one is better equipped to keep an eye on him. My father has a whole army of *wyrdi*, and Kaspar, and himself. Honir will not bother with a lone tiger. And I promise I will bring him back to you as soon as I am able, once he is better. "

Her vision swam. She bent down to kiss Kadj. "Thalja watch over you," she said into his fur. Then she pulled herself to her feet, squared her shoulders, and steadied her nerves. "If we're going to go, then let's go."

Neelie looked to Modorin, to her father, but shrugged. She

hugged Hosvar, who already seemed far steadier, then Ren. And then, just like that, they were leaving.

Sequestered in her room, Neelie was trying and failing not to think as she packed up for the journey ahead.

Although Neelie's parents had never once made her wish she'd been born without magic, there were certainly times where she'd hated herself for it. There had been nights when she'd prayed to Skï, hoping for some way to rid herself of it so she might be normal. They'd been small moments, doubts she'd never voiced. And it had been some time since she'd let them reach her.

Bard's magic had scared her more than she was willing to admit. And now that she'd had the night to think about it, she had come to accept her father's reasoning. It wasn't just about not having magic; it was about losing control, of coming face to face with that inescapable *najik* reality.

Neelie wanted to stay. Her magic burned in her veins, sparked at her fingertips. As they darted around the house to gather their things, every single Shadowman she passed woke something terrifying and harsh inside her. She wanted to rip the streets apart. She wanted to blast down *Freyr* Honir's halls with white-hot fire. She wanted to freeze the very blood in *Wyrdi* Bard's body. It terrified her, this lust for violence. She was afraid if she stayed, the temptation would break her completely.

So she threw spare clothes into a bag, too restless to fold them properly. Modorin helped her; he didn't keep much at the Raven's Head, and there wasn't time to run to his lodgings on the other side of town to fetch anything else. He packed what he had, including some things for Sarol, and she packed what she could, and then they went to the common area where a few badly wounded

Shadowmen continued to heal or slept off the spells. Kadj was on a low table there. Zyre stood over him protectively.

Zyre, of course, had nothing to pack. Everything had been sent to the *Lemanthus* last night.

Neelie stopped a few feet away. The other woman looked up from her sleeping tiger—whose breathing, Neelie noted with some relief, had slowed back to normal—and her eyes were steely. She kissed Kadj gently between his ears, and when she broke away, Neelie could tell it took a lot of effort, even as she stormed out of the Raven's Head.

She knew what it meant for Zyre, in a way, that determination to just *move*. It was either run away now or get stuck behind.

Neelie hurried to catch up, taking the lead so she could direct Zyre and Modorin through shortcuts. They weren't heading for the Sector of the Gulls; Honir would be watching for them there. But Honir didn't know half of what he should about his own city.

The roads grew less populated the farther away the three of them got from the Raven's Head. Everyone was either already waiting near her house for orders or else they were smart enough to stay inside. She hoped if it came down to it, they would remember who it was who had made sure they had food in their bellies and roofs over their heads. She hoped if her father called for aid, there would be more than just their *Hædros dir en Schadra* who answered.

The *Lemanthus* was moored in the very cove that Zyre had seen her magic tested in. It was small enough that it barely warranted the name, but it was secluded from prying eyes and often served as a hub for her mother's side of Shadowmen dealings.

As they reached the fringes of the city, though, Neelie gestured for them to slow their step. Honir would theoretically have the bulk of his forces patrolling Bijal, ready to swoop into the Shadow

Quarter as soon as the wards went down, but if he was expecting people to flee, she didn't want to run straight into his hands.

Crouching behind a building, she rummaged through her bag until she found her spyglass. To her left was the beach, eerily empty despite the heat pressing down on them. To the right, trees. She searched for any indication that soldiers were hiding in the shadows.

"I think we're all clear," she muttered.

Then, suddenly, the ground rumbled and pitched forward, and she nearly smashed her face into the cobblestones. She heard something crash and break within the building next to her and had to reach out to steady herself as another, smaller, wave of tremors came, sending her friends to the ground.

Neelie's vision flickered suddenly. Then again.

No, not her vision. The wards were breaking.

Scowling, Neelie trusted her hard-won sailors' instincts to keep herself upright as she hauled her friends to their feet. They had to get out of this city.

"Come on, before these buildings collapse on us," Neelie snapped.

They needed no further prodding. The three of them ran, Sarol flying on their heels, past the last few houses, angling toward the beach. The pavement gave way to red sand that shifted under her feet.

The forest crept up on the beach, skirting the edges of it. Her steady breaths ran in tandem with her footfalls. Then the sand fell away and they were dodging trees and underbrush, the alcove a pinprick of light that expanded the closer they got. The trees broke apart to reveal the cove. There she sat: the *Lemanthus*. A modest ship, a skimmer, it was nothing like the *Telaña dir Ansol*, but it would serve.

Best of all was the fact that, amidst its small crew, Neelie already recognized the figure barking orders on its deck.

"Vidar!" Neelie called out as they drew near the water's edge. The Shadowman broke off from his duties and trotted to the railing. "I hope she's ready!"

"Near enough," Vidar shouted back. "We haven't secured all the supplies, but everything is aboard save you."

"Then I suppose we'd best board as well."

She waded into the cold, foamy water, grateful that the *Lemanthus* had a shallow enough belly that it could skirt the beach. Vidar threw a rope over and helped haul them up. Modorin went last, Sarol draped over his shoulders.

Her trousers dripping water all over the deck, Neelie did her best to wring herself out. Then, suddenly, the water just fell, leaving her mostly dried. Modorin grinned devilishly, already dry, and turned to do the same for Zyre.

"Your father should really give me more warning when it comes to a thing like this," Vidar rumbled with a shake of his head. "Honestly. It's a wonder I was able to supply the ship as well as I did."

"We'll just have to make do. I don't expect this trip to take long, anyway."

In her periphery, she saw Zyre's blank expression. Neelie switched into Corvikan, saying, "You should probably go below deck for now. I'll send for you when it's safe."

Modorin was far more eager to reach the belly of the ship than Zyre. He wasn't looking green yet, but once the *Lemanthus* was out on open waters, he'd be miserable.

Neelie strode to the helm. She could not dwell. Until the ship had set its path, she did not trust herself not to jump out and run back home. Three days to sail, two more to walk. That was more than enough time for her mother to arrive in Bijal, settle things, and come fetch her. Her father had given her a charm, the same kind of spell as his bowl of ships so she could keep tabs on her mother's location.

Five days, by the looks of it, and then she could come home. Surely that was long enough for her to find her mind.

If Zyre could be courageous enough to leave Kadj behind, she could leave Bijal.

"Draw the anchor!" she bellowed to her crew. "The waves of Dûl swallow us whole!"

"And the light of Skï bring us home!" came the reply from a dozen voices.

The *Lemanthus*'s sails pressed into the wind, and the ship withdrew from the cove, bound, finally, for Las Corvika.

# CHAPTER 16

The *Lemanthus* sailed up the coast for three days straight. The scenery passed by with deathly slowness, but waiting below deck was even worse with nothing to pass the time. Zyre lasted all of one day before she took to the deck to practice her magic. Leaving Kadj behind had to mean something. If she still had no control, then she would have been better off keeping her tiger bound to her. So on the second day, in one corner that was as out of the way as could be on the small ship, Zyre faced the ocean, her back to the coast. She let her vision shift blue. The magic answered immediately and in force. It wasn't just the water around the boat; it was the air she was breathing, heavy with the sea spray.

She raised her hand, watching as the little blue orbs parted ways. With small, quiet gestures, Zyre let her magic course through her, shooting through her arms, sparking at her fingertips. The water in the air coalesced. A ball of it the size of her head dripped onto the railing. Curious, she hardened the sphere into ice and sent it into the empty space before her. It wasn't until the ice was fifty feet away that she found herself really straining to hold the magic.

Zyre let the ice go and watched as it was swallowed by the waves.

A laugh bubbled out of her chest. Blue turned to orange. She blasted a fireball at a distant wave, and it crashed with a steamy explosion. She let the smallest flame rest above her hand, warming her fingers, dancing harmlessly. Orange to silver. A gust of wind caressed the sails at her behest, and the *Lemanthus* surged forward.

Zyre tapped her fingers thoughtfully. She saw Neelie move in her periphery. Grinning, Zyre sent another, smaller, wind past Neelie, and the unbound tips of her hair waved in the breeze. The other woman frowned, glancing over her shoulder. When their eyes met, she raised a disapproving eyebrow.

Zyre dropped her arm and turned away quickly, feeling her cheeks burn. *Silver to brown, silver to brown,* she thought, hoping that if she ignored the footsteps, then Neelie wouldn't actually say anything about her foolish display. There was so little earth within her reach, but the *Lemanthus* was not without dust. She reached out —

"You should be careful not to use too much too quickly," Neelie's voice said behind her.

Her embarrassment surging, Zyre decided the safest thing to do was to keep gazing at the railing in front of her. "I was just testing my control."

"How is it? Does it feel much different now, without Kadj?"

At the mention of her tiger, Zyre's heart contracted. She hoped he was feeling better. "It helps, being at sea. It just feels like there's so much more magic out here."

"I'm glad. Just," Neelie began. She grimaced. "With your soulbeast, you didn't have to worry about limits. Without him, you do."

Oh, she was well aware. That was not something an *aljarne*

could ever conveniently forget. "I am just worried I won't know what my limits are until I've surpassed them."

Neelie barked out a laugh. "I think you'll know. The problem is you're most likely to hit it when you use big magic, and if you need to use big magic, well…. You may not have much of a choice."

Zyre frowned, eyeing her companion out of the corner of her periphery. "Have you gotten close?"

Neelie fell completely still, her expression unreadable. "Once," she said curtly.

Then she cursed over her shoulder in Venascan, yelling at some sailor as she strode away from Zyre. She didn't even look back once, and the poor soul who had directed her anger looked as lost as Zyre.

Well, practicing her magic no longer felt like a good idea.

Not knowing what else to do, Zyre surrendered and returned below deck, knowing Modorin, at least, would not deny her his company.

⁂

Zyre resurfaced at night, as her thoughts and fears made her restless. The crew's thundering footsteps had quieted some time earlier. She crossed Neelie's path at the stairs, Zyre going up as Neelie went down. The other woman was lost in thought. Her attention honed in on Zyre for a brief moment, though, and Neelie offered a ghost of a smile. Then they were outside of each other's view. Zyre stepped on the deck, comforted by the night's cool breeze.

She stayed there for some time.

Kadj would have loved it. Zyre would have had her hands full keeping him from the railing.

In only a few days, they would find her father's camp. Now

that they weren't trying to hide under the Bérangers' thumb, Zyre could be acknowledged as an Arnaud at last. How thrilling it would be, not having to hide anymore. However worried she was about everything else, she had that, at least, to look forward to.

Her moonlit wandering did little to calm her mind, but Zyre knew she needed to rest and eventually returned to her bed, somehow managing to find herself asleep.

The next morning was all abuzz with activity. The *Lemanthus* was to arrive at its destination around noon, and even Neelie's sudden standoffishness—which Modorin now fretted over, though he told Zyre not to push Neelie—couldn't keep her from pacing on the deck. Modorin hobbled up the stairs with her, Zyre watching him as nervously as Sarol. He hadn't been up once since they'd set sail. He said the fresh air would do him some good, but she was pretty sure he just wanted to keep an eye out on Neelie.

"Do you know of Haveil?" Modorin asked her, looking a little green.

Zyre shook her head.

"I'm not surprised. It's a small fishing town, nothing more. But there's a convenient little bay in the area. The ship will drop us off there."

They made good time, and eventually, just as Modorin said, the ship turned toward a small bay. When the *Lemanthus* dropped anchor, the water was waist-deep, which was not a problem for Neelie and hardly one for Zyre. Modorin had to steady himself against the side of the ship so the tide didn't send him tumbling, and Sarol leapt in without hesitation, heading straight for the beach.

Holding their heavy packs above their heads, the three of them followed Sarol.

Once they reached land and pulled the water from their soggy shoes, Neelie announced that the other two would both wait while she went into town to buy horses. Zyre was the least likely to stand out, of course, as a native Corvikan, but there was no way to be absolutely sure people wouldn't be looking for her.

Between Neelie and Modorin, the latter knew horses best, but between a Venascan and a Syfresian, it was the former who would draw the fewest looks. Most people fleeing the south went to Atlor or crossed the sea to Pailyr. Las Corvika was not a magnet for war refugees. But Venascan trade? That was another matter entirely.

So Zyre parted with a good chunk of her coins to help pay for the horses, hoping Neelie knew at least half as much about them as she knew about ships.

***

Haveil was not an impressive town. At this time of year, harvests should be bolstering the economy, yet far too many of the people wore clothes that fit a little too loose on their frame. Their smiles didn't quite reach their eyes, and the chatter was subdued. Someone was willing to give Neelie directions to a decent tavern, and she made her way there quickly. A quick gossip pitstop hadn't been part of the plan, but she wanted to know what they were walking into.

The tavern was called The Brass Knob and was appropriately empty considering the hour.

An old man in an apron bustled over to her. Neelie didn't miss the way his eyes darted toward the door or the way he frowned at the empty space around her. "Can I help you?" he asked, taking unnecessary care with his pronunciations.

Neelie rolled her eyes. "I'm waiting for a friend," she said coolly. Then, to appease him, she said, "I wouldn't mind a cup of ale while I wait."

Looking very much like a rooster with its feathers ruffled, the innkeeper hurried off. Neelie scanned the room, taking note of where the groups were and which ones might actually be talking about the things she was trying to listen for. Finally, she took a seat at one of the center tables where she was roughly equidistant from the three main groups. One had the look of merchants, their travel-worn clothes still a little too fine to fit in. The others could have been from Haveil or the next town over but were certainly all local.

The innkeeper set her mug down and darted off before she even realized he had arrived. Her annoyance spiked, and she was tempted to throw a candle-sized flame at him.

"We're not at war," a fellow from one of the local tables said insistently, snatching Neelie's attention.

"Then explain the soldiers my cousins saw marching out of the capital, Ivat," said another.

The man named Ivat slammed his cup against the table.

"Hey, watch it!" the innkeeper snapped from across the room.

Ivat's cheeks colored, but his voice was still vehement. "It's those thrice-cursed bandits that have been roving around the countryside, stealing poor folks' food and money, destroying fields. Regis Béranger, may the gods bless his reign, is finally putting a stop to it. He already chased off the band that's plagued us for months."

Ivat's little temper tantrum had gotten them more than just Neelie's attention now. One of the merchants turned in his chair, saying, "They aren't bandits! My cousin's friend was there a week and a half ago. He *saw* them heading north, enough to populate a small town! And there's been rumor, hasn't there, about the regis outside his castle and men pulled from their fields to march behind his banner?"

Neelie raised an eyebrow, taking a long draught of her weak ale. *What are you up to, Jervin?*

A week and a half ago… That would have been before he'd given Zyre his message. But if "we sit in the shadow of the Bérangers" didn't mean Les Stelvo, where else? She couldn't afford to go on a wild goose chase, searching through the entirety of northern Las Corvika.

"Marching north?" Ivat said incredulously. "Well, there you have it. They were fleeing the regis's men. There won't be a war; they're a bunch of cowards is all."

The merchant laughed derisively. "Do you know what is in the north? The Áit. Men have been congregating there, and rumor has it there are standards flying. I can't say for certain if there'll be a war, but there will most certainly be a battle. If you had any plans on traveling north anytime soon, you'd best forget them." At that, he returned his attention to his companions.

Neelie grinned, thanking Skï.

Unfortunately, she couldn't leave just yet, or else it would be pretty clear she'd only been here to eavesdrop. Neelie rifled discreetly through her pockets, letting them wrap around a cool metal disk. She set it onto the table and studied it, sipping her drink. The disk was engraved and painted, though it was clearly quick work, showing a map of the local waters from Bijal to just north of the Áit river and the entire coastline in between. A small metal piece in the shape of a whale, her mother's soulbeast, still sat atop Bijal. It had been there almost two full days now.

Well, her instructions were to wait in Las Corvika until things had settled down enough for her mother to come fetch her. They might as well follow the baron to the Áit. If they rode fast enough, they'd only lose a few days, and Adreia could follow her there.

*If my mother hasn't come to fetch me by then, though, I swear by Dùl, I'm racing back home and putting an end to* Freyr Honir's *reign even if I have to burn the whole city to the ground.* Neelie grimaced. *No. Not the whole city. But I will turn his house to ash.*

Neelie tossed a few copper *pengs* onto the table. She shook her head for good measure, as if too impatient to wait for the friend she'd mentioned to the innkeeper. With her disk back in her pocket, she hit the streets.

After only a few inquiries, she learned of a stable close to the edges of town, probably for travelers such as herself.

There was, of course, a chance that the stable wouldn't have what they needed. *Majican*-trained horses were not common, and they were not cheap.

Skï favored her this day, though, because the stable master assured her that he had a few. He was a little older, with gray in his hair and a quiet demeanor that was rare for such an occupation. He showed her four—two brown horses, a black, and one with a black-and-white pattern. The latter was restless, prancing around, shaking his mane. She liked that he wanted to run, like she did, but she had a feeling he'd be more than she could handle.

After Neelie exchanged an unfortunate amount of gold for the two bays and a black, the stable master had one of his sons put tack on all three, with a lead rope for the two she'd be taking to her friends. She mounted the taller bay, liking the feel of him under her.

After thanking the stable master and his son, she gave her horse a soft kick of her heels, setting the bay at a brisk trot. The other two's *clip-clop* was a satisfying echo. Neelie rode with intent, and the residents of Haveil were quick to get out of her way.

She had a war to catch.

⁂

After what felt like hours, Neelie came riding back to them on a gorgeous bay with kind eyes and legs built for speed. Two horses plodded behind her, already saddled up and ready to ride.

"What took you so long?" Modorin asked, eyeing the horses and seeming as content as Zyre.

"Following a line of information, you ingrate," Neelie replied as she dismounted. "Zyre, there's a map in my bag. See if you can find it. The rumor in town is that soldiers are congregating on the Áit." She peered over her horse's withers as she passed Modorin the black gelding.

"Here, I'll just hold the horses," Zyre said, leaping to extract them from Neelie. Better that than going through her things.

Neelie rolled her eyes as she passed them over. It did not take her long to find the map of Las Corvika, and she brought it back to Zyre. "If your father didn't mean Les Stelvo by his 'Béranger's shadow' comment, what else could he have meant?"

Trying not to look too closely at the edge of the map where Lasinia sat, Zyre studied the country thoughtfully. "You said the Áit?"

Neelie nodded.

She pointed to a fortress a few miles north of the river and its fork. "Mod Redel belongs to House Béranger. They must be camped somewhere near there." Zyre looked up from the map. "Why did you buy these horses if you knew he wasn't where we thought? You're not coming with me, are you?"

Neelie looked at her flatly. "Of course I'm coming. I promised, didn't I?"

"But it's going to take us days to get there. What about your mother?"

"She'll find me, don't worry."

Modorin shot Zyre a fake glare as he finished fastening his things to the saddle. "One might think you didn't want us here."

Zyre flashed him the rude gesture she'd seen Neelie make, but it only made him laugh. Neelie put the map back in her bag and took her horse from Zyre. They both made quick work of their own saddlebags, and then the three of them mounted up.

"How good is your riding, Zyre?" Neelie asked with a wicked grin. Before she could answer, Neelie heeled her horse into a trot.

Zyre urged her own mare faster to catch up. She would not be outdone by the seafarer. Careful not to ride too close to Sarol, Zyre passed Modorin and rode levelly with Neelie. Then, suddenly, the other woman kicked her horse's flanks, and the beast surged forward.

With a laugh, Zyre kicked her own horse into a gallop, and then it was a race on the open road, the path only big enough to fit two horses abreast. They thundered on, Zyre's mount quickly catching up.

They raced until they noticed how far back Modorin had fallen, unwilling to draw too far ahead from his soulbeast. Laughing, truly laughing, Zyre conceded the race, and they both walked their horses back to their slow friend. Already, Haveil was nothing more than a speck behind them.

⁜

Traveling cross-country was not as fast as any of them would have liked, and Zyre especially chafed at the pace.

Despite Modorin's protest, though, the horses did actually hurry things along. They alternated between trotting in the saddle and walking beside their mounts, both to give the horses and their own backsides a break. Zyre's guard shifts with Telpari had never given her saddle sores, and she learned they were even more unpleasant than they sounded.

With Modorin taking charge of the map, Zyre was allowed to tour her own country for the first time in her life. In a way, it almost felt as alien as Bijal. They cut through towns where people strode purposefully to and from their destinations. More than a few times, Zyre noticed glares being sent their way. It surprised her. She'd expected to draw curious stares, and there was certainly some of that, but the mistrust in some of those gazes really took her breath away. It broke her heart. There was so little music. The stone walls were too often crumbling. And the people, *her* people, looked harried in a way that contrasted so starkly from the easy confidence of the people of Bijal.

But the landscape was just as telling. In those first few days, the places in between towns held the normalcy that Zyre had been expecting. They passed houses with small plots of farmland, and they passed great fields of flowers. They even crossed a few oddly constructed garden houses with enchantments cast into the metal frames, where Zyre knew coveted fragrances like jasmine and ginger grew. If time had been on their side, she might've asked to tour one of them. No country did perfumes better than Las Corvika, and those garden houses were at the center of it.

There wasn't always a town in view as the sun began to set, and sometimes, it was a village they stumbled on, with an innkeeper who took one look at them and insisted on a sum too ridiculous for them to part with for such measly rooms. So, more often than not, they slept under the stars. The ground was hard, and sleep sometimes took a long time coming, but they would sit around the fire until the sun was well and truly out of sight, talking about things that didn't matter.

On one such night, after clouds had gathered throughout most of the day and with no chance that they would find an inn before nightfall, rain crashed down onto them before they could even set up camp. Neelie said something to Modorin, who gave her a strange look, filled with worry that Zyre probably wasn't supposed to have seen. Modorin enlisted Zyre's help, not Neelie's, to construct an earthen shanty to hide beneath. They made one for the horses, too, and by the end of it, her head was spinning and she felt a little cranky, the curious exchange already forgotten.

They started a small fire and withdrew some of their provisions, and in the course of their conversation, they somehow got onto the topic of gods and magic.

"I'm just saying, I don't get it," Modorin insisted. "How is Tholjun not the same as Dûl, if he is as bloodthirsty as you say?"

"He's not evil incarnate, you heathen," Zyre said in exasperation. Neelie snickered. "Oh, don't be rude, Neelie; you are just as lost as he is."

"Never said I wasn't."

Rolling her eyes, Zyre pressed on. "Tholjun is the god of life *and* death. In battle, he will protect the devout, but he is a god, and the protection of a god is not free. If you are lucky, it's the other side that pays the price. We bless all *sjarvisk* under Tholjun's name because their power comes from him. The fire they wield is his fire, and the destruction they cause is his to feast upon."

"And let me guess," Neelie said, still laughing. "We *aljarne* are blessed by Thalja the Merciful."

"*Aljarne* don't get blessed by the gods," Zyre said, her humor dying like fire by water. "Las Corvika prefers to pretend *aljarne* are just monsters from old stories. We don't exist."

Their small fire flared suddenly. Its light cast a dark, writhing shadow across Neelie's face, and when the rain slammed into their earthen walls, Zyre knew it was Neelie's doing. "Except we do," the *najik* said.

"Except we do," Zyre agreed, her anger dissipating as quickly as it had come.

Modorin shoved Zyre good-naturedly. Even Neelie smiled, her own anger gone.

"Thalja is the champion of the non-magic folk, actually. On

the battlefield, at any rate. She is their shield against an onslaught of magic against those who cannot defend themselves magically against it." She shrugged. "Thyljal the Creator is the benefactor of *kjarnik*, because what they make—it's not a weapon."

"Except it can be," Neelie said. "I know for a fact Las Corvikans use *kjarnik*-enhanced weaponry."

Modorin, unhelpful as always, gestured in emphatic agreement with Neelie's sentiment.

"Yes, all right, but they don't *make* the weapons. They just make them more dangerous. Which," Zyre amended, "I suppose that doesn't help my argument. But. *But*. I mean, just think about all the things that *kjarnik can* do. They can heal people. They can make things grow. There is art woven into their very enchantments. Maybe they don't create, exactly, but their sole purpose is not to destroy. And what are we, *sjarvisk* and *aljarne*, who burn and crumble buildings and kill, what are we but destruction incarnate?"

Neelie scowled, and Modorin drummed his fingers against his knee. Zyre found her shoulders falling, realizing too late that what she'd wanted was for them to prove her wrong. To be able to fight alongside her father knowing that, when it was all said and done, she could still have a use beyond doing the thing she detested above all else: killing.

And then Modorin raised a hand, one finger pointing up at the ceiling above their heads. "Does making a little house not count, then?"

They all laughed at that, and the tension dissipated.

After talking for just a little while longer, Zyre felt the familiar tug of exhaustion. They curled up on their sides of the fire, forming a loose triangle. Zyre found she wasn't as bothered by Neelie's proximity as she'd been during their last night in Bijal.

Riding for days in anyone's company would do that to a person, she supposed.

Either way, as soon as she lay down, she tumbled off into sleep.

The next morning, they were off again, leaving the little earthen shanties where they stood. And, later that very evening, they finally found the wake of destruction that came from traveling bands of soldiers. They had forged the road wider in some places, then left the path altogether, wandering into the trees. A few paces off, though, and all tracks of the army disappeared, leaving only strange fissures in the ground and the trees leaning. Modorin dismounted and inspected the trail. He walked along the road, searching the fissures for answers.

"I think they're trying to throw off potential pursuit," he said finally. "Do those marks look familiar to you?"

They did, but Zyre thought it was a ludicrous line of thought. "But why bother? They can't hide the entire army's trail for any length of time. That'd be a stupid waste of *sjarvisk* energy."

Modorin shrugged. "I can see the uses for the short term, though. Level an entire area, and any pursuers would have to search the entire circumference to figure out where the trail started up again. Laeris employed similar tactics to get in and out of hot zones."

Neelie urged her horse forward. "All right, then. What do we do?"

"Map."

Zyre passed it over, watching, with some level of amusement, as he tilted the page first one way, then the other. "Are you struggling to read it, then? I can take a turn if you need a break."

He lowered the map a fraction of an inch so he could glare at her over its edge, then returned to studying. "No," he said finally. "The road here will lead us to a town called Toritet. It winds a little, but it'll be faster to cover it than it would be to go cross-country. From Toritet, it's a short ride to the fork that sends the Gouvelle from the Áit, and as long as we can ford it, we'll find your father's army there."

"How long?" Zyre asked so Neelie wouldn't have to.

"Two days?"

Zyre's heart sank. In two days, she would finally join her father's ranks, help him win the crown, and free them of the danger of Béranger's army. She would pay back Nyli for the destruction of her home. "Then we follow the road," she said quietly.

In two days, her friends would leave her. If they didn't offer, she would make them. Zyre did not want them to witness the killer she would have to become to survive this war.

Modorin mounted, and they were off.

⁂

Ivanya held a small torn piece of a fine fishing net, running her fingers along the rough lines. It was time. Any minute now, one of their allies would walk through that door, lead them down some secret passage, and give them their freedom. Ivanya wasn't one to let her nerves show, but she held on to that square of net like a lifeline. Damari was trying to keep calm too, for Bernard's sake, but if they got caught, there would be no spinning this out of disaster.

They waited in the sitting room. The traffic that walked down this stretch of hallway had grown minimal these past few days, and each patter of footsteps made Ivanya tense, waiting for the inevitable fight to break loose. But this newest set sounded all wrong—thunderous and stormy, made up of at least a handful of men. Surely Fidou would have sent a discrete number, focused on stealth rather than power.

A muffled conversation took place on the other side of the

door. Ivanya looked at Damari, confusion and worry bubbling toward the surface. This was wrong. All wrong.

Ivanya slipped the fish net under her sleeve, and none too soon.

The door swung open, and Ivanya's hopes fell. Rasin Béranger stepped inside their room, accompanied by two of her honor guard. The rest positioned themselves with the guard already waiting outside.

Ivanya and Damari swept into a half curtsy. When they rose, Ivanya noted that Rasin was measuring them. A dozen scenarios ran through her head and, with them, a hundred different responses. Unsure what Rasin knew or thought she knew, Ivanya waited for the princess to make the first move.

Rasin surveyed the room, then, with a frown, closed the distance between herself and the two women. "We are going to sit on these comfortable couches my father let you keep, and we're going to talk about mundane things, and when my brother storms in here in the next five minutes, all he will see is his sister attempting to shift your loyalties back where they belong. Am I understood?"

Damari looked to Ivanya, trusting her decision. For Ivanya, it was interesting that, after everything, Rasin was more compelled to help them than she was to side against them. Maybe there was an ally buried in there yet.

Ivanya made a decision. She sat down, though the wary mistrust was not forced. Damari took a seat next to her, and Rasin claimed a high-backed chair for herself. Ivanya asked for mercy and protection from Thalja, hoping she had not just given up her only chance at freedom.

"I don't think you realize the freedom my father has bestowed upon the loyal nobility," Rasin began without preamble. "The Houses have been given the chance to govern their region with very little interference. Do you think they will thank you, a minor

House new to the greater nobility, for putting that very freedom at risk? I don't think so."

Rasin prompted Ivanya with a pointed stare. "Jervin doesn't care much for that end of the politics," Ivanya replied. "Notoyem Béranger took the throne with complete and utter disrespect for the traditions that hold Las Corvika together. If we disregard the very foundations of those traditions, it is to pull at a loose thread that undoes the entire country."

"Yours is a minor House," Rasin snapped. "And you, an outsider, married into it. Even with the full might of an extended family, it was nothing. It only ever had a small estate that pulled very little in the way of financials. So tell me why House Arnaud should have the crown when House Béranger, mighty on its own, considered greater nobility for *generations*, could lead the way?"

Before Ivanya could answer, angry shouts pushed through the thick wooden doors. They swung open, and Luc stormed inside, his expression murderous. Everyone froze, even Bernard, and Ivanya prayed the boy would not begin crying. The eldest Béranger son inspected the room, then said, "Rasin, a word."

Two of Luc's honor guard remained in the room with Rasin's while the princess joined her brother in the corridor.

Ivanya glimpsed outside before the door swung shut and noticed with a sinking feeling just how many men Luc had brought with him.

Damari leaned in and whispered, "What happens now?"

"We wait," Ivanya replied, her eyes glued to the door, "and see if Thalja gives us a way out."

The minutes stretched out into eternity. The raised voice of Luc could be heard through the door, along with the quieter, steely replies of his sister. Then, just as suddenly as before, the doors swung open.

Luc did not even look at the three of them as he said, "In

addition to the guards outside, I want two men stationed in the sitting room and four right outside their bedroom doors at all times. And Rasin… Don't fraternize with the enemy."

Behind him, Rasin did not say a word. She just scowled past Ivanya's shoulder.

The prince stalked out, and after a moment, his sister followed. Ivanya glared at the men, none of whom deigned to meet her gaze, and with a few choice Crasik curses, Ivanya rose and stormed with what dignity she could muster into the master bedroom. There was no way their allies would be able to fight their way through now, not with the added men, and until someone came forward with a better idea, they were stuck in this thrice-cursed castle at the mercy of the Bérangers.

Damari didn't join her, instead taking Bernard to bed. Ivanya couldn't find it in herself to care. She just didn't have the time. Any day now, Notoyem was going to find out she'd lied about Jervin's army, and Ivanya knew the regis wasn't one to make idle threats.

# CHAPTER 17

Being around Notoyem was to always wait for the other shoe to drop, and it had, the moment their scouts had gathered their count of Jervin's army.

"Send someone to the capital," he snarled as he paced. "I want Remy Arnaud executed. I want them *all* executed."

"Perhaps not the wisest move," Pierre Duvachelle said calmly. Kuval and their general, Josse Héroux, also joined them in their war tent. "There's the *vinjess* and the boy, Bernard. Some at court may find themselves more sympathetic to Arnaud's cause if we start executing toddlers, not to mention Venasca's response—"

"Sympathetic to his cause?" Notoyem echoed dangerously. "If they support him, they are traitors and deserve the same punishment. Dispatch a messenger. I want it known that *anyone* who wishes to undermine me will be dealt with swiftly and severely."

Nyli stood at attention, watching the exchange with some trepidation. He was angry too, in his own way. Why did these people continue to defy his father? Did they not know? Had they somehow forgotten, in a way that he never could, just how far Notoyem was willing to go when he was angry and certain that someone had wronged him?

Now Remy was a dead man. Rasin's heart would break to hear it, and Nyli couldn't bear the thought. Worse, although they'd managed to scrounge up just shy of nine thousand men from the royal army, the nearby outposts, and whatever minor lords they encountered along the way with enough men to call upon, they still only had eleven thousand men with Comte Duvachelle's own army. Had Ivanya been telling the truth, they could have crushed Jervin's army like an ant under their thumb.

The problem, as their scouts had just discovered, was that Jervin had fifteen thousand men at his disposal.

*Ants indeed. There can never be just one,* Nyli thought bitterly. They had already started conscripting men from nearby, but even doubling the numbers with poorly trained soldiers did not improve their odds overly much. And since they couldn't get an accurate read on the number of *sjarvisk* under the traitor's employ, Nyli wasn't even sure they had the advantage of magic.

Of course, his uncle across the river had at least another fifteen hundred he was willing to bring, but Notoyem refused to call on him.

"We should pull back to Les Stelvo," Nyli hazarded. Mentioning Elyx Béranger was a terrible idea just now, so withdrawing was the only other logical suggestion. Not that logic would matter right now. Nyli had the knot of the Commander of the Royal Forces tied right above his heart, but there were no other decorations. In this tent, his office meant nothing. A child playing at war.

Héroux was too smart to agree with Nyli outright, and his father opted to pretend his son hadn't said a word in the first place.

Mercifully, someone asked permission to enter. The tent flap peeled back at his father's curt response, and a young man, a proper Corvikan, strode in. He gave the proper honorifics and then rattled off his report.

"Your Highness, the duc has sent word. He will pass Obele tomorrow and estimates that he and his three thousand men will arrive in five days."

"Five days?" Notoyem growled. The unfortunate soldier flinched, but he got off lucky after all. The regis dismissed the man with an aggressive wave of the hand, and the soldier bowed hurriedly before making his retreat. "Jervin Arnaud is in that camp, the traitor. I want him dead, and I want him dead now. This is how he repays my mercy? I should have sent him to the headsman years ago, after we crushed the Ermengardes and ripped the rest of their allies apart."

"He is a fool," Kuval agreed, and Nyli tensed as he took a sip of wine. It was an Atloran vintage, a little sweet, but it was the kind his father favored, so it was the kind they drank. *Don't draw attention to yourself,* he wanted to warn.

The regis spared Kuval a glance, appreciative of the support. Nyli forced himself to relax. Talking to his father, even when he was angry, was not an immediate death sentence. If it was, the court would be full of ghosts.

"Five days gives our conscripted soldiers a chance to train," the comte added, unwilling to be outdone by his son.

Héroux snorted derisively. "Hardly. Your Highness, while I'd hate to retreat from traitorous scum, there's no denying that we are badly outnumbered, and five days is a long time. Worse, even with the duc's men, we'll *still* be outnumbered. You should return to Les Stelvo, where it's more defensible."

"Do not tell me where I should or should not be, General," Notoyem warned. "Leave that to my honor guard. We will hold this position and conscript more troops, and when Villeneuve arrives, we will run in and crush Jervin's forces once and for all." His burning gaze swept from Héroux to the comte to Nyli. Nyli toed the line between too little defiance and not enough strength—right where his father wanted him—unable to look away.

"Do not fail me," his father continued. He spoke to everyone, but his words seemed meant for Nyli. "I doubt I need to remind any of you what happened to the last person who did."

"No, sir." He was aware of the words coming out of his mouth, but he did not hear them, or the handful of voices asserting the same, their owners shifting awkwardly in their seats or on their feet. Notoyem's words hit him like a punch to the gut, like smoke that had hung back all this time finally reaching for him, its black tendrils like claws worming down his throat.

With a sneer that did not help his features, oblivious to the spark that had flared in his son's breast, Notoyem rounded on General Héroux. "All right, then. Tell me, what is the status of our supply line?"

The meeting droned on, and slowly, the tension in the room lifted. It did not dissipate, not completely. That was not possible when Notoyem Béranger was in the room. But supply lines, boring as they were, offered little chance of displeasing the monarch, and in that, at least, something went right.

⚜

They walked out of the tent some time later, he and Kuval, after the war council had officially convened. Kuval's father stayed behind to continue conversing with Notoyem. A blessing, because had the comte followed them out, he might've sent a soldier to tail them. However glad he might've been to see his son ingratiate himself with the regis's son, Nyli could also guess it made him retch in disgust to think what the two of them did when no one was watching.

The foot soldiers made way for Nyli and his honor guard. It

was the middle of the afternoon, and the number of comings and goings was especially irritating. "I can't wait for this to be over," he found himself saying.

"It doesn't look good, does it? Five days isn't long, but it's going to feel like an eternity knowing that Jervin could probably swoop down at any moment. Still, what is one traitor against the might of the throne? What is five days when compared to a single year? To the rest of our lives?"

To Nyli's honor guard and the soldiers they passed, it would have sounded like the philosophical nonsense that Kuval was sometimes known for. But Nyli knew Kuval. They had dreamed of the possibilities, of spending some time in Mod Redel with its lush fields growing food for the region and its vast floral gardens. There was plenty of room for hunting, or perhaps just a simple, quiet day-long ride free of looking over their shoulders. Uncle Elyx, the steward of Mod Redel, would not mind a visit from the two of them.

"Are you ready?" Kuval asked quietly. "To lead the men?"

Nyli's fists tightened at his sides. His father's threat loomed like a storm cloud ready to burst. The impossibilities rattled his chest like nearby thunder. If killing Jervin brought his father peace, then it would be worth it.

"I'm ready for it to be over," he repeated. "One last battle between the rightful regis and the wishful usurpers? I will do what I must, as will everyone else in this camp."

He studied Kuval out of the corner of his eye. The man was not built to be a fighter. He was tall, yes, but he did not have a soldier's muscle. He was soft and philosophical and worlds smarter than Nyli, all the things he'd never thought he'd fall for until he did. Nyli had seen Kuval with a sword, and it terrified him to think of the man on the battlefield, commanding soldiers without an honor guard to watch his back.

They came upon Nyli's tent. It wasn't all that far from his father's pavilion. Two of his guards broke away to search the tent and, finding it empty, returned outside while Nyli and Kuval ducked in. Everything was still in crates and trunks. No furniture had been brought in yet. Everyone had probably been too focused preparing his father's tent. His things would come later.

So he sat on top of a trunk, quietly studying his lover, the stubble on his cheeks, the way he favored his left side now that he had the sword to weigh it down.

"You don't have to be here, Kuval," he said softly. "I could find some excuse to get you back to Les Stelvo or send you to Mod Vjenaro, one that would not impugn your honor."

"Stop," Kuval said. Nyli flinched at the tone, not out of fear but rather out of habit, and hated how much he appreciated Kuval's immediately penitent expression. "These men are traitors, and you have my complete and utter loyalty. Is that not enough for you?"

Nyli studied the calluses on his hands. "I just want you to be safe."

Kuval knelt on the ground in front of Nyli, taking the prince's hands into his own. "You worry too much, Ny. Don't add me to your list of concerns." He brought Nyli's hands to his mouth, kissing them softly. A playful gleam twinkled in his eye. "I could use a drink. How would you feel about leaving camp for a few hours? We could sneak on over to Toritet and have the rest of the day to ourselves."

And just like that, his good mood was yanked out from under him. Nyli gently extricated his hands. "I can't. I have to oversee my troops. Jervin could choose to attack at any moment to take advantage of his superior numbers. And even forgetting that, my father—"

"It's just for a few hours." His dark eyes glimmered. "Come on,

Ny. It's gloomy here, and all I see in the men around us are dead faces. I need to get away, if only for an evening. Same as you; don't tell me it's not the truth."

Nyli hesitated. Five days. Five days he was stuck in this camp, waiting for Villeneuve to arrive with reinforcements, waiting too on bloodshed he would not be able to stomach, dealing with his father who would grow more impatient by the day. It might be nice to get out of the camp, if only for a little while, to have some time alone with Kuval. "Okay," he said finally. "Fine. Let's sneak away like we did way back when we were young boys. Do you remember?"

"Oh, the fun we had," Kuval said, brightening up. "Skulking down hallways like certifiable vagabonds. I'd almost worried you'd lost your irresponsible tendencies."

Well, and that was foolish of him. Pretending to be what they weren't had always dragged most grievously on the relationship, more than anything else. The honor guards, the propriety… Kuval rarely complained, but Nyli knew he hated it all. And yes, in public, Nyli wore whatever mask he needed to, but here in this tent, with just the two of them, Nyli would have promised Kuval the moon had he asked for it. Leaving his honor guard behind was child's play by comparison.

⁂

After six days of hard riding, the last thing Zyre wanted to do was stop at Toritet for the night. In a foul mood, wanting to prolong her friends' presence at her side yet wanting nothing more than to yank out the knife of unease for the family reunion, she kept quiet while her two friends bickered about the position of the sun and the distance they'd have to cross.

Neelie was the one suggesting they press on, that they wouldn't have to ride in the dark for that long, but her heart wasn't in it. Some of their things were still damp from the rain, and there had been no roof to sleep under last night either. Modorin desperately wanted a proper bed to sleep in for the night, and Zyre couldn't help but agree. Finally, Neelie caved to Modorin's persuasion.

"But we leave first thing in the morning," Neelie said. "If they don't have breakfast ready by sunrise, we ride on an empty stomach. Can you handle that?"

Modorin feigned horror. "But how will I stay on my horse without food in my belly to ground me?"

Neelie said something in Venascan, but Zyre must've misheard her, because it *sounded* like she'd said "Eat rocks," and that did not account for Modorin's red-faced laughter. "Come on," she said, again in Corvikan for Zyre's benefit. "I hear a bed calling my name."

"And warm food," Modorin echoed, grinning like a fool.

They rode to the entrance of town, where grim-faced guards directed them down the main road. The Lady Rose was not far, as promised, with a stable and a cleanliness to its exterior that suggested it was several steps up from some cheap inn. Zyre took the lead, dismounting as a young boy, no older than twelve with the tawny complexion and long face that would have fit in better in the south, ran out of the stables. He took their horses' reins and offered a curt quarter bow.

They dismounted and unfastened their bags from the saddle, and from her own, Zyre fished out some coins and passed him a silver *peng*. It equated to a few copper *delars* more than the traditional rate for his position and the number of horses they'd brought with them. The boy's eyes lit up, and he took the small coin with another bow, this time swooping to the half.

With a smile, she led the others to the main entrance. It did not go straight to the common room, but rather to a hallway well lit by candlelight. Zyre wiped her shoes clean of dirt on the fibrous mat at the door. Neelie stared at it, perplexed, before shaking her head in disbelief and following Zyre's example.

A young woman hurried down the short hallway wearing a full apron with a rose imprinted on the corner. She held a candle in her hand, and the fire never wavered as she fell into a half curtsy. "Welcome to the Lady Rose. Are you looking to stay the night?"

"Please," Neelie replied.

"And how many rooms were you hoping to acquire?" The woman searched between the three of them, uncertain.

"Three," Neelie said quickly, then added, belatedly, "please."

Zyre had warned them that innkeepers and their servants could be touchy here in Las Corvika. Be too rude or abrupt with someone, even the scullion, and word would reach the innkeeper. Next thing you knew, when it came time to pay, the innkeeper would inform you of a sudden shortage of beds or food or stalls that would invariably drive up the price of your stay. Sarol would already be an added expense to the price of Modorin's room.

The serving girl smiled and bobbed a curtsy, and Zyre let out a silent exhale in relief. No offense had been taken. Or at least, their coin would be enough to offset it. "Follow me, if it pleases you. I'll show you to your rooms, and then you may feel free to enjoy the comfort of our common room if you so desire."

She set a quick pace, glancing shyly at Sarol as the fox trotted by her heel. Toritet was an old town, located on an even older, disused, road. Merchants would come this way to buy and sell goods to the settlements south of the Áit, but *sjarvisk* would have few reasons to be sent this way. Zyre imagined the townsfolk were not happy about all the soldiers settled nearby.

Modorin was given a room on the second floor, and Zyre and Neelie, rooms on the third. It was a setup Zyre had heard of before, separating the men and women for propriety, though so antiquated she hadn't thought inns were still doing it.

"You ladies may visit your friend," the serving woman said with a dip of a curtsy before they left Modorin, "but we ask that no men roam the women's halls."

Zyre mouthed *sorry* over her shoulder to Modorin as they walked away, but the man just shrugged, then waved Sarol into his room.

More than a few doors on the third floor remained propped open, but the number of patrons at the Lady Rose was surprising. She had not expected so much travel, even during the middle of summer. The serving girl managed to find two rooms that sat next to each other. Neelie flashed her a smile before disappearing behind closed doors.

Zyre stepped into hers and shut the door, setting her things onto the floor while she surveyed the room. It was modest, just large enough to fit a small bed, a rug, and a washstand. The washstand was well made, its paint unchipped and the wood worn smooth. The bed, she learned after a few experimental prods, was satisfactorily lacking in lumps, and either way was a far cry to the hard ground they'd been sleeping on.

But the room, as small as it was, still felt impossibly empty. She was so used to Kadj taking up space. Sharing sleeping quarters with Modorin, and then having the entire outdoors on the way here, had made his absence less noticeable. Not forgotten, not ever, but less sharp of a loss.

Zyre's stomach rumbled, but she ignored it. She washed herself as best as she could, scrubbing dirt off her face, her arms. Then she collapsed into the bed, promising herself just a few minutes to consider what today meant for her. Starting tomorrow, she would be with her father. She tried to envision what it would be like to be in an army, leading men into a battle, *killing.*

But if the *Aretmor* was anything to go by, or the assault on Bijal's city barracks, it was hard to imagine Zyre would ever come to terms with it. Better just to rebuild their estate, to put its destruction behind them. It would even bring jobs to the area. She thought she might be willing to swallow insults from the regis if it meant she didn't have to kill anyone.

It was also hard to believe she'd been away from her father for a whole month. Spare change, she supposed, when, if things had been at all different, she might've spent the rest of her life in Bijal with Neelie and Modorin. The city was everything Lasinia could never be.

Zyre had never let herself contemplate another path, but now, just for a few minutes, she considered what her future held, Thalja willing. She imagined her fear and disgust of battlefields fading, of impressing Neelie by showing the necessary bravery and power and cunning it took to stay alive in a battle, her dance to keep her sanity.

Zyre would say in passing, in this future, how badly she wished to see the rest of the world—and she did; one small taste of Bijal was not enough for her—and the other *aljarne* would invite her aboard her ship. They'd sail and sail and sail, however far the ship could take them. And they'd stop for occasion in Bijal to see Modorin, because she could not envision a future where he was not somewhere in it.

And they'd get along, and they would kiss, and fall in love. Zyre could imagine that, if this was to be a dream.

She rolled onto her stomach, and that was her mistake, because it protested loudly. With a sigh, Zyre let her hopes for the future fade. She had to help her father win the war, first, before she could have any kind of future with Modorin and with Neelie. She rose, wound her way down the hall and down the flights of stairs that tumbled into the fringes of the common room. Food was, blissfully, still being served, and for all her love of Bijal, there was something to be said of familiar meats cooked with familiar spices, of stout potatoes and sweet carrots coated liberally in butter.

Unsurprisingly, Modorin had claimed a table for them, a plate in front of him and somehow already half-empty. Perhaps she'd been in her room longer than she thought. Stomach growling fiercely, Zyre joined him at the table, mindful of Sarol licking his plate clean on the floor.

"I see you enjoy Corvikan food with the same verve as Venascan cuisine."

"Just hungry," he said through a mouthful of food, shrugging.

"Do all Syfresians eat as much as you do?" she exclaimed with a laugh.

Modorin pouted. "Do you know how much energy I burn constantly worrying about the both of you? You can hardly blame *me*."

Still snickering, Zyre noticed a serving girl, different from the one who had shown them their rooms, drawing near with a plate full of food. The girl set it down in front of Zyre, and for all her teasing, Zyre attacked her food with just as much gusto as Modorin. Her friend's eyes twinkled. Just like that, her own good mood faded.

She had a question for him, one that had been burning on the back of her mind. In less than a day, they'd go their separate ways. Zyre didn't know whether she'd see them again, but she wanted to. She just didn't know where she belonged in this odd little group, and it felt important for some reason that she figure it out now, before they left her.

"Did you want to come to Las Corvika with us because you wanted to be with Neelie?"

Her question caught him off guard, and for a moment, he just sat there, his fork halfway to his mouth. Then he snorted. "Zyre, while I find Neelie's company enjoyable, we have an agreement when it comes to me and her various needs to travel, and I doubt I have to explain what I mean."

"So you did it to avoid the fighting in Bijal?" She winced. "Wait, that's not how I meant it."

He shrugged, taking another bite. "Maybe I just wanted to spend a little more time with a newfound friend before she went off to war."

"Friend," she murmured. "That is all we are, though, right?" He looked at her blankly. She surged forward. It was now or never. One last secret for her to reveal. "Because you're not exactly my type." She cursed clumsiness. He was going to think it was because he was Fresian. "I mean that I'm not interested in…men."

He blinked. Then blinked again. Suddenly her heart was racing, and she tensed, trying to calculate how fast Modorin was and what he might do if she fled.

"You know, I had wondered."

"I… What?"

His eyes bored into hers. "You like Neelie, don't you?"

"I don't," she said, too quickly, wishing she had kept her fool mouth shut. Some secrets were better left unspoken.

But then his eyes softened inexplicably. "It's okay. She's quite the force of nature, isn't she? It's easy to get drawn in."

This was not at all where she'd wanted this conversation to go. Cutting another bite of steak free, she tried to keep her tone flippant as she said, "It doesn't matter one way or the other, does it? Because something tells me I'm not the kind of person that she would like in return."

"That's something you should…"

Modorin kept speaking, but as two men stepped into the common room, she no longer heard him. They wore loose hoods, but she would recognize the shorter one anywhere. His sharp jaw, his hungry prowl—Nyli Béranger, as if Tholjun himself had sent the prince in her path.

She should kill him.

He had burned her house to the *ground.*

*Get up, you idiot. Get up and finish this,* half of her said. But the weaker, naive part of her was the one in control.

Zyre tore her eyes way from the newcomers, glaring pointedly at the plate in front of her. *Don't look, don't look, don't look,* she prayed.

"What's wrong?" Modorin asked, turning around to look.

"No, don't!" Zyre snapped. "Don't draw attention to us."

"Okay," he said, worry lacing his tone.

Zyre swallowed a lump in her throat. She should kill him. She should really kill the prince. He had no honor guard with him, just the twig-shaped man. It would be one less Béranger her father would have to contend with. She could take him on, surely. She had her magic, her sword. He had only one of those things. And it wasn't like he didn't *deserve* it, after Lasinia.

"Zyre, talk to me," Modorin muttered.

Through gritted teeth, she replied, "Prince Nyli just walked in with some man."

He cursed, growing tense. "Is he looking at you? Did he recognize you?"

"No, I don't think so."

"Good. That means we can still sneak out of here."

"But, Modorin," Zyre protested. *I made a promise.*

His eyes bored holes into her. "Zyre, are you really going to murder him here in cold blood? Could you?"

Zyre glanced at the table the two men had taken. Nyli was smiling at his companion. It made her heart ache, though she wasn't entirely sure why. It would have been easy to kill him. Kill them both, even. A blast of ice shards shot their way, or even a fireball. She wasn't entirely sure she could do it without killing anyone else on accident, but at least Nyli Béranger would be dead. She *should* kill him.

*But then, if you're so certain, why do you hesitate?* A voice asked her. *Nothing but a coward. Skill and valor indeed.*

No. If she started a fight here, her friends would get caught in the middle. Besides, it wasn't honorable. It wasn't *fair*. She couldn't kill him unless their odds were fair.

With a growl, she tore her eyes away from the pair. "Fine. How do we do it without attracting their attention?"

Modorin relaxed visibly. "Easy. You'll go up to your room first. When you get up, angle as quickly as you can so your back is to them, but otherwise, act normally. I'll wait a moment and then go to mine. There'll be a back entrance, I'm sure. You will grab Neelie and meet me in the stables. It looks like we'll be riding in the dark after all."

The problem was that it was hardest to act natural when circumstances demanded it. Gathering her courage and what was left of her pride, Zyre stood out of her chair, spinning as calmly as she could so that her back was to the prince. Her instincts shouted at her, but she ignored them, trying to remember how fast a *normal-paced* walk was. No one screamed her name or called her traitor.

Once she was out of sight of the common room, she bolted up the rest of the stairs and thundered down the third floor. Neelie's door was cracked open. Zyre didn't bother with pleasantries, hoping the other woman was at least dressed as she ran into the room.

"Zyre!" Neelie squawked. She was perched at the foot of her bed. Her fingers had been at her temples as if she had a headache, but all signs of weakness faded with Zyre's abrupt arrival.

"I'm so sorry. We can't stay. The prince is downstairs, and I think he'll recognize me if he sees my face. I should have killed him, but I didn't, and Modorin told me not to and said we should rendezvous at the stables and get out of town before a fight breaks out." The words came spilling out of her, and for a moment, Neelie just sat, frozen in place, as she processed everything Zyre had thrown at her.

In one fluid motion, Neelie rose and grabbed her things from where they sat on the floor. "Go get your stuff, then. I'll keep an eye on the hall."

At least men were not allowed up here, Zyre thought.

She ran into her room, picking up her bag. At the last second, she thought about payments for the room and blindly threw a few *delars* onto the bedside table. Then she reunited with Neelie in the hall.

It struck her, as they headed for the creaky staircase that the serving girls used, that if Nyli saw her, a fight would break out and she could kill him in self-defense. If he attacked her, it wouldn't be fair, but at least it wouldn't be her fault.

They couldn't run down the stairs without drawing undue attention, but Zyre moved as fast as she dared. Her heart hammered in her throat as fear waged war with hope, with *need*. It was only the knowledge that the town's loyalties were unknowable, and that the town's guards would be obligated to chase them down at the very least, that stopped her from turning back around and doing what she should have done from the start.

Nyli never appeared, and they walked out the back door unseen even by the serving girls or the innkeeper.

Modorin, true to his word, had somehow beat them there. Stablehands were already putting the tack back on their poor horses, tying down their bags for them. Passing over a few more coins, Zyre swung into her saddle, letting her friends take the lead.

*Tholjun, if you really want the prince dead, send him to me,* she prayed. *I swear if I am given a confrontation, I will strike him down.*

Modorin and Neelie urged their horses forward. Zyre hesitated, looking wildly for the prince. *Am I really going to leave him alive?*

"Zyre, come on," Modorin called.

Tholjun didn't answer her prayer. With gritted teeth, Zyre let her horse follow her friends, and they left Toritet with the setting sun.

# CHAPTER 18

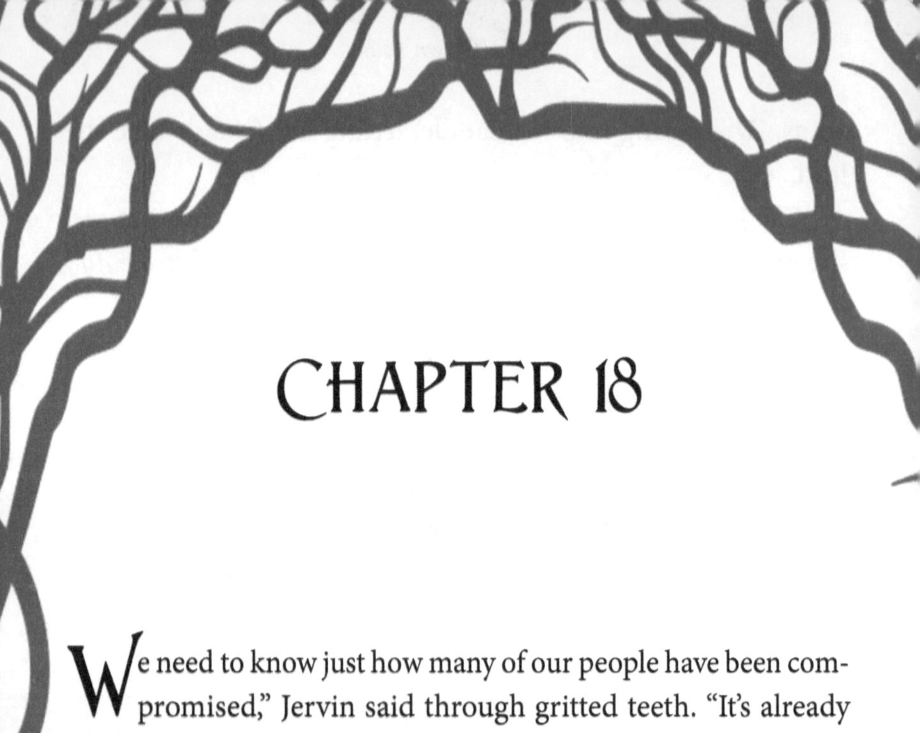

W e need to know just how many of our people have been compromised," Jervin said through gritted teeth. "It's already been two days. How much longer will Thalja grace my family with her protection?"

Jervin was in his personal tent, particularly crowded this evening what with General Tavere, Jervin's recently arrived daughter Aljeya, and Captain Merytz all crammed in there with him.

Aljeya had brought his chair out from behind his desk and was sitting on it thoughtfully. Tavere just stood out of the way while Jervin paced. His daughter tapped the arm of her chair. "I don't understand. Notoyem's men are camped on the other side of the river. We are about to be in open rebellion. Whatever men of ours who are situated at the capital should be told that their highest priority right now is to help the rest of our family. What other use could they possibly have?"

"Their continued secrecy might just be the difference between loss and victory, my lady," Tavere replied. "Les Stelvo's defenses are numerous. Without those men, the capital will not yield."

"Are you seriously going to prioritize the city over the safety of the baroness and the *vinje*?" Aljeya snapped. Jervin could hear the indignation in her tone. He wished he could agree with her on that front, but even as her furious gaze shifted from Tavere to Jervin, he could do nothing but pace, unwilling to argue.

The bulk of Notoyem's forces were just across the river; there was no denying that. Engage them now, kill the regis, and the country would be shaken, ready to fall beneath Jervin's banner. But there was Luc, who, by all accounts, remained in the capital. Luc, the Béranger wolf, whose hand of death had only been stayed by the regis himself. He was smart enough to hold the city against Jervin's forces, even with inferior numbers.

"Father, surely your family's lives are worth more than the crown!" Aljeya folded her arms in front of her chest. "Atlor would give you political asylum if it came down to it. Your pride cannot be so massive."

"Watch it," Jervin snapped. He was, after all, now a regis-un-crowned. He turned to Tavere. "We have the advantage of num-bers. How fast can we get to the capital with all these men?"

"Five days at best. A messenger could cross that distance in half that time, though," his general responded gravely. An Atloran guard, one of Aljeya's, poked his head inside the tent and muttered something to Merytz. "I'm inclined to agree with your daughter on this, Jervin, though perhaps for different reasons. We have never been closer to killing the regis. If we leave the regis alive here, this could quite quickly become a drawn-out war, even with Les Stelvo under our command."

Jervin knew this. The good news was that Les Stelvo was cur-rently empty of soldiers. It would be easy for them to capture and next to impossible for Notoyem to take back. But if they deployed to the capital, Luc would soon know his hostages had outgrown their use. And they had to assume the extraction mission had ended in failure. They would have heard otherwise by now if it hadn't. "Have we at least found our way into the city?"

Jervin was glad to see the grim smile the general offered him. Tavere searched around for a street map of Les Stelvo. A thick wall surrounded most of it save for a few sprawling districts that had tumbled out the city's perimeter like a burst grape. Just northwest of the center, the palace was a huge angular blob surrounded by more walls.

Tavere set a finger on the outer ring. "The walls have been under construction for decades. Charms are slowly being infused into the stone to prevent *sjarvisk* magic from punching through. But our informants say that here, here, and here," he said, gesturing to the different locations, "remain unfinished. With his numbers, Luc would be a fool to waste troops trying to hold them. With Tholjun's blessing, we'll enter the city with ease and encounter little resistance. Where things will get tricky is the inner wall. It doesn't have the weaknesses of the outer wall; *kjarnik* magic is going to slow us down and what troops Luc has will undoubtedly be waiting to pick us off as much as possible until we breach the gate."

In his periphery, Jervin saw a soldier poke his head into the tent and whisper something to Merytz.

"Then it's not enough to pack up and march," Jervin said, ignoring the disturbance. "We lose time if we pick either place of engagement. Before we leave, we should pay the regis a little visit. Cut off the head of the snake, and the tail flounders."

Tavere knew exactly what he meant. Jervin knew this, because Tholjun graced Tavere's darkly happy expression. "Tonight, sir?"

"However soon you can pull a team together."

Aljeya was blind if she thought he held no love for his wife and son. He would have set the entire countryside ablaze if it would have gotten them out safely. But both knew the stakes. Both had helped him plan this. It would be a disservice to give up his one chance to set this country aright.

"Pardon, sir," Merytz said, clearing his throat awkwardly. "There's been a disturbance on the outskirts of camp. Two women and a man, a *sjarvisk*. One woman claims to be part of Regis-Uncrowned Arnaud's guard, escaped from Lasinia, though she has no soulbeast and wears Venascan clothes."

Aljeya was suddenly on her feet. "Zyre?"

Jervin glared at his daughter but dared not chastise her in front of everyone. If she wasn't careful, people were going to wonder why she was so excited to see the family's *sjarvisk*.

He set his sights instead on his Guardsmaster. "Merytz, go see this group. If it's Zyre, bring her to me. Otherwise, turn them over to Lieutenant Vaudian and let him determine whether they can be of some use."

Merytz bowed and left. A few minutes later, another young soldier by the name of Reubod, one of the newest additions to his guard, took his place. His honor guard had been put together quickly and efficiently. Jervin had to give credit to Merytz; he took his job seriously.

Once everything had settled back down, Jervin turned to Tavere. "The regis is sitting right on our doorstep. We need to take advantage before he gets his reinforcements. Do we have any idea why his brother still has troops on the northern side of the Gouvelle?"

"I expect it's a warning. We engage Notoyem's troops, Elyx crosses the river and hits us from behind. And, with his brother's forces, Notoyem's got us almost evenly matched, and with us fighting on two fronts, well…"

A thousand men, maybe two. It didn't guarantee Notoyem the win, of course. Nothing about a battle was ever certain except that it ended and men died until it did. But sometimes it was the small things that turned the tide of the fight, a sword to distract from the knife plunged between the ribs.

Jervin ran his fingers through his hair. "I want to know as soon as your team has completed their task. Tomorrow morning, I want a full briefing. Bright and early. I expect a plan that will lead us to the destruction of the rest of Béranger line, my family safe from harm, and the Arnaud name attached to the throne."

"Yes, sir."

The general stepped out. Jervin looked at his daughter and sank onto a closed trunk with a sigh. This hadn't exactly been his plan when he'd set out to undermine Notoyem's reign. Everything had been placed just so, where a single prod would send it all tumbling.

But that was the problem with strategies: Nothing was fool-proof. Once the pawns started moving, it was adapt or die.

"If it's Zyre, I hope you are kind to her," Aljeya said, startling him.

Jervin took hold of himself. "She ran off."

Aljeya frowned, and that judgmental expression was so *Ivanya* that it hurt. "Were you there when she did? Right there, with her?"

"No, I was too busy trying to escape the Béranger brat." He shot a pointed look in Reubod's direction, warning Aljeya to watch her tongue.

"So you don't know what happened," Aljeya pressed, either oblivious or uncaring. "She's lost her soulbeast, Father. Whatever that means, I hope you will not send her away. She has every right to be here as you or I."

"That's presumptuous."

Aljeya glared in response.

The tent flap drew back, allowing Merytz to step halfway in. "Permission to enter, sir."

"Granted," Jervin replied.

Merytz stepped forward, but before he was even fully in the tent, Zyre tumbled in. Her hair was wild, unkempt, as if she'd just been running around in the dark, which, considering the hour, she actually might have been. But she looked well enough. In fact, aside from the Venascan clothes she wore and the absence of her great tiger, she looked much the same as she'd had the last time Jervin had seen her.

Two others followed on her heels. One was short, with blond hair that could only be found south of Venasca. He wore a blue scarf around his neck despite the late-night summer heat. The fox must have been his. The Venascan woman, Jervin had never met but knew by reputation and by the shape of her face. One could see the Pirate Queen in it if one knew where to look. This was the Viper, Neelie Hijaladreia.

"It's a pleasure to meet you in person, Captain Neelie," Jervin said, giving her a polite quarter bow in greeting. Aljeya offered a curtsy.

"Baron." She matched his bow. Something about the gesture felt like she was mocking him.

With a frown, Jervin turned to the shorter fellow. "I'm afraid I don't know who you are."

"Modorin Kal," the man replied.

"It's a pleasure, but I need to speak to my former employee. I'll have my men find you some place to stay the night, if you would like."

"I don't think so." Kal's expression didn't waver, but his tone was steel.

Zyre's hand brushed his arm, a thoughtless gesture that Jervin didn't miss. "There's no reason to kick them out. They already know."

It took everything in him to keep his composure. Jervin looked to Merytz. "It appears we're going to need more chairs. Have someone run and grab them, and give us some privacy."

"All due respect, my lord, but I insist on staying, for your safety." Merytz shifted uncomfortably, glancing at Zyre's companions.

Jervin studied the young man, hesitating on instinct. But if he couldn't trust Merytz with these secrets, then he'd picked the wrong man to guard his life. He nodded in acquiescence.

Merytz sent Reubod to the war tent to fetch a few spare seats for everyone. Zyre stood awkwardly with her companions on one side of the tent, Jervin and Aljeya on the other. The seconds stretched on like years. He could not risk asking Zyre the important questions until they'd secured their privacy, but they burned on his tongue.

He kept seeing flashes of a silhouette on a hill raining fire down in the valley below. Of fire, and the sharp echo of screams.

As soon as the chairs had been deposited and Reubod cast out from the tent, Jervin wasted no more time. "You've lost your magic, haven't you?"

"Father!" Aljeya protested.

Zyre brought up a fist by way of answer, letting a flame blossom above her fist. Her expression was harder, stonier, than he'd ever seen on her before, but he couldn't dwell on that. In the corner, Merytz looked like he'd swallowed his own tongue. Jervin hadn't thought to tell Merytz about his secret daughter before this. But he couldn't spare a thought for his Guardsmaster right now.

"It's still salvageable," he said, thinking quickly. "No one has to know. Beyond those you've already decided to tell, I mean." He looked pointedly at Neelie and Kal. "If you insist on staying in the camp, we can find some place for you. Maybe as a washer woman or a cook."

"Washer woman," Zyre repeated blankly.

Neelie crossed her arms, settling into a belligerent stance. "We did not sail your daughter all the way from Bijal just so she can—"

"I would ask you to watch your tongue," Jervin said, barely

keeping a grip on his tone. "That kind of information is danger-ous. If she trusts you with it, there's no going back on that, but there are people in this camp who would kill her because she is *aljarne*, and who will lose faith in our cause by knowing it."

"All for the cause," Neelie said icily.

Aljeya stood up suddenly, before Jervin could think of a response. "A long-lost cousin. Maybe a bastard, an unknown daughter of one of your brothers. If she doesn't use her magic, no one needs to know any different. She can be part of the planning, both in the war and in getting *our* mother out."

Zyre was still glaring at him for the washer woman comment. It seemed she had picked up on some bad habits from her new-found friends. He didn't like this new attitude of hers.

"That is risky, but doable," he said, if only because it meant he wouldn't have to throw away all of Zyre's soldier training. He didn't do it out of kindness. He couldn't. Something she never seemed able to grasp: Jervin was not just her father; she was a soldier under his command. Neelie mocked him for fighting for a cause? Yes, he would do anything for it. Vying for the throne was not child's play, where one could end the game at a whim. "Now, as happy as I am that you are back, it's late, and there are meet-ings to be had in the morning. We'll talk later about everything. Merytz, find them a tent, please."

"Wait, hold on," Zyre said quickly. "I want to help against the regis. Listen, I broke the *leiks* on purpose. It was the reason my magic was unpredictable, and I figured right now you need all the help you can get. I'm not some regular person. I have magic, and I'm willing to use it. To end all of this, I'm willing to do anything."

*Then why did you flee Lasinia, rather than do what I told you to?* Jervin wanted to ask. "We'll discuss it in the morning," he said curtly. "But I expect you'll need to brush up on your war tactics. You and your sister can be of help planning the battles."

He knew by the flash in her eye that she wanted more, but before it could become an argument, he gestured to Merytz and let his Guardsmaster usher them out.

Aljeya gave him a cold glare. "Goodnight, then, Father," she said, leaving Jervin on his own.

⚜

Nyli liked how quiet the camp got at night.

It wasn't that it became utterly still or lifeless; there were still the patrols, the sentries, the soldiers stumbling off to bed after an evening of gambling and drinking.

But their paths were mostly empty, and filling the space between each footfall was the rumbling of crickets, the occasional hooting of an owl.

Nyli hadn't had much to drink in Toritet. Truth be told, Kuval hadn't either. But then, it had been less about getting blindingly drunk and more about getting away from the tension at camp for just a little while. To be amidst people who had no idea who they were and had no reason to look at them twice.

The warmth in his chest and the lingering lightness of his steps were just an added bonus, but he hadn't taken the drinking any further than that.

Nyli bumped Kuval's arm with his knuckles, the closest they could come to holding hands out here. Kuval smiled and bumped him back.

As they finally got closer to the center of camp, his father's tent looming in the shadows as only seemed befitting for the volatile regis, Nyli saw something move in the dark.

*Great. The honor guard come to fetch their errant prince*, Nyli thought, steeling himself for the argument.

The dark silhouettes did not step into the light. Nyli couldn't make out their faces, but as the mysterious shapes stopped right beside Notoyem's tent, it struck him that something was terribly wrong.

Nyli pulled Kuval to a stop, pressing an urgent finger to his lips. Kuval followed his gaze and grew deathly still. They drew back, stepping away from the light before the assassins spotted them. For what else could they be?

He didn't notice himself taking a step forward until he felt Kuval's hand on his arm, begging silently for Nyli not to leave.

*I have to*, he wanted to say.

Three of Notoyem's honor guard stood watch outside. There would be two others in the tent. But the assassins were good, or enchanted, or both. Nyli hadn't heard them, only caught a glimpse by sheer luck, by Thalja's grace. And Nyli knew his father didn't like sleeping with the guards looming over him. They'd be in another section of the tent, listening for trouble they would not hear.

The shadows began to fade as one by one the figures snuck into the tent through a slit.

*Go, you fool*, he snapped at himself. *The man is a force to be reckoned with, but he is your father.*

*He is your father.*

But Nyli saw in his mind the glass vial, the green-tinted liquid. He remembered how his mother had taken it, her fingers trembling but her jaw set. The deadly calm in Notoyem's voice as he declared, "You've absolutely destroyed Nyli with your doting. He'll be a man afraid to kill, jumping at his own shadows, incompetent. Your destruction of the prince is nothing short of treason, and for it, I sentence you to death."

He remembered how he was forced to watch his mother the queen drink the poison, how her body seized for what felt like an eternity before she fell.

*You are betraying your family by your inaction*, he tried, but the other side of him, the side wounded by his father's cruelty, the side that hated the wrath that burned through him when he grew angry, that feared what legacy he might leave behind because of his father's influence on him, could not listen.

His father had begun it all. Notoyem had betrayed his son first.

Nyli's heart slowed nearly to a standstill. Time seemed to stop as he reached for Kuval's hand, quietly pulling him away.

The other man looked at him, as if to say, *Are you sure?*

Nyli was, but wasn't. But he had made up his mind. Let the gods decide his father's fate. If it was Notoyem's destiny to die tonight, Nyli would not intervene.

⚜

They waited in Nyli's tent in silence. The furniture had been brought in, including the bed, but neither of them sat on it. Neither of them could even think of sleep. Kuval had taken up residence on Nyli's chair, but Nyli himself was content to perch on his trunk, yet unpacked, and listen.

The alarm was never raised. Instead, the only warning he got was the way his honor guard filed in, the torchlight revealing their barely concealed lividness. Nyli's Guardsmaster didn't even try to hide it. After all, Nyli had left without them, had thrown himself carelessly into danger. But death came for them all.

"You're needed in the regis's tent, Your Highness," the Guardsmaster said, looking directly over Nyli's shoulder. "Your father has been assassinated."

Nyli stiffened. He knew. Of course he knew. So what was this foolish, mad lance of grief racing through his veins like a poison?

He didn't know how he kept his voice steady as he said, "Take me to him."

"Would you like me to come?" Kuval asked.

"I do, but it might be best to return to your own tent now so your father knows where to find you."

The two of them shared a look, Kuval's saying *this isn't fair* and Nyli's saying *I know, but this is the world we live in.* Kuval slipped out of the tent, and as Nyli followed his honor guard out, he looked over his shoulder, at the lone figure slipping away, and felt himself start to untether. Would it be so bad if the world knew? How was their love any different from anyone else's? He just wanted Kuval to be there when he stood over his father's body and wrestled with this double-edged grief.

Nyli didn't call him back. He turned, letting his honor guard corral him to his father's tent.

It was not pleasant to look at.

Nyli should have expected as much after finding the tent's entrance devoid of guards, the foyer as empty as a shadow.

Bodies were strewn across the floor of Notoyem's sleeping quarters. General Héroux was already there, directing two of his captains as they moved bodies of the assassins and the honor guard into another section of the tent. One or two of Notoyem's guards might've been killed by the assassins, but the rest had taken their swords to their chest for the shame of having let their charge die.

This was the dishonor Nyli had committed against his honor guard by leaving them behind. If something had happened to him, they'd have been honor-bound to do the same.

Nyli moved carefully around the captains, gesturing absently for his honor guard to help. He made himself walk to his father's bedside. Notoyem had very clearly fought back. His hands had been sliced from trying to fend off a blade, and there was a blood-slick knife not far from him, dropped, most assuredly, while he was fighting for his life.

"It was an enchanted blade," Héroux said, coming up behind him. "The thrice-cursed cheats struck him with an enchanted blade, and whatever sick spells were woven into it made fast work of him. I'm sorry, Your Highness. May Tholjun bring him peace."

*May Thalja protect my mother's soul from his*, Nyli thought, but he couldn't bring himself to argue with the general.

"Sir, the comte and his son are here," Nyli's Guardsmaster announced. "They would like to speak with you."

"Let them in."

He had no idea what he was going to say to Pierre Duvachelle, but the man had best be on good behavior, because Nyli wasn't feeling particularly charitable right now.

"So it's true, then," the comte said hoarsely as he and Kuval squeezed into the room.

Nyli didn't bother to answer.

Héroux's gaze swept across the people in the room, no doubt trying to decide where the power resided here. Eventually, he turned to Nyli. "What would you have us do, my prince? Do we wait for the duc's men, or do we return to the capital to support your brother's claim against this usurper?"

Nyli scowled. *Luc.* There was still Luc to contend with. Evil persisted because it was so easily replaced. He had let his father die, but Luc remained. "I don't support him," he muttered to himself.

"My prince?" Pierre squawked.

He should have taken it back, said he wasn't thinking straight in his grief, but why *should* he support Luc? He'd just condemned his father to die. Why not take it one step further? "I don't support Luc's claim. We will march to Les Stelvo, but not to aid my brother. We march to keep that crown off of his head."

"Nyli…" Kuval stepped closer, and Nyli didn't miss the disgust that swept across Pierre's expression. "That's a big decision.

You would take his crown in his place? Do you know what that means?"

He wasn't a fool. Of course he knew. It would mean seeing his brother dead, same as his father.

Pierre coughed. "All due respect, my prince, but the regis—the *late* regis—was always vocal about Luc being the heir apparent. The families loyal to the Béranger name would see that wish fulfilled."

"We have the men. And we can have the element of surprise. If Luc thinks we are, in fact, coming to support him, he'll let us into the capital with open arms. We won't even have to fight to take the capital." Nyli smiled grimly. He had to think this through now before he could start second-guessing himself.

*Would Rasin even approve? No, don't think that*, Nyli thought to himself.

"That's all well and good, but I'll remind you that you cannot have the crown without noble backing."

Nyli spun to face the comte, knowing what the man was going for. Pierre took a hasty step back, and Nyli felt nothing but vicious pride, knowing that he could intimidate Pierre as much as his father could.

Then he felt sick to his stomach for that pride. Making people afraid was nothing to be *proud* of.

"They will back the one most likely to win. And those who prove loyal will be rewarded, Comte Duvachelle. Think of what your family has to gain by helping shift the trajectory of our be-loved country? With you, Duc Villeneuve, and my uncle standing behind me"—and he *would* need Elyx's blessing to cement this mad decision—"the others will fall in line."

Pierre measured Nyli's words in silence. After a moment that lasted an eternity, he nodded.

Which only brought Nyli one step closer to something he

could not come back from. But if the gods cursed him for it, so be it. Notoyem had cursed him since the cradle, and Nyli had always hoped someone could come along and break it for him. His mother. Rasin. Kuval. But no one could break him free of this except himself.

He would not be the puppet on his family's strings any longer.

# CHAPTER 19

Zyre had worried she might sleep in late and miss whatever meetings her father had been talking about, but she needn't have. She was pulled unceremoniously from sleep by the clatter and shouts of an army readying itself for whatever it was an army did in between battles. Her two friends continued sleeping, Modorin curled around Sarol's small form and Neelie snoring just a little. She rifled through her bag, withdrawing the pieces of one of the guard outfits she'd ordered in Bijal. The shirt was in a vibrant blue with silver thread, and the pants were a matching blue with black paneling.

Merytz would be at the meetings. She wasn't looking forward to seeing him again now that her truths were laid bare. Last night, he'd reached out and grabbed her arm, stopping her from joining her friends in their newly claimed tent. "You're an Arnaud?" he'd asked dejectedly.

The fact that he knew the answer, that she knew he only wanted to hear her say it, didn't make it any easier. The betrayal was already evident. Zyre found she could only nod.

"And an *aljarne*?" His eyes had darted around them, searching for possible cavesdroppers.

Again, Zyre nodded. She found her voice. "Look, Merytz, no one outside my family knew. No one except a select few members of our staff who would have been impossible to keep it from. It's nothing against your character."

Except that, invariably, was a lie, and both of them knew it.

He'd let his hand fall away. When he bowed to her to the half, with the added honorific, it crushed her heart. "I'm your father's Guardsmaster now. I expect we'll be seeing a lot of each other. I bid you goodnight, *Vinjess* Arnaud." Then he'd spun on his heel and left her there.

If she and Merytz had ever actually been friends, that time was over now. Finally, someone recognized her noble blood, and all it did was divide them. How bitter that little truth tasted.

Once Zyre was dressed—quietly, so the other two did not wake—she slipped between the tent flaps and stepped into the weak light of the early morning sun. A man stood on guard outside her tent. He was young, roughly Merytz's age, dark hair loosely bound atop his head. She almost sent him away; she didn't need someone to keep an eye on her.

But then the soldier bowed. Only to the quarter, but with the added honorific. "Madame Arnaud."

Zyre tensed. How did he—?

*Of course,* she thought, remembering the lie that her sister had gifted her last night. It wasn't what she'd hoped for, but it was better than the alternative. "What's your name, soldier?"

"Veirole, Madame Arnaud. I was told you might want to see your uncle. He is in a war council, but I was given leave to bring you, should you wish it."

Zyre let herself look back to the tent, silently begging Neelie and Modorin not to go anywhere until she got back. At the very least, praying they wouldn't leave without saying goodbye. She had no idea how long they'd stay.

To Veirole, she said, "Please."

The young soldier marched them down a hard path that clearly hadn't seen rain in some time. Other men were polishing armor, sharpening swords, eating food gotten from who knew where, running. There was a surprising amount of running around. Many looked at her, but they gave her a wide berth, at least.

At the center of the camp, a large pavilion stood under the shadow of an even larger ancient silver tree. Its branches were recognizable, and it eased some of her nerves to see the velídas tree there. A young woman wearing divided skirts stood at attention beneath it, and an owl perched on a branch above her head.

The pavilion itself was surrounded by a dozen soldiers, three of whom stood out like a sore thumb with their Atloran garb. Merytz, fortunately, was nowhere to be seen.

Veirole walked by them all without a word, and Zyre followed, the quiet thrum of conversation pushing through the thick canvas walls.

"Madame Arnaud, requesting permission to enter," Veirole said, sticking his head into the tent.

"Granted," came the belated reply.

The young soldier stepped out of her way, holding the tent flap aside for her. She nodded her head in thanks and then took in the scene.

The pavilion held at least a dozen people of various ranks. The only people she recognized were her father, Aljeya, and, unfortunately, Merytz, who stood at attention in the corner.

An older man, with thinning hair and an impressive number of medals and knotwork decorating his uniform, spoke to Jervin while her sister listened nearby. The decorated soldier was almost certainly General Tavere. The others had knots, too, but Zyre couldn't have guessed what they meant. An otter rolled in the dirt between two men, their hands full of steaming bowls of porridge. Whom the soulbeast belonged to, she couldn't guess, but she hadn't expected to find a *sjarvisk* on the war council.

The pavilion, blessedly, was stocked with breakfast, and the very thought of food made her stomach rumble. She skirted the clusters of men, feeling more than a little outnumbered and overwhelmed, and grabbed a bowl of the bland but filling gruel. Modorin would be put out if this was the only thing offered, Zyre thought with a bitter smile.

"Zyre."

Zyre looked up, surprised to find her sister suddenly by her side. She grinned fiercely, glad to have another chance to talk to her. "Aljeya. How have you been?"

"Well. Better, to see you're here."

"Where is my… Where are my cousins? With Muldar?"

Her sister nodded, grief temporarily marring her beautiful eyes. "He can take care of them, of course, but I hate being away from them for long." She shook her head. Drawing closer, Aljeya said quietly, "I'm sorry about the welcome you received last night. It was unpardonable. I would love to hear about what happened to Kadj and what drew you from Bijal."

Zyre frowned at their current company. "Maybe later? It's a long story."

"That's probably wise. Come on, I think the meeting is about to begin," Aljeya said, dragging Zyre playfully by the elbow. They came to stand behind Jervin. Her father spared her only a moment's glance.

In front of him was a long table with two impressively detailed maps. One was of the country as a whole. The other showed the region, the Áit cutting straight through. On Las Corvika's map, little figures marked the locations of standing armies at outposts, in lords' manors, on patrol. The Áit map was far more populated.

Somehow, the rebel army outnumbered the royal one, although not by a particularly wide margin.

"Captains, Lieutenants." Jervin said, his voice taking on that sharpness of command Zyre had often heard when working as a guard on the estate. "We had hoped to appease Tholjun with a battle on these fields, killing the regis and all his men in one fell swoop. But he has granted us another opportunity, one that brings Notoyem's tyranny to the ground where we might plant our banners instead. *Eris bi eljers!*"

"*Eris bi eljers!*" Zyre echoed warily, her voice drowned out by the cheers of the men inside the pavilion.

"I cede to General Tavere's judgment for the battle plans."

The general nodded his head in thanks as the tent fell to silence once again. "Les Stelvo has become as vulnerable as it's ever been, manned by five thousand troops if we're being generous. But our lady and our *vinje* are in the griffon's beak, so to speak, and any force wishing to save them would have to be the stealthiest Las Corvika has to offer. The comte and his cavalry couldn't make it to the meeting, so that leaves us sad dogs."

The men laughed, but Zyre could only frown, wondering if it was a soldier's joke or if it just went over her head because most things did.

Vjeronin Tol was a middle-aged man with more than a few scars and a missing finger. "What of the regis, sir, and the forces across the river?" he asked. Other voices rumbled beneath his.

The general motioned for silence. "We called for Thyljal's favor last night. Our informants are late to bring back news but—"

A soldier ducked into the tent, bowing. "Pardon the interruption, sir. Scout Rodier is back with his report."

"Ah, perfect timing. Let him in," Tavere said.

The soldier ducked back out, replaced immediately by a wiry

man with sharp eyes. He bowed, breathing heavily. "Pardon the tardiness, sir, but I have more news to report than we'd hoped."

"Was the team successful?"

Rodier nodded grimly. "The regis was found dead late last night."

The men burst into cheers. And, despite herself, Zyre smiled. But there was more to it. She could see it in his expression. Things could never work out perfectly, could they?

Jervin noticed it too. "You said there was more?"

Again, Rodier nodded. "A small party of fifty has snuck out of the royal army, Regis-Uncrowned, General. Two nobles bearing the comte's sigil were among the retinue, and I'm certain Nyli Béranger was with them too. It appears they're heading for Mod Redel."

Zyre scowled. She heard her father respond, something about Elyx Béranger and a pincer move that might at least rob them of some of their advantage. But hearing and listening were two very different things, and for Zyre, the words were drowned out by a single sentence played over and over in her head. *I should have killed him. I should have killed him. I should have killed him.*

She didn't hear, at least not at first, her father's declaration for attack. And by the time her brain caught up, it was too late.

Tavere faced the captains and lieutenants. "All right, change of plan. Captain Ricard, grab your strongest *sjarvisk*. Have them pull the bridge. We make the crossing now. *Eris bi eljers!*"

The men roared their agreement.

"Tavere, a quick word," Jervin said as the men filed out.

Zyre waited with the stragglers, her sister among them. She watched as her father took Tavere's arm, brought him close, and whispered in his ear.

"Send word to our spies. Their one and only directive is to get Ivanya and Remy out of the capital through any means necessary."

"Jervin, your wish is my command," Tavere said, "but the gates—"

"We'll find a way. See it done."

The two men stared each other down until Tavere bowed his head in acquiescence.

And then Aljeya was pulling on her arm, ushering her out of the tent. Zyre's mind was already whirling. Her magic was now unbound. With a battle coming, perhaps she could finally show just how useful her magic could be. She was more than just something that got in the way. She was more than some *washer woman*. She was Zyre Arnaud, daughter of Baron Jervin Arnaud, rightful regis of Las Corvika. The gods had graced her with *aljarne* magic. Why else, if not to help her father secure his throne?

"Zyre," Aljeya said before Zyre could find her friends, say her farewells. Aljeya's tone was cutting. "You should wait out the battle with me. Father's little spies and advisors might have a way to free Remy and our mother, but I'd much rather have my own plan in place. I could use your help. My tent is big enough to accommodate your friends, too, if you'd like."

"I'll have to find them first," she replied with a laugh.

Her sister looked at her suspiciously. Even after all these years, Aljeya knew her too well. "Okay," she said finally. Then, suddenly, she smiled. "I'm glad you've found some people you can trust, *ehzi*. I look forward to learning more about them."

Aljeya gestured to her guards, and they began to press their way through the camp.

As soon as she was alone, Zyre stopped the closest soldier and demanded to be told where the armory was. He directed her to the east side of camp, though he frowned at her as he jogged off.

Zyre sprinted past the *velídas* tree, turning right at the fork. Everywhere she looked, she saw men donning leather armor, belting water flasks at their waists, stringing their bows or sharpening the tips of spears and edges of swords. She was surprised at how many men had bows in addition to the close-range weapons. There were no fumbling fingers, no slowness of movement. It was an army used to viper strikes, one that had done battle over the course of five years and pretended it was nothing more than banditry.

Even as they ran to meet their captains, it was purposeful and direct. Her mad dash was the only thing that threw them off, chaos amongst order. She clipped several men's shoulders, was nearly knocked down by others, and, all the while, tried to fight off a growing, insistent panic that she was doing the wrong thing.

The armory itself abutted the largest part of camp, squatting next to the clusters of foot soldier unites. It was not full of traffic, but the area surrounding it was even more intense than the rest of camp. It was like a small delta beside a rushing river of movement.

They gave the armory a wide enough berth, at least, and once Zyre was a few paces away, she could finally stand still. It was more a pavilion than a tent, with only a canvas wall on the back. A workbench separated the blacksmiths from the soldiers, swords propped against the short end of the table and pikes leaning on a rack farther in.

She watched, half-intrigued, as the few men received spears and pieces of armor. There were a few older in years, but mostly, they were young, younger even than her. Their fingers fumbled with the knots, dropped the spear, or held its shaft too tightly. This would be their first battle, then.

Finally, it was Zyre's turn.

The armorer and his team took one look at her and gave her a strange look. "Do you have a permission slip?" the armorer asked.

"I—what?"

"You lost your soulbeast, did you not?"

For a moment, a wild moment, Zyre thought he was talking

about Kadj and wondered how in Thyljal's name he could have possibly known.

The armorer continued, oblivious, "Women who have lost their *sjarvisk* are allowed to fight only if they have a permission slip from their commanding officer." His eyes narrowed. "But I cannot just get you a new set of armor. You will have to use the set already assigned to you."

"I am the…" Zyre snapped. She bit her tongue before she could blurt out the truth. "I am the niece of Jervin Arnaud, the daughter of his brother, not some common *sjarvisk*. I know how to fight. I need armor, and I need a sword. Quickly!"

The man just laughed in her face. "Yes, and I'm the cousin to the regis."

"Zyre!"

She nearly jumped out of her skin at the voice behind her. Zyre turned from the infuriating man to find Merytz, of all people, charging toward her. *Thalja's breath*, she growled. "You should be with Baron Arnaud."

He drew to a stop before her, several paces separating them. "*Regis-Uncrowned* Arnaud, now. And he sent me to find you. He was worried—rightly, apparently—that you were going to try to fight in the battle."

"Do you intend to stop me?"

"Those were my instructions, yes," Merytz said. He stepped closer. "Zyre, battles are no small things. You would have to fight it on the merits of your sword fighting alone, and it gets chaotic out there."

As if she didn't know what a battle was like. "I sank the *Aretmor*, and I stormed a city barracks in Venasca. I'm not new to conflict; I know how to keep my head." That she had to use her magic for the former and that she'd relied on Modorin to keep her own kill count to a minimum in the latter was not worth mentioning.

Merytz blinked, stunned, but he recovered quickly. "I like to think that we were friends on Lasinia. Whether or not you're experienced at fighting, that doesn't change the fact that you hate bloodshed. I know you do. Unless losing Kadj…"

"It didn't," Zyre snapped, knowing where he was going with that train of thought. "This is about playing my part and about making up for all the times I ran away or couldn't do anything to help keep people safe."

The Guardsmaster sighed. "I get that. Trust me, I do. What if we make ourselves a compromise? Sit this battle out. Just listen," he pressed when she made a move to argue. "Sit this battle out. There will be others, trust me. Once this fight is won, I'll put together some men who can act as your honor guard to watch your back in the next fight."

Zyre crossed her arms. "And what if they need me in *this* battle? They don't actually know what they're walking into, and we don't outnumber Notoyem's men so much that luck might change the tides."

"One person cannot change the course of a battle," Merytz said gently. Except that wasn't strictly true, and that was more terrifying than anything else. "Please, Zyre. I promise, I will find you an honor guard, but until then, stay out of this."

She grimaced. Lies were to be her friend today. "You promise I will be able to fight in the next battle?"

Her old friend nodded.

"Then I swear on Tholjun's blood, I will sit this one out."

His relief was evident. "Then I must leave you." He turned and trotted away.

"Merytz!" she called out after him. He slowed and turned back toward her. "Go safely."

The man gave a ghost of a smile. He fell into a half bow, fist over his heart. And then he was gone, lost in the crowd.

Zyre made the mistake of glancing back at the armorer, who was looking far too smug for his own good. She flashed him an obscene gesture that wiped the grin from his face. Then she walked back to her tent.

Already, many of the paths were starting to clear out, as the troops had found their commanding officers and were waiting in the field. Those she passed were stragglers, slow to rise, tripping over their feet in their haste to get where they needed to be. With little trouble, Zyre found her friends. They were not sleeping any longer, but rather sitting outside the tent, watching the chaos with some curiosity.

"Zyre!" Modorin called as Sarol unfurled from his lap and trotted a few steps toward her, tail wagging. "What's going on?"

"Modorin! Neelie! I was looking for you." She steeled herself for the words she was about to say. "There's going to be a battle."

Modorin sobered. "So this is it, then? You're really going to fight?"

"I have to." *To save my mother and brother. To pay back the Bérangers for destroying my home. And to make them pay for these years of hiding.*

Zyre hoped to find respect or pride in Neelie's eyes, but the woman's expression was shuttered off from her.

She filled them in as they followed the last of the men to the banks of the Áit, facing the miniscule earthen bridge that the three of them had crossed just last night.

Seeing the army, though, made both her mouth and her mind go silent. Zyre was dumbstruck by the massive congregation of soldiers before her. If this was fifteen thousand strong, what was the hundred thousand the bards always sang of in their epics? They crowded the banks in an organized manner, so many banners flying her father's sigil. Words buzzed behind her, but she did not pay attention.

Zyre had no idea how she was going to sneak into *that*.

A hand tugged her away, and she tore her eyes from the massed army back to Modorin. They stepped off to the side for some privacy, though it was unnecessary. Neelie watched but did not follow.

"You're going to sneak your way onto the fight, aren't you?" he asked.

"Maybe."

Modorin groaned. "That's a terrible idea, Zyre. Do you know what armies do to people whose allegiances they don't know? Battlefields are all 'kill first, ask questions later.' Your own men would turn on you."

"They won't when they see that I'm killing Béranger men."

"That's one hell of a risk, Zyre. In any case, how are you going to fight? As *aljarne*? Have you even figured out how you're going to use your magic on an open field, *without* a soulbeast, and still keep your magic a secret?"

Zyre opened her mouth to argue, then, with a growl, snapped it shut. She hadn't thought about that. "So I don't use my magic."

He stared at her. "You know I was there with you when we went to rescue— You know what, never mind. Look, Neelie and I are leaving in a few days. Sit this one out, for me? We can even figure out how you can fight in the next battlefield without revealing your magic."

Gods, she should have said no, or better yet, lied. However much Zyre hated bloodshed, she could do this thing for her father. It was bad enough that Merytz and Jervin were both intent on keeping her off the field, but her friend? Modorin?

How could she say no to him?

Cursing silently, she said, "Fine. We may as well see the army off, and then we'll go find my sister. She has a rescue mission she needs help planning, and I'm sure she'll be able to help with my problem too."

Modorin broke out in a grin. He gestured behind them at a tall tree. The tree offered ample footing, and the three of them scrambled up it. Neelie was a strong climber and matched Zyre branch for branch. Modorin got left in the dust, at least until the limbs thinned and both Zyre and Neelie had to stop. He grinned victoriously as he clambered up a little higher, the thin branches able to support his smaller frame.

Sarol was on the ground, of course, keeping watch.

The army had been milling into its final place as they climbed, and the three had just gotten settled when a voice muffled by the distance and the height and the sounds of thousands of troops shouted a command. A handful of figures detached from the army. Beasts trailed after them, though Zyre could only make out the largest, a brown bear judging by the height. Then, suddenly, the ground began to tremble and the water began to roar. The earthen bridge rose, growing wider and wider until it spanned a hundred feet across.

The company of mounted soldiers crossed first, shouting to Tholjun over the thunder of their horses' hooves.

The foot soldiers crossed next, compressing their ranks. From this distance, she couldn't see their faces. She saw only their slow, methodical march. But she knew her father was there, near the forefront, one of the few mounted men. He would bring the army to the battlefield, then let one of the captains lead the charge.

The archers folded in on themselves next, and the smaller units of *sjarvisk*. The cavalry had already disappeared, but everyone else waited for the entire army to cross. Only then did they follow after the others.

Zyre whispered a prayer to her gods, especially to Tholjun, surprised at how far the sound of a marching army carried.

When the forces met, she heard that too, the thunderous clash of bodies, the war cries, the screams. Though it shamed her, Zyre was a little glad Modorin had talked her out of fighting in that chaos. In the thunder, she heard the groan of the *Aretmor* as she ripped a hole in its belly. She heard the terrible thunk of the man's body crashing into the guardhouse in Bijal. She'd have to face that fear eventually, and she tried to steel herself against it now. She really did.

But, gods, how their screams made her tremble.

⁂

Mod Redel was a welcome sight after spending half the day in the saddle. Nyli and his group had left early, traveling three miles downriver just to make sure their party didn't stumble across some of Jervin's men, and even then, the journey had been made in silence so their voices would not betray them to the enemy.

It wasn't much of a traveling party. Kuval and the comte were both with Nyli, of course, along with his honor guard. General Héroux was the only man of rank left behind in the camp, waiting for Nyli's return so they could start discreetly telling the commanding officers their plan of attack. If word spread too fast, some of the soldiers would desert, and Luc would know not to grant them entry into the capital.

The hope was Elyx's support might be enough to hold the loyalty of the troops under their command.

Elyx was waiting for them in the courtyard, and as Nyli's horse trotted in, he began to feel the full weight of his nerves. For all his bold talk, this was no sure thing. Elyx did not get along with Luc, but it was one thing to stay out of his way and another still to outright oppose him.

Only a few years younger than his brother, Elyx had the sharp

Béranger jaw, the intense brown eyes, the lean figure. The defining difference between the two men was that Nyli had never once seen any harshness, any wrath, in Elyx's eyes. Today, though, might prove to be the exception.

"Welcome to Mod Redel. I'd offer you pleasantries, but considering the sudden increase of soldiers in the area, I'd first like to know if this is a matter of urgency." Elyx's dark gaze flicked between the comte and the prince.

Nyli dismounted and allowed a stablehand to take his horse's reins. "The regis is dead, assassinated in the night. It is about as urgent as it gets, Uncle."

Elyx was momentarily at a loss for words. His eyes darted from one member of Nyli's retinue to the next, perhaps hoping one would prove him wrong. "Notoyem's dead?"

Nyli nodded even as Pierre said, "Yes."

Elyx turned away from Nyli, taking a step toward the fortress, halting, stepping again. Then Elyx spun again to face them. "You'll pardon me. This is unexpected." His face was unreadable.

Nyli, who'd been given a handful of hours to process everything and still felt as unsteady as he'd been standing over his father's body, sympathized with his uncle. "We're here on a matter of succession. I hate that these things must happen so quickly and give us so little time to mourn, but that is the nature of being noble."

"You want to oppose your brother?" It was the only logical conclusion, and if Elyx disapproved, it was still kept tightly in check. "Comte Duvachelle, I hope you'll pardon me, but I should speak to my nephew alone. I'll have my servants show you where you can take your respite."

The comte did not protest, and although Nyli wanted nothing more than for Kuval to stay by his side, he said nothing while the two men and Nyli's honor guard were led away.

A nearby servant took Pierre, Kuval, and Nyli's guard to a sitting room near the entrance. Elyx took Nyli farther in, clearing a few clerks out of an office so they could have some privacy. His uncle withdrew a chair and sat behind one of the desks, motioning for Nyli to bring a spare to the opposite side.

And there, finally, Elyx slumped forward, letting his head fall into his hands. It made Nyli's throat burn to see this grief. Out of the entire camp, his uncle was the one who understood Notoyem's poisoned love best. And who, truth be told, would understand the position Nyli was in better than anyone in the world. It had never struck him until this moment to wonder what Elyx had felt the day he'd learned his brother—his volatile, proud, dangerous older brother—was pursuing the power that came with a throne.

"What happened?" his uncle asked.

"We think Jervin sent some men into the camp while it was late. They snuck in and struck him with an enchanted blade before his honor guard could realize what was happening. It appears there was a scuffle, though, and the assassins were killed."

Elyx nodded numbly. "I, ah. I suppose it shouldn't surprise me. He always seemed to have more enemies than friends."

"I'm sorry," Nyli blurted out. Then forced himself back into some semblance of calm. "I wish I'd been there with him, I mean."

He didn't, and Elyx knew he didn't, because the two of them understood one another. It was why Nyli loved his uncle even though they couldn't see each other often.

"So you will march against Luc." It was more statement than question, Elyx pulling his grief inward so he could look more like the stern uncle he often tried to play. "And you want me to stand in open opposition against him? The gods always favor the eldest, Nyli. You know this."

"But the gods have put me in an unlikely position of power, Uncle," Nyli said, pulling himself to the edge of his seat. "The capital is drained of troops, troops that *I* currently hold command of. Comte Duvachelle stands behind me. With luck, so shall the duc. Even if he doesn't, I have more than enough troops to fight my way through if I have to, and I'm hoping I won't have to."

His uncle sighed, scratching at the graying scruff near his ear as he settled back into his seat. "Your brother only grew up the way he did under pressure from your father," he said helplessly.

"Our father pushed the same pressures on me, and yet I'm *nothing* like him. I don't find joy in making people terrified." The words came out hotter than Nyli had meant them to. He didn't want to seem *eager* to betray his brother, because that wasn't exactly true. It seemed unfair that one could hate a person so strongly yet love them too.

Nyli felt the weight of his uncle's gaze as the man studied him thoughtfully. "Thalja forgive me, but it would still be an easy answer, Nyli, if your brother didn't hold Les Stelvo. Even with a small contingent of soldiers to man it, the capital will not fall easily—at least, not with the troops that you have. And he who holds the capital—"

"Holds the country," Nyli finished glumly.

"The duc and his son have always been closest to Notoyem and Luc. They may not be eager to betray them for you. You do realize this? They might fight you or rush to Les Stelvo to fortify the city against your attack."

Nyli understood, but he remained silent.

"You'll have to kill Luc, too, you know."

"I know."

There was that piercing gaze again. Elyx didn't believe him. Nyli met his uncle's stare, imagining, if only for a moment, a version of himself that could do whatever needed doing.

His uncle caved. "All right. All right. What troops I have are yours to command. But do not ask me to march with you, Nyli.

I do not want to have a direct hand in my nephew's death, no matter how much he takes after my brother."

Nyli let out a breath, not sure why he suddenly felt like crying. Or screaming. "Thank you, Uncle."

"Don't thank me yet," Elyx replied. He stood. "Come on. I suppose we should bring the news to the comte."

They walked toward the sitting room and were just about to turn a corner when they heard a crash. Elyx and Nyli shared a look, then hurried toward the source of the sound. Just outside the sitting room, Pierre stood with splinters of wood around him, the remnants of some piece of art. A green-clad soldier was frozen before him, eyes wide at the mess on the floor. Pierre's eyes were fury as he turned to face Elyx and Nyli.

"Jervin's somehow found our ruse. Our army is under attack."

Nyli's mind spun, searching for purchase. A bold, foolish plan tumbled into place. If they were quick, it just might work. "Uncle, I need the horses saddled. Have the men ready to march, but don't send them into the field yet. I'm going to demand a parlay."

Pierre spluttered. "Are you *mad?*"

"Maybe," Nyli said. "But if all our men die today, then our dreams for a better nation die with them."

Behind his father, Kuval offered a supportive grin. But Nyli couldn't hold on to his elation. Things were turning out the way he'd hoped, but it could all still be torn apart by Jervin Arnaud.

*Thalja, give wind to our horses' hooves today. It's the only chance we have.*

# CHAPTER 20

The camp was eerily silent as Zyre led her friends back to the war tent. The only folk who remained were the medics, and they were in their own section of camp, preparing for the end of the fight.

"You're going to be stuck doing small magic," Neelie was saying. "Things that either look like they could've come from a nearby *sjarvisk* or that they wouldn't even notice. Minor tremors in the earth to make your opponent stumble, or a flick of air to turn his blade away from you. That sort of thing."

"And you're not going to be able to just knock people out on the field, either," Modorin warned as the war tent's flags became visible ahead.

Zyre rolled her eyes. "I know that."

"I'm just saying. Everything moves so quickly during a fight. Even more so than it did when we were in the barracks, because on the field, it's just facing one man and then the next. Although you Corvikans rank your troops, don't you? Move the men in the front to the back for a break?"

Zyre nodded. "When there's space. In confined quarters, it's a bit difficult. What, they didn't do that in the Syfris army?"

"Laerans use hit-and-run tactics," Modorin said with a shrug. "Fighting them was always chaotic."

They came to the tent. Zyre was surprised to find that two men stood at attention; she didn't think there was any point in leaving guards. But, then again, there would be plenty of secrets kept within the confines of this canvas that her father probably wouldn't want to risk getting out.

Of course, that didn't apply to Zyre. The soldiers saluted and waved them through, holding back the flap for them.

A small flame flickered above Modorin's palm, offering a little more light in the hazy darkness. "What are we looking for, again?"

"Any information there is about Les Stelvo. Especially the palace. We'll need to know how many men are stationed there, its layout, things like that."

They began to rummage through all of the papers and maps stacked on the tables and kept in the chests. Fortunately, Jervin was very strict about his organization. All they had to do was find the right area, and the rest should follow.

After several minutes, Zyre, sitting at her father's desk, found a map of Les Stelvo, pieces of its walls shaded in. Interestingly, the entire inner wall was completely darkened. "I got it!" she said.

Modorin and Neelie abandoned their own searches and came to join her. Together, they looked through the notes, the maps, everything. There was a roughly drawn map of the palace with small corridors wedged in odd places. Supply closets had little marks drawn against the wall, though Zyre didn't know what it meant beyond the fact that they seemed to lead into the corridors. There was also a map of the palace grounds. She didn't know what else they might need, so they took those three pieces and left the rest.

Finding Aljeya was the next challenge, but it proved easier than expected. In an army camp emptied of its troops, the Atloran guard stood out. Aljeya's tent, it seemed, was not all that far from their father's.

The Atloran's equivalent of Guardsmaster made them wait outside while he announced their presence. Only then did he let them pass.

Aljeya's tent was sparse, but what was there spoke of comfort. The cushions on the floor looked plush. A tray of food sat in the center—fruits, sweet breads, and soft Atloran cheese. Aljeya herself was on her feet, scowling at a piece of paper. She set it down and smiled at Zyre. "You actually came," she said, sounding surprised.

"With company, and information." Zyre waved their maps in the air. "We raided the war tent."

Her sister looked impressed.

They settled down on the cushions and considered everything they knew about Ivanya's situation, what allies they had to work with, and what escape routes were open to them. For the better part of an hour, they plotted, until Zyre remembered there was a velídas tree on the grounds.

"Maybe we could replicate Neelie's rescue!" Zyre said excitedly. "I could travel through Velídas and clear open a path or something."

"Yeah, that's probably off the table," Neelie replied with a wince. "You don't have your *leiks* to protect your mind."

"A beautiful sea in which to drown, remember?" Modorin added.

Zyre deflated.

Aljeya's eyes darted across them all curiously. "All right, who's going to be the one who fills me in on all of my sister's antics?"

Hearing the words *my sister* made her thrum with joy, and Zyre launched into the tale with a reckless abandon. She did try to gloss over the full extent of her destruction, both with the

*Aretmor* and Bijal's barracks, but her friends piped in, painting her as some stranger, brave and selfless.

It was good that they were so quick to talk over each other, though. In the few quiet moments that lapsed, the sounds of battle continued to boom across the fields, bouncing amidst the tents. If Zyre strained her hearing—and she tried not to—she swore sometimes she could hear their screams.

Despite Jervin's little ambush, Notoyem's men were holding out with surprising tenacity. Well, perhaps not *so* surprising; General Héroux was considered one of the most cunning battlefield commanders alive. Either way, Jervin took pleasure in knowing he was right; their attack had caught the Béranger men off guard.

When a messenger came running up with reports of Nyli returning from Mod Redel, though, Jervin wasn't surprised. What *did* surprise him was the messenger's insistence that Elyx did not ride with Redel's reinforcements. Then the messenger said something even more unexpected.

Nyli was flying the flag of peace. He wanted a parlay.

Jervin contemplated the offer. People generally didn't ask for a parlay unless they were desperate. And even if the prince was trying to lure him into some trap or delay the inevitable, Jervin's men had still established the upper hand on the field.

"What do you think, Tavere? Should we hear what the Butcher has to say?"

Tavere shrugged. "The battle is in our favor, but the fight will cost us troops we will likely need in the fight to come. I say hear him out. Best-case scenario, he falls under our banner and we have enough men to crush Luc's. Worst-case scenario, we kill him where he stands and we'll have only lost an hour."

Jervin nodded in agreement. He turned back to the messenger. "Bring him here. Tell him we'll hear what he has to say."

The messenger bowed and ran off.

They had however long it took for the soldier to return to Nyli and lead him back to their pavilion, and Jervin made the most of it. They immediately sounded the horn, signaling their troops to stand down, and the opposing side echoed the sound, though whether it was on Nyli's orders or simply from relief at the possibility of a reprieve, there was no way of knowing.

Merytz led the honor guard as they cleared away any sensitive information, flipping pages over, tucking them in drawers. Then Merytz sent runners to the lieutenants on the field, requesting some men to guard the pavilion. Small units of soldiers filed in, reporting for duty, numbering a hundred strong. Tavere positioned them around the pavilion while Jervin drew three chairs from the corner: two for them and one for the prince.

None too soon, Nyli and his retinue appeared. He did not arrive with the duc or even the comte. Instead, it was the comte's young son, Kuval, who accompanied the prince. Jervin couldn't quite decide the political implications there. Kuval walked so close to Nyli that his hand bumped against the prince's thigh, though Nyli didn't seem to care.

"So, the Butcher has resurfaced," Jervin said, sliding into his chair. Tavere followed, sitting more stiffly on his own.

A flash of Béranger wrath burned and died in Nyli's eyes. "And come with a proposition."

Jervin scoffed. "Proposition? What could you possibly have to offer me? The only thing I want is the crown, and you're not the one who can give it."

"Considering the regis fell last night, I disagree," Nyli said coolly.

Jervin snorted. "I will not cede the crown to your brother. I have no intention of bowing to another tyrant regis."

Nyli's expression darkened. "I am not here on behalf of my brother. You're right, Arnaud. Las Corvika does not need another tyrant regis. I do not intend to let one claim it." The prince looked sharply at Jervin. Jervin scowled when he realized Nyli's implications—the *audacity*, to call *him* a tyrant. "I have taken claim of my father's men. Our forces combined would make a pretty frightening figure, don't you think? All the forces in the world could not save Luc from defeat, then."

Tavere frowned. "You would turn against your own brother?"

"In a heartbeat," the prince answered quickly. *Too quickly?*

"So you would be willing to give up the crown, to swear your allegiance to me?" Jervin challenged.

Nyli glanced at Kuval. The comte's youngest son nodded. It was such an odd gesture that Jervin didn't know what to make of it. Then the prince turned his attention back onto Jervin and Tavere. He wore a dangerous grin. "No. In fact, that is the very opposite of what I've come to do here. I wish *you* to swear your allegiance to *me*."

It took every bit of willpower not to let his jaw gape open.

"My father won the crown, Jervin Arnaud," Nyli continued. "House Béranger holds the throne. The Ermengarde reign is over and has been for twenty years. Or do you really think battlefield Right of Precedence would hold any weight? No. I don't even need you. My brother would welcome me into Les Stelvo, oblivious of my intentions, and I could bury a knife in his chest before he even knew what happened. And if you really think we'd leave Les Stelvo defenseless, you're a fool. You have, what, fifteen thousand? Larger forces than yours have tried and failed to take it."

Jervin grasped at what he could from Nyli's mad speech. "I know for a fact that Les Stelvo had to empty most of its troops to populate your army, Butcher. The very one we were about to destroy. Don't insult my intelligence. The capital is more vulnerable than it has been in all those other attempts to take it."

Another flash of anger crossed the prince's face before he shuttered it behind a stony expression. "You want to claim the crown for the Ermengarde name, to avenge the men Tholjun claimed unfairly. It's an understandable sentiment. But even if you win Les Stelvo, you are backed by predominantly minor Houses. They will not help you rule the country. And I know House Villeneuve and House Duvachelle will not back you, because they know what their alliance to my father's cause will cost them if they do. Every day of your leadership will be plagued by unwilling Houses refusing compromise. And for what? I cannot give you regency, but I can give you all the power that comes with being a direct ally to the regis. I can grant you Right of Precedence, the lands and power that come with Ducship. You could create a new home in Obele to function as your base. Although," he said slowly, "I'm not one to turn down wisdom in its many forms. I should hope you would spend more time in the capital."

Silence fell.

So, the prince would just throw this at him like it was nothing? In those first years after the Succession, Jervin had fallen in behind Notoyem, betrayed *everything* he stood for in the name of peace. He'd endured insult after insult, hoping if he could just prove to Notoyem how dedicated he was to the idea of peace, the regis would welcome him into his circles where a man of his station belonged.

And here Nyli was, offering the titles and respects that Jervin had been denied, the very titles Nyli himself had taken in those days when the Arnaud House finally fell from grace.

How dare Nyli mitigate every effort Jervin had made these last five years of rebellion?

The prince, apparently, had even more left to say. "I do not have to sit here and treat with you, Jervin Arnaud. I do it in the hopes of unifying Las Corvika, letting it become what it was meant to be. Not a place of tyrants, but rather, a country that rivals Venasca, Pailyr. Is it the country you fight for, Jervin, or is it your pride? Because only one of those things will return Las Corvika to its former glory."

What a pretty picture the prince painted for them. But it seemed an insult to all the men who had died these past five years to give up the cause to this upstart.

Growing up, Jervin never would have thought a House as small as his would ever have the chance to take the throne. But their power had grown exponentially under the Ermengardes. Tholjun himself had graced their armies, their cause. And for what? He was winning this fight. He could win the battle, too.

Still, he hesitated. Not for the reasons Nyli likely hoped— Jervin did not consider himself sentimental in that regard. He wanted to build a country he could be proud of again. He would have ceded to Notoyem all those years ago, forgiven all those slights. It was Notoyem who had shut that door, but his son was willing to open them again.

But Jervin had learned from the last. He would not give it all up in the name of peace. One could not fix a broken country if one was amidst the shards. He had to tie himself to the regis somehow. Something more binding than borrowed armies or words on paper.

A thought came unbidden. Or perhaps it was sent by the gods themselves.

Five years ago, Notoyem had destroyed their chances of unifying their families and bringing peace to the land. It was only right that Nyli remedy that situation now.

And when, after a lengthy, incredulous debate, the prince

finally conceded to the argument, Jervin rose and offered a full bow, a symbolic promise of fealty to the newly chosen Regis-Uncrowned.

It felt like he was signing away something irreplaceable, more than just a crown. But he had cast his dice. Now it was time to see how they landed.

Zyre had heard the horns in Aljeya's tent, though none of her companions seemed to know what they meant. It wasn't until the first hour had rolled well into the second that the ground trembled and the healers were summoned to the Áit to meet the soldiers. With nothing more than harebrained schemes and half-formed plots to show for their effort, the four of them—plus Sarol—followed the flow of traffic to the approaching army.

"What are the chances that Nyli's army won and is about to wipe us all out?" Zyre whispered to her sister.

Aljeya's expression darkened. "If that's the case, make it clear immediately that you're the daughter of a nobleman. Even traitors can be worth a nice ransom." She turned to look directly at Zyre. "Use your magic *only* if it's a matter of life and death. There's no putting that bird back in its cage."

Zyre nodded, a small amount of dread building in her gut.

They arrived on the banks of the Áit, but Zyre's fears quickly proved ungrounded. The standards the men held had bloody tips and torn fabric, but the Arnaud fish were still clearly discernible. And the soldiers themselves, roughened, bloody, and mud-spattered, wore Arnaud uniforms. Not blue, but rather, dark green with black patches to better blend into their surroundings.

The air was thick with the metallic scent of blood and dirt and sweat, crowded with the pained groans that clashed with the exhausted but victorious grins of the troops well enough to celebrate.

One of them, with knots decorating the space above his heart, broke away. Zyre recognized him from the war meeting earlier. For all the signs of victory, he looked surprisingly downcast.

Zyre had a bad feeling about this.

Aljeya marked the officer, too. She marched over to him, and Zyre struggled to keep up. "Where's my father?" Aljeya demanded.

The captain wiped his sleeve across his damp face. "Alive and unharmed, my lady. There are simply some things he needs to tend to. But I'm afraid I'd best leave that to him to explain."

"And the prince?" Zyre pressed before he could make his escape.

"I'll leave that to him, my ladies," he repeated uncomfortably. "Now, if you'll excuse me. I have duties to tend to."

The officer hurried off.

"That was odd," Aljeya said.

Zyre nodded in agreement. She pressed a hand against her sister's arm, signing, "*I'll be right back.*"

Her sister waved absently.

Zyre rejoined her friends at the edge of the field, where they watched the healers tend to the wounded soldiers.

Modorin was scowling. She thought she could understand his sentiment. The men were happy. Despite the blood on their clothes or bubbling out of gashes, this was a good day for them. There was an incongruity to bloodied men cheering.

It was different from the joy she and Modorin had shared that last night in Bijal, with Neelie freed and both of them safe again behind Hosvar's wards. They hadn't run in with the intent to destroy as many lives as possible. They'd gone in, rescued Neelie, and run out. What she was looking at now was nothing less than a two-sided massacre. Victories should be somber things, not joyous celebrations.

"Look at them go," Modorin said with disgust, startling Zyre.

"Sorry?"

He gestured to the healers, their familiars bumping noses against the leg or palm of whichever soul the healer was tending to. "They'll patch them up as best as they can, and the commanders and lieutenants will pretend that all of their surviving troops are as good as new, ready for the next battle, where they can once again risk their limbs or their sanity or their very lives. It never ends, not really. Maybe for a year, maybe five, maybe ten, but always, someone's greed for power sparks it all again."

"You make it seem as if humanity is always destined for war," she said.

Modorin shrugged as if to say, *Aren't we?*

"I do not accept that."

She glanced at Neelie, hoping for backup. The other woman refused to side with either of them, just studying the proceedings blankly. *Does she see her Shadowmen in these soldiers?* Zyre wondered.

"You don't have to stick around," Zyre told her friend quietly. "Your mother hit the Áit, didn't she? You could travel upriver and meet her there."

Neelie's eyes went back into focus. As she looked at Zyre, a strange expression flitted across her eyes. But when she spoke, there was nothing in her tone to reveal more. "She's only a day out. One day's not going to lose us anything."

"Your family, Neelie. I thought you were in a hurry to get back to them."

"I am," Neelie said softly.

Zyre waited for her to continue, uncertain why her heart felt like it was fracturing in the silence. "Well," Zyre said finally, "you might as well head back into camp. I need to wait for my father, and I'm not sure how long he'll be."

"Are you sure?" Modorin asked.

"I'm sure."

Even though she didn't mind, not really, it still stung to watch them walk away together, their heads bent, already deep in conversation. It was a bitter reminder that all she'd ever been was a temporary addition. Bijal was not her place. Las Corvika was.

Zyre meandered back to her sister. After a few minutes, when it became obvious Jervin wouldn't be reappearing all that soon, they found shade underneath the tree she and her friends had climbed earlier. Time dragged slowly.

There were fewer men injured than she would have expected—those who were unhurt, or whose injuries were minor, pressed on to the camp so they could get out of the way of those who needed the most attention—but the range of wounds was surprising. Lost arms and legs, missing ears, missing eyes. One bleeding so badly at his nose that it took her a moment to realize he'd lost it completely. And all of them bearing rumpled, muddy, and blood-spattered uniforms that had been so pristine earlier. She'd never considered just how *dirty* a battle could be.

Finally, a small group on horseback trotted across the earthen bridge. Merytz rode on Jervin's right, bearing the Arnaud flag. Both wore surly expressions that matched the captain's from earlier.

Aljeya rolled to her feet in a single fluid motion. She helped Zyre up, and the two of them hurried over.

"How did we do?" Aljeya asked cautiously.

Jervin swung down from his horse. He passed the reins over to Merytz and drew them off to the side. "It was a draw," he said finally.

"A draw?" Zyre exclaimed. "It doesn't look like the battle went as bad as all that."

"Keep your voice down," Jervin snapped. His expression was harder than she'd ever seen before. "Do you both trust me?"

Zyre and Aljeya shared a worried glance before they both nodded.

"Nyli approached with a peace treaty. The two of us had a lengthy conversation about the future of this country. It was not an easy decision, but I have sworn allegiance to him."

"You *what*?" Aljeya snarled as Zyre shouted, "You can't have! To *Nyli*? He burned down our home!"

Jervin silenced them both with a gesture. "I'm well aware of that, thank you," he said curtly. "My allegiance did not come cheaply, I assure you. It was the only way to guarantee our family's well-being. Even now, Nyli is writing a letter to his brother saying I have surrendered to him. Luc won't know he's under attack until it's too late to do anything about it."

*They wouldn't even be in the capital if it wasn't for him,* Zyre wanted to scream. But she kept her mouth shut.

"I wish you would have consulted us, Father," Aljeya said quietly.

Jervin snorted. "To what end? Neither of you are directly involved in the war. I appreciate your input, of course, when asked, but these decisions are mine alone to make. Now, we don't have time to just sit around and talk. I need to get myself cleaned up for the council we'll have to call. Tomorrow, we begin the march to the capital."

"So soon?" Zyre asked, startled.

"Is there a reason to delay?" Jervin crossed his arms in front of his chest, waiting.

There was only one answer he would accept. "No, Father," she said dully. But she remembered Modorin's words. *They'll patch them up just to send them off again.* What an unfortunate, bloody cycle.

⚜

In a darkly lit corridor tucked behind the throne room, Ivanya listened to the buzz of conversation on the other side of the wall and felt disheartened by its volume. Everyone seemed to be converging in that room. But not Ivanya. Not Damari or Bernard. No, they waited under guard in the servants' corridor, like a bride waiting to be debuted.

Except there was no way this would be a merry occasion.

Two days. It had been two days, and Ivanya had not heard a single message from any of her unnamed friends here. There had been nothing from Jervin, nothing from Roch. She didn't know what had happened to Remy or why Luc suddenly wanted to show their faces to the court, but it did not bode well.

And then, as if to answer her prayers, she heard the distinct rattle of chains. There Remy came down the dark corridor, accompanied by two other prisoners and a small contingent of guards. As he shuffled closer, everything else fell away. The chatter. The guards. The other two prisoners. Ivanya had eyes only for her son, his face busted and bruised. Gods, he'd lost weight.

They'd been fools to go against the likes of Notoyem Béranger. They should have fled to Crasea, to her home in the white-capped mountains. Zandua pride aside, at least her son would not look at her with such empty eyes.

"Remy—" Ivanya found herself saying.

"Quiet!" one of the guards barked, looming over her, hand falling to his sword.

As relieved as she was to see him, Ivanya could only guess one reason Prince Luc would have gathered his Arnaud captives here.

Her only hope now was that one of these guards was among the few Fidou had converted to their cause.

Ivanya fell quiet, not wanting to press their patience. She studied them all, hoping for some sign that Fidou had a plan. Nothing. The guards settled into a bored wait, and not a single one pounced on the others' distraction. She fervently prayed that Fidou was still alive, moving through the castle in his haste to free them. Until then, she could spare some concern over her son.

"*What happened?*"

With his hands bound, he could not do much to respond without alerting the guards. But he gave her one word, enough to make her heart sink: "*Caught.*"

Ivanya inspected the two prisoners behind her son. The man still wore the clothes he'd been arrested in, marking him from one of the minor houses. Cheron Vesour, if she recalled correctly. One of their allies. The other prisoner, the woman, she didn't know by name, but the woman wore servant attire. These must've been the people Fidou had assigned to rescue Remy. But if Vesour had been caught, what of Fidou?

A deafening silence fell on the other side of the wall. The guards around them stiffened. Whatever had brought them here, Ivanya was about to find out.

"As you all know, my father, the regis, has left the capital with Prince Nyli to quell the beginnings of an uprising." The voice was undeniably Luc's. "House Arnaud demands we waste your hard-earned taxes on levying troops and weapons, even knowing that my father, the regis, earned the gods' approval for the throne in the Succession. Imagine the arrogance."

There was a pause, and although she couldn't hear it, Ivanya could imagine Luc snorting, as if the Béranger family had not used every single trick in the book to *steal* the throne.

"I'm sure this talk of rebellion has made at least some of you wonder what Las Corvika might look like under different leader-ship," Luc continued. "Remember who the gods favor. Remember what happens to those who went against them in the Succession, and remember the rubble where Mod Adeirno once stood."

Silence fell. Luc had delivered a threat, and he wanted his au-dience to take it in. *Remember Louis Ermengarde*, he was saying. *Remember how my father obliterated his House.*

"Today I remind you what loyalty looks like. House Villeneuve has stood by our side since the beginning, and never once did their loyalty waver, not even when it seemed my father might be losing the Succession. These past twenty years, still their loyalty has not flagged. I offer them a gift—and remind you what you stand to gain by remembering your loyalties. Eduoard Villeneuve, please step forward."

Ivanya glanced behind her, hoping to hear some telltale signs of a group of soldiers en route.

"We will bind your House and mine. I offer you my sister's hand in marriage."

"I willingly accept," came the muffled reply of the Villeneuve heir.

"I did not, however, bring you all here for a simple marriage proposal. Guards!"

The men snapped to attention, and then suddenly, Ivanya found herself being ushered into the throne room. Luc stood before his father's throne, flagged by his reclusive wife and son on the one side and his dagger-eyed sister on the other. The look on his face was disgustingly *pleased*. He and his retinue stood side by side, with Luc in the center, the lot of them facing a crowd of nobles, royal *sjarvisk*, even folks in servant attire… She searched the crowd, unsure if she wanted to see Fidou there or if she hoped he wasn't.

Then she found him in the crowd, near the front. Their eyes caught, and Ivanya's heart plummeted. She knew. She *knew*.

No help was coming.

"There are those among you who may have sympathies toward the Arnaud cause. Whatever hopes you may hold are nothing more than delusions. Remember the Béranger fury. The winds are rising, and they will cut through any opposition swiftly and severely."

His boots thundered slowly toward them. Ivanya turned instinctively at the rasp of a sword drawn. Luc nodded to their guards, his blade sharp and cruel. She watched as Remy was shoved to his knees along with the other two in chains.

"Luc—" Ivanya began, trying to step between the prince and her son. A guard dug his fingers into her shoulder, pinning her in place. "Please."

But even as the word spilled out of her mouth, she saw his blade flash silver.

The tip slid through Remy's chest, jutting out of the other side, red and dripping as if it were melting. A chorus of screams crashed against her ears, but she could barely hear it, didn't notice that one of the voices was her own. Rasin lurched forward as Remy collapsed in a pool of his own blood, but Ivanya couldn't move. She couldn't think. She could barely even breathe.

With a gesture, Luc sentenced the other two to death, leaving it to the guards. Rasin shouted at her brother, but the pounding in Ivanya's ears drowned it all out.

Remy.

Her view was blocked suddenly as Luc stepped over his body and came to stand directly before Ivanya. "I am not without mercy," he told her, loud enough to be heard by their audience. Loud enough, even, to be heard over the pounding of her own heart. "You three, I shall let live, for what do women and toddlers know of warfare or treason?"

*More than an arrogant boy like you could ever know,* Ivanya wanted to say. Tight fists curled around her wrists before she could even think to bury her nails into the prince's eyes, the guard's grip like iron. *You Bérangers and your misplaced mercies. Tholjun will feast on your blood.*

"*Oderta neg rasin det pieterad!*" Luc crowed. The crowd parroted him back. Ivanya stared silently at him. If only she were an *aljarne* like her daughter, she could kill him where he stood. The guard's vice grip on her wrists didn't even allow her to stoop over her son or whisper her Crasik farewells over his soul.

Then she was being pulled away, back out of the throne room, away from Remy's still form. She caught Fidou's gaze on her way out. Ivanya wanted to kill him too. What was the point of allies if they did not react when they were most needed? Fidou, Roch— they should have saved her son. Now they were complicit in his death, and they would pay for it.

They were ushered directly back to their quarters, the guards immediately filing into position. Damari took Bernard and disappeared behind closed doors, her eyes stained red.

Ivanya held on to her composure until she was alone in her bedroom. She set her sights on a pitcher. With a shriek, she threw it toward the wall. It exploded in a shower of porcelain and water. Next came the wash basin. Then a stool. That did not break as easily, not until she slammed it again and again into the tiled floor and finally the wood splintered and fell to pieces in her hands. Then, suddenly, her own body could not bear the weight of her grief, and she collapsed into a pile of fabric. Her son. Her *son.*

She remembered him when he'd taken his first steps across the carpeted floor of his nursery. She remembered how, a few years later, his small form had peered over the crib at his baby sister

Aljeya, and then, a few years more, how he had stood protectively over his baby sister Zyre. He would follow his father all around the estate whenever Jervin was home, and he was so dedicated to his studies, especially when Jervin was off at court groveling at Notoyem's feet so their lives might be improved.

And when Jervin took Remy to court, she remembered how he'd spoken in awe of the princess, of her intelligence and cunning and, of all things, her kindness. He'd been inconsolable those first few months after being cast from the court and absolutely unforgivable to Damari in the first months of their marriage. Ivanya could still remember the day she and Jervin had pulled him aside and spoken to him of the nature of nobility, of fickle regises and secret rebellions. How determined he'd become then.

Ivanya remembered, too, his first bumbling swings of a sword and how quickly they turned to viper strikes. On the day Nyli landed on Lasinia, when all hell broke loose, Remy had killed no fewer than ten soldiers. Luc couldn't hold a candle to Remy's skill. Had there been time, had she just been able to *think* quicker, she might've bought Remy a chance to duel the prince.

A knock rang against the door, and Ivanya cursed. She pulled herself to her feet, scrubbing at her eyes even though she knew it was of no use.

Ivanya did not know who she expected, but it was not Princess Rasin, carrying a small sewing box in the crook of her arm. Her own eyes were red, cheeks flushed.

Ivanya grabbed at a stool, brandishing it even as Rasin's honor guard drew their swords. She didn't care if they tried to kill her now. At least one of them would pay with their life if they tried. Maybe even two or three.

"Pardon for intruding on your grieving," Rasin said. Her voice was hoarse. "I just… I wanted to give you something."

"My son back, alive and well?" she spat.

Rasin flinched. "I would if I could. Truly." She swallowed audibly. Then she walked to a small table and set the sewing box atop it. "They whisper that my brother has no heart. This is not true. Everyone has a heart. His is just black and twisted. I hope you find it, Baroness."

Rasin turned away and strode out before Ivanya could question the oddity of her words.

The door shut between them, leaving Ivanya alone once more. She glanced at the box, snarling at it. It was ornate, embroidered with thorny vines and beautiful flowers. The lid swung easily on its hinges, revealing small needles and a few colorful spools of thread. Folded on top of them was a note. "The best pieces of art are those done by hand. With luck, this will even the scales. - Rasin"

Roaring, Ivanya smashed her fists against the box. It slid across the table and crashed onto the floor. The spools rolled free and the needles scattered, but a much larger flash of silver caught her eye.

A knife tumbled loose from a small bundle of fabric. Frowning, she grabbed it. The hilt was simple, nothing more than old, worn leather. The blade itself was nothing ornate, either, but she tested its edge and found it sharp.

Even the scales? No, she thought not. But certainly, it was a start.

Luc Béranger was a dead man walking.

# CHAPTER 21

Neelie was not the type to hang around battlefields, and the more time she spent in Jervin Arnaud's camp, the more she was beginning to understand why Modorin had been so determined to leave Syfris's army. It was noisy all the time, and not even the same kind of noisy that a city could be. Healers could only do so much when it came to blood loss or missing limbs, and the groans of the still-injured haunted Neelie no matter where she was. And there was music, yes, but it wasn't the lifeblood sounds of Venasca. It was fast-paced and bawdy with strident chords to match. Half the time, the lyrics didn't even make sense. Neelie didn't mind bawdy music, but this didn't even sound good.

There were other complaints—the bland food, the grim faces, the uncomfortable pallets they slept on—but it was the discordant noise that sent Neelie rushing for solitude late that night while Modorin and Zyre slumbered listlessly in their tent. Neelie rolled to her feet, beelining for the tent flaps. Zyre shuffled slightly, but if she woke, she said nothing.

Truly, how either of them could sleep in this cacophony was baffling to her. The men were still celebrating their victory, or commemorating the fallen. Maybe both; Corvikans were odd folk.

They watched her as she walked past. One was foolish enough to call out to her, but a glare silenced him. She could weather the hungry stares, and hell, some of the men were kind of cute, but she was not some dog to be summoned.

Neelie reached the north end of camp, walking past the sentries. The path continued on a short distance until she came across the Áit's daughter river, the Gouvelle.

She set her shoes next to her, burying her feet in the cool sand.

It was rougher than Bijal's beaches, the sand, and darker too, but the familiar feeling quieted her uneasy pulse.

Reaching into her pocket, she withdrew the charmed map. She held it in one hand and allowed a tiny flame to burst above her other, casting the map in an orange glow. The whale floated above the Áit, wherever her mother had dropped anchor for the night. As she'd told Zyre earlier, it likely wouldn't take more than a day for her mother to reach the camp. If only staring at it would make the time run faster. Shaking her head, she let the fire wink out and pocketed the charm.

The Gouvelle rushed past. It wasn't the ocean; there was no salt in the air or rise and fall of the waves. But when she closed her eyes, she could at least remember the pitch of the deck beneath her, hear the billowing of the sails when the wind had finally caught. She had been too long with Zyre. She needed to put herself to sea, to set sail and leave all signs of the coast far behind her. Maybe she could go to Pailyr or Darsenia. Or she could tour Onaris. The things that *wyrdi* supposedly could do there…

She opened her eyes at approaching footsteps. In the soft glow of the moonlight, Neelie could barely make out Zyre as the woman shook her head. "Did I wake you?"

Zyre sat down beside her. "I'm just having trouble sleeping."

The Corvikan noblewoman was admittedly beautiful by moonlight. Neelie was fascinated by her hair, wavy rather than coiled, and her warm, coppery skin that was only a few shades darker than Modorin's. Zyre wasn't particularly sharp-witted or fierce like Modorin was, but she was quiet in an empathetic sort of way.

Supposedly, the army would break camp tomorrow or the day after and begin their march on the capital. If they were lucky, Zyre would have one big battle to fight in, and if she could keep her head, she might make it.

But *najik* magic always led them to the same destination. There was no hiding this magic. Either people killed them out of fear or used them out of ambition, but either way, their lives were doomed to be short.

They were fools to waste it on anything that didn't matter.

Zyre leaned back, watching the stars.

"Are you truly going to fight?" Neelie asked softly. The quiet rushing of the river seemed to urge them to speak of secret confessions, willing to whisk them all away.

"You don't think I can do it?"

Neelie shrugged. "Not everyone is made for it. I didn't mean it as an insult."

Zyre sat up, twisting her lithe body to face Neelie. "I have to, Neelie. My entire life, the only thing I've been able to do for my family is pretend that I'm someone I'm not. It's different for you; your family would wage war with the city to see you safe."

"Exactly."

"My magic obeys my commands now," she pressed on. A flame burst like a flower above her palm. She scowled into it. "If I can use it to end the war faster, to save lives, then why wouldn't I?"

*Because you're not a warrior*, Neelie wanted to say. Some people were born with a speck of Dûl in their hearts, and they would set the very world aflame if that's what it took to get what they wanted. But Zyre? Somehow, Zyre had been born with a piece of Skï. If it was possible to use *najik* magic to create, Zyre would find it.

"And when the war is over?" Neelie asked gently. *If you still have your sanity?*

Zyre hesitated. "I had a dream. To travel. But," she added quickly, "with everything that's going on, how can I leave? Las Corvika is my home."

"As Bijal is mine," Neelie said quietly. She reached out, then stopped herself, cursing her heart. "However much I love the city, I love the sea more. A lifespan is but a heartbeat; ours, barely a flutter. I can't let duty pull my strings from birth to death; some of it must belong to me alone. My mother found a way to make it work. So can I. So should you. I know you fell in love with Bijal, and I hope you will not let your duties keep you shore-bound."

The flame winked out, casting them both in darkness. Zyre inhaled. "It wasn't just Bijal I fell in love with," came her voice, so quiet Neelie didn't catch it at first.

"I cannot stay in Las Corvika," she said gently.

Zyre exhaled slowly. "I know. It never crossed my mind that you would."

A sudden rage burned through her, and for a moment, fear grappled with it as she thought her magic had turned her mind against her. But the fear faded, leaving behind only the anger. Zyre had grown too used to bending her whims to the needs of other people. Neelie loved her selflessness as much as she hated those who had taken advantage of it. She could not stay in Las Corvika because war was a death trap for *najik*, and she would not die in a war that was not her own. But she wanted to give Zyre something, anything, a bit of reciprocated selflessness.

Behind them, the camp began to crawl like a disturbed anthill, but Neelie ignored them.

Their lives were short, and her pride did not matter.

She looked into Zyre's eyes and leaned.

Then a horn blasted nearby, echoing across the expanse of the camp, and Zyre's head whipped around, her brows furrowed. She scrambled up, her eyes wild.

With a sigh, Neelie got up too, and they ran back to camp.

"Are we under attack?" Zyre asked a passing soldier.

"Don't believe so, my lady, but we are getting ready to march." The man's expression was grim, but he didn't stay to elaborate.

For a second, Zyre watched slack-jawed as the soldier disappeared in the crowd. Then, hollowly, she said, "I need to go find my father."

⚜

Zyre knew things were not good when she heard her father's shouting rolling past the thick canvas walls. His guards stood ill at ease outside, and even Aljeya's, normally stone-faced, looked on edge. Zyre almost couldn't force herself to walk in. If it wasn't an army swooping down on them, then Zyre dreaded to think what awful news had sent her father into such a rage.

Her heart only began to hammer harder when the guards refused to let Neelie through. She found herself suddenly wishing Kadj were by her side. Whatever news she was going to hear in there, she did not want to face it alone.

Neelie gave her an encouraging smile. Gathering what little resolve she had, Zyre stepped in.

It was chaos. Papers were scattered across the floor. The little army figurines had joined them. Merytz stood at attention in the back, but there was something wrong with his eyes. It wasn't until Zyre found Aljeya, looking desolate in her chair, sharing that same strange look, that she recognized it and named it as grief.

Jervin took notice of her arrival. "Where were you?"

*On the beach, saying more than I should have*, she thought. "I was having trouble sleeping, so I took a walk. What's going on?"

An odd noise escaped her father's throat. He snatched a paper off the table and shoved it into her hands. The handwriting was his own. The message was not long. She noticed another piece of paper, ciphered, lying on the desk.

"Grave news," the note began. "Prince moved without warning. Public execution. *Vinje* Remy Arnaud dead."

It was strange, the way loss hit a person. Zyre didn't quite understand at first. Her brain knew what the last word was, but it didn't want to accept that *dead* and *Remy* might ever be used in the same sentence.

That last moment of ignorance was long and blissful. And then her knees gave out and she hit the floor. *Took too long*, she thought dully, but it was a passing thought, lost behind a replay of the last day she'd seen her brother. She tried to remember how he'd been, to fill in the gaps of how he'd gotten to the palace so she might know what had happened in these last weeks that had led to this awful reality. If she couldn't connect the dots, then that meant it couldn't possibly be true.

Her brother, who had been there when she'd learned how to use a sword, who had always found ways to steal time with his little sister so she didn't feel so alone. They didn't always get along, but wasn't that just the way things were between siblings? She was the *aljarne*. She was the one who was supposed to fall first. It made no sense, no sense at all.

"Our allies are likely catching wind of this as we speak, or will soon," Tavere said gently. "If they learn you are without a male heir, we may begin to lose support."

"Who cares about allies?" Jervin snapped. "My son is dead."

Zyre tuned them both out. Numbly, she returned the paper to

the table and walked toward her sister. Aljeya wasn't even shaking as the tears rolled down her face.

"Aljeya?"

Her sister's eyes focused on her, burning sharply. Her voice, though, was hollow. "I wish I'd never left home." Then Aljeya's entire body finally began to shake. "Why did I stay away for so long?"

The tears were contagious. The emptiness shattered like broken glass, each shard gouging holes into her heart. Zyre found herself sitting abruptly at her sister's feet, unable to stop herself from crying, mourning the future moments they could no longer share with their brother even as she still fought to deny the truth.

She'd been *so close.* So close to a life where she didn't have to hide, where she could have been who she was without fear of being discovered. Mere weeks separated her from being able to form a proper, careless relationship with her brother, and Tholjun had snatched it all away. Her grief threatened to choke her. She was certain she would drown.

She didn't think it would ever end, but when the tears subsided, Zyre slowly grew aware of the discussion Tavere and her father were having. The army was preparing to move *tonight.* They had already dispatched a messenger to Nyli and they would begin their march on the capital, using every bit of stealth they had learned these past years so they might arrive in Les Stelvo's shadow before Luc was even aware they were marching. Word would be sent to their spies at court so that, when the attack began, Ivanya, Damari, and Bernard would be protected from Luc's wrath. They, at least, could still be saved, should Thalja look down upon them fondly.

Zyre wanted to scream. *You made that pact so that Remy would live. He's dead, now, dead! What's the point? Kill Nyli and be done with it!* But the anguish welled up in her throat, and she knew she would never get the words out.

Tavere said if they could rescue both Ivanya and Bernard, then their allies at court would hardly shake in their loyalty, because as soon as Jervin was regis, he could start the process to adopt Bernard as his heir as well as promise future sons through Ivanya. He spoke to a wall, though, because no one else in the war tent cared for anything more than making sure Luc found a sticky red end.

If time could have stopped in that tent until they were ready to face this bleak new future, it would have been a gift, but all too quickly, a lieutenant by the name of Oretnir Valade arrived with the news that the men were packed and ready to march. Zyre was forced to follow her father out. The skeletal remains of an army were all that was left: smoking fire pits, indents in the ground where tents had been, and an eerie silence. The velídas tree's silver bark seemed to glow at night. She hadn't noticed that before.

Wherever their tent was located, Zyre had no way of figuring that out now. Even if it had been light outside, the way through camp felt eerie and strange without any of the structures remaining. Not knowing where else to look, Zyre ran to the Gouvelle.

Her instincts proved right, because Neelie had returned to the banks, and she'd brought a haggard-looking Modorin with her. Zyre slowed, another lump forming in her throat. They were going to ask what was going on, and she wasn't sure she could form the words.

Modorin saw her first. He frowned. "Zyre?"

She thought there must've been a limit to how much a person could cry, but that single question, said in the same tone she had said Aljeya's name, was all it took to procure more. "My brother," she managed to get out. "They killed him."

Zyre was only numbly aware of Modorin's sudden proximity and of Sarol pushing his forehead against her calf.

Her whole body trembled. "Luc, the prince," she tried to say. It took too much effort. She abandoned the sentiment; there was another, more important, that she had to get out. "I could not save him."

Anger surged, and behind her eyelids, she saw pinpricks of orange. Fireballs exploded above her fists. Modorin cursed.

"Zyre…" said another voice. *Hers*. Neelie's. It cut like a knife.

Zyre snapped her eyes open. She had saved Neelie, but she could not even save her own brother. *Took too long*, she thought again. She felt like she was exploding on the inside. "They killed him, Neelie. And for what?" she shouted, spinning so her friends could not see how much it hurt. "For a crown? For a throne? Tholjun's blood, is it worth it? Is it?"

"Zyre," Neelie said again, softly. Zyre wanted to rip apart the earth for the way she said it, wanted to lash out—until Neelie said, "I'm sorry," and the pity in her voice was too much for Zyre to bear.

The noise that came out of her throat was not human, and suddenly, the tears were there again. She sank to her knees on the sand, letting the tremors wrack through her body once again.

Modorin knelt beside her, wrapping his sturdy arms around her. She knew, though she could not see his face, because Neelie would never in a hundred years offer her the same.

"Modorin, move," Neelie said quietly, surprising Zyre enough that the stone in her throat eased its pressure. She blinked past the tears and saw the other woman sit on the sand in front of her. She glanced behind Zyre's shoulder, but there was no one around. Everyone was too busy preparing for departure.

"I didn't know your brother very well, but I know he cared about you. He was the reason I stayed in Lasinia's port. He wanted you to get off the island, if the chance presented itself, to be free and safe away from the dangers of your family's war."

There it was again, that awful pressure in her throat, threatening to choke her.

"The love we have for our family is irrational. It is a flame that burns hot and bright. I know I would level Bijal to the ground for mine, so I know I cannot ask you to stay off of the battlefield. But I ask that you remember yourself, and remember the person that your brother loved you for being. I ask that you remember there are those amongst the living who love you and whose loss would devastate them."

Despite Neelie's vehemence, Zyre was startled when the other woman reached out and clasped her hands in her own.

Zyre squeezed tight. Neelie didn't complain but instead squeezed back. Then she extricated one of her hands gently from Zyre's grip and put a soft, suggestive finger under Zyre's chin, drawing forward in a way that Zyre had only ever thought she'd see in her dreams.

And in the wake of her brother's death, she grasped blindly for any proof of *life*. Zyre leaned in.

The kiss was slippery and tasted of salt and copper as their lips met with urgency, someone's tooth colliding into the other's lip just hard enough to draw blood. But she didn't care. She didn't care, because her brother was dead before she could ever have a proper relationship with him, and here Neelie was, throwing her a lifeline as she drowned in a sea of ineffable grief.

When they broke apart, Neelie squeezed Zyre's other hand once more.

"Remember this, Zyre," she breathed. "We are made for more than battlefields and mourning songs."

# CHAPTER 22

**P**olitically speaking, news of Remy Arnaud's death should have crushed Nyli's chances for the throne. After all, despite what he'd said to Jervin, maybe he didn't *need* the Arnaud forces on his side to take Les Stelvo, but he needed it to forge peace for Las Corvika.

Jervin somehow knew before he did. The conversation that had ensued had been less than comfortable, and even with his honor guard by his side, Nyli was convinced Jervin might try to stick a knife into him. He wouldn't have blamed him. For this was the strangeness of it all: Remy's death was more of a personal wound than a political one. Whether it was from guilt or grief or some bleak certainty that his family was full of poison, Nyli couldn't shake the terrible emptiness in his chest. Poor Rasin. She'd had to witness it, too.

And now Jervin was without an heir, and his wife's own life was on the line, and it was all Nyli's fault.

He had just wanted to make his father proud of him for once. Root out the corruption and the treason. If he'd caught Jervin in the first place, perhaps Remy could have lived. Married to a woman who was not Rasin, true, but alive nonetheless. And

Notoyem would have been able to settle into Les Stelvo, secure on his throne, and maybe it would not have been a progressive and stable Las Corvika, but it would have at least become a quiet one.

Now, Notoyem was dead, Remy was dead, and Nyli was marching against his own brother with an army full of people who would have rather seen him dead than fight for him.

On the first night, after a disastrous council between all of the lords and high-ranking officers of all their camps in which Nyli tried to prove his dedication to their cause by outlining the weakest parts of Les Stelvo's defenses, he and Kuval retreated to his tent. Discrete, even now, because there would be many who would disapprove, who would desert if they didn't try to kill them first. There would always be cause for a courtly mask; that hadn't been simply for his father.

For a while, he was silent. He sat on the bed, untying his shoelaces in the dim torchlight, listening to the soft rumblings of the soldiers around them.

Nyli couldn't help but wonder if this was the price they paid for their throne. Behind the prominence of the Béranger name was a long list of dead men, of which Remy Arnaud was only the most recent. There would be men in this camp—too many of them, even with the advantage of numbers, Nyli was sure—who would die in the days to come, all because of him. He had not escaped the curse of his family name after all.

Maybe he'd been wrong after all. Maybe he should have fallen in line behind Jervin Arnaud. If he swore fealty to him, then maybe the other Houses would too, and Las Corvika could have its peace behind a House that wasn't so tainted by dead men.

"Are you worried about your brother?" Kuval said, breaking the silence as he came to sit next to Nyli.

"About beating him?"

Kuval nodded.

"Of course I'm worried about it," Nyli said quietly. "Though whether I'm more worried about winning or losing, I can't tell. It all feels so wrong. I think… Kuval, I think I might be just as much of a monster as my father."

Nyli startled as Kuval scooped up his hand, taken aback by the fire he found in the man's dark eyes.

"Your father never once feared what he was or second-guessed his actions, even when he should have. Neither does your brother. The fact that you fear to be one just proves that you are not."

Nyli pulled his hand free, pushing distance between him and Kuval. He didn't *get* it. The worst thing that had happened to Las Corvika had been Notoyem taking the throne. It had not been his to claim, and now the country was divided and war-torn, and *gods,* he just wanted it to be over. Why had he let his father die, if not to end this bloody conflict, to spare as many people as he could? Who else would die for this insane belief that the wrathful Bérangers should have been allowed anywhere near the throne?

"Where are you going?" Kuval demanded, his words laced with concern.

"To Jervin. To tell him I will give him his throne after all."

He reached for the tent flap, only to find Kuval barring his way, pulling him back. "To what end, Nyli? Is this because of Remy? Why is this affecting you this way?"

For the first time ever, Nyli heard a twinge of jealousy in the other man's voice.

"My family is poison, love. Even me. Everything would have been better if I had just left it alone. I am not fit to rule, Kuval. It was a delusion to think that I was."

He extricated himself from Kuval's grip, his heart breaking, because he could feel the disappointment in that last brief moment before his love's fingers dropped away. Nyli turned his back, waiting for the other man to leave in disgust.

"It's a beautiful dream you have in your head," Kuval said instead, his voice steely. "That in transferring power to Jervin, everything can magically get better. It's funny, because the man I fell in love with had this grand hope of undoing all the evil things his father had done. And even knowing that wasn't how the world worked, I found myself believing just as fervently in that dream. In you."

"Jervin can do the job worlds better than I," Nyli mumbled.

"No. He can't."

There was a soft *whoosh* of the tent flap falling behind Kuval as he made his exit. Nyli stumbled to the edge of his bed, collapsing onto it with something terribly close to a sob. He wished Notoyem were still alive, because then none of this would have fallen on Nyli's shoulders. But it was a terrible thought, a wicked one, because then it would have just given Notoyem more time to create the chaos that Nyli had always wanted to undo.

Jervin wanted the throne to right the wrongs done to him. That was what Kuval meant. Nyli knew this, because they had talked about it before. His end results might be the same as Nyli's, but they would always be based on selfish desires. That was no better than his father. Las Corvika needed an impartial regis. He just wished to the gods that it didn't have to be him.

Nyli couldn't bring himself to stand up, to follow through with his threat. At some point, he curled up hopelessly on the bed itself, but sleep never came. And in the early hours of the morning, before the sun had even risen, when the call sounded to move out, he mounted his horse and rode out to the front of the army where Kuval was so sure he belonged. Jervin met him there, flanked on one side by his daughter, Aljeya, and by Zyre on the other. Zyre would not meet his gaze, but Aljeya had daggers in her eyes. She reminded him of Ivanya.

Ivanya.

Luc hadn't killed them all. Remy's son, Bernard, and Ivanya and Remy's wife—some Venascan woman whose name he could never remember—they still lived.

If they could escape this war alive, then maybe Nyli was good for something after all. Their survival would be his proof. If he could save them, if he could save even *one* of them and right his own wrongs, then maybe there was hope for him and for his country.

⁂

It was said of Adreia Hijalcaelan that she'd been born with the sea in her veins and the wind on her side. It was all nonsense and fable, Neelie knew, but there were perks to being a *majican*. If Adreia hadn't been using her magic to help the wind find her sails before, she certainly was now, the little whale inching closer and closer as the day wore on.

When dinner drew near and Modorin began shuffling hopefully through what supplies Jervin had spared for them, she again found herself consulting her father's charmed map. It was close now. Unbearably close. As much as she hated dealing with grief, Neelie hated to leave Zyre to deal with it alone.

There was no delaying the inevitable, though. "Modorin, best not fill your stomach just yet."

Modorin glanced up, frowning.

"My mother is almost here," she said, flashing the map. "She seems intent to race the wind."

Modorin looked desolately at some dried fruit lying in his palm.

"You're just going to be throwing that right back up, you know."

Modorin muttered in his native tongue, which she pretended

not to understand. Then, in Corvikan, though Zyre was no longer there, he said, "I feel like a terrible friend."

Neelie decided not to tell him how tempted she was to take off after the army once her mother told her of how things fared in Bijal. She didn't want to give him any chance to convince her that she belonged by Zyre's side, no matter how deadly wars were for *najik*. She was perilously close to convincing herself and felt selfish for not letting herself even think on it.

A ship slid into view. It was an ugly Corvikan vessel, squat and squarish with plain white sails. It certainly wasn't the *Doleir*, Adreia's favored vessel and the one equipped with rich black sails painted with the skeletal hand.

"That's a river barge," Modorin noted as if it were a riddle rather than a statement of the obvious.

Neelie rolled her eyes and got up, gathering up her things as the barge rowed closer. "A sea vessel is too deep to travel through water like this. We'll sail down the Àit and then return to her ship once we reach the open waters."

The figures aboard the river vessel began to take shape as it pushed itself upstream. Her mother stood at the helm with her thick gray locks tied loosely behind her head. The ink that ran down her arms and crawled across her neck were too far away to see the details of, but Neelie knew them well. She knew the tattoo constellation on her right forearm that her mother had gotten after Neelie was born, and on the left, the wren that stood for Neelie's brother. A skeleton hand wrapped around just below her elbow for the first ship she'd ever captained, the parts of which had built the framework of the *Doleir*. The raven, of course, was there, too, tucked just underneath the collar of her shirt.

Pride swelled in Neelie's chest, and relief. Seeing little figurines on a charmed map was not the same as seeing her mother in the flesh. It had been far too long.

The call to drop anchor was given, and the barge stopped just shy of the resubmerged earthen bridge. Her mother came to the prow, scanning the area, her gaze settling on Neelie. Before the barge had stopped completely, Adreia had leapt waist-deep into the water. She waded to shore with a slow, easy grace, and as soon as her feet touched dry ground, she sent the water crashing into a puddle at her feet.

Neelie resisted the temptation to run up to her mother. She forced herself to walk calmly, but when she drew near, both of their composures cracked. Adreia threw her arms around Neelie.

"You have sent me on quite the chase, Neelie," Adreia said sternly as they broke apart. "And for what?"

"I was taking Zyre to her father and his army." Neelie swept her arm behind them, showing the emptied campsite.

"Jervin Arnaud was here?" Her mother scanned the scarred remains of the army's camp as if the baron himself would appear out of thin air.

"He was, yes. They left in the dark hours of the morning, southbound."

Her mother finally slid her intense gaze over Neelie's shoulder, inspecting her two companions. "Greetings, *Magi* Modorin."

Neelie rolled her eyes again when Modorin swept into a bow. "A pleasure, as always, my queen."

*Suck up*, she mouthed. He laughed.

"How are Father and Ren?"

Adreia waved away her concern. "There will be time for that on the trip home." At Neelie's crestfallen expression, her mother clapped her on the back and added, "Don't worry. They are well. Inoger himself would be hard-pressed to win a fight against the Shadowmen."

The Pirate Queen beckoned them to follow, and they waded into the water.

It felt good to have a ship under her, even if the quiet river made the deck feel too tame by half. Neelie wove past the crew as they shifted the sails, drew the anchor, readied themselves at their oars. Adreia kept track of it all at the helm, and Neelie was happy to see Raylir serving as her mother's first mate. He tipped his hat at her, and she grinned. But it was short-lived.

It had almost been a fortnight since they had fled Bijal, and at this point, she was almost, almost too afraid to ask. Neelie steeled herself for news, then pushed the burning words out of her throat. "How bad is it at home?"

"*Freyr* Honir came to his senses about a few things," Adreia replied grimly, keeping her eyes on her milling crew. The anchor was heaved back onto the deck, and the river barge began to make way downriver even before the oarsmen got to work. With the drummer pounding rhythms onto his instrument serving as a backdrop, Adreia filled Neelie in. She had arrived in Bijal only a day and a half after Neelie had left, finding much of the Shadow Quarter and even some of the Deckhand's Quarter in shambles. Honir's men had torn through the Raven's Head searching for Neelie and the men who had attacked the city barracks, but even Ren had gone to ground already.

Neelie feared her father might've been arrested out of suspicion if Honir had already taken it so far, but the Shadowmen had drawn the line. Minor scuffles had erupted through the neighborhood as its men defended it from Honir, but the *freyr* apparently wasn't stupid enough to try arresting Hosvar.

Honir was lucky. Her mother had wanted to burn the Serpent's Quarter to teach Honir a lesson. "I didn't, of course," Adreia said smugly. "But I could have, and that *marosen* knew it, and that's all that matters."

From there, Adreia had used one of her contacts in Honir's inner circle to set up a meeting. Risky, but Honir already looked bad before his king, and if matters escalated any further, Honir risked being stripped of Bijal.

When Adreia outlined the details of their discussion, Neelie almost did not believe her. The Shadowmen held a lot of power over their respective districts, enough to make it more effort than it was worth to wrest power from her father, but the fact that Honir was willing to admit defeat showed just how desperate the *freyr* was. Inoger was too distracted by the war in the south to put any real focus on his own city, and the *freyr*'s might was underwhelming, especially against the force of Adreia Hijalcaelan's wrath.

In the end, Honir had caved. He'd offered Hosvar a semi-official title, granting him leadership over both the Shadow and Deckhand's Quarter. It was all pomp and circumstance, of course; all it did was save face for the *Freyr*. They had come to some agreement regarding what resources would continue to flow into the two districts from Honir's coffers and what had to come from Hosvar's. "The *Freyr* is foolish only in some things, it appears," Adreia said. "Essentially, very little changes beyond technicalities. Honir won't delve into the specifics of your father's business, and Hosvar agrees to an acceptable tax on our income. Undesirable, but inevitable, I suppose."

"And me?" Neelie hazarded.

"You. Yes. You cannot use magic in Bijal. Whatever happened before is in the past, but Honir warned us that the law on *najik* comes from higher up than him. If anyone reports a use of unbound magic, they will have to investigate."

Neelie nodded. Few in the Shadow Quarter would report on

her, but the warning was appreciated nonetheless. There were always those who thrived on chaos or who prioritized gold over loyalty. She would take care.

"Tensions are still high," Adreia continued. "Honir is not happy that he had to agree to so much. You know he'd rather see your father and me completely out of the way. And the city watch feels slighted. They wanted payback for the assault on their headquarters. It's not over yet."

"Things can never be simple," Neelie muttered to herself. But her mother heard and nodded in agreement. "I will help rebuild our district if it won't cause problems. I can put a few things on hold." *Besides, I have a promise to keep*, she added. *I want to make sure Kadj is okay.*

Adreia nodded again, absently. She did not say anything about helping rebuild, but then, that was her way. Here one day, gone the next. At least she couldn't disappear until they reached Bijal. That, at least, brought Neelie a small smile.

***

The arrival of the duc's forces served as a test for Nyli's already tenuous relationship with Jervin Arnaud. It had been a stressful three days of traveling; fights kept breaking out between soldiers of each army, and none of the commanding officers did much to stop it. Jervin's officers blamed Nyli for their *vinje*'s death, and Nyli's did not trust the loyalty of the traitors.

Everyone was convinced that Josef Villeneuve's arrival meant that there would be a battle. As if either one of their armies were likely to take the capital on their own.

It was with some trepidation that Nyli mounted his horse, accompanied by Kuval and Pierre. Jervin would stay behind; they had to do this delicately, and the baron's—soon to be duc's—presence could quickly ruin their chances.

Josef's army was stationed a safe distance away. He would be waiting for them on the edge of it, where Nyli had said they'd meet to discuss the terms of allegiances for Las Corvika's upcoming coronation.

As they neared Josef's contingent of men, a small party broke away from the rest of the troops, marching toward them. Josef Villeneuve and his retinue.

The duc was at least a decade older than Notoyem had been, maybe two, but unlike Nyli's father, he was not prone to excess. His wiry, sun-dark figure suggested he was as fit to fight as some of Nyli's best honor guard.

As Nyli and his men dismounted, he felt the duc's eyes boring into him. The duc bowed to the quarter. "My lord. An unconventional meeting, if I may say so."

"Unconventional meetings for unconventional times," Nyli replied carefully. "We appreciate your haste."

Josef looked nonplussed. That all-seeing gaze was what had gotten him sent away from the capital several years ago. Notoyem thought he was too clever for his own good.

Josef reached into his pocket, and as Nyli's honor guard went nervously toward their weapons, he took note of that too. It took some effort, but Nyli kept his expression neutral. Uncaring.

The duc withdrew a piece of parchment. "As I'm sure you are aware, Luc already promised your sister to my son. Are you also aware that he promised to expand my region farther south, as well as granting me the title of General of the Royal Forces?"

Losing the title of general was a relief, not a burden. It had never been a position for Nyli to begin with. But the marriage? Nyli's blood ran cold. *Rasin.* His motives for turning the duc to his side grew that much stronger.

"I thought not. I know you march with Jervin's men and that you told your brother that it is all some trick so that the traitor can be collected in Les Stelvo and meet his sticky end in public. I will also tell you that Luc is not entirely sure if he believes you and that he has asked me to spy on you and turn on your forces if you end up betraying him."

"Luc is the eldest and the heir apparent," Nyli said cautiously. *He wants me dead. He wouldn't give my title to the duc unless he didn't think I was going to survive this.*

Josef snorted. "Yes, this is true. But do you know what I am, my lord?"

Nyli shook his head warily.

"I am a man who likes to fight for the winning side. And I know Luc's suspicions are right. I know you are planning to take the throne from him." His too-knowing gaze flicked onto the comte. "House Villeneuve is going to fall far by siding with you. I'm afraid I know what numbers Duvachelle has given you, and I know I have more. Enough to damage your forces and warn Luc of your betrayal. My loyalty is worthy of a *comte* at the very least, I must presume."

Nyli didn't even feel remotely guilty for nodding. Kuval's position would fall with his father's, technically, but in reality? Not even close. And Pierre could stand to be knocked down a few pegs.

"I'm afraid I cannot promise Rasin's hand in marriage, but the title of General of the Royal Forces will be yours. That agreement, I can match. I need a general I can trust, and the Villeneuves have always been loyal to the Bérangers," Nyli said. "In addition, I know House Dorellier's lands, and the ownership of their mines, have been long contested. But the Dorellier family has grown so small as to become obsolete. I give you leave to absorb the minor House into your fold and take the riches that come with it."

Josef's stony expression never wavered. "I find these terms to be acceptable, but I have one last request to make before I can agree."

Nyli swallowed his relief alongside his fear. "Name it."

"I would like to return to the capital and reclaim my courtly duties from my son," Josef said with a grimace. "Too long have I been confined to my estates. Allow me to pass stewardship back to him so I might return to court and offer my wisdom and my services."

Nyli let a smile break free. This was a request he could easily grant. Notoyem had grown too secure in his power, pushing away his allies and enemies both. Nyli wouldn't make the same mistake.

"I welcome you to my cause with open arms," Nyli said.

Josef was too formal to smile back, but the full bow he gave Nyli was precise and respectful. "Then I'd best see to the consolidations of our armies. *Oderta neg rasin det pieterad.*"

Nyli echoed the words and, for the first time in his life, felt proud.

# CHAPTER 23

A mere four days after news of Remy's death, the army woke in the shadow of the capital. Zyre's sleep had been listless, just as it had been the past few nights, but she found comfort in the old familiarity of her sister's elbow digging into her side pulling her into consciousness.

A flash of dim light, and then, "*Sinomi, mu kidya,*" said a deep voice from the other side of the tent. One of Aljeya's personal guards. "*Illo ri deró eivai hrotima eb kitheíni.*"

"*Xei, ikarí,*" Aljeya replied, her voice still hoarse from sleep.

The canvas rustled, and then the light disappeared. "What did he say?" Zyre asked once the guard was gone. Her sister was already drawing back the thin sheets. The bed moved as she rolled out of it, and candlelight flooded their sleeping quarters.

"The army's getting ready to move." Aljeya knelt in front of her chest of clothes, looking grim.

So. It was time. Zyre stepped out of bed and went to her bag, rifling through it for some clothes, unsure what to wear. *They're going to be bloody beyond repair by the end of the day,* she realized.

They both got dressed quickly and stepped into the controlled chaos of the camp as it broke down tents, readied the nobles' horses, and smothered fires. In the dim torchlight, Zyre felt tension so thick she ought to have been able to touch it. Merytz waited impatiently nearby, holding a torch in one hand and using the thumb on his other to tap against his thigh. He stopped as soon as they stepped out.

"Shouldn't you be with my father?" Zyre asked, unable to explain the surge of annoyance she felt.

Merytz frowned, his thumb hovering over his thigh as if he'd just forced himself to stop tapping. It made Zyre uneasy; Merytz had nerves of steel. "He sent me to fetch you. Come with me."

With him at their helm, it was easy to navigate the tide of soldiers that parted around them. They arrived at the war tent, Nyli's griffon standard flying over her father's. It made her sick to her stomach. Aljeya marched right in, either not seeing or not caring, but Merytz grabbed Zyre's arm, stopping her in her tracks.

"Zyre—"

"Not now, Merytz."

Zyre tried to break free, but his grip only tightened. She stared at him, thinking of all the things she could do to that hand if he didn't let go. Merytz wisely returned her arm. She reached for the tent flap.

"Zyre. I'm sorry, but you can't fight."

She stopped. "I beg your pardon?"

Merytz threw his shoulders back, assuming an air of command that she'd seen him use on his men before, but never on her. "Jervin Arnaud has directly forbidden it, and as I am his Guardsmaster, I must comply. You'll stay with your sister when the fighting starts."

"Tholjun's blood, I will," she snarled. "You made me an oath. I don't care if I have an honor guard or not. I will fight."

"Why are you being so stubborn?" Merytz exclaimed, his

fingers balling into fists. "You always said that you hate the very idea of killing."

"And maybe if I didn't, Nyli never would have gotten his hands on my brother or my mother." Her tears threatened to choke her. She fled into the tent before they drowned her completely.

The tent was bustling with most of the ranking officers of the camp. The number of enemies that included kept growing, with Pierre Duvachelle and Josef Villeneuve. But it was their liege, Nyli Béranger, who made her stomach roil most of all.

Zyre shoved all thoughts of her brother as far down as they would go and pushed past people so she could stand by her sister.

"What's going on?" she asked.

Aljeya glared daggers at Nyli. "Apparently the prince has something to say."

Right on cue, Nyli broke away from his conversation and gestured for silence. His was not a particularly commanding presence, but everyone in that tent was aware of him, either because they didn't trust him or because they trusted him overly. The discussions died away.

The prince started with a sad smile that Zyre didn't know what to do with. "We are only a few miles from Les Stelvo. This is not a statement of the obvious. It is a warning. Luc certainly knows we're here, and he knows his defenses and his numbers just as well as we do. Those walls were built to defend against armies, even with a skeleton force to hold it.

"I have been right alongside you all these past few days. I know tensions are high between the men. For good reason, admittedly. It's hard to put the past aside. But we all fight for a common goal today. We all fight for a better Las Corvika. If you believe nothing else, believe that. If we do not stand together, that dream will die with us. Whatever reservations you have about me, or about those standing opposite of you today in this tent, set them aside, or else we will lose and this will all have been for nothing. If you hear rumblings with your troops, quell them, and do it quickly. We march now."

"Yes, sir" echoed down the ranks.

"Good. Dismissed."

The men scattered to pass the message along. Zyre wove past them, ignoring Merytz's warning glance. "Fa—" She stopped herself. "Uncle. I've been told you won't allow me to fight in the battle."

A few of the remaining men shot her looks, but she ignored them too.

Her heart sank when he shook his head. "We've talked about this, Zyre. The battlefield is no place for a lady, especially one of your… constitution."

"I'm good with a sword. Give me command of some soldiers. Just a single unit. Let me help lead the rescue mission."

"Don't worry about your *aunt*," Jervin said, the emphasis on *aunt* feeling unnecessarily cruel. "We already have plans in place."

"I can help. You know I can!"

"No," Jervin snapped. Zyre took a startled step backward. "You will help by staying in camp, out of the way. Now, I have an army to lead. Merytz."

The Guardsmaster stepped forward, expression stony.

"Leave a few good men with Aljeya's guards. Make sure the ladies—*both* of them—remain safe and secure in their tents when the battle begins."

Zyre seethed. Jervin strode out without another word, and Merytz had the audacity to look at her as if to say *I told you so.* Zyre glared at him, half tempted to punch the smugness off his face. But, with her father's words still echoing in her ears, she held her temper and followed Aljeya to their horses, falling in line at the back of the army. Aljeya's Atloran guard pressed tightly around them, and a handful of Merytz's men added to their ranks. The army began marching.

The sun was still a few hours off by the time the army stopped, and even from the back, Zyre could see the great city of Les Stelvo sprawling out before them.

Dimly, Zyre was aware of a few attendants setting up Aljeya's tent while the rest of the army resettled for the first strike. With Merytz's men keeping a close eye on her, Zyre could not disappear into the ranks of soldiers. She dismounted, watching the men settle into their positions. She marked where the horses were hobbled and, as soon as the tent was set up, followed Aljeya inside. Cushions had been splayed out on a rug. Zyre took one and listened as the army's marching feet faded.

"Why do you want to fight so badly, Zyre?" Aljeya's voice cut into the silence. "Do you realize how dangerous it is? Not just for an *aljarne*. For any soldier. A stray arrow, a lucky swordsman… battles are death fields for whoever enters them. Would you leave me without any siblings?"

Zyre's throat made an involuntary noise. "My life is no more important than those of the men following Father onto the battle-field. Some of them are going to die, regardless of numbers. They will leave behind families of their own."

"You are an Arnaud," Aljeya snapped with surprising vehe-mence. "And they knew what they were getting into when they signed up for this."

Zyre flinched as if Aljeya's words were a physical blow. Everyone stood against her, then? "Aljeya, I had to give up ev-erything because of my magic. Everything. I didn't get to learn languages with you, or study politics. I didn't get to tease you or Remy like other siblings get to. I didn't get to tell Remy that I loved him." Her tears threatened to choke her, and she had to pause to regain her composure.

Aljeya was barely holding on to her own.

"I love you, Aljeya, and I'm sorry that we live in a world where we don't get to see each other very often. But this isn't about you or me. This is about what we get to leave behind. You married an Atloran noble and used his influence to shape a country. Father is about to change the trajectory of Las Corvika's own future. And maybe I can't change nations, but I can save lives by being on that battlefield. I'm an *aljarne*. There is danger for me everywhere. I just want to do some good—save *someone*—while I'm here."

Aljeya's eyes shone with bitter tears. Resignation washed over her. She stood, walking serenely to one of her many chests. The wood creaked as she opened the lid. It did not take Zyre long to identify the pieces she withdrew. "You're about my size. You should fit into these," Aljeya said, handing the leather armor to her.

"Thank you," Zyre said, taking them. Her sister threw her arms around her, and they embraced awkwardly but fiercely. Something warm dripped onto Zyre's shoulder, and she realized her sister was crying. When they broke apart, she looked into Aljeya's eyes and wished she knew what to say.

Instead, she turned her attention to the armor. Her hands remembered the placements, the knots. She made quick work of it, wishing she had a weapon, if only to have that familiar weight on her hip.

"Zyre? My men will not stop you, but Father's men will try. Do your best not to harm them. They're only doing their job." Aljeya produced a knife from somewhere and cut a slit in the back of the tent.

"I will," Zyre swore.

Sheathing her knife, Aljeya hugged Zyre tightly. "Go safely, sister. May Tholjun watch over you."

They broke apart, and Zyre ducked through the slit.

In the dark of the early morning, all she could see were the vague silhouettes of the soldiers. She crouched down and waited for her eyes to adjust. Their horses were fastened to a thick, low-hanging branch, and their tack had already been removed, piled into two small lumpy mounds. Between her and her mount were their ten guardsmen. One stood at attention only a few feet from the horses.

Zyre felt a prickle of doubt. Merytz was right. She wasn't a killer. Sinking the *Aretmor* felt like a massive stain, and here she was, about to bring an entire city to its knees.

She could still return to her sister. She could still…

*No*, Zyre thought, shutting down that line of thought. *No. Even if the part I play tonight in saving my family is small, I insist on being there to see Luc Béranger fall. And if I see Nyli, I will kill him too. My father should never have given him rights to the throne. I don't have to be a clever tactician to know that.*

With her resolve stiffened, she charted the bits of cover between her and her horse. Then she flew, keeping low, rushing on quiet feet. The soldier was only a stone's throw away. Zyre crept closer, wary of any stray sticks or dead leaves that might give her away. The horses did not even fidget as Zyre stepped beside them and grabbed the rope that held the nearest one. Keeping her sights on the soldier, she called to magic, felt a spurt of shivers run down her arms. In the summer heat, there was little water to draw from, but Zyre could sense it there. She summoned a small stream of it, turning it to dense ice even as it touched her palm. The ice crackled softly. Zyre held her breath, urging the ice knife to form quickly. The soldier only had to turn his head a little and she'd be seen.

The knife became sharp and sturdy, and when it was ready, Zyre attacked the rope with a fervor. There was no masking that sound, and within moments, the soldier glanced over his shoulder. The rope snapped in half.

Zyre vaulted onto the horse's back, conscious of the man's eyes suddenly on her. "My lady!" he shouted as she threw her arms around the horse's neck and kicked her into a gallop. The men cried out in alarm as Zyre thundered away.

Hooves followed after her as she streaked across the empty fields that surrounded the capital. Zyre marked the great hole in the wall around the city and the thick, billowing smoke that rose above it. She couldn't see her father's men, but she heard them. The crash and clatter and screams rolled across the fields as if the gods wanted to mark all of the tragedy of war.

The horse was no sprinter, and the fields were a few miles long, but the guards had been slow to follow. Zyre looked over her shoulder. They were far behind, but they were gaining on her.

She kicked the horse's side, urging her horse to give everything she had. Its neck was already dark with sweat, but it gave another feeble burst of speed. They could make it. They were close. She'd lose them in the streets. The horse could take however long it needed to catch its breath. Zyre would take to the roofs from there, where the vantage point would make it easy to see where the fighting had progressed.

The two of them came to an abrupt halt just past the hole in the wall. She jumped off the horse, praying the gods would watch over the beast tonight as she scrambled up the side of the nearest roof. She kept her senses tuned, not just to the shouts or the tremors of the earth in the short distance, but also for any royal troops that might be taking the same routes as her, hoping to surprise Jervin's men.

The roofs were a sight taller than those at Nolasi, and less friendly to climbers than those in Bijal. She was panting by the time she was up the first one. She ducked low, trying not to let her heavy breathing give her location away as the guards searched for her below. Another roof sat adjacent to the one she stood on. She clambered over the divider and kept moving, angling toward the battle.

The army had already advanced some distance, leaving a trail of flame and half-collapsed houses that Zyre could only hope were empty.

She heard her father, once, shouting orders. She kept low and jumped onto the rooftop a street over, out of his view.

A soft curse was her only warning before something went swinging at her head. Zyre threw herself backward. She fell. Her palms burned as they collided with the harsh scaffolding of the roof. A boy stared, perched in front of her with a cudgel between his spidery fingers. In the early dawn, she could see his pale face, his threadbare clothes, his frightened eyes. He was not a soldier. He was just a city commoner. He scurried forward, swinging it again, admittedly determined for one. Zyre rolled to the side, using her momentum to gain her feet.

"I'd really rather not hurt you," she said, raising her hands up as a sign of good faith. "Lay down your weapon, and I'll be on my way."

"Treasonous scum!" he squawked as the cudgel arced toward her head. Cursing, Zyre dodged, darted behind him, and knocked him out with what she hoped was a gentle blow. She took his cudgel, broke it in half, and threw it off the roof onto an empty street.

Men were going to die by the thousands tonight if Luc had forced his city folk to defend their streets. Fury burned icy hot in her veins. These people didn't know how to hold a sword. They didn't even know how to use a pike. They were nothing more than obstacles to be thrown in front of her father's men, to stall them and tire them as much as possible. It was sickening.

But as she made her way farther into the city, closer to the front lines, it became abundantly clear that Tholjun was hungry for more than just the blood of soldiers. Below her, a handful of armed men wearing Béranger green led a ragtag group of incensed, unarmored civilians bearing little more than cudgels, quarterstaffs, or butchers' knives.

Against the Arnaud troops, they fell in waves, but there was nowhere for them to run even if they'd wanted to. Those in the back pushed against the people in front of them, shoving forward even as their lines were forced back. It was madness.

From her vantage point, Zyre watched her father's army progress quickly through Les Stelvo's streets. The gaping hole in the outer wall hadn't been that far from the palace, and their opposition thus far could not hold them back long. The front lines were foot soldiers, though Zyre had seen a few Arnaud cavalry units sweeping through Béranger lines, picking off men, lowering their morale.

As she tried to decide what she could do to help, something arced through the air, flashing silver, crashing into the Arnaud ranks. It exploded, throwing soldiers outward with a terrible force that nearly sent Zyre off the roof.

Everything fell to a ringing silence. With a groan, she rolled slowly onto her stomach and pushed herself onto her knees, barely registering the next flash of metal or the second explosion that followed. She fell heavily onto her rear, dimly aware of voices barking urgent orders to reform the lines. The explosions paused.

She crawled to the edge of the roof. Jumping onto the neighboring building was not easy, but she needed to see who was throwing those enchanted metals.

The milling masses of civilians made it difficult to make out, even as the morning sunlight began reaching its way into the city, but... *there*. Another silver flash spat forth. Zyre gripped the edge of the roof to steady herself and called to magic.

It didn't answer. As the silver charm began to descend, she yanked again at the magic.

Bright orange flames flared across her eyes, nearly blinding her as the explosion rocked the streets, but she was ready for it this time. Seething, she searched the area she'd seen the metal be thrown from, scanning farther out. The crowds shifted oddly, and between them, Zyre was able to make out the form of a dog.

Finally, her magic answered her summons. She gripped the edge of the roof with one hand to steady herself as her vision took on a blue tint. With the other, she formed an ice spear and waited for the *kjarnik* to reveal themselves.

A weathered old woman in the crowd withdrew a small silver ball, disturbingly similar to the shape of those old *mutalguen*. She drew her arm back.

Before Zyre could even think, her ice spear hurtled off her palm and flew straight into the woman's chest. Blood pooled around the melting ice, and she could hear the dog's frantic howl. Zyre's stomach turned as she let flame light up her vision. She braced herself as she threw the fireball, and when it crashed into the silver charm, the force of the explosion was enough to nearly knock Zyre off her feet.

She hastily let go of magic and flattened herself against the roof. Her eyes took an eternity to adjust. She needed to move.

Below, the Arnaud forces regrouped and continued to press, practically trampling over the large swath of civilians knocked over by the explosion. The inner wall was only a half-mile in front of them. Zyre still saw black spots dancing across her vision, but people would be wondering where that magic had come from. She followed the army as it moved toward the palace, her heart aching. Thalja had been dragged into this battle tonight.

Ivanya was expecting men to barge into her rooms, but she still pretended to be wrenched from sleep—as if anyone could have slept through the sounds of battle only a few miles off—to give herself an excuse to grab the knife under her pillow.

Her would-be murderers numbered five.

"Excuse me!" Ivanya squawked, her fingers curling against the cool hilt of the knife.

"Pardon the intrusion," said the man at the back, stepping forward. "The city is under attack. Regis-Uncrowned Luc Béranger demanded you be kept under careful watch." He gestured at the door, and one of the men jumped to close it. One of the men… with a badger trailing at his heels.

Ivanya bit back a sigh of relief. Whatever rage she felt toward Roch Allais, a spy of her husband's, she could set aside for now if it meant surviving tonight.

The guards shifted, hands falling easily to their hilts, once the door latched.

From across the room, Roch shared a look with Ivanya, and a ghost of a smile twisted his features. For the briefest moment, everything fell still, and then chaos befell the Béranger soldiers. The badger lunged across the distance as Roch drew his sword and jumped into action, slicing the chest of the nearest soldier in a single arc. The soldier fell, clutching his chest, screaming, but Roch was already moving, leaving the man to his badger.

At the sound of screams, more guards filtered into the room. Ivanya threw her knife into the eye of the nearest soldier and pounced on his sword before anyone could get between her and another weapon. *Finally, time for action,* she thought, falling into forms she'd learned years ago. She tore her knife free from the soldier's still form and spun just in time to meet the downward arc of another soldier's sword. With a grunt, she shoved him off and swept to the side, running the edge of the blade against the back of the man's knee. He fell with a cry, raising his sword valiantly. She sent her knife into his throat, then shoved his gurgling body off.

As Roch dealt with the last man, she fetched the robe off of her chair and crossed into Damari's room.

Her daughter-in-law stood by the foot of the bed. A broken stool lay a short distance to the side, its missing leg held tightly in her fist. Bernard was nowhere to be seen.

Damari lowered the stool leg a fraction, her eyes widening. "What's going on?"

"My husband has provided an opportunity for our escape. Where's Bernard? We need to go."

After a moment's hesitation, Damari set the leg on the bed and knelt onto the floor. She murmured a few quiet words, and a few seconds later, her son's head popped out from underneath the bed. She helped him the rest of the way, then scooped him up, settling him on one hip so she could carry her makeshift weapon with the other. "All right, I'm ready."

Ivanya led them back into her sleeping quarters, where Roch stood nonchalantly amongst the carnage. Damari covered Bernard's eyes.

"We'll take you through the servants' quarters," Roch told them as he led them into the sitting room. "Luc doesn't have the men to patrol them."

They wound through the rest of the Arnaud quarters, Ivanya letting Roch take the lead. At the main doors, Roch motioned for them to wait. He pulled the doors open a crack, peering through. His badger pressed his nose in the opening, snuffling loudly.

Confident, Roch pulled the door open further and urged them through. He shut the door behind them, and then took charge, leading them through hallways that had grown eerily quiet. Faintly, if she strained the edges of her hearing, Ivanya could catch hints of the preparations being made: orders being shouted, men getting into position, furniture being moved to form barricades.

They eventually stopped in front of a supply closet. The halls were empty, but Ivanya searched for any signs of trouble as Roch and his badger stepped through first, checking to make sure the coast was clear. He ran his fingers along the wall. There was a soft groan that came from the wall, and then a door-sized chunk of it swung backward, revealing a dimly lit hallway.

They hurried out of the main corridors and into the dark, abandoned hallway. A handful of people waited for them. Her grip tightened on her sword for only a moment before she recognized the man at the forefront as none other than Jehan Fidou, a gray-haired mouse of a man with eyes that revealed his intellect. He was joined by the matron—the head of the castle's maids—and a group of men. The matron was armed with nothing more than a cudgel, but the rest, at least, had swords.

Ivanya didn't know who the soldiers were, but four of the armed men in the hall had Fidou's hawk sigil stitched on their breasts. There was a *kjarnik*, too, his cat sitting on his lap, but it was the two turncoat soldiers that surprised her most.

She met Fidou's gaze and saw his failure reflected within them, his grief that he hadn't been able to save Remy.

Well. There would be time for questions later. But for now, she supposed, she could work with him. There were still Damari and Bernard to save.

Roch reached for something in the wall, and the entrance groaned shut.

Ivanya turned to Fidou. "Do we know where Luc is located?"

"My assignment was to take you someplace safe until the battle is won," Fidou replied, shooting her a knowing glance.

"Crasik women do not cower while the men fight," she replied stiffly.

"That is good to know, as I expect there will be some bloodshed between here and our destination. It's a perilous journey between here and the kitchens, Dirige-Uncrowned. As for Luc, well. I expect I know why you're asking, and you should know you will not be able to get within a hundred feet of him. Your life, and the promise of more heirs, may be the only thing that keeps your husband's alliances intact." Fidou grimaced. "Vengeance won't bring back the dead."

Ivanya scowled. She was a Crasik woman. They did not bow and bend, accepting their fate as little more than baby bearers or more support for their husbands. They went out and they *acted*.

But his words called to something in her. She was not the only one who'd lost something to the Bérangers.

*Oh, what I wouldn't give to have my daughter's abilities right now. One* aljarne *could kill the prince, of that I'm sure.* She, on the other hand, needed to focus on getting out of Luc's reach so he could not use her against Jervin. There would be time for vengeance later.

Ivanya jerked her head in assent. "Very well, then. Lead the way."

# CHAPTER 24

The battle was going smoothly so far, by Nyli's estimation, but of course saying the battle was going smoothly was like saying the winter season would be warm just because it hadn't snowed in the first month.

At the moment, they were at a bit of a standstill as their *sjarvisk* tried to find ways around the enchantments written into the metal chips nailed into the gate and surrounding walls. Luc's archers and a handful of his remaining *sjarvisk* clogged the space above them, raining down magic and metal, but Nyli's *sjarvisk* now so outnumbered Luc's that it was a useless attempt. Those not trying to bring the wall down with earthquakes or batter the gate down with flying rocks had dispersed through the rest of their soldiers to protect them from Luc's projectiles.

Nyli could barely make out the details from where he was at the back of the army, with the houses and shops blocking his view, but runners were constantly delivering messages from the ranking officers on the ground. Both Pierre and Josef were out with the troops, thank the gods, giving their respective archers and cavalry some morale boosts while Jervin and Nyli oversaw the two generals directing the ebb and flow of battle.

Héroux and Tavere worked well together, which came as a surprise. Tavere deferred to Héroux when he had to, but Nyli's general listened to Jervin's as if they hadn't just been at each other's throats not a few days ago. Before the battle had started, he'd heard Héroux try to corner Tavere to settle the chain of command. But what had started off as an antagonistic meeting turned into a friendly pact to keep as many of their respective troops alive as possible.

Nyli would never say so out loud, but he was glad that neither of the men wanted to waste lives.

A group of men bearing the Arnaud crest pushed past the ring of soldiers protecting their flanks, past both Nyli's and Jervin's honor guard, even past Nyli himself. The captain bowed to Jervin. "Pardon, my lord, but our charge was insistent about participating in the fight. She snuck out, and when we tried to pursue her, she disappeared. We believe she took to the roofs and made her escape there."

Jervin looked up from the report he was scanning. "What do you mean, she took to the roofs?"

The poor fool shifted uncomfortably. "I mean, sir, that she took her horse and ran into the city. By the time we caught up to her horse, though, the beast had been abandoned, and your niece, gone."

A slew of curses tumbled out of the baron's mouth.

"We've had reports of…anomalies on the field," Tavere said carefully. "Disruptions in the ranks. I had assumed they were sympathizers from within the city itself, but they could well have been Zyre. Should we send someone to find her?"

Nyli had to admit, what little he'd gleaned about Zyre Arnaud had not suggested she was the type to chase after a fight. Perhaps it was just grief shining through—he tried to imagine what he'd do if something happened to Rasin, but it was too terrible to fathom—but he found himself mildly impressed. And disgustingly hopeful.

A battlefield was an unpredictable place.

Jervin called for a man named Merytz, and the young man with the sandy hair, the so-called "Guardsmaster" of Jervin's "honor guard," hurried forward.

"You know her better than anyone, Merytz. Find her."

The soldier bowed at Jervin's command, but the baron gripped his arm and drew him close. He whispered something into the soldier's ear, too quiet for Nyli to make sense of. Something about a valley, and sending someone to Tholjun. The soldier paled but nodded, and Jervin released him.

Merytz disappeared. Jervin dismissed the captain curtly, telling him and his men to return to Aljeya Nyelin and ensure her safety. Then it was just the sounds of the battlefield, the rumble of the earth as *sjarvisk* tried to dislodge the gates, the *boom* of the earthen battering rams, the cries of dying men.

Then a loud crash brought all of their attention toward the wall. A cheer cascaded through their ranks. Within moments, a messenger stood before them, panting as he said, "The gates have fallen. We're through."

Ahead, the army was already surging through. Someone ran to collect their horses, and then the lords mounted up, riding to the forefront. Kuval fell in beside Nyli, his face grim underneath his helmet. They were close. They were so close to Nyli's throne.

They were so close to Luc's downfall, to destroying the last bastion of the poisonous Béranger wrath. There was Luc's son to contend with, but he was young yet. There was hope for him.

None for Luc, and no mercy, either.

Zyre, carefully tucked away atop some poor shopkeeper's roof, watched her father ride into the palace. Her kill count was at least fifteen, including the eight who had fallen as a result of the *kjarnik's* explosives. That most of them were untrained civilians sat sourly in her stomach. The fifteen felt just as much a crime as the hundred she'd left to drown on the *Aretmor*.

*Best not to dwell*, she told herself. The army poured into the palace grounds. If she intended to follow them, she was going to have to leave behind the safety of her roof. She climbed down off her perch and peeked around the corner. Two soldiers had been ordered to remain at the fallen gate.

The problem was that there was no hiding the fact that she was a woman. Her face and long hair would give her away. Even if they believed she had been a *sjarvisk*, women were discouraged from fighting once their beast died. They would not let her through.

Her only other option was to commandeer a helmet, but the very thought threatened to empty her stomach. She'd have to take one off the dead.

*You are a useless soldier*, she told herself harshly. *After all that stubbornness about being allowed on the field, you're really going to make a big deal of stealing some poor dead man's helmet? It'll only prove Merytz and your father right—that you are too much a coward to be here.*

Zyre forced her resolve to stiffen as she retreated into the shadows and backtracked, using the slowly rising sun to keep her bearings. She had to be cautious. The armed city folk had stopped trying to flank her father's men, but that didn't mean there weren't some still out and ready to kill.

Zyre didn't need to go far. The battle left quite a lot of destruction in its wake. Few of the fallen had any amount of armor on at all, but there was an unfortunate number of Arnaud casualties, and all of them were outfitted with some cheap helmets.

Zyre took care looking around the corner. Men and women wove through the bloody scene, checking the bodies. They didn't have any familiars with them, but Zyre felt relieved to see that healers were tending to the wounded, even if they weren't equipped with charms.

Then a wounded man reached out and grabbed at one of the new arrivals, a gaunt gray-haired man who yanked his arm back with disgust and moved on to something definitely more corpse-like.

The realization crashed into Zyre with a determined ferocity.

They weren't helping the wounded. They were robbing the dead.

Zyre stepped out from the shadows, her anger flaring. "What are you doing? You should be helping these people!"

The dozen men and women all jumped at her voice. A few skittered toward the shadows before locating the source. The gray-haired man stood his ground. A haunting sneer marred his features, and there was a wildness to his eyes that made Zyre take a step back.

Without realizing it, Zyre called to magic, seeking the faint throb of power that wanted to answer. She snatched at it and let fireballs grow above her fists. It didn't take long for people to notice.

"*Aljarne!*" someone shrieked. They began to scatter before Zyre could even throw her magic toward them—even the gaunt old man fled—until Zyre was the only one left standing there. The flames died. She closed her eyes and inhaled, seeing the cobblestones in her mind, painted in the dark red of drying blood. The cloying smell of blood and death hung heavily in the air.

"They'll be back, you know," said a reedy voice behind her.

Zyre jumped and spun around, reaching for her sword. But

she found only a white-haired woman, her hair tidy, her dress neat. She had a leather bag slung across her shoulders. "Why?"

The woman shrugged, kneeling beside a body. She pressed her fingers against the side of his neck as she said, "Desperation makes monsters of the best of people. Luc promised a fortune for every Arnaud slain by the common folk. Of course, there'll be no way to prove which of the dead belonged to which side." She sighed and stepped over the body, moving to the next. Before she knelt, she inspected Zyre. The old woman must not have been far away to have arrived so quickly. Had she heard the city folk name Zyre *aljarne*? She did not seem afraid. "What side do you fight for, then?"

"Does it matter?" Zyre asked. There was no way she was telling this stranger that she sided with the invading force. She didn't want to have to fight off another civilian like she'd done with that boy on the roof.

The woman frowned, but a man in front of her groaned, drawing her focus. As she set her leather bag on the bloody street and opened it, Zyre took the chance to disappear. She swiped her helmet off the body—then, feeling guilty, pressed her own fingers against the dead man's neck, relieved when she found no signs of life. "We will come back for you. Give you a proper burial," she told the dead man. It did little to assuage her guilt. She scampered away, running back the way she'd come.

When she neared the wall, Zyre did her best to shake the image of the dead-littered street. Soldiers didn't care about bloodshed. They didn't care about Tholjun's price, so long as they weren't the one paying it. She tied up her hair and put on her stolen helmet. It was big, comically so, but it was the best she could do. Better than it being too small, she supposed. She marched straight toward the blue-clad guards, unsurprised when they hefted their pikes in warning. Zyre raised her hands and deepened her voice. "I fight for Jervin Arnaud."

"Why aren't you in the palace, then?" the guard on the left asked. "*That's* where the fighting is."

"Personal assignment from Arnaud himself," she lied. "Now, are you going to let me through or not?"

The two guards glanced at each other, then the one on the right shrugged. Zyre hurried through before they could change their minds.

The battle had been a constant cacophony. The noise bounced off the buildings, through hallways, down to the very courtyard where she stood. She wanted nothing more than to find her mother, but standing before the castle, she realized what a foolish endeavor this was. It was a vast structure, and even with the blueprints imprinted in her mind, the castle would provide more of a maze than she had imagined. *Tholjun guide me*, she prayed.

The dungeons, she supposed, would be the first place to look, but even after studying the map a few days ago with her friends, she could not remember where they were. It seemed logical that perhaps they'd be under the castle. She strode toward the great doors.

Immediately, she was met with carnage. Massive fissures ran along the floor. Some beautiful artwork had streaks of blood or char. Several bodies littered the hall, some of them soulbeasts. It was worse than the city. There were few shadows and no dark cobblestones to hide the horror. There was no open air to cut at the scent of the dead. It broke her heart.

*Find my mother, get her to safety.* Zyre told herself, stiffening her resolve. She stepped lightly, gently, around the bodies, both Béranger green and Arnaud blue.

At the first intersection, she listened for signs of the battle. Maybe it was the confines of the building making the sounds echo, but it seemed as if shouts were coming from all sides except behind her. The right side seemed to be the quietest, so she followed that route. She padded through the halls, searching behind any doors she came across that looked large enough to fit a war council, doing her best to skirt the hottest fights. *Aljarne* or not, she didn't want to get into a fight where she'd be greatly outnumbered.

Unfortunately, Luc had his men running about, sending reinforcements where they were needed. Zyre didn't know if it was the castle's size playing tricks on her, but Luc had more men than it seemed he ought to have.

On more than one occasion, Zyre had to dart down a side hall and duck behind an art pedestal or in a supply closet as a whole unit of soldiers marched through. Once, to escape a unit of soldiers, she nearly ran into a half-dozen *sjarvisk*. A door provided her salvation. She sprinted through it, surprised to find herself outside, on the fringes of a beautiful garden with a great silver tree at its center. Zyre's breath caught, but shouts behind her reminded her she didn't have time to gawk. She threw herself behind a squat hedge of lavender.

The voices followed her. The door opened, and Zyre's heart leapt into her throat.

⁂

Nyli had lost the baron. He'd lost track of most of his men in the warren of halls. Now, it was just him, Kuval, and their honor guard with a handful of soldiers they'd picked up a few minutes ago. They were far from where Nyli meant to be; they'd been heading in the direction of the throne room when they'd run afoul of some of Luc's men. The palace was tricky like that, and now Nyli was being jostled against his honor guard as they slashed down the last of yet another unit of soldiers. Kuval grabbed his arm, and they ran forward together, both of their swords bloody.

"We need to get to the council room," Nyli said to his Guardsmaster. "We're going the wrong way."

"Lower your volume, my prince," the Guardsmaster hissed. "We don't want to attract any attention to ourselves until we find more men."

Nyli could hear the distant shouts of the other men and doubted Luc had enough troops to prowl the hall at random. Still, he fell silent and was glad he did as they turned down the lengthy corridor that held the apartments of House Villeneuve. A handful of honor guard stood at the ready. Nyli frowned. Those were *Rasin*'s honor guard.

"Secure the hall," Nyli ordered his honor guard, then strode toward Rasin's. They shuffled uneasily, and he supposed he didn't blame them. He offered his sword hilt-first to her Guardsmaster. "Permission to see my sister?"

The gesture worked. Devoid of his sword, Nyli motioned for Kuval to wait outside and let one of Rasin's honor guard lead him in.

The drawing room was empty, but the honor guard led him farther in, to the less formal sitting room where two guards in red uniforms bearing the Villeneuve kraken kept vigil. Rasin paced along the carpet while the second-eldest Villeneuve daughter, the mousy Everi, watched with some trepidation.

"Rasin."

His sister spun around, her jaw swinging open. "Nyli?"

Everi scrambled to her feet to make the proper curtsy, but Nyli ignored her. "What are you doing in the Villeneuve apartments?"

Her expression was filled with such derision that Nyli thought she was going to lash out at him. She drew close, dropping her voice to a snarled whisper. "I could ask you much the same. You invaded Les Stelvo with Jervin Arnaud. What did you do, brother? Father…"

"I'm sorry. I did what I thought was right. It seemed like long-overdue justice for our mother. And Luc…"

"So you did kill him." Rasin exhaled. "I can't say he didn't deserve it."

He heard her grief buried deep just the same. Familial love was a horrible creature sometimes.

"You'll have to kill Luc, too, you know. Do you really think you can?" Rasin asked. Her voice was small, but the question thundered in his ears.

"I expect so," Nyli said hoarsely, turning so she could not see his face. "If Luc will not submit, then I suppose I'll do what I must." He risked a glance over his shoulder. Her expression cut to the bone. It was pity, and grief. They both knew Luc would never bend the knee to his younger brother. "Stay here," he said. "It'll be safer. I'll send some men to make sure no rebels bother you."

Rasin stepped closer and wrapped her arms around him, seeming not to care about the blood that now stained her dress. "Go safely," she said. Then she let him go.

⁂

A strange gurgling sound and a scream cut short made Zyre peek up over the shoots of blooming lavender. When she called to magic, it answered her summons with surprisingly little restraint. She saw a familiar form standing over the body of one of her pursuers. Captain Merytz yanked his sword free. Then he saw her, and his expression grew stormy.

"Come to fetch me like an errant dog?" Zyre asked sharply.

"I've come to fetch you like the unprotected lady that you are," he replied, marching through the lavender. "You're risking the entire country by being here."

Zyre might've laughed if she hadn't been startled by his sudden steely grip on her arm. She shoved him off of her, marching toward the center of the garden. "Unprotected lady? Merytz, have you forgotten the sparring we did together? Did you forget my magic? Don't insult me."

He hurried after her. "You don't even like fighting," he snapped. "At least, you didn't. Tell me, have you gone mad? They say the madness makes you more bloodthirsty."

Zyre screamed in vexation. "Merytz! I'm not mad. I am just trying to help my family, and no one will even let me do that! Tholjun's blood! What else am I supposed to do?"

"You could become dirige like your father has planned!" Merytz snarled. "He's going to marry you to Nyli to forge an alliance with the new regis so there can finally, *finally* be peace!"

Merytz kept talking, but Zyre didn't hear a word. Her mind got stuck on *married to Nyli*. Nyli, who had tried to arrest her family, who had gotten Remy killed. Nyli, the Butcher, who had burned her home to the ground, who had slighted her brother, her father, forced her to keep her secrets that kept her separate from her family. "No. No, I won't marry him."

"Not even to save the country?" Merytz shook his head. "The Zyre I know would do anything in the name of peace."

"Anything but that," she whispered.

Then it dawned on her. Whether she followed Merytz or fought in the battle, if she survived, she'd been promised to the prince. *I guarantee you, the price of the throne did not come cheaply*, her father had said. He'd said it as if Nyli was the one who had to pay the price, but no, Zyre did too. And it wouldn't end when the war was over. In fact, that was when it would *begin*, as if everything she'd done up to this point was nothing more than delaying the inevitable.

All this time, she had thought that once the war was won, she could do as she wished. Be with her family the way she'd always dreamed but free, also, to chase her dreams and see the world. Was she really willing to dedicate the rest of her life to this?

Merytz took a step toward her. He would do what he had to in order to force her compliance. She could see it in his eyes. Doomed, not just to marry a man, but to marry the prince, the *Butcher*.

She could not.

She would not.

Any fate was better than that.

Even, Zyre realized, catching a glimpse of the velídas tree in her periphery, even an *aljarne*'s fate.

Zyre bolted for the tree, felt the whispers of Merytz's fingers as he tried and failed to grab her. She fell headlong into Velídas.

The waves of magic crashed into her so violently, so quickly, that Zyre didn't even have a chance to prepare herself. She stepped into that beautiful, burning sea, and in it, she drowned.

***

Tholjun favored them, for although Jervin had lost sight of most of his army, reports were flooding in that skirmishes continued to end in their victory. The palace was torn apart: doors broken off their hinges, rooms searched, soldiers killed. Hall by hall, the palace fell.

Taking respite in a now-empty corridor, Jervin drank from a waterskin. A runner sped toward them. "My lord!" the runner said, snapping into a sharp salute. "Luc's been spotted, my lord.

He's heading in the direction of the throne room. There's a major holdout there."

"Boosting morale, I suppose," Tavere muttered.

"Or preparing to make his move," Jervin countered. He turned to his men. "If Luc is heading to the throne room, then that is where we must go. *Eris bi eljers!* For House Arnaud!"

The cry echoed down the halls, and the hundred men he had with him fell into formation. They began to march, repeating the epithet. Drawn in by the noise, more Arnaud men found their retinue and joined in. They met little resistance. Perhaps the rest of Luc's forces were waiting for them in the throne room.

Captain Ricard joined them with what was left of his *sjarvisk* forces. Jervin remembered the way. The old soldier, Noam Rodier, stood at the end of the hall, watching the great green doors of the throne room. Jervin motioned for the soldiers to halt, and then he, Tavere, and Ricard joined Rodier. The doors to the throne room were shut, displaying the golden griffon and the Bérangers' House words. *Oderta neg rasin det pieterad.* Old words. Beware the fury on the winds.

"Any eyes in there?" Tavere asked.

The grizzled soldier shook his head. "They shut the doors before I could get a good look, sir. I saw more than a few animals, though, and archers and swordsmen."

"Numbers?"

Again, Rodier shook his head. "I can only say that the room looked rather full, sir. My best guess is five hundred strong."

On an open field, the odds would make it an easy win, but only so many men could engage in such confined quarters. Luc was still unlikely to win, but he'd evened the odds considerably.

Tavere tapped his sword hilt. "Nyli said Luc doesn't have many *sjarvisk.* He'd want to conserve them. What do you think—foot in the front, archers in the middle, *sjarvisk* in the back?"

"That's what I'd do in his place," Jervin confirmed. "There's only one main entrance into that room. And he'll be in the back, protected by the *sjarvisk*. Let's mix our *sjarvisk* into our ranks, or else the foot will be a pincushion for magical attacks and arrows. Ricard, I will need a handful of *sjarvisk* to join me, though."

Tavere blinked. "Where are you going?"

"Most of the noblemen don't pay much mind to the servants' quarters, but I am not most noblemen. There's an entrance near the back, close to the throne itself. Give me five minutes to get into position, then blast that door open. I'll sneak in during the bedlam and find Luc."

Tavere nodded. "Be careful, my lord."

"Certainly." He gestured to Ricard and let the man choose a few *sjarvisk* to fall in line behind him. Ricard barked the names Deitral Vaudian, Horadon Jorvik, and Boreil Edvjorni. A woman with a wolf and two men, one with a weasel and another with a mole, of all things, stepped forward. He frowned, but he trusted Ricard.

With several of his makeshift honor guard, a unit of foot soldiers, and Ricard's assigned *sjarvisk*, Jervin marched down a nearby hall and found a supply closet. He ran his fingers across the coarse brick until he found the knob that opened a hidden doorway, revealing a dark hall. It was eerily silent. Jervin's honor guard took the lead, following his direction.

Before long, they came before another door that Jervin knew would lead to the throne room. That was where their luck ended. A handful of guards stood between them and their quarry.

As the words *eris bi eljers* met with *oderta neg rasin det pieterad* on the other side of the door, Jervin motioned his men to follow. They charged at the soldiers with a war cry of their own. The *sjarvisk* fell behind, launching fireballs ahead of them.

Two men fell, screaming, and the acrid scent of burnt flesh rolled across the space.

Jervin drew Eris as they bridged the gap. The sword hummed beneath his fingers, growing light in his hand. It felt like an extension of his arm. There was almost no resistance as he buried it into the chest of the first soldier, the sword cutting through the leather armor like it wasn't even there at all. The rest of his men fell in line around him, and by the time he'd killed his second soldier, the rest were dead.

Gods, he'd forgotten how alive he felt during a battle.

His adrenaline still coursing through his veins, he felt along the wall for the knob. The door swung open. His men poured through.

The back of the throne room had not yet fallen to chaos. Better yet, Tholjun favored them, for Luc himself stood surrounded by his honor guard, watching the battle with a pale face. He spun to face Jervin's men, oaths dripping like poison from the prince's lips. His men engaged Luc's honor guard, leaving the prince for Jervin himself.

Jervin hefted Eris, the family sword sharp and glinting. *It's only right that this should be the weapon that kills you*, he thought. This was for his brother, who had fallen in battle, and for Louis Ermengarde and all the others who had died that day in Kullen Valley. This was for Remy, his son. It was for the endless insults he had endured.

Jervin struck out like a viper, and Luc barely deflected the blow that had been meant to take off his head. But the prince was an agile swordsman. He fell into the offensive, twisting his wrist so that Eris was forced upward, and Jervin had to retreat as the sharp edge of the prince's blade slashed at his chest. Jervin ducked, his sword's edge racing against Luc's knee. The prince shouted in pain, his leg giving out.

"Surrender," Jervin ordered.

The prince's expression only darkened. He struggled to his feet, his balance unsteady. "You will never take the throne, Jervin Arnaud. *Oderta neg rasin det pieterad!*" he shouted, lunging forward.

His sword was easy to deflect, and for that short-lived moment, Jervin could not believe Luc would be so stubborn. Deflect, then attack. Eris buried itself in Luc's chest.

Then a sharp pain bloomed in Jervin's side. He glanced down, surprised to find a knife there, Luc's fingers dropping lifelessly away. With a pained grunt, he pulled Eris free.

A terrifying grin plastered across the prince's face.

Wincing, Jervin surveyed the scene around him. The *sjarvisk* near the back had begun to realize they'd been flanked. They turned to face their enemy. Jervin drew up his sword, ready to sound the retreat. Then he staggered. Fire burned through him, raging against the knife in his side. Dark spots flashed across his vision. *Enchanted blade*, he thought sharply, suddenly terrified. Somehow, he was aware of his men falling around him protectively, but he barely had time to be startled before he fell to the floor, unconscious.

⚜

The woman who prowled through Velídas had no name. She used to, once, but she had lost it. Everything was silent and drab and colorless. The only thing that pulled at her was a pulsing in her heart, her bones, her skin. Something sang to her in a way she'd never heard before.

This place was strange, but to the woman, it felt *right*. It felt *whole*, like a new food that filled one's belly or riding a wave across the sea or sharing a space with people who knew you, *really* knew you.

The woman's palms burned. She had fallen earlier, but she didn't remember it now. She barely even gave much thought to the throbbing scrapes.

Beneath her feet was the lifeblood of the world. Magic in the shape of branches formed a latticework of pathways that the woman barely noticed. She didn't mark her path. There was no reason to think of where she'd come from and no way to know where she was going beyond that constant tugging on her heart.

The silhouette of a velídas tree appeared before her, no taller than her knee. Through it came the comforting scent of salty ocean air, the musical creak of a ship cutting through the waves. The pulsing came from there, begging, demanding. She tried to get through. She just wanted to silence the summons. But no matter how small she tried to make herself, the silhouette would not give.

The woman once named Zyre looked thoughtfully at the silhouette, picking apart the summons. Underneath the thundering pulse came a smaller throb, one that drew her away from the little tree. She walked on until the throbbing intensified and a larger silhouette blinked into existence.

She stepped through, and this time, the tree gave.

As soon as the woman was back on solid ground, the magic tore itself away, eager to remain in Velídas where it belonged. The woman fell to her hands and knees, only vaguely recognizing the yard she was in and the house that towered before her. Distantly, she heard a voice shout in surprise, and then everything went dark.

# CHAPTER 25

The *Doleir* was as splendid as Neelie remembered it. It was an impressive four-masted barque, one of the fastest ships Venasca had ever put to sea even without her mother's magic to encourage the wind. They had left behind the *Holeny* yesterday afternoon after a quick two-and-a-half-day journey downriver. The *Doleir* was a hell of a lot noisier than the *Lemanthus*, its crew numbering thirty strong, many of whom now ran about their tasks behind Neelie.

A short distance away, something moved in the water. Adreia's soulbeast, Kesnit, broke the surface. A watery spray shot up, and then the whale disappeared beneath the waves.

Right on cue, her mother's steady footfalls thudded across the deck. Neelie didn't bother to look up at the movement in her periphery. "You missed it. Kesnit just said hello."

Adreia chuckled. "I saw." She leaned against the bulwark.

A bird's cry tore both of their attention from the water. A blur of black feathers flew above deck. Adreia, seemingly by instinct, raised her arm, and the raven landed on it.

*Berhôt?* "How…?"

Adreia spared Neelie a glance as she unfastened a white slip of paper from its harness. "I like to keep a small velídas tree on my ship for emergencies," she said with a shrug. She unfurled the paper and read it. It was not a particularly long note. She passed it to Neelie, frowning.

If Berhôt was the one bringing bad news, surely it had to do with the Shadowmen. Neelie tensed, preparing herself for some grave announcement like *Ren's been arrested* or *The Shadow Quarter is in flames.*

Instead, it was about Zyre, of all people.

*The Arnaud girl returned to our home through Velídas. I don't know what happened... The magic has clearly taken its toll. I've used a spell to send her to sleep for the time being, but I cannot make it last forever. If you've reunited with our daughter, and I'm hoping you have, then please ask her what she would like me to do. I'm hesitant to reach out to your friend the baron until I know what sent the girl into Velídas to begin with. Safe travels, -H*

"She's back in Bijal?" Neelie asked, looking up at Adreia. Her mother only shrugged again.

Neelie's fist tightened around the note, and she ran. The crew cursed at her as she bumped into several, leaping down the steps below deck that led to Modorin's sleeping quarters. She knocked but didn't wait for an answer. The scent of sick was faint. Modorin himself lay on his cot, arm over his eyes. "What do you want, Neelie?"

She didn't give him the satisfaction of asking how he knew it was her. Instead, she slammed the paper onto his stomach. Not hard; just hard enough to get his attention. He made a noise in his throat and sat up, glowering. But he took the paper and read it. His face, already pale, turned ashen. "Not possible. We left her at the Áit..." He trailed off. It was Velídas. Of course it was possible. "Ski's breath. I can hardly believe it. What do you think happened?"

"I don't know!" Neelie snapped. "Why in Dûl's name would she travel through Velídas? She knew the dangers! No. It doesn't matter. I need you to help my mother, Modorin. Please. Two *majican* manning the sails will get us back to Bijal that much faster."

Modorin swung off the bed, his cheeks going green. "I didn't know you cared about her this much, Nee."

"I…" *I kissed her before we left. Does that count?* She shook her head. "We're friends, you ass. Of course I care. What should I tell my father?"

He shrugged, though it didn't carry his usual swagger. "Zyre was marching for war. There's a good chance this means they lost. There may not be anyone for him to tell." Neelie hovered close to her friend as he fought with the stairs, careful, too, not to step on Sarol. "He should send in Kadj, though, if it's safe for the both of them."

"Thank you," Neelie said. Then, as they surfaced, she shouted, "Mother! I've got an extra pair of hands to help with the wind."

If Adreia thought anything about it, she wisely kept it to herself. Neelie wrote back what Modorin had said while her mother showed him how to put wind in the sails without upsetting the weather overmuch, and when she was done, Adreia took Berhôt and Neelie's message below deck. When she got back, the bird was gone and the *Doleir* was cutting through the waves with a recklessness that matched Neelie's own bleak mood.

⚜

Ivanya and her companions had the misfortune of taking up residence in a cramped secret room in the kitchens. Emptied of servants and behind a false wall in one of the pantries, they'd had the lovely honor of being able to hear the muffled sounds of the battle taking place above their heads. There was a little more room now, and a lot less noise, ever since a horn had sounded not ten minutes ago. The *sjarvisk* Roch Allais had taken his badger to investigate.

Damari sat on the floor, murmuring softly to Bernard, keeping him quiet. All the fake walls in the world would not protect them if the boy started crying, but Bernard, thank Thalja, had never been fussy. Jehan Fidou helped, letting Bernard toy with his graying mustache. One of Jehan's soldiers waited inside the room with them, but it wasn't big enough for all of them, so the rest had taken up residence in the kitchen, playing at cards so as to seem less like guards and more like apathetic soldiers. The *kjarnik* had gone with them after Bernard had petted his cat a little too roughly.

This was all to say that the hidden compartment was nearly silent, and when the rhythmic knock announced Roch's return, she was not the only one who started at the sudden noise. When the door slid open, the *sjarvisk*'s expression was grim.

"We didn't lose," Ivanya surmised, "or else you'd be rushing us out of the palace."

"I'm not entirely sure we won," Roch replied. "Your husband the baron killed Prince Luc but took a blade in the process. *Kjarnik* healers are working on him now, but in the interim, it appears Nyli Béranger has laid claim to the throne and seems to be backed by House Arnaud and all of their forces."

Ivanya blinked. "I highly doubt that."

"If I hadn't spoken to your daughter, I would have said the same. But she was there, with your husband. It should be safe for me to take you to her."

"My daughter?" Ivanya echoed, taken aback. She dared not utter Zyre's name.

"Aljeya Nyelin," Roch insisted with a nod. Ivanya's heart contracted sharply. Roch continued on, mistaking her confusion.

"Apparently she joined the rebel forces less than a fortnight ago with a small contingent of guards."

Ivanya rose, grabbing her borrowed sword with one hand and smoothing her ruffled skirts with the other. "Very well. Let's go see what my daughter has to say."

She wished she could reunite with her eldest daughter under better circumstances, but at least Aljeya could help Ivanya pick up the pieces in the aftermath of this battle. And perhaps she'd have news of her sister as well.

Roch bowed to the half. Everyone else in the room scrambled to their feet, eager to get out. Jehan Fidou and his guards fell into position around them, joined by the two Béranger turncoats and the *kjarnik*. They formed an odd procession out of the kitchens and into the main halls of the palace. Already, *kjarnik* swarmed, stooping over blue- and green-clad soldiers alike. Ivanya glanced at Damari out of the corner of her eye and saw the woman's expression flushed but determined. She was trying to shield Bernard from the worst of it. Ivanya herself looked at the wounded and dead soldiers with pity.

They did their best to avoid the piles of dead men, and eventually, Roch stopped them in front of some minor lord's apartments within a stone's throw of the throne room. Blue-clad guards swarmed outside of it, a small area around the door cleared out to make room. Roch announced their party, and the soldiers, eyeing her and accepting Roch's testament, opened the door. Ivanya signaled for everyone to remain outside. Then she braved the room.

Jervin had been placed on a table in the drawing room just inside the lordling's apartments. Two *kjarnik* bent over the table, one with a spotted dog and the other with a rabbit. From where she stood, Ivanya could not see the wound.

Roch was right about Aljeya. Ivanya's daughter sat helplessly in a chair. She immediately leapt to her feet at Ivanya's arrival, though, her eyes red. They embraced, and if Ivanya squeezed a little too tightly in relief, Aljeya seemed not to mind.

"Come," Ivanya said quietly, pulling Aljeya farther into the apartments so as to not disturb the healers. "I hear you joined your father two weeks ago. What's happened since then? How are we allied to the Béranger brat? No, that's not important. Tell me first. How's he doing?"

Aljeya wiped at her eyes. "He killed Luc, Mother. Killed him with the family sword. But he got stabbed, too. It's not… The healers say if the knife had been a normal one, it's possible it would have been an easy fix, but the blade was enchanted. It's destroying Father's body. They've stopped the spread, even hope to reverse some of it, but they don't know yet what the effects will be."

"Will he live?" She should not have sounded so desperate in front of her daughter, but, well, these were desperate times.

"The healers seem hopeful, but they said it's too early to be certain."

Ivanya sighed heavily. It took a surprising amount of energy to walk across the room and fall into one of the chairs. "I haven't heard a single word about Zyre. I'm afraid to ask."

Aljeya followed her over. "I don't know much."

Her eldest daughter spent the next few minutes speaking of exploits that Ivanya could hardly believe belonged to Zyre. Part of her wished Zyre had stayed in Venasca, or gone across the sea to Pailyr. Zyre would thrive there.

But that was not all there was.

Stealing a glance at Captain Merytz, Aljeya inhaled shakily and added, "Nyli Béranger came to Father with a proposition. In order to gather the favor and support of all Houses, Nyli would claim the throne but place Father at his right hand as Duc. To cement the alliance, Nyli would marry Zyre. Father said he claimed her as his bastard daughter, though I doubt he told Nyli of Zyre's magic."

"What?" Ivanya snapped. After ten years of hiding Zyre, denying her very own daughter, whom she had carried for nine months in her womb… to throw all that away for politics? If Jervin hadn't been lying unconscious and wounded in the next room over, she might've stabbed him herself.

Aljeya shrugged as if she too had felt the same. "The family's position is tenuous, though. Zyre wanted to fight and I… I let her."

It was impossible to fathom at first, her little girl going out and fighting. For so many years, Ivanya had worried Zyre wouldn't be able to take care of herself, but after everything, she wished her youngest daughter could have held a little tighter to her own beliefs, if only to keep her away from the dangers of politics and warfare.

"A battlefield is a dangerous place for an *aljarne*," Ivanya said in lieu of those dark thoughts. "Do we know where she is? What happened to her?"

"Merytz said Father sent him after her. She… disappeared. Through a tree. At least, according to Merytz. He's not one to lie, but it doesn't make any sense." Aljeya shook her head in confusion, but Ivanya knew it made perfect sense.

Velídas. The garden.

It was possible, she supposed, though what would drive Zyre to do such a thing was beyond her. The story of Teirolac's demise was one told even in Crasea. "Do we know where she might have gone?"

"Well, if she *went* anywhere, I might wonder if she returned home or to Bijal. She made friends there."

Ivanya nodded and tucked that information away. "I have to find Prince Nyli. I need to know what kind of man he is and if we can patch up this fiasco." She rose, looking down at her daughter. "Keep an eye on your father. I may have words for him later, but he has to stay alive to hear them. Let me know if his condition changes."

"Yes, Mother," Aljeya replied quietly.

Ivanya embraced her daughter fiercely, then braved the bloody corridors again to find the boy-regis.

Nyli stood over his brother's dead body, set carefully on the small bed that occupied the room, and tried to find it within himself to be pleased, to sneer like Luc probably would have done had their places been reversed. To be merciless like Luc had been after Nyli had witnessed his mother's execution. But he just couldn't find it in himself to be cruel, even with no one there to see it. "May your soul find peace, brother," he said.

Feeling surprisingly wretched, he wandered out of whatever minor lord's bedroom they'd placed his brother's body in—he hadn't bothered to look on the way in—and found himself face-to-face with Luc's family. Essir had always been mousy in the quiet sense, and it hurt more than facing Luc's death to see the emptiness in her expression. Her son stood behind her, hand squeezing her shoulder in solidarity. Alexandre held some of that Béranger wrath, and Nyli expected to see some of it now.

When the boy stepped forward, Nyli steeled himself for the argument. Alexandre was too young to take the throne, and he was now illegitimate since Luc died before the proper crowning ceremonies could be done, but a case could still be made.

Then, inexplicably, Alexandre fell to one knee. "Regis-Uncrowned Nyli Béranger, I recognize the tenuous position I put you in," he said, well-spoken for a twelve-year-old. "My father would certainly want me to take the throne. He told me so. But I am not ready to take the crown. I do not even think I want it. So I gladly swear fealty to you as the new regis and ask for clemency on my mother's behalf."

Nyli glanced at Essir. Her focus had sharpened. She nodded. Looking back to the boy in front of him, Nyli said, "This is something I can easily grant. You and the Lady Essir will return to Mod Redel, and when you come of age, Elyx will relinquish his stewardship to your care." He couldn't, after all, keep Alexandre at court. Not until he was certain, at the very least, that Alexandre did not take too much after his father.

The boy seemed to understand. He nodded graciously, and Nyli gave him leave to stand.

"You may, of course, wait for Luc's burial." Nyli added, realizing it would be cruel to do otherwise. With a curt nod of his head, Nyli fled the apartment, closing the door behind him with relief.

Kuval and his retinue were waiting for him, but to his surprise, Kuval had company. Eduoard Villeneuve spoke quietly with him. Nyli noted the blood on his armor and wondered if Eduoard had fought for Luc. He scowled and strode toward them. As soon as Eduoard caught sight of him, though, he broke away and hurried to meet Nyli halfway.

He bowed. "Regis-Uncrowned, I apologize for interrupting you in your grieving, but I have a request to make of you."

"Is this about my sister?" Nyli asked, not bothering to hide his disgust.

"It is," Eduoard replied. He fidgeted. "With all due respect, Your Highness, your brother, may Tholjun grant him peace, made demands to bind our two Houses together to strengthen our alliance."

"I am aware. You're here to ensure that the marriage is still going to happen?"

"Not quite." He hesitated, offering up a smile that looked more painful than anything else. "You and your brother had more than a few differences, your relationship to your sister being one of them. Luc wished to see Rasin and I wed, but as you hold the throne now, it seemed pertinent to know about your own desires."

"Eduoard," he said sternly, "I find it unethical to force a marriage onto anyone." He certainly knew how disgusting it felt to give into Jervin's demands with his *sjarvisk* daughter.

The Villeneuve heir straightened, his grin turning into something a little more genuine. "I'm relieved to hear you say so, truth be told. I would be lucky to marry your sister, make no mistake; I think she is as impressive as she is stunning. But it would feel cheap to take her hand rather than earn it, if you don't mind my saying so."

Nyli blinked. He found himself looking at Kuval, trying to determine if Eduoard had spoken to him about this at all, but Kuval seemed as clueless as he. Nyli suddenly wondered if he'd denied himself of a worthwhile friend these past years Eduoard had been at court. The man had spent a considerable amount of time in Luc's company, but perhaps it was only a measure of survival to befriend the next likely regis.

Suppressing a small laugh, he said, "If she asks my opinion on you, Eduoard, I'll be sure to speak favorably. But know she's not easy to impress."

"I find no fault in that. By your leave?"

Nyli nodded, and Eduoard strode off. He nearly collided with a small party marching through the corridor, Ivanya Arnaud at its head. He grimaced. An inevitable tangle, he was well aware.

His Guardsmaster led Ivanya toward Nyli. The rest of her retinue remained at the other end of the hall. As Ivanya fell into a low three-quarter curtsy, Nyli asked, "To what do I owe the pleasure of your visit, Duchess Arnaud?"

"It pleases me to hear that title," Ivanya said coolly. "There are a few matters that require some discussion. Is there somewhere private where we can speak?"

There was, although moving farther into the palace meant gathering both his honor guard and Ivanya's retinue, walking some short distance through corridors still full of blood and, in several cases, the bodies of the fallen. Then, of course, his guard and hers had to ensure there were no troops hiding out in the room, ready to lash out.

They'd found themselves in a large office with several desks that clerks would normally occupy if today were a *normal* day.

At Ivanya's behest, Nyli dismissed everyone, even Kuval. When the last of them had shut the door behind them, Nyli turned to Ivanya. "Well, you have your privacy. What can I do for you?"

Ivanya steepled her fingers. She took her time in answering, surveying the room and finding a chair to slip languidly into. "I understand you made a bargain with my husband prior to storming the city. Considering I was not present at the time of the bargain, I would like to go over the terms with you in full."

"To what end?" he asked.

"I'll remind you that your family was going to offer my husband false terms to lure him back to the capital so you could have him executed."

Nyli shifted uncomfortably under her gaze. Not because that had been his plan—far from it—but because it seemed willing to carve out his very soul. It had been surprising enough to learn Jervin had been unfaithful to his wife and that it had resulted in a *sjarvisk* daughter—though the gods made him pay for it with her uselessness. It had been a far less pleasant surprise to hear Jervin Arnaud demand Nyli wed the bastard girl. But his distaste was a lesser thing compared to the peace his country might finally hold.

"This bargain was not a ploy, Duchess. I am willing to prove it however you see fit. Bring in your husband's bastard daughter. We can be married by the end of the night if you'd like and hold a proper ceremony later."

Strangely, Ivanya flinched at his mention of Zyre Mescal. So, she held ill will toward the girl? Maybe that part of the bargain wasn't the right place to start.

"Look, everything else will take time to write up. I cannot officially give you the title of duchess until I am crowned, and it will take *weeks* to get that ceremony—"

"Stop," Ivanya cut in.

Nyli fell silent. He didn't realize how bad that looked—the regis taking orders from a noblewoman—until it was too late. He scowled at the floor.

"I believe you," she said with a tone as sharp as steel. "Unfortunately, I cannot allow you to marry Zyre."

He pushed down the hope that bloomed at her words, waiting for the bargain that Ivanya would insist on taking its place. "Why not?"

Ivanya glared at the wall behind him. With a grimace, she turned her back on him and found a chair to sit in. "It was an unfair bargain on our part. The girl took the loss of her soulbeast poorly. I'm afraid she's lost a piece of herself. In fact, during the battle, she seems to have given her guards the slip and has disappeared, but it's no matter. I would rather see a full Arnaud connected to the throne, if it pleases you."

Nyli followed the Arnaud woman's example and bought himself some time by winding through the room and grabbing a chair so he could sit nearby. If only it were possible to delay this question inevitably. "Who else did you have in mind? There are, after all, no other unwed Arnaud women for me to marry."

*Thalja have mercy, if she means to marry herself to me... I thought Jervin was likely to survive his wounds.*

"It's not really a marriage I had in mind," she said quietly, and Nyli stiffened. "Remy's widow, Damari, has a son. If you were to wed her and adopt him as your own, then in the eyes of the gods, Bernard would have both Arnaud and Béranger blood."

Well, *that* was certainly not where he'd expected her to go with this. "Marriage isn't a requirement for adoption," he said.

"Maybe not," she said, eyes turning to ice. "But you need a dirige to help you rule. And in the eyes of the gods and the law, Damari became an Arnaud as soon as she married my son. You need a woman to marry, and you need an heir."

*Except for the fact that I have to marry a Venascan woman several years my senior who will no doubt blame me for the part I played in her previous husband's death.* The irony wasn't lost on him, either, that Damari had only wed into the family because Remy had been ripped from Rasin and that if his father had just let things be, Bernard would have already shared Béranger blood and Nyli wouldn't have had to marry any Arnaud at all.

Even worse, this wouldn't just affect him. This would affect Kuval, too. He hated how he hadn't even been crowned yet and he was already being forced to make decisions for other people, people he cared about.

"Unless Damari's and Remy's was an unhappy marriage, I cannot imagine she'd be thrilled with this agreement," he said. "Moreso, I can't imagine the rest of the nobility will look kindly upon it. There are suitable options within the Houses to strengthen the peace, or at the very least, foreign princesses that might buy us favorable relations with neighboring countries." It made his stomach squirm, but at least he could put off those marriages for a time. Ivanya, on the other hand, would be harder to distract. "Damari seems like a nice woman, but she is not of noble blood, and I have already offered House Arnaud more than a few gifts of good faith."

"Nevertheless. You would have neither crown nor throne without my husband's intervention. If the other Houses wish to air their concerns, they can always put themselves to use by making these political marriages you worry so much over." Ivanya sat back, watching him coolly. If she could have killed him with looks alone, she would have. "I'm afraid I must insist on this, Your Highness. Titles can be taken, rights of precedence rescinded. I doubt you'd be so quick to end a marriage."

The words cut deep. He was certain she meant them to.

He let loose a quiet sigh. If they were to have any chance of having peace, he was going to have to make amends. The price of Béranger wrath was apparently quite high, and it fell to him to foot the bill. But his mind had snagged on the idea of the little boy that clung to Damari's skirts. He, raise a child? A terrifyingly exhilarating concept.

"I accept your terms, Duchess Arnaud, on one condition. I speak to her first."

"To what end?"

He laughed coarsely. "Common courtesy, I suppose. Should the meeting prove satisfactory, we shall plan a date for the wedding after her mourning has ended."

"Very well." Ivanya rose to her feet, falling into a full curtsy with the added honorific. It felt almost mocking. "By your leave?"

Nyli wished he were brave enough to say how sorry he was that his actions had led to Remy's death. He wanted to tell her that his dream was to create a Las Corvika that left such things behind.

But underneath her carefully kept mask of neutrality was unadulterated hate. The words would sound empty.

So instead, he let Ivanya go with the words unsaid.

Over the course of the next few days, Neelie exchanged letters with her father with the help of Berhôt while the *Doleir* churned through the waves, rushing toward home. Hosvar wasn't making any progress with Zyre. He said his enchantments refused to come alive, and even Kaspar Gehrig was at a loss.

But her father was also still trying to tinker with Kaspar's false-*leiks* enchantment in the hopes of finding where Kaspar's magic had gone wrong. *Fix the kinks in the false-leiks, and maybe Neelie could avoid the same fate as Zyre.*

The day after Hosvar sent that first letter, Neelie was in her mother's quarters, reading the newest message her father had just sent.

*Kaspar assumed that the* leiks *only needs to have one non-magic being and one magic being to make it work. Human and soulbeast. But clearly there was something missing. A stronger soulbeast, perhaps? Something with more potential than even a tiger? Except a* najik *has far more power than a soulbeast could ever handle. I believe that is why they never get one.*

*But it leads me to a question: Why do soulbeasts choose the humans whom they choose? Why is it that* majican *get wild animals like wolves or bears or whales, while* wyrdi *only get creatures like cats or snakes or ravens? Why is it that there is more magic at sea or in a forest and that most* wyrdi *are born in the city? You were born at sea, Neelie.*

*I believe that a* leiks *requires both sides of the bond to have magic. Soulbeasts and familiars can use magic without ever bonding to a human, and of course, some never do. But the human must have some latent ability. They serve as a conduit, like a lightning rod for their soulbeast's electricity. This means you can't just throw a random human and animal together. The tiger didn't have the metaphorical lightning rod to pull the Arnaud girl's magic safely between them. The only beings we know would have that lightning rod are unbound* majican. *One must wonder if that's the path that will lead to your freedom.*

A pit formed in Neelie's stomach at the idea. What was the difference between a *majican* bound to her and a *gortien* watching her every move? Besides, where would they find an unbound *majican*? Her choices would be to either find a kid—assuming her father could make up some kind of charm to identify them *before* their soulbeasts appeared, and that did not seem like a safe magic to release into a world where so many places took advantage of their *majican*—or to hope she could bind herself to someone who had already lost their soulbeast.

Either way, she refused to do it with someone she didn't trust, *really* trust. And the only people she had faith in to such a degree were Modorin and, inexplicably, Zyre.

Her stomach dropped. *Zyre.*

They said that when a *najik* lost their minds, they became wild, like a soulbeast that had just lost their *majican*. It was insane, absolutely insane, to think that two *aljarne* could form a *leiks* and have it be enough to save their sanity, but surely it was worth a thought? If she could save Zyre *and* herself, she'd be a fool not to.

Neelie pulled out a piece of paper and began scribbling.

She was halfway through her logic when Adreia stepped in and fell dramatically into her bed. "What news?"

Neelie rumpled up her father's note and tossed it to her mother. Adreia caught it easily, and the parchment crinkled as she straightened it out.

"I was thinking that a wild *najik* like Zyre might prove a possibility," Neelie began. Adreia put up a finger while she read the note.

When she was done, Adreia sat up and set the note on the bed beside her. "That's a lot of magic getting shared between two people. It wouldn't really dispel anything." She frowned. "As usual, your father is on the verge of understanding but doesn't make the leap. Kaspar Gehrig forged the *leiks* on land. Even in the middle of the wildest forests, magic cannot be as strong as what it is at sea, and Gehrig's *leiks* was not forged in the wildest forest. Ask him to reconsider what might happen if the animal bond was created at sea."

Unfortunately, her mother had a point. But as Neelie wrote Adreia's thoughts to her father, she kept her original response off to the side. She sent Berhôt through Velídas with the letter and waited impatiently for a response.

Fortunately, Hosvar must not have been in the middle of anything back at home, because the response was quick to come.

*Theoretically, it's possible, but the problem comes in the inter-pretation. The biggest hurdle I found in breaking the Arnaud girl's* leiks *was that I had to use my* wyrdis *magic to breach a* majican *bond. The magic of both comes from the same place, but* wyrdi *magic is at a far, far smaller scale. I will have to consider how to take that particular lesson and expand it further if your mother's idea is to hold any merit.*

Neelie sent Berhôt back through Velídas without a response. She needed to think.

She went up to help Raylir and the crew. Her mind always worked best when her hands were busy. The day wore on. Sometimes she thought about it, sometimes she let the idea come and go as it pleased. Her mother had returned to the helm well before Neelie had stumbled across any major breakthroughs.

When the sun began to set, Neelie had parsed out the major obstacles they'd need to overcome. First, the obvious: Two *najik* could not serve as the other's soulbeast. At least, not without an actual soulbeast present. Second: Even if they could, two women who could use magic without a soulbeast would *look* like two *najik,* and there would be some dangers to that. Technically, this would be true whether Hosvar found some random unbound *majican* or if he managed to find some way to use Zyre.

If Neelie was going to make a *leiks* with Zyre, then it stood to reason that Kadj ought to be their soulbeast. Which made her wonder: Could some sort of enchantment give Kadj that lightning rod he needed to serve as proper soulbeast? They were already creating false *leiks*. Surely her father could do this, too.

Kadj had worked as Zyre's soulbeast. It might've made her magic explosive, but she had still been able to *use* it, and Kadj had protected her mind. So one must wonder, could they make a three-souled *leiks*? Could Neelie and Zyre serve as each other's soulbeast if Kadj was there to take the excess?

Neelie hastily finished her task before thundering down to Modorin's quarters.

"I need to borrow Sarol," she announced.

Modorin, lying on his bed with one arm draped over his face, waved her off half-heartedly.

"Thanks."

She scooped up the little red fox and slipped back into her mother's quarters. Back at the desk, Neelie began to scribble down her note as quickly as she was able. It was a good thing Berhôt wouldn't be taking this note, because it ended up being several pages long. She tied it gently to Sarol.

"Take this back to the Raven's Head, please," she told him, although Neelie wasn't sure if the fox could actually understand her.

Sarol scrambled onto the large pot that held her mother's velídas tree, and within the space of a heartbeat, he vanished.

Neelie paced back and forth, grateful that her mother's cabin was quite large. She knew it would take her father several minutes to read it even if he wasn't in the middle of something, but her impatience spiked regardless.

When Sarol tumbled back into the cabin a short while later, Neelie scrambled to free the small—worryingly small—note attached to his leg.

It seems highly unlikely, Neelie, and I'm not sure it's wise. But I will see what I can do.

Neelie exhaled. That was all she wanted to hear.

Transitions of power were more complex and time-consuming than Nyli ever would have thought possible, especially with his soon-to-be-appointed *duc* in recovery. Several days after taking Les Stelvo, he'd yet to find himself alone with Damari. In fact, it was by mere happenstance that he stumbled upon her in the library at all, on his way to meet Kuval for some book he'd been told would help him with one of the issues that had already cropped up.

It was not a large library, a fact that he hoped to change, but even so, Nyli almost didn't see her amidst the looming shadows. Her son, Bernard, sat on a nurse's lap across the table, watching aptly as the young girl read a book for him. Bernard took after Remy. He could see that in his eyes, his smile. But it didn't bother him that he was handing the Arnauds control of the throne once he died, so long as the person who this child grew up to be could continue to rebuild all the broken things this country had made.

As for his mother, well, she was beautiful, objectively speaking. Nyli remembered from the journey from Lasinia that she was just taller than him, with thick hair that framed her face almost naturally. Her night-black mourning dress lay expertly on her dark figure. Had Ivanya sent her here on purpose, hoping to ensnare him?

Well, be that as it may, this wedding was likely going to

happen either way, and it did neither party any good to put off this meeting.

Carefully tucking away all feelings into a box, he approached Damari like he would a startled canine. "*Vinjess.*"

Only the nurse was taken by surprise. Both rose from their seats and curtseyed, Damari as cool as ice.

"May I have a word?"

The nurse glanced at Damari, and after a moment, the *vinjess* nodded. Bernard was ushered a short distance away, giving the two of them some privacy. Nyli gestured for her to sit, and he took the nurse's chair opposite her.

"I'm sure you're aware by now that our marriage was part of an agreement that the duc and I made."

"I am."

There was nothing, no indication at all, what she thought of it. Nyli tried again. "Bernard is the other. He'll become a prince." He smiled thoughtfully, glancing the boy's way. "He looks the type. Someday, he'll even be regis."

"Power brings enemies," she said. Her accent, he could hear now, was still present. It added a clip to her *r*'s.

"Oh, certainly. I'll ensure the very best honor guard is picked out for you and him promptly; there's no need to wait until the wedding in that regard."

Damari didn't reply. He got the sense she was waiting for him to flounder his way to the end of this conversation.

"I'm sure you have mixed feelings about becoming my wife, Dirige-Uncrowned Damari." He liked how her title sounded, and there was a flash of something in her expression that made him wonder if she felt the same. "But, in truth, thanks to Bernard, I do not need a wife. I only need a dirige, and with luck, a friend. Someone to help me rule this country and turn it into something better."

She shifted slightly. He'd surprised her, he could tell.

"The wedding won't be for some time yet, but I hope you'll allow me to come speak to you before then on matters of state. Get used to each other, at least?"

Damari was about to answer when the nurse said, "My lord, pardon, but I do not think they wish to be interrupted."

Nyli spun around to see Kuval frozen in place near the nurse, his eyes caught on Bernard. He wanted to smile, to tell him, *I know*, but he didn't. "Kuval."

"You were supposed to meet me by the—" He trailed off, glancing shyly at Damari. "Pardon, Your Highness. I'll return with the book later."

Kuval retreated, leaving Nyli alone with his dirige-to-be. The woman, strangely, held less animosity than before.

"*Evlo Venascan?*"

It took him a second to realize what she said. *Do you speak Venascan?* Whatever she wanted to say, she didn't want to risk being overheard.

"Yes," he replied in her tongue. "A little."

"What role will he play in our marriage?" she asked.

He stared at her. And then, out of instinct, he glanced at the nurse, but she was fully preoccupied with Bernard, and even so, it was highly unlikely she knew Venascan.

"Venascans care little about bedroom politics, Your Highness." There it was again, that peace offering. A secret unspoken—acknowledged and accepted. "I have met the baron's son. He is here quite often. How long have you held this secret between you?"

He swallowed, wondering how much he was willing to share. If the gods were being kind or playing a trick on him. "A long time." Nyli didn't know why he didn't refute her claim, but who held power over him now? Who could terrorize him for this love he held for Kuval Duvachelle?

Damari smiled. It almost felt genuine. "Do you truly wish for a better Las Corvika?" she asked, finally speaking in Corvikan again.

"I do."

"Then I am honored to join you in this dream, wherever you would have me in it."

It struck Nyli then, fully, just what all of this meant. It seemed wrong that the gods would favor him in this way despite the role he had played in his father's and brother's deaths, but *gods*. This future Kuval had tried to paint for him, it had been so cloudy and blurred before. Now, though? With Damari and Kuval both at his side, and the little Bernard to care for between them, what couldn't they do? What couldn't they make Las Corvika out to be?

# CHAPTER 26

After a week at sea, it was a relief to arrive home. Their house wasn't quite back to where it had been before Neelie had left. Some furniture was missing, some smaller items put back in the wrong place. But *Es Hædros* had their heads held high.

Adreia wound through the crowd of Shadowmen populating the Raven's Head. The men whooped and hollered at their return, and she waved at them with grace. Neelie was grateful. As she and Modorin trailed behind her mother in silence, the last thing she wanted was to be the center of attention.

She knew she should be glad that everything had worked out. She *was* glad. It was just hard to celebrate when one very important thing had gone horribly, horribly wrong.

Hosvar had, of course, known they were coming, and both he and Ren were waiting for them in the office. Regardless of her fears, it was good to see them both. Her mother had been right; they'd gotten out of the fight unscathed, but she hadn't been willing to quite believe it until she saw them with her own eyes.

After hugging them both, Neelie stepped back.

"Do you want to see her?" her father asked.

Neelie was grateful beyond words that she didn't have to vocalize it. She shared a look with Modorin and said, "Yes. Please."

Hosvar nodded and motioned them to follow. "I'll be back in a few minutes, Addy."

Her mother broke into a grin.

Neelie, Modorin, and her father delved deeper into the Raven's Head. There were more signs of Honir's raid, little scars littered here and there, but the Shadowmen were a fierce lot. They'd already started to rebuild, and when it was done, it would be even grander than it was before.

Finally, Hosvar stopped before a closed door. He turned his back to it, his expression grim. "She's been kept in an enchanted sleep as much as possible, but whatever we do with her, it'll have to be done soon, or else the magic will start having a negative reaction. If I can't figure out the enchantments in the next day or two, we may have to send her back through Velídas and hope she finds someplace isolated, somewhere in the mountains or something, to make her home."

"She's not an animal that needs to be released into the wild," Modorin said cuttingly.

Hosvar only shrugged. "You did not see her when she arrived, *Magi*. Don't be so sure."

He stepped out of their way. With some trepidation, Neelie let the door creak open.

They'd put Zyre in a guest bedroom, one that didn't have much in the way of furnishings. It was more of a place for *majican* to sleep off their magic than for anything else. Beyond the bed that Zyre slept in, the rug that her tiger dozed on, and a nightstand, there wasn't much else. Neelie was grateful to see that Kadj was with her, though. When the great cat lifted his head, it seemed as if he'd gone back to the way he was before.

Neelie knelt onto the floor and scratched Kadj's head. He chuffed happily.

If Kadj could be all right, maybe that was a sign from Skï that Zyre could be all right too.

Modorin sat on the foot of the bed. "Do you really think your father can help her?"

Neelie studied Zyre's sleeping form. Zyre was surprisingly still and peaceful. Asleep, she looked the same as she had those nights traveling across Las Corvika. But Neelie believed her father. Bad things happened to *najik* who traveled through Velídas, and Neelie hated to think what desperation must've sent Zyre there. "I hope so."

*Skï*, she began, then stopped herself. Neelie wasn't one much for prayers, and she didn't want to offend the goddess in praying only for a favor. But for Zyre, she was willing to risk it. *Skï, please help her. She's one of the good ones, and she doesn't deserve this fate.*

Neelie swallowed a lump in her throat. "Stay with her, okay? I need to go have a conversation with my father."

"Are you all right?" he asked.

"I suppose that's going to depend."

"On?"

"If he can save her," Neelie replied. She hated how distressed she was at seeing Zyre, at how helpless she felt.

Modorin nodded in understanding.

She marched back through the Raven's Head to her father's office. The door was closed, but she didn't hear anything untoward, so Neelie took a risk and knocked.

"Father? It's me."

"Come in, Neelie," came Hosvar's voice.

Neelie opened the door. Adreia was perched on Hosvar's lap, her arms draped across his neck. The intimacy was strangely painful to see. It reminded her of the kiss she'd shared with Zyre on the beach.

"I need to know how far you've gotten with your experiment."

Hosvar extricated one of Adreia's arms and pinched his nose. "Several of the enchantments have worked so far, but I won't know for sure until I finish all of the pieces and link them together. I haven't had a lot of time to devote to it, Neelie. There's still a lot of work that needs to be done."

"What if I take over some of your tasks for you?" Neelie asked desperately. "As you said, we don't have a lot of time to work with."

"That would be helpful, yes." He grinned pathetically when Adreia gave him a quick peck on the cheek. "I promise, I'll work on it later today. Go find Ren. He can tell you some of the work that needs doing in the meantime."

"Thank you, Father," Neelie said from the bottom of her heart.

Not wanting to deprive her parents of their happy reunion any longer than she had to, Neelie made her escape.

Over the next two days as she ran errands for her father, Neelie kept tabs on the number of white-clad guards populating the streets. She didn't see any with Inoger's crest, which meant Honir had sent them back to the High King in Veridhol. Neelie wondered with a smile if Honir was in hot water for the agreement he'd made with her father or if he'd managed to wriggle out a lie to save his own skin.

There were still a lot of guards with Honir's crossed swords, but not in the Shadow Quarter, and hardly at all in the Deckhand's. Mostly, they populated the Sector of the Gulls and the Whale's Belly. Honir didn't want any of the gangs in the Whale's Belly to get any ideas.

The only tragedy was that she'd missed out of the last week of *Preze od Kerig*. The street musicians had faded back to their homes or to the inns and taverns they'd been playing at before, and everything seemed unfortunately silent.

*Zyre will miss getting to listen to them*, Neelie thought, then banished it from her mind.

Then came the day when she returned home from a job and was greeted by her father, the biggest grin plastered across his face.

"It worked?" She could barely get the words out of her mouth. "Yes."

A noise escaped her throat involuntarily. So she'd been right. If this worked… "Father, if this works, you will truly be the most famous *wyrdis* in all of history. The man who didn't just figure out how to protect a *najik*'s mind, but who also figured out how to bring a lost *najik* back from the madness."

"*If* it works. You need to prepare a crew and set sail as quickly as possible," Hosvar said, some of his excitement diminished. "Are you truly certain you want to do this with her? You barely know the girl. Modorin would work just as well and—"

Neelie shook her head. "He doesn't like the sea, Father. I would have to be land-bound, or he, stuck at sea, and neither of us would be happy. Besides, if I won't do it for Zyre, no one will. I trust her."

Hosvar grimaced but said nothing.

"I'll find a way to get us out of the city by morning," Neelie said softly.

Then she went to find Modorin. He was in with Zyre again, a jaw harp fitted against his teeth. He struck it dismally. *Twang, twang, twang.* She knocked so she wouldn't scare him.

"Did you hear?" Neelie asked.

He nodded.

"I'm going to set sail with a small crew tomorrow morning. I want you to stay here."

Modorin frowned. "As much as I hate being out at sea, Neelie, I think I ought to be there. She's my friend, too."

"And if everything works out, we'll sail right on back. The trip should only take a week. But if it doesn't, if she sinks the ship, I'd rather you be safe here." He looked on the verge of arguing. "Modorin. Please. I promise we'll come straight back."

"If she tries to sink the ship, you'll need someone to help combat her. It. Her magic," he amended. "I may not be as powerful as either of you could be, but I can do more than you can without the risk."

"Modorin…"

"I can handle a week at sea, Neelie. Besides, you're in no position to deny me this."

She was. Neelie didn't have to let anyone on her ship whom she didn't want there. But she couldn't say no. And if it didn't work, maybe it was for the best if someone was there with her to pick up the pieces of her broken heart.

⁂

Neelie's *Spider* was back at port where it belonged, and just as she'd promised, she managed, just before dawn broke, to scrounge up a crew and fit it with the resources they'd need for their trip.

The charms did not require Hosvar's participation, but both he and Adreia tried to convince her to let them come. They were worried what Zyre might do when she woke up. But Neelie pointed out that things had not settled down so far that Honir wouldn't pounce on the opportunity to swoop in if her parents gave him one. Besides, Modorin would be with her.

When the *Telaña dir Ansol* set sail, it was just the three of them—two *najik* with their *majican* friend, a fox, and a tiger—and her crew, led by Raylir.

They sailed for three days, directly west. The weather was mild, and the crew far too capable. They barely needed her, and with Modorin below to monitor their slumbering passenger, Neelie was restless.

On the third day, Neelie reached for magic and was pleased with how eager it was to answer her summons. She told Raylir they'd gone far enough, fetched Kadj, who was enjoying the ocean breeze, and then the two of them braved the cargo hold. Modorin's green-hued face was illuminated by the one lit torch, its light revealing an empty hold save for the barrels of water and food they needed for their trip and the bed that Zyre slept on.

Neelie didn't want to do this out in the open, and this was the most contained space on the ship.

"Is it time?" Modorin asked.

She nodded. He unsteadily got to his feet, bracing himself on the sturdy wooden walls.

Neelie reached for the small heavy sack resting by Zyre's head. One by one, she withdrew the carefully wrapped charms, their annotations written in the neat lettering of her father's hand. *To wake*, said a small iron disk with Skï's symbol etched into its center. *The tiger's lightning rod*, with a pendant on a metal chain just a little larger than Kadj's head. Then three more pendants, one of them sized for Kadj, all annotated with *To forge the* leiks, *wear these and throw the large disk into the air between you.* The last was the large disk like the one he'd used to break Zyre's *leiks* in the first place.

She sucked in a breath.

Zyre would want this. Neelie *knew* Zyre would want this. But it didn't feel right, making this choice for her. She glanced at Modorin. He nodded encouragingly.

There was nothing else to do.

She unfurled Zyre's fingers and pressed the small disk into her palm.

For a moment, nothing happened. Then Zyre's eyes fluttered open. Her eyes grew wild, and she bolted upright, scrambling unsteadily to her feet.

Neelie worked fast. She looped both of Kadj's pendants over his neck, then slid hers on. She cursed herself for not putting Zyre's pendant on first, but Zyre was still slow, dazed. She slipped Zyre's over her head, then grabbed the large disk and retreated a few steps.

"It's okay, I'm just trying to help," she said soothingly.

Pricking her finger, she let her blood fall onto the disk. It lit up like the sun. With a shout, she threw it in the air.

The pendant grew heavy around her neck, but Neelie couldn't have torn it off if she'd wanted to. She was rooted to the spot, her very limbs weighed down by the force of the magic. Something solid and constricting formed in her chest, then unfurled toward her shoulders, down her arms, to her very fingertips. It rolled downward, feeling like it scraped against her legs, her ankles, her toes.

Distantly, Neelie was aware of her magic pulsing, of the disk spinning, casting its light across the entire hold.

Then something flared within her, chasing away the heaviness. Her magic skated across her skin, lighter than it had ever been, like a kiss of the wind.

The disk fell onto the floor with a clatter, and Neelie was suddenly aware of… a connection of some kind. Nothing visible, nothing tangible, but something she could sense like a phantom itch.

Neelie dared to follow it, to look at Zyre. She steeled herself for the wildness that might still be there.

She found fear, uncertainty, confusion. Was this what madness looked like? How would she know? Modorin seemed as clueless as she, frozen in place, eyes wide out of worry or concern or both.

"Neelie," Zyre breathed. She stared at the space between them, at the phantom link bridging the two of them and Kadj. "I don't understand."

Zyre looked down at her fingers, and inexplicably, she fell to her knees, crying.

⚜

Zyre felt like she was a thousand burning fragments. There was so much she didn't understand, and the only anchor she had was this feeling of emptiness, of being lost within herself or outside herself. It was difficult to explain, even to herself, and that made it all the worse.

Because the only piece of herself she seemed able to recall with any vividness was the piece that had emerged from the magic of Velídas, and she did not recognize the person she'd been there at all.

"Zyre," Neelie said gently. Her very voice seemed to crush Zyre into even more pieces. Neelie's hand fell onto Kadj's shoulder in a way that Zyre recognized, because it was what she'd always done when she found herself on unsteady ground. "We're bound. The three of us are. My father helped bring you back."

"Bring me *where*?" she found herself saying. "Back from *what*?"

Something slipped into her periphery, and Zyre scrambled for her magic, her vision tinted orange before she saw that it was Modorin, only Modorin, sliding to his knees next to her with an earnestness that was impossibly grounding.

"Velídas, Zyre," he said quietly. "Back from Velídas."

The problem was, that still wasn't the answer Zyre was trying to find. In Velídas, she'd had no name. Everything she'd known about herself had vanished. Was she still the person she'd been before she'd walked into the sea of magic? Maybe it was a different brand of madness now.

And why, *why*, had Velídas drawn her to Neelie when everything else had faded away? There were two explanations, and she didn't like either of them. The first was that she was always meant to pair with Neelie the same way Sarol was always going to have paired with Modorin or Berhôt was always going to have paired with Hosvar. But that meant this pairing would only work because she'd been a beast, an animal.

The second was that, to her very core, she loved Neelie. More than that, she loved Neelie more than she loved her mother or her sister or her brother, more than she loved her home, more than she loved herself. But that didn't feel right. She couldn't love a woman she'd only known for a month and a half more than anyone else in the world. Zyre liked Neelie. She really did. But not that much, not yet.

Which brought her to the other thing she was grappling. "It appears you'll never stop saving me," she said, braving a glance at the other woman.

Neelie stood a good few paces away, studying her. "Modorin, can we have a few minutes, please?"

Her friend hesitated. Out of fear? Were they both afraid of her now?

He gave Zyre an encouraging smile, like one would give a shy beast, hoping to convey they posed no threat to it. Then he left. As the door opened and shut, she saw Sarol sitting impatiently on the other side, but Modorin scooped him up before he could slither in to say hello.

Neelie knelt in front of her, drawing Zyre back to the matter at hand. "You think that I saved you here?"

"I don't know what else to call it."

She exhaled. "Zyre, this *leiks* doesn't just benefit you. It's going to save my mind as well. Which means we're saving each other."

Zyre crossed her arms in front of her chest, not believing Neelie for a second. "Are you really trying to tell me that I was the only one you could have bonded with?"

As she'd expected, Neelie did not reply.

"Right. But here's the problem, Neelie. You've made it so that we're always going to have to be near each other. I have to follow you wherever you go, because if you don't, my mind will slip again. Won't it?"

Her silence was confirmation enough.

"Why didn't you do it with Modorin?" she demanded, almost begged. "Or someone else? Anyone else! We are two very different people, Neelie! I know who you are and what you're capable of, and I'm glad for it, because I want you to be safe, but that is not the life that I want. I don't want to be Tholjun's hand for the rest of my life."

"You think I'm only good for destruction?" Neelie snapped. "You think I don't want to build, too, to make this world a better place than how I left it? Then what would you call my risking my life, my *crew*'s life, to get you off Lasinia? Was that a destructive act, helping someone in need?"

Zyre felt like Neelie had missed the point. "I'm saying you're willing to do whatever needs to be done. But me? I balk. I hesitate. I'm not strong like you."

Neelie reached out, saying softly, "That's not true, Zyre. There's more than one kind of strength. Its definition is as varied as a human can be."

Zyre pressed on. "I will always need saving, Neelie, because it's just who I am. And you will get tired of it the way you got tired of Modorin. You will get tired of *me*." Zyre's voice cracked, and she turned away so Neelie could not see the tears.

*I think I love you. Or, I think I want to. But that makes the thought of losing you hurt even more. I have no one else.* Zyre clenched her fists at her side.

"Maybe I could have chosen someone else, Zyre," Neelie said softly to her back. Her tone grew bitter. "Maybe I could have chosen one of my *majican* crew members, one who could follow me wherever I went and who would take orders from me and never make things complicated."

Neelie's boots thunked against the floor as she crossed the distance, putting a hand on Zyre's shoulder, turning her around. Her deep brown eyes flared with determination. "I chose you because you deserve a chance at life just as much as I do, and this was the only way I could think of to give it to you."

"*Ìr liora*," Zyre said, feeling like if she didn't say it now, it would burn a hole in her heart. And it was easier to say in Venascan than it was to admit the truth in her native tongue, to hear the words ring against the silence, irrevocable.

Neelie smiled bitterly. "I love you, too, I think. But you're right. I don't know what this *leiks* will mean for any relationship we might've had. So we'll go slow, okay? Figure it out together."

Hearing Neelie say the words back sent a thrill down her spine.

"I'm going to go up and let Raylir know we're heading back to Bijal. Are you okay?"

Zyre nodded, hoping Neelie didn't sense the lie.

"All right. Come find me if you need anything. Oh, and you

can move to my quarters if you want. It'll be more comfortable there." Neelie offered Zyre a shy smile before stepping out of the hold, leaving the door cracked open behind her like an offer.

⁂

Zyre couldn't stay below deck for long. For one, she knew she'd loved feeling the ship pitch and fall beneath her, and she wanted to prove to herself that Velídas had not changed that about her at least. For another, Kadj was as restless for the same fresh ocean air as she was.

She scanned the deck and found Neelie at the helm with Raylir. Kadj bounded up the steps to join her, but Zyre hesitated. How foolish she'd been to admit her feelings out loud. She still couldn't believe she'd said that. Maybe Neelie had just been messing with her when she'd said it back. Maybe she *did* mean it, but not in the way Zyre did.

Careful not to bump into the sailors, Zyre wandered over to the railing. All around her was an endless stretch of sea. The world seemed so *big*, so impossibly huge. She liked how small it made her feel, like she could keep on messing up and it ultimately wouldn't make a difference.

She stayed there for a while, reveling in the feeling, awed by the sight. Then, before her courage could abandon her, she followed Kadj up to the helm, to *Neelie*. Modorin sat right next to her, holding Sarol, no doubt fighting with his stomach.

It was easier with him there. Less intimidating. She sat next to him, looking up at Neelie.

*I love you too, I think.*

Those very words made Zyre's own stomach rebel. To quiet it, she asked, "Do you know anything about the war?" However much she hated her father, she had to know.

"I made some inquiries before we left," Modorin replied for her. They both turned to stare at him, and he shrugged. "I felt a bit helpless, to be honest. Figured we should know eventually."

Touched by his consideration, Zyre gestured for him to go ahead.

There was to be a marriage between Nyli and Damari, once Damari was out of mourning. Zyre didn't envy her. She did feel a little guilty for putting her in that position, though. Kaari from the Siren's Haunt had also heard both of Zyre's parents had survived, but Jervin had taken an enchanted knife to the side and had lost the use of his legs because of it. He was alive and otherwise unharmed, though, and if nothing else, Zyre was grateful for that. And there was no news of her sister, which she took to be a good sign regarding her health.

Zyre moved next to Kadj and let herself mull over the news. After losing herself to Velídas, it was hard to know if she should be more happy than she was or less. She was grateful for their victory, but there was no forgetting what it had cost her.

Her grief over Remy remained intact, at least, reappearing like a gaping wound in her heart. It ached, but she clung to it, because it proved she was capable of feeling anything at all.

She didn't know how much time passed. Long enough for Modorin and Neelie to wander over to the rail, Neelie holding on to Modorin's arm to steady him. With her other hand, she had her spyglass. They spoke quietly between themselves while Zyre tried not to feel excluded, accompanied as she was by a very attention-hungry fox and a happy tiger.

Eventually, there was the familiar *snick* of a spyglass shutting, and then suddenly Neelie was looming over her, a grin plastered across her face. "Come here. I want to show you something."

Neelie offered her a hand up, and Zyre took it. They went to the starboard side, facing south, and Neelie passed over the spyglass. Zyre glanced at Modorin, hoping for some indication of what was about to happen, but although he offered her a weak grin, he didn't spoil the surprise. Zyre took the spyglass, sweeping it across the horizon until a distant patch of green filled her view.

"What is it?" she asked, lowering the glass.

"It's a little cluster of islands, uninhabited, and unclaimed by any nation as far as I'm aware. I've been there once or twice; it seems like a nice little haven."

Well, that seemed unlikely. "If it's so nice there, why is it uninhabited?"

Neelie grimaced. "It probably has something to do with the maze of shoals that surrounds them. They're not easy to get through if you don't know what you're doing. But that makes it even safer, don't you think?"

Zyre was definitely missing something. "Safe for whom?"

"You said you wanted your legacy to be something that you built. Well, there's a lot of people like us out there who can't live their lives the way they want to because others want to use them." Neelie leaned against the railing casually, but Zyre couldn't miss the tenseness of her body or the steel in her voice. "I already have people who are willing to help me get them out, but it's where they go from there that sometimes causes problems. Modorin and I, we always wanted to find somewhere they could go if they had nowhere else. Maybe we could make this island that safe place for them or, at least, a stopping point for them to get their bearings."

Zyre listened in silence, but when Neelie was finished, it was obvious she wanted her to say something. Zyre passed the spyglass back to her, refusing to look at either of them. "This is what I was talking about. You're giving up on your own plans to accommodate mine. That's unfair of me to ask of you."

Neelie pocketed the spyglass. "Zyre, you're not asking *me*. I'm asking *you*. I'm not giving up on my own plans. I'm building on them so that it might be something we can work on *together*."

"A group project," Modorin interjected. "A way for us to all do some good. I, for one, hate feeling like I'm stuck in place, unable to help those who need it. Please say yes, Zyre. It'll be dull without you to tease."

Zyre bit her lip. Trying to buy herself some time, she asked, "What would we even name such a place?"

Neelie broke into a grin, elbowing Modorin with a laugh. "I don't know. This one said we should do something in Dosperic. I was thinking *Ilusia Somev*. That's the correct interpretation, isn't it? For Island of Dreams?"

Zyre couldn't help herself. She smiled right back. "It's whimsical. I like it. Ilusia Somev."

Something settled in her at saying the name. It wasn't that all her little fragments fused into a single whole; she wasn't sure what it would take for that to happen. But it was as if a few of the more vital pieces got sewn back together.

Tholjun had lost his hold on her. She was not the bringer of death and destruction any longer; her magic would not be used to dictate who got to sit on a throne or who got to live or die. Instead, it was hers to use as she saw fit, to protect people and create a better future for them. She belonged to Thalja now.

Neelie reached out, offering Zyre her hand, and bravely, Zyre took it. For the first time in a long time, she couldn't wait to see what the future had in store for her.

# CHARACTER GUIDE

Allais, Roch—al-LAYZ, Rohk. An undercover *sjarvisk* for the rebels. Badger soulbeast

Arnaud—ar-NOH

>Bernard—ber-NARD. Firstborn son of Remy.

>Damari—DA-mar-ee. Wife of Remy. Hails from a Venascan merchant family.

>Ivanya—ih-VAHN-yah. Jervin's wife, and mother of Remy, Zyre, and Aljeya. Hails from *Rosema* Zandua of Crasea.

>Jervin—YER-vin. Baron of Las Corvika, leader of the rebels.

>Remy—REM-me. Firstborn son of Jervin.

>Zyre—ZEER. Youngest daughter of Jervin and Ivanya. *Aljarne*, but *sjarvisk* in appearance. Tiger soulbeast, Kadj. Also known as: Zyre Mescal, Ange Duval.

Bard—BARD. A *wyrdis* under High King Inoger's employ. *Ed gortien*. Dog familiar.

Berhôt—bear-HOTE. Hosvar's raven familiar.

Béranger—bear-ahn-JER

>Alexandre—AL-ex-ander. Firstborn son of Luc.

Elyx—EE-lix. Notoyem's older brother, steward of Mod Redel, the seat of the Béranger family.

Elodja—EL-oh-dee-ya. Notoyem's first wife, mother of Luc.

Essir—ehs-SEAR. Luc's wife, mother of Alexandre.

Luc—LUKE. Firstborn son of Notoyem and father of Alexandre. Heir apparent.

Maryn—MARE-inn. Second wife of Notoyem, mother of Rasin and Nyli.

Notoyem—no-TOY-yem. Regis of Las Corvika. Father of Rasin, Nyli, Luc.

Nyli—NIGH-lee. Second son of Notoyem. General of the royal forces.

Rasin—RAH-zin. Daughter of Notoyem.

Duvachelle—DOO-vah-shell

Pierre—PEE-yare. Comte of Las Corvika.

Kuval—COO-vahl. Youngest son of the comte.

Edny—edd-NEE. A *wyrdis* working for Hosvar. Black-and-brown dog familiar.

Edvjorni, Boreil—ED-vyorn-nee, BOAR-reel. A *sjarvisk* in the rebel camp. Mole soulbeast.

Elowarin—EL-oh-wahr-in. A *sjarvisk* under Nyli's command. Snake soulbeast.

Ermengarde, Louis—ER-men-GUARD, LOO-iss. The nobleman chosen by Fjeron Tavere to succeed him as regis.

Jehan, Fidou—YEH-han, FID-oh. An undercover courtier from a small noble family. Nephew of Maryn Béranger.

Hæfnir—HAYF-near. Innkeeper and owner of the *Huerdi dir ed Níete* (The Siren's Haunt). Husband to Kaari and loyal to Hosvar.

Héroux, Josse—hair-OO, YOSS. General leading the royal troops.

Hijaladreia, Neelie—HE-yal-ADD-reyah, NEE-lie. Daughter of Adreia and Hosvar. *Najik*. Captain of the *Telaña dir Ansol* (the Water Spider).

Hijalcaelan, Adreia—HE-yal-KAY-lin, ADD-reyah. Wife of Hosvar, powerful *majican* with a whale soulbeast (Kesnit). Leader of the Shadowmen's pirate fleet.

Hijolhosvar, Ren—HE-yol-hos-VAR, Ren. Firstborn son of Hosvar and Adreia.

Honir—HOE-near. *Freyr* of Bijal.

Hosvar—hos-VAR. A powerful *wyrdis* with a raven familiar (Berhôt). Leader of *Hædros dir en Schadra* (Shadowmen).

Inoger—INN-oh-ger. High King of Venasca.

Jorvik, Horadon—YOR-vick, HOR-a-don. A *sjarvisk* in the rebel army with a weasel soulbeast.

Kaari—KARR-ee. Wife of Hæfnir and co-owner of the Siren's Haunt. Loyal to Hosvar.

Kadj—KADJ. Zyre's false soulbeast.

Kal, Modorin—KAL, Mo-DOOR-in. *Majican* with a fox soulbeast (Sarol). Friends with Neelie and loyal to Hosvar. Hails from Syfris.

Kesnit—whale soulbeast of Adreia's.

Merytz—captain of Arnaud soldiers, loyal to Jervin Arnaud.

Nyelin, Aljeya—NEE-yell-IN, ah-LAY-ya. Daughter of Jervin and Ivanya, married into a royal house in Atlor.

Oharyn—OH-har-in. A *majican* loyal to Hosvar with a chamois soulbeast.

Ortigan—OR-tih-GAN. A captain of Bijal's forces.

Raylir—RAY-lear. Acting first-mate for both Neelie and Adreia. Longtime friend of Adreia and her family.

Ricard, Erez—RIH-card, AIR-ehz. A captain in charge of the rebel *sjarvisk*.

Rodier, Noam—RODE-ee-yer, NOHM. A skilled scout in the rebel army.

Sarol—SAIR-ohl. Modorin's fox soulbeast.

Soderi—SOH-dehr-ee. Ren's fencer for illegally obtained items.

Sten—STEN. A sailor on Neelie's crew.

Tavere—tah-VEER

> Mahieu—ma-HUE. A General of the rebel forces

> Fjeron—FYER-on. Previous regis before Notoyem took the throne.

Telsadt—TEL-sadt. Guardsmaster of the soldiers in Jervin's guard.

Tol, Vjeronin—TOLL, VYEER-ohn-in. A ranking officer in the rebel army.

Tormod—TOR-mohd. A sailor on Neelie's crew.

Valade, Oretnir—VAHL-lade, or-ET-neer. A lieutenant of the rebel army, originally charged with rebel branch stationed near Obele.

Vaudian, Deitral—VAW-dee-yan, DEE-tral. A *sjarvisk* in the rebel army with a wolf soulbeast.

Vesour, Cheron—undercover courtier loyal to House Arnaud.

Vidar—VEE-dar. Loyal to Hosvar. Accountant for the naval business under Adreia.

Vigdis—VIG-diss. A *majican* loyal to *Freyr* Honir. Badger soul-beast.

Villeneuve—VILL-nohv

Eduoard—ED-oo-ward. Courtier in Les Stelvo.

Josef—YOH-seff. Duc of Las Corvika and loyal to House Béranger.

Zandua, Doran—ZAN-doo-ah, DOOR-ahn. The family head of a powerful Crasik *Rosema* (House). Ivanya's father.

# Translations

**Dosperic**

*Eris bi eljers*—By skill and valor.

*Ilusia Somev*—Island of Dreams

*Oderta neg rasin det pieterad*—Beware the fury on the winds.

**Venascan**

*Anodev*—When?

*Baraschion*—Ship

*Beikotel*—acorn

*Burriot dir schadra*—Shadow Quarter

*Ed Vodaría dir en Loræden*—The Guild of Magic

*En kurat thola*—the Coral Room

*En ssorvælo enya es borde dir ed theurvo*—I take her under the raven's wing.

*Es gortiens*—the guardians (in context, the name given to *wyrdi* who pair with *najik*)

*Es mueven estad gerroten*—The docks were closed off.

*Ethere. Velguir. Cor su perima*—Wait. Follow. Please.

*Etherodden en ssamena*—We await the call.

*Evlo Venascan*—Do you speak Venascan?

*Hædros dir en schadra*—Shadowmen

*Holte Barol*—High Bluff (a dice game)

*Id ed pejo ledri es wydonis dir ed furto*—It sticks to her like an octopus's tentacles.

*Ír dezi ke oveleori ed baraschion sil iezt geor mod*—I told you to get back to the ship if anything went sideways.

*Ír liora (téano)*—I love you (too). Familial.

*Ĭz*—Yes.

*Marosen*—a derogatory term loosely meaning "backwater rat"

*Medias*—Thank you.

*Oriete*—Hot

*Preze od Kerig*—Peace to Kirig (a summertime celebration)

*Probua ed lesyra dir zkife*—Try the disk of reading.

*Púo irudavit*—Can I help you?

*Telaña dir ansol*—the Water Spider

*Uda moteya, cor su perima*—One moment, if you please.

*Vierno adelne*—Coast ahead

**Atloric**

*Sinomi, mu kidya, illo ri deró eivai hrotima eb kitheíni*—Pardon, my lady, but the army is preparing to move.

*Xei, ikarí*—Okay, thank you.

# ACKNOWLEDGEMENTS

It takes a village to raise a child, as the saying goes, and it's hard not to think of of one's book as one's baby. After all, we writers watch them grow from infant ideas into fully-fledged manuscripts. But though *As the Crown Falls* may be mine, it would not have existed without the help and support of many.

First and foremost, of course, would be my parents, who were kind enough not to call me crazy for wanting to make a career out of writing. A special thanks to my dad for cultivating my passion for reading and for the fantasy genre. And thank you, Mom, for being my personal little cheerleader. Seriously, you guys are amazing, and I can't thank you enough.

I must also give an honorary mention first to my writing buddy, Kelly. Partnering with you has helped me improve my writing, and even my story-telling. I'm so glad we met. Additionally, I must give an honorary mention to all of my friends and coworkers whose support and intrigue with my writing kept me from giving up.

And now for the wonderful people who helped me polish up my manuscript and get it ready for publication: a big thanks to Laura Josephsen, my amazing editor, who went above and beyond to ensure the story not only read well, but made sense too. Next, to Viviencreis, my Fiverr partner who turned my book cover vision into reality, and who helped with the book formatting so I didn't have to. And last, but certainly not least, is my second Fiverr partner, Luanbittencourt, my map artist. You all have made publishing a book so much easier for me, and I thank you.

Lastly, a big thanks to you, dear reader, for picking up this book and going on this wild adventure with characters I can't help but love and care for. May this be the first of many.

*Eris bi eljers!*

www.ingramcontent.com/pod-product-compliance
Lightning Source LLC
Chambersburg PA
CBHW022020300726
48970CB00003B/968